Murder at the Mill

By Lynn Marron

A Mystic Witch Triplets Mystery

Book Designer: Leonard J. Bloom, Jr.

Published by Kear Press
Stratford, CT

LIBRARY OF CONGRESS: 2019943844

ISBN:  978-1-942888-19-2

Ebook ISBN: 978-1-942888-20-8

This Book is Dedicated to:

**Debbie, Jeremy,**

**Heather and Kristan Alston**

Who willingly shared

Birthdays and

Holidays,

Music and Meals,

And sometimes

Just a place to

Sleep.

Thank you!

You are truly lovely people

May all your

Happiest Dreams come

True!

# Chapter 1

Sitting in their cheery kitchen, Evvie waited until her husband finished his reheated pork chops and mashed potatoes before she brought the problem up. "Paul's run-away bride is back in Connecticut."

"Yhep."

"You knew?"

He didn't look happy, it had already been a long day. "And Paul's ex-closest friend, ex-fellow officer, and ex-best man is also back."

With big trouble coming up, Evvie worked it out by getting up to polish her new full-sized refrigerator unit and a full-sized freezer unit in her modernized kitchen, which still had its walk-in fireplace left over from 1769. "Well, of course, he's with his wife."

"Actually, I hear they're divorced. Dietrich has moored his shiny new yacht at the marina club, and Margaret showed up two days later with a new guy in tow. She and the boyfriend have connecting rooms at the Mystic Motel."

Evvie was shocked. "Alice is a friend of Paul's–she shouldn't have let Margaret stay there!"

"Alice is a manager of a public accommodation. She has no choice," pronounced Stan, sounding like the Chief of Mystic police he was.

"What does he look like? This boyfriend of Margaret's?"

"Brandon Uberstat? He's a look-a-like to Paul and Jim. Six foot plus. 200 lbs. Dark haired like Jim. Muscular chest, with strong features. A lot younger than her. Might be underage."

"Stan, can't you do something?"

"Run them out of town on a rail for fornicating? Not within the purview of the Chief of Police."

"Does Paul know?" she asked.

"I called him in yesterday and broke the happy news."

"What if he goes after, Jim?"

"He's not. Paul's a police sergeant."

"But after what those two did to him!" Restless, she looked about her yellow, hand-painted tiled kitchen. "I was hoping he'd be engaged to Althea by now."

"I don't think that is going to happen with Officer Rogers."

"Why not? Althea brightens up whenever he comes near. She's beautiful and smart. Has family connections. They've been going out."

"But last December our boy was down dancing publically naked at Grace La Fleur's!"

That seemed silly to Evvie. "Everybody there was nude. Old Craft worship is skyclad."

Stan wanted off of this topic. "Paul Travinski is a sergeant in the Mystic Police!"

"But that Yule's was a religious ritual, being celebrated at Grace's Church of Nature's Bounty."

"Church of Booty! It's an orgy of moon worshiping, chicken- sacrificing nutcases! What Miz Le Fleur runs down there with condom foils decorating the altars is not a religious service!"     Evvie hated it when Stan went in stubborn mode. "It's Old Craft. It's the religion I was born to as a Fuller. The religion of many generations of the old New England families around here, like the Scofields, Coreys, Le Fleurs, Fitzgeralds, and the Hoyts."

**"You're *First Congregational*!"** He thundered. "At La Fleur's Paul wasn't looking for a religious experience. It's that blonde with her curves and blue-green eyes that lured him down to that basement!"

Suddenly Evvie was hyper alert. "Althea?"

"No!"

"Who is this girl?"

Stan ignored that. "There was a murder down there in

Caddemfield–that's what she got him into!"

"Paul doesn't know Old Craft..."

"Well, his lady friend's hip deep in it! Now the spring rites are coming up. I bet Grace is planning to get Paul on that altar couch to perform as the 'Horned God' with the 'Earth Goddess of Carnal Knowledge.' Paul's twenty-eight. High priestess Le Fleur is old enough to be his mother!"

"They'd pair Paul with one of the younger women. Maybe this blonde he likes will be the surrogate Goddess?"

Stan exploded again. "**No Sergeant of mine is going to be 'paired' with anyone!** No more rituals! Sergeant Travinski goes back down to Caddemfield--he's out of a job!"

She waited a few minutes, to let things cool before saying, "Stan, Beltane is a loving festival to renew fertility to the earth. To bring back abundance, increase the earth's energy, reunite the universal forces... "

Wanting to end this, he carried his plate to sink. "I don't think that Corey girl is really interested in advancing his religious education."

"Corey?" Evvie's eyes opened in surprise. "Holly Corey? One of the other triplets is back with Frost?"

Not looking at her, Stan said, "Both of them are back."

"Noel too?"

"Noel Christmas Corey now calls himself 'N.C..' He's going for his doctorate in marine mammals while working at the Aquarium. Brother Frost is still working as a guide at the Mystic Seaport Museum. And their triplet Holly has opened 'Witch House' as the 'Corey Mansion Bed and Breakfast.'"

"No one told me," said Evvie, sounding hurt. She stared out their wide porch, overlooking the river as she painfully remembered. "The Corey triplets–when their mother died, they were separated. Farmed out to relatives for over....how long was that?"

"Seventeen years," he supplied.

"Those babies shouldn't have been separated," Evvie

murmured.

"Would you have had them living with the man who slaughtered their mother?"

Evvie knew her voice sounded dead. "They said that Hester committed suicide."

"My uncle never believed that. Nobody on the force ever did!"

With a concerned frown, she looked to him. "So now the Corey triplets are asking questions?"

"No. The lady's got your fair-haired boy, my Sergeant Paul Travinski investigating her mother's murder!"

Evvie looked frightened. "Paul wants to know what happened to Hester?"

"There's nothing to investigate!" He looked at her and said firmly, "Hester died in one of those crazy witchcraft rituals."

"Beltane." In a dreamy voice, Evvie continued. "It's is coming up at the end of the month. Old Craft holidays start at sunset. Hester died before dawn on May 1st."

"Hester Corey waltzed out to the old mill and got herself stabbed to death at midnight. What could be simpler than?"

"It's still an open case, Stan," she said tightly. "Nobody was ever arrested."

He looked at her hard. "And you want Paul opening up that can of worms? Knowing what could happen to you and me?"

\* \* \*

Relaxed in jacket and khaki pants, Paul Travinski parked his blue F 150 king cab truck on the white gravel of the marina parking lot. Deeply inhaling that salt water aroma, Paul wanted to be out on Henry's boat and fishing. He went around and opened up the gate to the truck bed with his fishing poles, tackle box, and white cooler.

"Paul."

He turned to see the tall man with dark hair. Not Henry. Not anyone Paul ever wanted to see again, his 'old buddy,' Jim Dietrich. "Heard you were back in town," Paul said coolly.

"Yhep. My boat's docked over there."

Paul turned his attention to unpacking his truck. This was not a conversation he wanted to continue.

But Jim was persistent. "Look, Paul. What I did was wrong..."

Might as well get it over with, Paul turned back to him. "Eloping with my fiancee on my wedding day?"

"Yeah." Jim grinned lopsidedly. "I don't know what got into me. I divorced Margaret. Hell, I've even got an Order of Protection against her."

Paul frowned. "I hadn't heard that."

Seeming to stall for time, Jim looked over Paul's truck. "Nice. Knowing your Boston bullheadedness, you probably paid cash." He indicated the dock below them. "Take a look at the seventy footer I've got in Slip 27, the 'Sea Hag.' Named it after Margaret."

"Paying for it on time for the next hundred years?" commented Paul cooly.

"Leased to the business. It's a legitimate, tax-deductible expense."

"Sounds like you got it all worked out."

Jim looked at him, earnestly. "Look. We were friends at Camp Lejeune, in the Marines in Afghanistan, and on the force here at Mystic. I got you here to Mystic."

Paul wanted to change the flow of the conversation. "What are you doing now?'

"Remember when we talked about setting up that secure courier service?"

The way Paul remembered the business plan was

entirely his idea, but he just said a level, "Aaup."

"Well, I set up Targeted Security."

*Didn't even bother to come up with his own business name, Paul silently noted.* Carrying his fishing gear, Henry was walking over to them, asking in a friendly tone, "Hi, Paul, is your friend coming with us?"

"No," said Paul turning back to Jim. "Gotta go."

But Jim just turned to Henry. "I'm James Dietrich. A...former friend of Paul's."

Henry hesitated as if recognition hit, then he offered. "Officer Henry Mackay." Paul had never before heard Henry announce he was a cop when he was out of uniform.

"Mystic Police?" a surprised Jim asked.

"Yes, sir."

Paul explained, "Actually, Jim, Henry took your place when you left town." Paul slammed up the gate of his truck and picked up his poles. "Those fish aren't going to wait around."

Jim nodded but kept talking. "Paul, Targeted Security is just me now, but I'm making big bucks, and I need to expand. I'm up here couriering diamonds for a Brazilian conglomerate."

"Blood, diamonds?" Paul asked coolly.

"My job is to protect their transport here. It pays very well, in cash. All the paperwork goes through Customs–all of it on my end is legal. I just don't ask questions."

That's the way Paul had planned it years ago over pizzas at La Luna. "I'm sure doing work for guys who transact business in diamonds would pay well. Laundry work usually does."

Jim wouldn't let go. "I need someone I can really trust to work for me."

"Why don't you keep it in the family. Hear Margaret's got a new playmate. How about him? "

His ex-best man frowned, looking over Paul's

shoulder. "They've followed me here. Margaret wanted me to get back with her again. For 'us' to take off with the diamonds."

Paul raised an eyebrow. "Does she have any idea who you're doing business with?"

Jim continued to push. "I could use a guy with your skills and instincts. I'll pay twice your sergeant's salary to start with. And if it works out, I might take you on as a full partner."

Paul didn't hesitate. "I'm happy where I am. But as law enforcement, if Margaret and friend are hanging around, I suggest you find someplace safe to secure those diamonds!"

Henry shifted uneasily. "Paul, we ought to get going."

Jim stepped a bit back. "Think about my offer, Paul, it's a good one. I'm here for another week. Come on down to the boat, and we'll have a drink, and talk about old times...and about Margaret, I'm sorry."

"Don't be," Paul answered, sincerely. "I think you did me the best favor of my life!"

*   *   *

Friday evening, the sky was dark as Paul parked his truck at the end of the line of cars in front of his chief's rambling, white clapboard house. Meeting of the informal blue shirt club must be in full swing. Since he was late, most of the food Evvie had put out would be wolfed up. Paul headed to the side entrance to Evvie's big yellow kitchen. He just went in without knocking. The remodeled kitchen had South-facing windows overlooking a glassed-in porch that spanned that long side of the house–Stan's man cave. It had been outfitted with snooker and pool tables, two big screen televisions, and comfortable reclining leather couches.

From the sound of the game on t-v and pool balls hitting the cushions, the 'meeting' was in full swing. In the kitchen, next to the stone fireplace, Sally his old, piebald border collie was sleeping on her corduroy pillow. He decided to just let her sleep while he joined the guys.

Facing away from him was Evelyn Lewis with her golden hair short and perfectly styled. His chief's wife had put a few pounds on over the years, but still had a womanly hourglass figure in her green pants suit. Evvie was rapidly working on a purple cabbage, that had an already lighted Sterno can in its hollowed-out top. Now she was sticking cocktail weiners, pineapple chunks, and mini-meatballs on long cooking sticks stuck deeply into the cabbage leaves. Paul snuck up behind her and started grabbing a few of the weiners.

Exasperated, she turned to him. "Can you just let me get it on the table?"

"Nope," said Paul chewing. "I'm starved!" She shook her head as Paul moved over the kitchen sink where she'd left the faucet dripping. "Didn't have dinner." He tried to turn the faucet tighter, but it was locked in position. "This thing's leaking."

"I've got to call a plumber. Stan's got no patience. He'll just get mad and hit it a few times with a gun butt. All it needs is to have the washer changed."

"They don't make 'em with washers anymore, Evvie. You have to change the whole fixture."

She held out a plate of wheels of wrapped up ham and cream cheese. "Honey, try these."

Paul looked for the hook. He knew it was in there. "What else has to be fixed, Evvie?" He said just before popping a cream cheese hors d'oeuvre into his mouth.

"The shower in our bedroom..."

"It's leaking too?" He reached for a second ham roll up.

"A little." Evvie was looked to up to him, with those deep indigo blue eyes that matched her husband's. "But what I was thinking, they have those lovely 'rain shower heads' that hang from the ceiling. Have you seen them?"

"Aaup. But you're talking major renovation. I'd have to rerun the plumbing lines."

"But you've done that for me when we put water out to the little greenhouse."

"Redoing the master bathroom plumbing would mean ripping open the wall and ceiling, taking out the tiles, and replastering the wall and ceiling. Won't get tiles to match anything that old. Probably have to retile the whole stall to make it look decent."

"If I made you pirogies every Friday for a month?"

"Your husband's got me pulling double shifts. Don't have that much spare time."

"But Stan's back's been spasming so much lately. A shower like that could help him. Maybe you could fix it like a steam cabinet? You do some work, and I bet I could make a few more beef dinners with roasted potatoes?"

He'd give in—eventually. But not just yet. "Just pick up a new kitchen sink faucet. Make sure you get one with a side sprayer. Monday after work, I'll see if we can get the kitchen fixed, and then I'll take a closer look at the bedroom."

Loud male cheering came from the long man cave. Paul looked up eagerly, but Evvie wasn't finished. "I hear Margaret's back in town?"

Not meeting her eyes, he reached down to pick up her fire cabbage platter to carry in. "Understand she's staying at the Mystic motel."

"But not with her husband?"

He had to get through this. "Nope. They're divorced. Jim's living on a boat. She's at the motel with her new boy toy. And I mean the 'boy' part literally."

"So your old buddy Jim followed her to the seaport?"

"Actually, he came into Mystic first. We've met. Talked." Evvie paled, but Paul continued casually. "He admired my taste in trucks. I suggested that his divorce was a very good idea." Evvie looked like she wanted to hear more, so he added. "Yeah, the day of my supposed wedding, I would've beaten him to a pulp if I could've gotten my hands on him, but I got over that years ago."

"Why did he come to talk to you?"

"He wants to hire me."

"Hire you?"

"For '*his*' security transport business. Didn't even change the name I thought up, 'Targeted Security.'"

"Transporting what? Drugs? Illegal aliens? I never trusted that man. Can't you just stay away from them? Margaret always seemed to have some sort of a weird hold over you."

"That's over," Paul said with finality.

Just getting off his cellphone, Stan Lewis had walked into his kitchen,. Even in khaki pants and a red polo shirt, he walked like the Chief of the Mystic Police. Now seeing Paul, he didn't break into the usual welcoming smile. "You're late for the meeting," Stan said evenly.

"Aaup," Paul hefted up the heavy flaming cabbage platter to balance it, but Stan wasn't getting out of his way.

"Why were you late?" his chief asked.

That seemed to stop Paul. "I didn't know we were doing a roll call tonight?"

"Why are you asking?" Evvie sounded concerned.

Stan just looked at Paul. "I want my sergeant to tell me where he was."

"Do I need a lawyer?" Paul was trying to joke, but it fell flat. Behind Stan, Henry and a few of the other guys were coming into the kitchen and listening with curiosity. Paul didn't appreciate the public grilling. "I was on a snipe hunt."

"A what?" Evvie asked.

"Some guy called me," Paul started.

"Who?" questioned Stan.

"I don't know. A deep voice. No name. Asked about

the reward for the Deli man's killing. Said he '*might*' have some information. Wanted to meet me at the Town beach."

Evvie asked, "If he didn't know you, how did he get your phone number?"

Stan answered. "He's not unlisted."

She looked at Paul. "Honey, that's not a good idea for a policeman..."

Her husband cut her off. "This man—you went to meet?"

"You went there alone?" asked Evvie.

"Aaup," said Paul, really getting annoyed at the team questioning in front of the rest of the guys.

"Anybody see you?" asked Stan.

"There were some people on the beach."

"Paul, that beach is closed at sunset," said his chief staring at him hard.

Paul glared back. "It's a surprise to you that a bunch of teenagers don't always obey signs?"

"So someone saw you?" asked Evvie hopefully.

"Nobody I recognized."

"And no informant showed up?" said Stan in measured tones. "Did you make a record of this in your duty book?"

"There was nothing to record."

Stan still persisted. "Did you also stop by the North marina dock?"

"No. Why are you asking?"

"So that's a negative? Is that your statement?" Stan carefully emphasized.

"What's this about?" Evvie asked, staring at her husband.

"Got several reports that a tall, sandy-haired man in a blue uniform was seen on the North Marina dock tonight. One witness thought he saw sergeant's stripes on his shirt. Was that you, Paul?"

"I just told you, no," Paul spoke with a touch of anger.

Stan just watched him. "You knew that James Dietrich has his boat docked there?"

"Yes. I spoke to him."

Stan watched him carefully. "You're admitted to seeing him?"

*What the hell was this*? "He came over and talked to me."

"Tonight?"

"Wednesday."

"Anyone witness this?" Stan asked.

Paul answered in a measured tone. "Henry was there. We ran into Jim on the docks when we were going out fishing."

"And?"

"We talked."

"**About what**?" yelled an exasperated Stan.

"He apologized for running off with my bride-to-be. We both agreed he was punished enough."

"That's all?" Stan pursued.

Paul shrugged. "Jim is here on business...and he also wants to hire me."

"For what?"

"His security company." The cabbage's blue flame was smoking a bit, causing Paul's eyes to water. "He's paying better than you, Stan."

His chief ignored that. "Did you fight? Did he threaten you?"

Henry spoke from the back. "They were perfectly amiable. I even heard him tell Paul to think about his job offer."

"You heard the whole conversation?" asked Stan.

Henry confirmed strongly. "Yes, sir."

Immediately Paul corrected. "Actually, he came over when we were already talking, but Henry heard most of it."

"Then, what happened?" Stan continued in an officially detached tone.

"Henry and I spent the day out fishing." This full interrogation treatment was annoying Paul. "Sir, what is the problem?"

More of his brother officers were coming into the kitchen, staring at them, as Stan spoke professionally. "Dispatch called. James Dietrich was found on his boat–shot."

Paul looked at Stan in disbelief. "Is he in the hospital?"

"He's dead."

Everyone looked to Paul, who stood there with that stupid flaming cabbage sputtering in his hands.

# Chapter 2

Neither of her brothers was working at the Aquarium or Mystic Whaling Museum today, but Holly still had to drive down to deliver the bakery goods to Alice. They always needed more money for the mansion, so if Holly helped Noel with the baking, maybe they could spread out and sell to other motels?

A stop sign. She should have been paying attention and slowing. She pressed the brake pedal. To the floor. Then pumped it frantically as the heavy 1956 Cadillac hearse kept rolling. The brakes were so slow. Lately, she'd have to take it in for repair, but first, they had to pay the last two months of the electric bill before the shut-off date.

To the annoyance of the traffic behind her, Holly was going a dead crawl when she turned right into the parking lot alongside the Mystic motel. It had an A-framed office lobby, followed by a white brick, two-story, double row of rooms, accessed by outside balconies on either side. On the west side, it had more parking and a fenced swimming pool that backed up onto the pool of the next tourist motel alongside it.

Three of the long cardboard boxes were heavy but used to it, Holly carried all of them into the lobby. Red haired, fortyish and trim Alice Seymour was checking out a salesman at the desk. When she finished, Alice walked over to Holly, who was loading muffins into the plastic cases in the breakfast area. "Did you hear about Paul Travinski?"

"W-w-what about Paul?"

"You know Paul was engaged to be married, and then Margaret left him on the wedding day?"

"Y-y-yes."

"Well, her husband and Paul's best man, Jim Dietrich, moved into the marina last week. Then the lady herself and her new boyfriend checked in here."

Holly automatically looked up, past the office to where the second floor of the motel was. The other day she'd felt jangling vibrations and looked up to see a redheaded woman coming out of a room. *A scheming, evil woman who hates.* "They're on the second floor, on the East side?"

Alice looked at her peculiarly. "213 and 214."

Holly spoke in a trance-like voice. "She hates Paul. Hates all men. Can you make her go away?"

The hotel manager ignored that. "The big news is someone just shot her ex-husband, Jim Dietrich."

"He's dead?" Holly asked, already knowing the answer.

"It probably was a robbery that went bad, but I've been told because of what Jim did to him they're questioning Paul."

\*   \*   \*

After his shift on Monday, Paul went back to his apartment that was cut out of the old Victorian building standing on land where the river meets the harbor. There he changed from his blues to jeans and a t-shirt. He wouldn't have time for running tonight. Instead, he got his plumbing toolbox from his basement storage locker, then headed outside to the back to the asphalt parking lot overlooking the river. He was just unlocking his truck when he heard a woman calling out. Not a voice he really recognized, but one he vaguely remembered, one he knew he should know. A voice that was coarse. Older. He turned. Brassy hair, full figure. Still shapely, but not the goddess he once saw. "Hello, Margaret." A tall kid Paul figured to be her toy boy was standing away by the building, watching them closely.

"Paul." She gave him a sunny smile. "Still at the old apartment? You didn't keep the house?"

"I sold it."

"For how much?"

"I've forgotten."

As her smile widened, he noted her front teeth were crooked. "I left phone messages for you," she purred.

*Aaup. He'd have to get that unlisted number.* "You'll have to excuse me. I'm running late."

She moved her head to the side, looking up seductively from under her heavily mascaraed eyes. He used to find that such a turn on. Not any more. Especially since her brown eyes were now a contact lensed washed-out milky-violet. "Half of that house was mine," she said sweetly.

"How do you figure that? You never paid anything on it."

"I helped fix it up. Sweat equity."

"Sweat equity? What exactly did you do? You didn't find the house. You didn't repair the holes in the walls. You didn't nail or scrape. You didn't paint. What did you do, Margaret?"

"I picked out the colors."

"Actually you never got around to picking out the colors. You just objected to the ones I painted."

"Paul, that house was a marital asset."

"Margaret, we were never married."

"I think I'm going to have to speak to a divorce lawyer about that."

"You do that. But remember since you were never my wife, you'll have to pay for that lawyer out of your own pocket. Now if you'll excuse me." As he started to turn away from her, she grabbed his arm. Years ago, that would have given him a tingle. Now? Just a feeling of revulsion.

She moved uncomfortably close to him. "Jim and I were married."

"And divorced, according to him."

"But I think I may still be in his will."

"I doubt it," said Paul. "He told me he'd placed an

order of protection against you."

She stepped back a little. "Jim had a shipment of diamonds on that boat. Have your police found them?"

He shrugged. "I'm not on the case."

"They said they haven't. Would your guys have stolen them?" Margaret demanded.

Anger flashed through Paul. "Unlike some people I know, my cops are honest."

Seeing 'old times' wasn't working, she changed tactics. "My divorce from Jim actually wasn't legal. There's a technicality. So I'm still his wife–his widow," she finished with a sad catch in her voice.

"Great!" said Paul. "They're looked for someone to pay for his funeral. I'll tell them where you're staying."

Her toyboy was moving closer. Paul found himself evaluating him as a possible threat. The kid was Paul's height of six four, and from the muscular chest, he too obviously worked out, and this kid's body language was showing protectiveness toward Margaret. *Might have a problem here.*

But Margaret was staring deep into Paul's eyes. "I need access to Jim's boat."

"No can do. It's a crime scene."

Her hand hanging on his arm made his skin crawl, as she murmured, "You're a policeman. We can search together. Share what we find." Margaret was lowering her voice, trying to create intimacy in that windy parking lot. "Paul, leaving you, I made the biggest mistake of my life. What we had...what I felt for you was such an overwhelming passion that I was drowning in it, losing my very soul. So on our wedding day, I panicked and ran from you. Ran from all that meant something to me–and I've regretted it ever since!"

"I haven't," he said.

She tried harder and lowered her voice to almost a whisper. "Can't we go upstairs to your apartment and talk about this?"

"Nope."

Seeing the hardness in his face, Margaret finally pulled back, letting go of his arm. Returning his hardness with some of her own. "I intend to put a claim in. Those diamonds are mine."

He just smiled. "You know where Police Headquarters is. Just go in and fill out the paperwork."

The kid had come closer and was possessively putting his hands on Margaret's shoulders. "Sweetheart, shouldn't we be going to dinner?" he asked her.

An annoyed Margaret glanced back to him. "Paul, this is Brandon."

"Oh," said Paul smiling warmly. "I didn't know you and Jim had adopted a kid. Congratulations!"

She ignored the dig. "Paul, don't be this way. We can hunt those diamonds together! Share them. Jim owes both of us!"

He looked at her. "The only diamonds I want from you are on that big engagement ring I paid for. That one you're now wearing. It's customary that when you jilt a guy, you return his ring."

As she returned his glare with flinty eyes, Paul noted those pale violet contacts were a bit surreal.

"You gave it to me. It's legally mine." Margaret spits out, then on schedule, the tears began. "Jim understood how much it meant to me, so it became our wedding ring. It's really the last thing I have of my husband. Paul, I'm a widow now, I'm alone in this world."

Brandon flexed the hands on her shoulders. "No, you're not, sweetheart. You've got me!"

Margaret didn't appear that consoled and Paul found himself grinning as he climbed into his truck and headed for his chief's house.

Inside the cheery kitchen, he could smell corn beef in the crockpot, and Evvie was getting the pan out for the homefries he liked to go with it. Paul put the toolbox down by the sink, and he went over to his old border, collie thumping her tail on the floor. These days Sally mostly just laid out on her cushion bed, with her grayed muzzle matching the black, grey and tan splashes on her white coat. "Hey, Sally. How's my girl?" Paul squatted down to scratch her ears. He looked up at Evvie. "She eating?"

"Yes, but on damp days her rheumatism acts up. The vet gave me more pills."

"I owe you for that."

"No, you don't! Sally's got a job here. Working as the house guard dog. She barks at any stranger."

"If she gets to be too much for you, I can keep her at my apartment?"

"With the overtime, you constantly work? And have her sore old paws walking on cement sidewalks? No. Sally likes the grass and sitting out in the sun with me when I garden. And she can't make the staircase to your second-floor place anymore."

"I can carry her up and down," Paul said as he moved to the round kitchen table with its box from Home Depot.

"As a twice-retired, seeing-eye dog Sally deserves her rest." Evvie looked out the windows through the porch and out to the river, then started slowly. "Paul, with Margaret in town..."

"My fascination with Margaret has been over for years. And I don't even know why I ever wanted her." He was unpacking the faucet she bought. Brushed pewter with an elegant curve. Evvie always decorated well. "Going to have to shut down your sink for a while."

She wasn't letting go. "Paul, some people see a kind heart as a weakness to be exploited. Giving your mother money she'd spend buying more booze..."

"You and Stan talked me out of that."

"Your mother hasn't starved. Your sister Rosalyn is

still managing to feed and clothe her kids–without her boyfriends or you paying the bills."

"Hey, my other sister Josey is working out fine-and very thankful for that job in Boston with the D.A. that the chief arranged."

"Josey's like you–a hard worker. But I don't want you to ever see Margaret again as a '*wounded victim needing saving.*' I don't want you slipping back under that conniver's sway."

"Not gonna happen." He laid out the faucet's parts on the table. Placing his toolbox on the floor by the sink, he turned the cold and hot water taps on and let them run before he got down on his knees before the bottom cabinet.

Evvie persisted, "She eloped with Jim because she realized in the long term she couldn't control you. But if she can, Margaret will try to use you again."

The outside door opened up as Stan came in, still in uniform. Looking older and tired and not walking with his usual swagger, he ran his hand through his white hair. The chief immediately focused on the new faucet on the table and Paul's toolbox. "I said I'd fix that."

"Paul just dropped by and had his tools in his truck," Evvie explained.

Stan shook his head. "And four hours ago you just happened to put one of his favorite meals in the crock pot?"

Paul knew the signs. "Is there something the matter, sir?"

Stan tightened his lips, then spoke with a touch of anger in his voice. "Tomorrow, my detectives are going to question you again about the Dietrich murder."

"Why?" Paul asked.

"The District Attorney is getting pressure from Hartford. He's putting pressure on me and my detectives. Apparently, Jim Dietrich was transporting diamonds for some Brazilian guys. No diamonds were found. The alleged owners have put in a missing property report, and they're claiming my officers might have '*accidentally*' removed the diamonds and said nothing. "

"How much are we talking about?" Paul had gotten down with his back on the floor, trying awkwardly to reach in under the sink. At least Evvie had emptied everything usually stacked in here.

"Eight large, cut diamonds, unset. Insured at twenty-nine million," Stan continued.

Paul whistled. "What would that look like?"

"They said a leather courier pouch about fifteen inches by ten inches."

"Not that easy to find," Paul said as he stretched his arms in that tight cabinet. Evvie was bringing a cushion to put under his back as he rested painfully on the cabinet frame and tried to turn the shut off for the hot water line. As per his luck today, it stuck.

"Yeah," said Stan as he moved to the other side of Paul. "I've got some Coast Guard drug guys coming with special equipment to go over the boat. See if they can find a cavity we didn't."

The hot water handle finally gave, and Paul closed it tight. Then he started on the cold water line as he was remembering that last conversation. "Jim seemed concerned about Margaret being around. He said she knew about the diamonds. That she wanted him to steal them and run away with her."

"**That's not in the transcript of your questioning!**" exploded Stan angrily. "Why didn't you tell Hiram that?"

"It's not admissible in court. It's hearsay. And Jim was always a little paranoid." The cold water line handle was sticking too. Paul put more pressure against it.

Evvie now stood on his other side, teaming up on him. "But it would have made the case for your innocence look stronger!"

Paul pulled his head out of the cabinet, as Stan barked out a command. "When Hiram questions you tomorrow, get that on the record! Then I'll get the detectives to go after your ex-fiancee again."

Evvie sounded concerned. "If Paul is to be questioned again, he needs a lawyer!"

Stan stared at Evvie, with both of them ignoring Paul. "That'll just make him look guilty!"

Paul reached for a smaller wrench on the floor. "Anybody care how the chief suspect feels about this?"

"**No!**" They answered in unison, glaring at each other. Then Stan compromised. "Paul will talk to the detectives without a lawyer, but before that, he'll go and talk with John Hagen about how best to protect his interests. I'll give John a call now. Evvie, you got his home phone?"

A pissed-off Paul crammed back into the cabinet and gave a stronger twist to the cold water line shut off. The corroded handle broke off in his hand, with the cold water tap above his head still running. "Stan, are there shut-offs for the kitchen water lines in the basement?" he asked wearily.

"Don't think so. That's still the old plumbing from before we remodeled the kitchen."

Evvie's family, the Fullers, had owned this farm on the river before the Revolutionary War. The rambling one-story building had been added on to generation after generation, resulting in multiple basements, built in multiple centuries. Paul had pushed Stan into removing the sections of lead pipes from the system, but Stan's plumbing technique consisting mainly of stopping leaks with pipe clamps or packing everything with aviation bondo.

With shoulders painfully wedged in that narrow cabinet frame, Paul visualizing what it would take to go down in that stygian maze of pipes to shut off the entire house and drain the whole stinking system before he could put in a new shut off valves here. *And what else would burst when he pressured* up? Maybe, just maybe, if he got lucky enough, he could get arrested for murder before he had to go down into that black hole of a cellar!

# Chapter 3

The next morning, Holly carried three boxes of baked goods into the lobby of the Mystic Motel. The redheaded manager, Alice, was already filling the coffee urn. "Hi, Holly.Umm...tomorrow cut the weekend order to weekday levels."

*Less baking for Noel, less money for them.* "In tourist season?"

"Gas prices up. Tourists down," said Alice. "How are you guys doing?"

Holly looked down in shame. "Only two rooms rented. No advance bookings. A-Alice, uh....y-y- you need any extra help?"

"Sorry. I've had to cut back Dorrie's hours. But..." The manager finished with a confident smile. "Two months to June. Then the kids are out of school and tourist season will really start warming up." She held out a green magazine. "I've got a giveaway you guys might advertise the mansion in. A lot of the senior citizens who would like to stay in a Bed and Breakfast don't do the Internet."

Holly nodded. To get business, they should advertise the Corey mansion more—but without guests, they didn't have money to advertise.

"You're still dating Paul Tranvinski?" Alice asked a bit too casually.

"We're going out Friday," said Holly feeling the happiness lighting up her face. Alice looked down at her computer. Holly had the definite feeling her friend wanted to say something but wasn't. "W-w-what, what is it?"

"Paul's a great guy, but since Margaret dumped him, he's not stayed long with any one woman."

Holly couldn't understand that. "Why did she give him up?"

"I don't know. I never could figure out what Paul saw

in her," said Alice with disgust. "Margaret and Jim were more of a matched pair. Surprised he didn't get shot earlier."

"Do the police know who killed him?"

"I hear there are valuable diamonds missing. They're questioning Paul because a man looking like him was seen running from the docks after the shot. I hear the D.A. is pushing Chief Lewis to put Paul on the rubber gun squad. They should be..." Alice pointed out to the motel's second story rooms. "questioning her and the boy wonder."

"They haven't?' Holly asked with a sinking feeling.

"They have. But supposedly Margaret and boyfriend have an alibi. The pair are still here."

"Did the police search their room?"

"They have connecting rooms. And no. They would have had to come through me to do that." Alice glanced to Holly, and her face stiffened. "Don't even think it! I know you figured a few things out the police didn't in those past murders, but I'm not giving you the passkey card! Paul will be fine." Again Holly sensed Alice had stopped before saying something she wanted to.

"What is it, Alice?" Holly asked.

"Oh, honey. You know that new, blonde policewoman? Althea Rogers?"

"I saw her with P-P-Paul once," said Holly cautiously. Althea was taller than her. A great shot and never seemed to have a dyed blonde hair out of place as she pursued Paul. *Holly hated her.*

Alice was continuing. "I heard Paul took Althea out to dinner at La Luna last week. They were dancing."

"She dances?" Holly lowered her head.

"Very well, I hear. But you know, Paul's been dating you more than anybody else for a long time. So make him really happy on Friday, and maybe he'll forget Miz Rogers."

Still, with her head lowered, Holly smiled shyly as she finished putting the donuts out.

A brassy-orange red, over-permed woman and a younger man, entered the lobby. Holly found her aura vibrations dark and unpleasant, like the odor of an unwashed body. The woman stared at Alice. "We haven't had a complimentary newspaper delivered since we moved in!"

Usually, Alice tried hard to please the guests, but Holly noted a cool shortness in her answer. "We don't give newspapers."

"The motel on the hill gives free newspapers," the woman said sharply.

"But their rooms cost more," Alice answered sweetly. The redhead walked over to Holly. "The usual garbage for breakfast?"

"It's free," said Holly. She found her eyes drawn to the outlandish ring on the woman's left hand. Square center diamond with six, narrow supporting diamonds radiating from it with baguettes all around the band. Holly wondered how the redhead managed not to have it catch on everything she wore? And something else Holly felt from her again: a hatred from deep within. A hatred of all around her.

Picking up her empty boxes, Holly nodded goodbye to Alice and headed out. She didn't need to be introduced to that couple; it didn't take a witch to intuit that woman was Margaret, Paul's ex-fiancee.

# Chapter 4

On Friday, as Thor's thunderous barks reverberated. Paul knocked at the pantry door of the kitchen wing of the Corey mansion. Aaup, another gauntlet to run through. Before Noel opened the back door, the rottweiler would be locked up in Frost's room off the kitchen. Holly's white-blond haired brother Noel just glanced at Paul's brown suit and tie. "Holly didn't mention you two were going out tonight?"

"She did to me," said Frost, who was a physical twin to his triplet, with freckling from working outdoors added to the Corey's fine features.

"Aaup, might be having some more time off soon," Paul tried to joke, but it came out sounding bitter.

Noel didn't look happy, but he went to call his sister. It was Frost who kept staring at Paul, looking like he was concentrating. "Paul, what's the matter?"

"Nothing," Paul said, not sitting.

Frost kept staring at him. "I heard a guy was murdered at the North Marina?"

"Aaup."

Frost studied him with gold-flecked, blue-green eyes, so like his sister's. "I heard the killer was supposed to be dressed in a blue uniform?"

Just returning, Noel looked to Paul in surprise. "Like you? They're accusing you of murdering someone?"

Paul tried for humor. "Maybe I'm gonna wind up in jail–at least I know a lot of guys there."

"Yes," finished Frost with a worried look on his face.

"Guys, I can assure you I didn't do it," Paul said lightly, thinking that should be all that was necessary.

Frost looked at Noel. "My brother has found a car he wants to buy."

"Do you have a VIN number?" Paul automatically patted his suit, looking about for his duty pad. It wasn't there.

Frost shook his head. "A local dealer is selling it. This one won't be stolen."

*Were the Corey brothers actually so far out of it that they trusted a used car dealer?* "Give me the number anyway. Did you pay for a carfax on it?"

"It's not needed," said Noel. An answer Paul could've figured, but Noel gave him a card with the VIN number written out.

Holly walked in gracefully, wearing a pink shell dress, topped with her usual sweet smile, and her silly red-framed eyeglasses. He never got tired of running his eyes down her shapely body. Tonight her shoulder length blonde hair was pinned up in a french twist with small, pink silk-flowers pinned in. She wore nylon stockings, red heels, and she lowered her head as she smiled shyly to see him.

\* \* \*

After they left, Frost stared at the pantry door, frowning. It annoyed Noel. "Why didn't you tell me he was coming?'

"You'd have started stewing earlier."

"He's using our sister!"

Looking off in an unfocused manner, Frost said, "Paul's afraid."

"Of what?" Noel asked.

"This murder. He's joking, but he's afraid he's going to be arrested. Be confined in jail with people he's imprisoned."

"He did it?" asked a shocked Noel.

"No, but remember when you didn't do it but were accused?"

Noel, too, looked to the door. There was a little more reluctant understanding in his voice. "He's a cop. They'll protect him." Noel looked back to Frost, who still stood staring. "But why are you so upset?"

"He's registering on me, N.C."

"What?"

"When something bad happens to you or sometimes to Holly, I feel kinda sick inside."

"Maybe you're coming down with the flu?" The relentlessly practical Noel suggested.

"No. Now I've got that sick feeling with Paul in trouble, it's as if he was one of us."

\* \* \*

Paul drove South on I-95. "We're going to Weston. It's pretty far down, but Cobbs Mill is one of my favorite restaurants," Paul explained. "Tonight they've got a live dance band."

It was so perfect to be here with him, Holly shouldn't say it–but she did. "You've got the wrong girlfriend. It's the other blonde that dances."

He ignored that. "I hear N.C. thinks he's found a car?"

They talked about that for a while, until they reached the restaurant. The pre-Revolutionary grain mill had patios on the dammed river, long wood banquet halls attached to a two-story Inn building. They were early for one of the tables overlooking the tree-ringed mill pond, so Paul ushered Holly down narrow wooden stairs to the bar area, alongside the fifteen or so foot curtain of falling water over the stone dam.

They sat at a small table overlooking the falls as fat, white ducks and green-headed wild mallards swam beneath them. Paul looked down, shook his head sadly and said, "If you order the duck l'orange, a guy comes out with a hook and a sack..."

"That's terrible!" Holly laughed. They ordered drinks, then Holly hesitantly asked, "Alice said they were questioning you about that man shot on the dock? Surely they know you wouldn't have killed him?"

He did not want to talk about this. "You were taking

a college extension course on Marine History at the Seaport Museum? How did you make out?"

She shrugged modestly. "Okay."

"What's okay?"

"I p-passed. With a B-B-B."

Paul smiled proudly as the waiter brought over his whiskey and water and her apricot sour. Paul held up his drink. "Then we're really celebrating. I toast you, my lady." They clinked glasses and sipped, then Paul said, "What are you taking next?"

"Next?"

"What college course? You're going to work for a degree, right? Two years at least? What was your major in California?"

She lowered her head and looked down at her drink. "It was art. And I fl-fl-flunked out."

The bartender told Paul their table was ready. Picking up their drinks, they headed upstairs again. The main dining room had a stone fireplace on one long wall and a row of small, wood-framed paned windows on the other side overlooking the smooth mill pond. As they were escorted to a window table, a regal family of swans was serenely gliding across the green-black water beneath them.

The maitre d' held out a chair for Holly as they settled beside a candle-lit table. When the sky darkened, lights across the pond came on to illuminate the water and trees.

Paul was continuing. "History and art? A lot of would-be artists and historians chasing only a few jobs. Maybe we can find something more practical? Do you want to be an art teacher?"

As she sipped the sweet apricot brandy, it warmed her. Sitting opposite the man she loved, being in this wonderful restaurant, Holly wanted to make him as happy as she was. "Maybe I could go into Police Science? Become a policewoman, and work with you?"

Paul got a painful mental picture of him trying to get Chief Lewis to hire Holly Corey. "Police work–just passing the Academy--that requires discipline. Holly, honey, that's not your long suit."

She lowered her head, looking down at the menu. "Paul, why can't you accept me as I am?"

He was tired and getting annoyed."Why? Because you keep holding on to that anchor of a sinking mansion?"

"We're getting guests," she said defensively.

"How many?"

"Uhhh...t-t-two..." she admitted.

"Not enough to make it, self-supporting?"

"You sound like Noel."

"N.C. is speaking sense. He's wanted to sell the mansion, for the three of you to get a smaller place with the money. Then, you could go back to college and get some sort of career. Honey, you haven't held a real job since the Rainbow Realm closed."

The waiter came. Paul ordered plank salmon, and she ordered scallops provencal with a shrimp cocktail. Holly didn't feel guilty about running up his bill since she knew he was going to get lucky tonight. When the waiter left, Holly pointed out. "Frost has gotten me jobs at the Seaport Museum."

"You think dressing up as a 'white lady' for the Halloween Festival week is employment? What did that pay–minimum wage and getting free membership for parking your hearse on the property?"

"Oh, Paul, you should-should've seen me in that crepe de chine gown. I looked so beautiful!"

His face softened as Paul said sincerely, "Honey, you'd look beautiful in anything." He stopped, then started carefully. "But we're talking about your life here. Doing a stint as a holiday ghost doesn't get you a social security account or a medical plan. Weeding the mansion's herb gardens are a lot of work, but..."

"The Hoyts said they will pay for my rosemary, basil and lemon verbena. They'll sell what they don't use at their farm stand."

He was getting a headache. "They pay you in eggs."

She shrugged prettily. "Well, a least it's not income the government can tax."

"Actually the IRS would disagree with that. There are rules about barter payments. Holly, let's not get into your tax situation, aaup?" On a small raised platform in the far corner, a drummer, piano keyboard guy, and the saxophone player were tuning up. Paul looked up expectantly, then he frowned again. "Your brother, N.C.'s trainer job at the Aquarium probably doesn't pay much, but he's working on his doctorate. But Frost's guide job at the Museum..."

She interrupted. "He's also designing displays for them! Doing ship's carpentry work building boats. Frosty is studying ancient Polynesian navigation with Tarus..."

"Is he on Mystic museum's books as a full-time employee?"

"I-I don't know."

"Or is he just considered a private contractor?"

Lowering her head, she just shrugged. "W-w-why would that matter?"

"If he's a full-time employee, the museum must pay into a social security account for him."

"My brothers and I are only twenty-four years old. We're not worried about collecting Social Security."

"You should be planning out a life for yourselves. Setting up your finances."

"We do need more money." She looked up excitedly. "Paul, Beltane is coming up."

To him, her train of thought often derailed, but he tried to follow along. "That's some sort of Old Craft ritual, right?"

"The Spring fertility rites. May first. Well, it starts at

sunset the night before. Surrogates recreate the union of the Goddess and God to renew the fertility of the earth. Ensure abundance..."

He looked at her in shock. "Are you talking about us as a couple screwing on Grace Le Fleur's altar couch, while a coven of nudies watch? No way, Lady! Even if I wanted to, Chief Lewis would have my badge if I get caught up at Grace's again!" He hated the disappointment on her face. The band was playing *Happy Together,* a foxtrot. "Let's dance." He suggested, starting to get up. If he could get his arms around her, it would all work out.

She wouldn't get up or meet his eyes. "You know I can't dance."

"I can teach you," he said firmly.

"No! You can't t-teach me. Or o-or-order my life! Or com-command me! Paul, I'd like to go home."

"We haven't even gotten dinner yet?"

"That-that blonde cop dances, right?" She looked at him defiantly. "Someone saw you dancing at La Luna. Was it with that cop?"

*How the hell did they get into this?* "Cop at La Luna's? Oh, you mean Henry?" Paul deadpanned, trying to joke her out of it. "He's always stepping on my toes. Trying to lower his hand down my back to get a cheap feel."

She stared at him, furious. "The blonde! A-Alegre...Alicia..?"

"Althea. Aaup, that lady can dance." Officer Althea Rogers could follow his long legs in the waltz's swirls, looking like a regal Viennese baroness. "Listen, we never spoke about dating exclusively..." But maybe it was time. He wanted her to change, so maybe he should first. Since Paul wanted Holly, it was time to take the plunge and commit to her alone. "Let's talk about it."

Holly lowered her head again, looking at her salad miserably. "Your chief wants you to marry her, doesn't he?"

*How did she know?* "Who I marry is not Stan Lewis' business. Honey..."

"He's pushing you! That's why we go so far away to have dates. You can't be seen dating me in Mystic?"

He was not going to admit that. "Please lower your voice. The waiter's bringing the entrees."

"I want to go home."

"Can we finish dinner first?"

They ate in silence. Holly just pushed her food around her plate. Paul didn't even suggest stopping at his apartment when they got back to Mystic. He wondered how a night that started so wonderfully went so bad? He parked the truck in the huge, empty parking lot behind the Corey Bed and Breakfast. Only Holly's hearse was parked there now. Meaning no paying guests. He'd barely rolled to a stop when she had the door of his truck open and was hopping down from the high cab. "T-thanks."

He was out the other side, catching up to her with his long legs. "Holly!"

She stopped. Head bowed, not looking at him. "You don't have to walk me to the door."

"Honey, please. Can we talk?"

"Maybe I should pay for half the dinner. You didn't get anything tonight."

"Get anything?" Paul asked sarcastically. "Dinner was payment for going to my apartment? Since tonight was such a wash, are you going to reimburse my gas too? Mileage on my truck?" he finished angrily.

"Paul. U-Us. It's not working out. I-I'm not what you want."

"Aaup, Miss Corey, I get it. I'll leave you alone--when you are safely inside."

\* \* \*

Irrationally, she wanted him to stop her, beg her to change her mind. Instead, Holly just unlocked the door to the pantry and left him standing with hands in his jacket on the dark step.

When she was inside the kitchen, tears started to run down her cheeks. Frost was sleeping in the next room, so she cried silently. Standing there on the linoleum, crying to the sounds of the kitchen ghost's mocking laughter.

# Chapter 5

The next day, Paul followed John Hagen's advice, and the detectives kept his questioning brief and professional. Hiram had even led him a bit, asking if Jim Dietrich had expressed any worry about the safety of the diamonds he was carrying? So Paul got it on the record that Jim had been concerned about Margaret and the boyfriend, but he found himself resenting that his coworkers playing all the old good-cop-bad-cop games to trip up his testimony. Before he started the morning roll call, he grabbed a mug of tea. The guys were unusually silent in the booking area. Men he worked with were looking at him with concern and outright curiosity: *Did he do it?*

Officer Althea Rogers came over. "Sir, I've been assigned bridge repair security. I'll have to change my unmarked car for a cruiser."

Paul nodded and looked over. "Mary, is 706 fixed?" The chief dispatcher nodded.

Althea said, "I'll get the keys from her." Then she spoke in a lower voice. "Paul, are you free for lunch?"

They never did a date on duty, so Althea must have something she wanted to talk over. "The Wok? 1 p.m.? I'll pick you up so we can leave the patrol car at the bridge with its flashing lights on."

At one, Althea insisted on Dutch treat. "This is not a date." Soon they settled down for plates of stir fry. He started on his beef. She just looked at hers, then in a strained voice asked, "They questioned you again?"

"Interrogation 101. Keep the suspect constantly repeating his statements. Compare answers. Find discrepancies. Demand the suspect explain discrepancies endlessly–all to trip him up," said Paul with a touch of bitterness.

"They say a tall, light-haired man in police uniform was seen on the docks before and after the murder. If it wasn't you, who was it?"

He shrugged.

"I understand the murdered man's ex-wife is in town?" she persisted.

"Aaup, my ex-fiancee, Margaret."

"The murdered man had an order of protection against her. It's on the computer."

Paul nodded. "Jim told me he thought she was after his diamonds, but that hearsay statement is worthless in court."

Althea started at him intently. "Margaret and her boyfriend alibi themselves. They were in their motel rooms. Around the time of the murder, they ordered food. Margaret got into a fight with the delivery guy."

"So I'm sure he remembered her. How convenient, " Paul commented.

"She claimed they'd gotten the order wrong. Had the deliveryman wait in her room while she called the restaurant, demanding they send out more food before she paid."

"The boyfriend was there?"

"That's what was written." Althea looked hard at him. "But when you read the record carefully, Brandon was allegedly taking a shower in the connecting room. The delivery man heard water running. Saw Margaret go into the room, heard her yelling to him. Then Margaret came back. She called the restaurant again, argued that her boyfriend said the whole order should be free since they were inconvenienced. She insisted that the delivery guy stand there while they waited for the owner to call back. At the end of this, Brandon came out in a bathrobe with damp hair and tried to calm her down. Paul, it sounds like there was a lot of time for Brandon Uberstat not to be in that adjoining room."

"So you think he was off murdering Jim?"

"It's five minutes down the road. And the delivery man may have come early?"

"Awful tight," he said, thinking about it. "And

Brandon's dark-haired. The witnesses described a light-haired man in a police sergeant's uniform."

"Witnesses are often mistaken. If you had an aggressive lawyer pushing, the police might shake Margaret and Brandon's alibis, at least enough to give some doubt in court..."

"What motive would they have? Margaret was bitter about the divorce? So bitter, that in less than a month, she ran out and got herself a new boyfriend?"

Althea looked down at her plate. "The detectives aren't coming up with anyone besides you!"

"Where did you get this information?" Not answering, Althea continued looking down at her stir-fry chicken. He slipped into stern sergeant mode. "Officer Rogers, sounds like you've been looking through the detectives' files?"

She colored. "As a member of the police force, I am supposed to be on the lookout for any criminal activity."

"You're a rookie here! Stepping on detective's territory in an open investigation is a career killer! Unauthorized viewing of restricted case files can get you fired. Don't do it again!" He softened his expression. "Althea, I know you want to help me, but don't try, aaup?"

She stabbed at a piece of tofu. "The detectives aren't even looking for someone else."

*Knowing Chief Stanley Lewis' anger when he was frustrated, Paul figured those detectives were desperately looking for anyone else.* He chewed on some water chestnuts and found himself studying Althea's fine features. She had a classic face--it reminded him of old movies, like Grace Kelly in *To Catch A Thief.* Why didn't he want to commit to her, instead of the flaky Holly Corey?

"You need a good criminal lawyer," she finally said. "I have a cousin who is willing to talk to you for free."

"Can't be much of a lawyer, if he's working for free," said Paul dryly. He did not like the drift of this conversation.

"Nathan doesn't need the money. He's a retired judge."

"Ever do any death penalty cases?" he asked flippantly.

"Connecticut's dropped the death penalty," she snapped. "And my cousin doesn't think you should be allowing them to question you without a lawyer!"

Paul finished the conversation. "For a cop, lawyering up is not considered a sign of innocence."

# Chapter 6

Driving the hearse to a job interview she wasn't qualified for, Holly was late as usual, and hurrying. Ahead, she saw an unexpected stop sign. Holly should've been going slower! She slammed down on the brake, feeling the pedal go to the floor. The heavy hearse was slowing, but not stopping. She was rolling right through the stop sign!

A cherry red Town and Country van was coming on the intersecting road. He had the right of way. Holly desperately pumped her brake pedal and twisted at the Cadillac's stiff wheel. Still, she headed straight for him! At the last moment-as, he hammered his horn- the van driver pulled into the left lane and just managed to slide past Holly's bumper. At the same second, lights flashed, and she heard the sirens of a cop's car. *Oh, shit!*

After such a close miss, her hands were shaking as she covered her mouth, wanting to scream. A ticket now would mean their insurance rates would be going up--another bill she couldn't pay. *Please let it not be Paul!*

A black officer she didn't recognize had come over to the car. "That was your fault, mam. Running a stop sign."

"I-I-I know. I saw it-it too late."

"License and registration?"

She dug them out and, sick to her stomach, waited while he went back to his patrol car.

Finally, he came back and handed her papers back. "You registration is clear. So is your driving record, Miss Corey, but you understand you could've caused a serious accident?"

"I'm so sorry."

"You're dating Sgt. Travinski aren't you?"

"N-N-no. W-w-we w-were. But we aren't anymore."

The officer looked sternly at her and said. "I'm only giving you a warning this time, but I will be speaking to Sarge about this."

"Don't." She didn't want that. "Paul doesn't c-ca-care about me anymore. He's said so."

"Uh, huh." He left her with the warning citation. If it meant he was going to speak to Paul, she almost wished he'd given her the ticket instead. The job interview went just as badly. The man she talked to said he liked her resume, but Holly read his aura. He would not be hiring her.

Back at the mansion's parking lot, she slowed properly, so the hearse just rolled to a stop. In the kitchen, Thor wanted out. She clipped him to the chain outside and went back into the mansion. He wanted a run, but Holly had to get some money. She must get the hearse brakes fixed and the other bills paid. The Corey Mansion Bed and Breakfast was making money; more each month, but it wasn't enough. And to make more money, they had to get the bathrooms renovated, and they needed fancier linens and more advertisements.

She walked through the dining room into the main parlor. Was there another painting she could sell? Great-grandmother Julia's ornamental clock on the carved marble fireplace? Oil painting of the China Clipper, her great-great-grandfather captained to bring tea from Cathay? Noel said dealers should be interested in the Empire couches, chairs and tables. But what would their guests sit on? And if they lost the mansion? Her brothers talked about trying to stay together, maybe renting a three bedroom apartment, but she couldn't afford rents around here. And Noel and Frosty couldn't afford to support her, and she wouldn't let them if they could.

But if the three of them left Corey House, they'd be separated, just when they were getting to know each other again. Holly felt sick as she looked about. Should they sell the mill property to Lilith Hoyt? And have that bitch poisoning the air around them?

Holly thought about that. Like Lilith, she was

supposed to be descended from witches. There must be a charm or a spell that could draw money? Frost might have learned something from their grandmother or the uncle who raised him after she died? Noel was raised by a military cousin, and he wouldn't even acknowledge extraordinary powers existed.

Skye Rainbow had told her to search for her mother's Book of Shadows. She hadn't found it. There were books all over the mansion on tarots, phrenology, herbs, palmistry, and astrology. She needed to sit down and start reading some. Maybe there was something there, but she didn't have time to read! April bills would be coming in, and she had already skipped paying the March electric and Noel's credit card. They needed money for the bills now!

Could she ask Abby or Sarah Hoyt how to use Old Craft to get the money? Somehow she didn't think Sarah would approve of that. Set inside a slanted desk in the alcove was Noel's laptop for her to check reservations on the Corey Mansion website. Noel paid for the Internet for his studies. Somebody must have put spells on the Internet. She pulled up Google and typed in *Spells for Money*. Site after site rolled up. She opened up the first one. They offered spells for money, love, beauty, but when she tried to pull one up, she found they wanted a credit card.

Holly went back to the Google home page and typed in *Free Spells for Money*. Again sites rolled down her screen. She tried the first. Promised a lot, but when she tried to pull up a spell, it switched to another 'paid for' site–spells promised to work, with a year's money back guarantee!

She pulled three more sites before Holly found what she was looking for. Then she had to skim through pages of *'money drawing spells.'* Holly studied them. When she had thought about putting a love charm on Paul–but didn't– Abby Hoyt had told her that it wasn't really the words or the ingredients, or the ritual movements that made a spell work.

Those only focused the practitioner's mind. That the simplest spells were the best, and that she should trust her inborn instincts to work them.

Scanning the pages, Holly found a formula she felt drawn to. It required nine white candles and nine green ones, green paper cut like money and patchouli oil. You placed one white candle nine inches from one green and anointed them with patchouli oil. On the green bill 'money' you wrote the bills that you must pay or what you needed to buy and put three drops of patchouli oil on that. Then you placed the candles nine inches apart. You lit the candles and repeated: *"Money, money come to me in abundance three times three. May I be enriched in the best of ways, harming none on its way. This I accept, so let it be, bring me money three times three!"* You let the two candles burn out, then repeated the ritual the next night, moving the candles an inch closer to each other. You did this for nine nights. Then on the ninth night, you burnt the green paper on a fireproof plate.

She had green blotting paper from the roll top desk she could cut up. Holly had a box of white tea lights, but she needed nine candles of green. Then she needed a list of her bills and patchouli oil. What was patchouli oil? And more importantly, where did she get some now that the Rainbow Realm was gone? There was probably someplace she could order it on the Internet, but she needed it now!

As Holly scanned down the site's pages, she saw more patchouli spells. Love spells. She had given her virginity to Paul Travinski. He was the first when she was twenty-two. She had had other earlier chances; Holly's looks attracted men all the time, but she read the auras of those others–she knew what they were after! Paul wanted pleasure, but he wanted it for her too. If only they could both go to Grace's Beltane. If they could be on the altar as surrogates for the Earth Goddess and Horned God in the sacred union. Then she wouldn't need Googled spells for abundance. But Paul was too worried about his career advancement with the police to ever let that happen.

Still, her body ached to have him lying by her side. Even if he didn't want her. Even if he was going to jail.

She had to pick up her brothers, then to her impatience, they wanted to borrow the hearse while she made dinner. Holly had finished her run with Thor, started some sloppy joes, and was now impatiently waiting outside for the guys to return her hearse. They came in late, with Noel struggling against the steering wheel and rolling to a long stop. Seeing Frost and Noel get out, the Rottweiler wagged his tail and ran up to get his ears scratched.

"That convertible was cool!" said Frost.

"But a soft roof is not practical for winter," responded Noel.

"You two looking at cars again? I thought it was settled, and you were buying the blue one?"

"Your boyfriend called N.C." started Frost.

"Paul? He's **not** my boyfriend anymore," said Holly a bit too vehemently.

"Well, you non-boyfriend called and said that he'd pulled carfax on the one N.C. wanted. It had been totaled in a coastal town in New Jersey after the hurricane. Which means it was probably in a flood area."

"Underwater? Would that hurt it?" she asked.

Noel nodded sadly. "Salt water is especially corrosive. It could play havoc with the electrical system farther down the road," said Noel. "So we're back hunting again."

"You lost your deposit?" Holly asked Noel anxiously.

"No, Paul talked the salesman into giving it back. He wasn't in his police uniform and didn't really threaten anything, but Paul talked a lot about '*misrepresentation*' and, with that grim face of his, scared the guy. So we've got the money back. But we've got to get something soon--the brakes on your hearse are really getting bad."

"As soon as we get some money we'll have them

fixed," Holly said defensively.

The three of them were looking at the long, black 1956 hearse, with its crimped tail fins. Noel pointed out, "You, know, Holly if you took those blue draperies out of the back windows, it'd look less like a hearse..."

A deep, long, sad sigh came from the back of the hearse.

Noel looked to his siblings. "What was that?"

Frost looked at him. "We could say it's the sound of metal contraction in the cooling engine, or we could say it's the resident ghost groaning. Which do you want to hear?" Frost looked back to the long black Cadillac, with its red velour interior, blue-gray curtains and stand up tail fins. "And, N.C., even without the drapes, it still is gonna look like a hearse."

The days were getting longer, so Holly still had some daylight after dinner. She told her brothers she had to get some eggs and milk verbena, so she slipped the hearse out. If she was going to help Paul, she needed an Old Craft practitioner. Two of them--who were a lot more knowledgeable than herself.

Soon, she drove down a tree-lined road, that opened up on to farmer's fields, now planted, soon to be growing blade-leafed corn. She passed the small, rock-walled family cemetery, and Holly finally pulled in past a wooden farm stand, closed until the crops started coming in. As Holly struggled to maneuver the stiff hearse, she noted a silver Acura was parked in front of the two-story, white-wood farmhouse.

She looked at the plates, as Paul had taught her. Rental. Holly had a good idea of who would be visiting the Hoyt sisters. For a moment she hesitated, it was only through the help of Sarah and Abby that Holly was able to throw their sister Lilith out of her Bed and Breakfast. But if Lilith was staying around here, she'd have to face her some time, so

Holly marched up and knocked on the door.

It was opened by tall Abby, with dark brown hair plainly parted at the top of her head and tied tightly in a bun at the back. They entered through the small draft porch. While outside the saltbox farmhouse looked like a classic 1800's New England Christmas card, inside the lower floor had been gutted, leaving beam and posts, two stone fireplaces and wide planked floors of gleaming yellow oak, with a modern, open kitchen in the rear. Now, facing three sets of strange gray eyes, Holly walked in. "I've just come for another dozen eggs, a quart of goat's milk, and some herbs."

The bench of Sarah's seven-foot loom stood empty today. On the walnut and chrome framed couches and chairs, with their moss silk cushions, two figures sat opposing each other–red-blonde haired Sarah and her golden blonde sister Lilith. The tea tray set before them had a clear glass teapot and anisette cookies. Regally Sarah indicating that Holly should sit down next to her on the couch across from Lilith, while Abby walked to the light oak cabineted kitchen in the back for another cup and saucer.

Sarah was not smiling but did make room for Holly as she came over slowly.

"Hello, dear," Lilith said, smiling brightly to her. "Since you are still refusing to sell the mill property to me, I've found a lovely house to rent over in North Stonington."

"That's good." Holly smiled back. It was surreal. Sitting here, talking with Lilith, after throwing her and her warlock friend out of the Corey Mansion. Both the mansion's and Holly's luck seemed to go down when Lilith Hoyt left. She and her brothers didn't have money to keep their home going. Now Holly was thinking about breaking up with Paul–thinking about him being put in jail for murder. That restless runner of man, caged in a tiny space. Holly found herself cycled farther and farther down into a cold grayness. Paul being penned up with dangerous inmates he'd arrested.

Locked behind bars like an animal. Being stabbed by some homemade knife.

Walking almost silently, Abby returned with a violet painted, bone china cup and saucer which she set before Holly. Abby poured a lemon-smelling tea for her, then stayed standing by Holly. To keep from talking, Holly sipped some. The tea tasted of licorice and clove. *Abby's mixes were always strangely satisfying and infused you with positive energy.* Holly took another fortifying sip of tea, then she realized what was happening. Yes, she had concerns about Paul's legal problems and money and losing her brothers again, but those were being projected and magnified by Lilith's powers of mental control. Holly had thrown off Lilith's nasty *mind-snake* control once, she could do it again!

With a satisfied smile, Abby moved to the other chair facing the couch, but still did not sit as Sarah asked, "Holly, what herbs do you need that you aren't growing?"

"Patchouli."

Sarah looked at her steadily. "We don't have any in stock."

Lilith looked interested. "Patchouli? For prosperity or ...a love spell? Still pursuing that big policeman of yours?"

Holly lowered her head. "I just need it for cleansing."

Lilith wasn't letting that go, saying archly. "You must be preparing for the Spring renewal of Beltane?"

"I don't think so," said Sarah setting her cup down firmly and staring at Lilith significantly. "Since none of us will be going to Grace Le Fleur's Church of Nature's Bounty."

"There are other places that celebrate Old Craft rites." Lilith turned to Holly, holding her with those penetrating, gun-metal eyes. "To buy patchouli, just go to The Lady's Cauldron in North Stonington. It's not far from here at all."

Sarah looked to her middle sister. "I don't think any of us would be welcomed at the Fitzgerald's farm."

"Actually, I am," said Lilith proudly. "I've been

renting a house near there. Since I was driving past it, I went in and visited with Maeve. No hard feelings at all." As she listened, Holly looked from sister to sister. Those supremely controlled faces revealed little emotion as Lilith continued, "I will be attending The Lady's Cauldron's Beltane ritual." Both her sisters eyed her skeptically, but Lilith had turned back to Holly. "You know of Beltane?"

Holly answered mechanically, "It's the Spring renewal rite–when surrogates reinvigorate the earth's energy by re-enacting the union of the Earth Goddess and the Horned Hunter."

Lilith continued in a deep voice, "And any other unions for those who wish to celebrate their gifts from the Goddess. I remember the old Beltanes that were held at night. In the darkness, so many of us could go into the woods and celebrate our lives. Reveling in their unbound sexuality, then coming out and switching partners. All celebrating the life force within."

In reminiscence, Abby smiled sweetly. "Remember the year we first brewed honey mead for Beltane? When there were thirty worshippers down in the Le Fleur sanctuary? The God and Goddess renewed the earth on Grace's couch, while we danced to drums and Egyptian sistrums?" As Holly watched, Abigail unconsciously swayed her body so sinuously in that long blue denim skirt.

Sarah looked up frowning and said in a disapproving voice, "I remember one Beltane, when the group healer had to go to the doctor she worked for and get thirty-two prescriptions for penicillin."

"B-b-but," Holly started. "I thought it was only for the main couple to reenact the union of the Goddess and God?"

"No," chimed in Lilith. "You could be the Beltane Goddess, Holly...with your policeman."

Abby sighed dreamily. "When he was up at Yule–oh,

you should have seen Sgt. Travinski. Such a marvelous, manly chest, with those strong arms and those long, muscular thighs."

Her sister Sarah raised an eyebrow. "You were there for worship, weren't you, Abigail?"

Not hearing that Abby was continuing, "I always knew the sergeant would look that good, just seeing him in those blue pants, walking away with that square, tight rear..."

A grim-lipped Sarah cut her sister off, **"We get the point!"**

As Abby reddened, Holly tried not to laugh. "Yes, P-P-Paul does have a nice exit." But she ducked her head. "But he can't go to Grace's. He'll lose his job. His chief won't allow it."

"Religious prejudice is so unfair," said Abby vehemently, but then looked to Holly. "But you shouldn't go unescorted to Grace's! Remember the trouble last time."

Lilith looked to Holly. "Celebrating Beltane is her birthright!" In a brief second, Lilith and Sarah exchanged gray-eyed glances. Holly found herself picturing two female cougars circling each other, one black, one sun yellow, judging the strength of their opponent before attacking. That image immediately appeared foolish, as Sarah turned to Holly, saying, "Without an escort, a young woman should not be attending skyclad worship anywhere."

"It's perfectly safe to attend Beltane at The Lady's Cauldron. They hold their worship outside, in a woods screened pasture above their farm. Closer to Gaia."

As if the very idea was unpalatable, Sarah asked, "Maeve still celebrates, after everything...?"

Lilith rose imperiously. "Of course, the Fitzgeralds are not cowards, hiding on their farm from the Witchkiller." She turned to Holly and said, "The Lady's Cauldron is just off Route 184 in North Stonington. You'll see the hand-carved signs. Follow them, and you'll find what you're looking for."

Then as she gave a brief triumphant smile to her two sisters, Lilith picked up her blue shaded mohair shawl and walked out.

The sisters said nothing for a time, then Sarah spoke wearily, "Holly, I know it's probably worthless to tell you, but you do understand that going to The Lady's Cauldron would not be in your best interests?"

But Holly was focused on something else. "That name, Maeve Fitzgerald...it sounds familiar, but I don't know why?"

The sisters exchanged conflicted looks, then Sarah spoke firmly. "You were only five, but you might remember Maeve as a member of your father's coven."

Holly thought about that. "I'd like to talk to her."

Abby sat down before her and reached out an appealing hand. "But just the fact that our sister is trying to get you *there* should be enough to warn you away."

"Lilith's power over me is finished," Holly said confidently.

"But I don't think Lilith is finished with you," pronounced Sarah darkly.

"Why?"

Again that exchange of significant looks between Abby and Sarah. Finally, it was Abby who answered her, "In the past, Lilith has spoken about wanting to control the power of the Corey triplets."

"W-w-we have power?" asked a confounded Holly.

Abby spoke gently. "Separately you all have certain raw talents, but if you were to meld your energies together..."

"Which would not be the best of ideas!" Sarah cut in firmly. "There are innate forces, but they should not be accessible to you or your brothers until you are trained!"

Holly thought about it. "N.C. resists any thoughts of psychic gifts."

"Which is best for of all you," finished Sarah firmly. "You and Frost are very undisciplined and should certainly not

be playing with things that you have no idea how to control!
You certainly should not be going to The Lady's Cauldron on
Beltane or any other day!"

# Chapter 7

The next morning, after driving her brothers to work, Holly dropped off Noel's baking at the Mystic Motel. She walked behind the desk counter to lay their bill down. The manager Alice was deeply involved with booking a large wedding party with the mother of the bride, the bride, and the mother-in-law-to-be all disagreeing over the arrangements.

Holly saw the maid's key card pass on the counter, and just slipped it under her hand and headed outside to the stairs. She knew where Margaret's rooms were. The second floor, Alice had said 213 and 214. The two large windows had their blinds pulled closed, so feeling like a sneak thief, Holly knocked on 213. When she got no answer, she knocked on 214. No answer.

Looking around to see that no one watching, she walked back to 213 and inserted the card key. Inside the room was dark. Holding her breath, Holly turned on the light. The bed was freshly made, but the room was messy, with paper cups of coffee, and clothes were strewn about. Freezing from the high air conditioning, she realized the double connecting door was open. Holly moved to check if anyone was in the next dark room. Then heart pounding she started hurrying about, opening drawers, looking in the closet and the bathroom. What was she looking for? Anything strange. There were a pile of books on the desk; Margaret didn't seem to be the reading type. Holly studied them: *Diamonds History and Lure*, *The Diamond Market*, *Hunting Diamonds*. She looked quickly in the waste can: used makeup tissues, sticky condoms, and candy wrappers. How much time did she have?

Holly stepped into the other room, fumbling for the light. She tripped over a large pair of men's sneakers, this must be Brandon's. This room was neater, no books, but the t-v guide was open on the desk. She looked in the bathroom--a leather bag with razor and lotions. The shower was wet, and

Holly noticed the drain had a yellowish stain. She was tempted to wipe it down--Alice's maid wasn't doing too good a job. Holly looked in the narrow closet: Brandon's Hawaiian print shirts, brightly colored golf shirts, and a plain blue, long-sleeved shirt, then a row of casual cargo pants, camo shorts in green, gray and blue. And then a pair of blue slacks. Those plain slacks were not Brandon's style at all. Holly looked back at the blue shirt, pulling it out. She could see something along its sleeve–a black thread, as if something had been sewn on and then cut off.

Steps outside and Holly froze. How could she ever explain being in here? She held her breath until the steps moved on and faded, then Holly hung the shirt back up, gave a fast look through the empty drawers, turned off the light of 213 and headed back into the first room.

Again she scanned the room, taking a closer look. Medicine bottles by the bed, there was a cosmetic case in the closet...which was strange, because there was another one in the bathroom. Holly pulled out the closet one, resting her hand over it. The flower print bag seemed to give off an evil vibration. She unzipped it and saw three white cloth dolls. Magical poppets! The first had a blue cloth scrap pinned to it, with red wax drippings and some sandy hair taped on; The next had black hair taped to its head, this one was crossed with a red painted 'X' and had black wax over the red drippings; the last doll also had black hair taped on with red candle wax dripped on its head. This one was wearing a doll-sized Hawaiian shirt.

Margaret was trying to control someone–three someones--, but Holly couldn't report it to the police. She touched the blue-clothed doll–it had no feeling of Paul, but she ripped the taped hair off and stuffed it in her jeans pocket anyway. There was a black candle and some herbs at the bottom of the case and a knife. The whole thing revolted Holly as she stuffed everything back into the makeup bag, and returned it to the closet. She had to get out of there.

Shutting off the light and not looking, Holly opened the door and headed out to the balcony walkway, and found herself facing Margaret and Brandon.

"That's your room," Brandon started.

"What are you doing in there?" demanded Margaret.

"I-I-I'm the m-m-maid."

Brandon looked at her. "The rooms were cleaned this morning."

He moved toward her and Margaret narrowed her eyes, but Holly only shuttered. "T-to-towels. You were short. I got more for you."

From behind them came an authoritative voice. "And now you have to finish the downstairs. 103 needs to be cleaned before I can rent it." It was Alice standing there, not looking too pleased.

Holly quickly pushed past the couple and started downstairs, with Alice following closely. When they got down, Holly turned to explain, but Alice was holding out her hand. "The key card."

Blushing Holly pulled it out of her jeans pocket, "I-I-I..."

"Wanted to help Paul. We all do but stay away from those two."

Margaret and her boyfriend had frightened her, but Holly had to calm down. If Margaret was using witchcraft, Holly had to counteract it! Getting gas for the hearse, Holly took 27 to Route 184 North. Her hands were sweating, and she felt a little sick. Because Brandon looked like he was going to grab her? Or because of Margaret's controlling dolls? Or because Sarah had said not to do this? *Was Sarah like her sister Lilith--deliberately trying to mentally control Holly?* Holly didn't think so.

She nearly missed the flat wooden sign cut in the shape of a black, three-legged pot, elegantly lettered 'The Lady's

Cauldron.' It was by an old mailbox. She must've passed it before and never noticed it. Holly couldn't stop the hearse in time, so had to drive past it, find a wide area, laboriously turn the long van around, and drive back to the whitish dirt lane.

Here the land sloped downward to a small stream. On the right side, higher on the hill of the private road, she saw a two-story, white wooden farmhouse. Farther down, across the wooden bridge, was a series of barns and buildings. There was parking to the left in front of a three-story high red barn that was now converted with small paned windows to form a country-type store. The hill sloped down to other barns and buildings, set around a square, fenced paddock area.

Beyond that, there were two or three commercial-sized, metal- framed, plastic-covered greenhouses, and then spreading brownfields under cultivation. Here the narrow valley started to climb up again, and the neatly plowed land gave way to the thickly forested hilltop.

She parked and looked around. In front of the barn were tables of plants for sale.: lavender, lemon verbena, mint, sage, and parsley–all stuff she had hoped to sell them. A rooster with iridescent black feathers strutted about, with some coal black hens picking at the grass behind him. Walking closer to the barns, Holly smelled hay and manure and heard laughter as two men in jeans were unloading hay bales from a truck into one of the smaller sheds down below. She saw a dark-red haired guy, nearly six foot, and a taller black man. They had their shirt sleeves rolled up, showing strong muscular arms shining with sweat as they tossed hay bales.

Holly walked into the barn store, breathing aromas of the Orient. She estimated that the salesroom took up two-thirds of the length of the old barn, with a stock room and restrooms set in the back. The ceiling was unfinished up to the beams holding up the steep roof. In the left corner, she saw a two-doored florist's cooler. They apparently sold flower arrangements here too. The Hoyt sisters knew she was always looking for a place to sell or trade herbs. Why hadn't Sarah or Abby mentioned The Lady's Cauldron before?

Inside the barn was gray wood, with some of the stalls left there, now used to hold up sales goods. Multiple-paned windows in the walls gave light to the large room filled with tables of hand-dipped candles, kiosks of essence oils, pyramids of souvenir mugs, and incense sticks. She passed a four-sided, revolving floor display of big-headed, cartoonish, cloth VooDoo dolls. Each was on its own card, with three long hat pins, and cutely labeled *for your ex-wife, for your boss, for your mother in law...* Remembering Margaret's poppets, Holly shivered.

Sounds of a soft thump, then another. Holly turned and saw a huge cat. It had green eyes, long, spiky gray fur with dark tiger stripes, touches of tan and a ruff about its neck–a Maine Coon cat. No, there were two of them. There was a smaller one, dark black with light gray markings meandering over, swaying its dark plume of a tail. They both were staring at her as if they were the shop's guardians. Holly started to reach down to pet the biggest one. The female raised her nose and smelled Holly's fingers, then regally turned her plume of a tail and walked away.

The other younger, thinner one, with darker fur, cautiously came closer. It seemed as if he was assessing her motives. Finally, he moved forward and rubbed his head and body against her jeans leg. Holly reached down and petted his long, stiff fur. The cat purred deeply and looking up at her as he walked away, headed to a wall. The cat looked back over its shoulder as if to see if Holly was following.

She did. Bookcases here held saints' candles, books on herbs, palmistry and crystals, hand blown glass pitchers, and jars of local honey. Walking that end wall, she saw a cork-board labeled *Community Connections*: Business cards for trash haulers, astrologers, plumbers, portrait artists, tarot card readers, baby sitters, herbalists, reiki massage therapists and reincarnation readings. There was even a schedule for meetings of 'The Lady's Caldron's Coven' right out on the bulletin board!

Well, Grace La Fleur had a publically accessible website for her Church of Nature's Bounty. Holly studied the board more. Maybe they would let Holly pin a business card here for the Corey Mansion Bed and Breakfast? At the bottom, she saw a neatly lettered index card that read: *Male Worker Wanted for Lady's Cauldron: Three days a week, but must be flexible. Sales, Stockroom, some farm chores, flower delivery. Florist experience a plus, but will teach. Must have a clean driver's record. Apply at the sales counter.* Maybe she could be the 'male worker'? It'd be great to work in a place like this. It wasn't that far from the mansion, and they had a lot of fun stuff. She started walking around, taking a closer look.

Displayed in the windows were not the usual sun catchers, but masterful designs of stained glass: translucent pink lady's slippers, scarlet rhododendrons, wild pansies, toadstools and several large Amish hex sign rounds done in clear, colored, and translucent milk-glass. Hanging from square forged nails in the old chestnut posts were pairs of hand-dipped bayberry candles. Above that, ice tongs, antique farm implements, and tinwork candle molds hung from the barn's cross beams. What was that? Holly moved under it, to get a better look. A saddle hung over the rafter, but she looked at the 'U' shaped horn. A lady's side-saddle, with leather that wasn't too dusty or dry–it looked like it had been recently oiled and used?

She walked around the room. Hand-crafted wood bowls next to a table of stuffed toys with Mystic's nautical theme. Some tree funguses with crudely painted farm scenes next to finely crafted, locally blown glass in rainbow colors. In the center was a square of sales counters. Two sides were fronted with glass cases for jewelry. She saw the usual abalone shelled turtle pins, gold plated cat earrings and silver porpoise pendants for the tourist trade, but mixed in were elaborate silver Celtic crosses, pewter Pentagrams, Thor's hammers, Watching Eyes, a bronze Caduceus, and Egyptian Ankhs. Holly realized this store was a strange mixture of tourist garbage, witchcraft paraphernalia, and finely wrought handcrafted items.

Walking to another wall, Holly found a gleaming, cherry cabinet carved with Wiccan symbols, holding about fifty little 2" x 4" slots for two oz bottles of oil essences. It was stocked with a mixture of homemade, hand-written labels and commercial brands. She looked through: Cinnamon, Green Apple, Witch hazel, Lavender, and what she was looking for!

From a mini-ramp with a black wire gate, Holly pulled out the small glass bottle labeled 'Patchouli.' It had a clear liquid inside. She untwisted the cap and inhaled an earthy, exotic whiff that made her envision the smoking censers of a sultan's harem. She rotated the small vial in her hand and saw a price label. Twenty-one dollars–a lot more than she wanted to pay. That she could pay. That she should pay!

But for those prosperity spells that she felt attracted to, she needed patchouli. There was no one here to buy it from. Should she go down to those guys working? She could hear their laughter in the distance. Holly walked to the large central counter built in as a square, with a wrapping table in the center. There was an ornate, old fashioned cash register on one side and a newer digital one on the other side. She looked to see if there was some kind of buzzer or bell she could ring to bring out some staff. Nothing. Should she knock on the storeroom door? That male cat had jumped up on the counter and was rubbing against her arm.

Then Holly saw the green cash box with its neatly printed sign taped on it: *If nobody's here, just leave the money in the box. Thank you.* Holly opened the unlocked box. There were some ones, a five, a few tens, and some change already in the unlocked box. These people were that trusting? The Corey Bed and Breakfast already had one couple that scrammed before dawn without paying, and two others that left bounced checks. Now, Paul, had her writing all their license plates and driver's license numbers on their check-in card herself.

With no one in here now, Holly started pulling out her money. She had twenty. But she had to pay the last one dollar in change. Two quarters, three dimes, she dug deeper into her purse. A nickel. Another dime. And pennies. Okay. She had twenty-one dollars.

Sound of boots of wood. The two workmen were coming in. The solid black guy was saying, "I'll get the sodas," as he headed for the door labeled 'storeroom.'

The other man nodded to him, then moved to get behind the counter, explaining, "I'm sorry, mam. We're short-handed today." He had tanned skin, even white teeth, and dark, reddish hair that would've needed a haircut if it hadn't coiled in lazy waves. "You look familiar? Where did I see you before?" He had lively, happy green eyes that seemed to see into her soul and like her. "Did we meet at the Big Y? Town Hall? Or at the Battle of Fredericksburg in one of our past lives? By the way, in this life, I'm Colin Fitzgerald."

"H-h-holly Corey," she said, lowering her head in shyness under his barrage of friendliness.

"You got the hearse out there?" he asked, smiling broader.

She blushed, lowering her head even more in embarrassment. "Y-y-yes."

"The guy in the back is really muttering because my ATV splashed some mud on it. You always ride around with a grumpy ghost?" he asked casually.

# Chapter 8

Holly looked up in surprise, directly into those emerald green eyes. "That's B-B-Bernie. The spirit of the hearse's last owner. Bernie worked at the funeral home and always loved driving a Cadillac. He bought it from the home, and when Bernie died, he didn't want to leave it. So I got it cheap. Most people don't hear him unless he really howls, but they feel uncomfortable in or around the hearse if Bernie doesn't want them there."

The younger cat on the counter was rubbing against Colin. He scratched its ears and said, "This is Horus, and that Maine Coon cat over there is his mother, Bast." He looked at the money she had been counting out on the counter. He picked up the small vial. "You're getting patchouli for a spell? For love or luck?"

"Prosperity spell."

"That'll work for you," he said firmly.

"W-w-what is patchouli? I grow herbs, but I don't know it. But I've seen it in spells on the Internet."

He laughed. "You're practicing from what you read on the computer?"

Holly found herself blushing more. "I-I'm stupid, I know."

"No." He face softened. "You are not, mam, I can tell that from the way you soak in everything around you. Patchouli is a weed in India. Like sage, rosemary, and thyme, it's in the mint family. In oil form, it's got a very heavy, earthy scent that is long lasting. It was popular in the 1970s with the hippy crowd--supposed to raise your enlightenment or your pleasure."

Holly was listening carefully. "It's grown in India? You can't grow it in North America?"

"No, it has been cultivated successfully in North

America since the 1900s. I had a small, experimental plot of it–that got wiped out with the cold winter and spring freeze we had this year. I don't think I'll plant it again, it's easier to buy it as an oil from my wholesaler."

"It's twenty-one dollars?" she asked, pushing her money toward him.

"Plus Connecticut's 6.35 sales tax which brings it to 22.31." He answered easily.

Her face fell. Embarrassed, she started to pull back her change. "I-I-I really don't know if I need..."

"You know," he said, quickly looking around. "That's why they don't let me work the desk here too often. The oil essences are on sale today. Only fifteen bucks—even."

She gave him her sternest look. "Thank you, but I don't know if your boss would be happy with that."

He looked furtively about and whispered, "Actually, I am the boss."

Lowering her head with a slight smile, Holly pulled back her coins and let him give her change. Putting her small bottle in a white bag, he asked, "Now tell me, how you do spells by the Internet?"

"Google them," she said simply.

He looked at her blankly

She smiled. "Google is a search engine on the computer. You click on your Internet Icon. If the screen doesn't come up with it, you type in 'Google,' and when the box comes up, you type in your request. Say, *Spell for money*. Hit enter, then Google brings up a choice of sites to look through. Some sites will want you to pay before they give you the spells. Just go back and type in *'free spells for money'* in quotes. But don't let them switch you to a for-pay site. Just keep looking, and you'll get screens and screens of spells, charms, poppet instructions, and places to buy the necessary ingredients."

This quiet man seemed to be paying more attention to

Holly's blue-green eyes than her instructions, but he finally asked, "How do you know if these spells are any good?"

"I search through them. And print out the ones that call to me. Then you just have to try them."

Colin looked doubtful. "It's that easy?"

"N-n-no," said Holly. "A lot of the spells don't have amounts of ingredients or proportions; they say cinnamon and patchouli and sage, but it's not like a cooking recipe that says two teaspoons of vanilla, a cup of flour, and three eggs whites."

"So how do you work it out?" Colin crossed his arms over his wide chest, studying her.

"I asked Abby. She said to lay out the ingredients on a table and hold my hand palm flat above them, and I would feel what was needed."

"That's Abigail, Hoyt?"

"Do you know Sarah and Abby?"

He seemed to answer cautiously. "They come in here sometimes when they need something."

"They never told me about you," said Holly feeling a little left out of the loop.

Colin looked to the door of the storeroom, then looked back to her. He seemed to look older and bit sadder. "Miss Corey, how did you find your way to The Lady's Cauldron?"

"Their sister told me."

His eyes narrowed a bit. "Yhep, it would Lilith Hoyt."

"She doesn't really like me," Holly started.

"Lilith doesn't like anybody," finished Colin with a slight smile. "Did Abby tell you to cast a protective circle before you were doing your spell?"

"N-n-no."

"Abby probably does it so automatically she doesn't even think about it. And are you keeping a careful record of every spell you cast? Write up the ingredients, the words, date, and phase of the moon and most importantly, the results. You keep that in your Book of Shadows for future use."

"Skye Rainbow kept asking if I had my mother's Book of Shadows?"

"Your mother?"

"H-Hester Farrington Corey. We live at..."

"Witch House," Colin supplied, his friendly aura disappearing. Not that he was hostile, but he had become totally unreadable.

"The C-C-Corey Mansion Bed and Breakfast!"

He took a deep breath before he spoke again. "I'd heard about your mother. They say she was a fine lady." He looked to the back storeroom door and seemed to listen, then he appeared to be just a friendly farmer again. "Your mother's Book of Shadows. You probably have it somewhere. You'll find it when you're ready. Will you be needing anything else today?"

Holly hated to ask for something she really wanted–needed-- especially when she was sure he would turn her down. She took a deep breath and tried to speak slowly, "Your ca-ca-card. You want to hire a man? I was interested."

He looked at her from head to toe. "With that figure, if you telling me you're really a male, preparing for your sex reassignment, I'm not going to believe it. Even we farm boys are not that gullible."

She reddened under his scrutiny. "I-I-I can drive a truck. Do farm chores. I've shelved stock. I used to be a saleswoman at the Rainbow Realm in Mystic. Did you ever go there?"

Again his face took back that guarded look, and she instantly felt his friendly radiations were damped. "That was Skye Rainbow's store in the Ye Olde Mystic Village? No–Maeve, and I never went there."

Belatedly, Holly looked to Colin's finger for a wedding ring. *He didn't wear one, but of course, a hunk like him would be married.* "M-M-Maeve's your wife?"

He flushed a bit, obviously sensing her personal interest as he explained. "No, Maeve's my mother. We've always had an adult relationship." He looked to the woods outside, saying ruefully. "Well, more my adult to her kid at times. Maeve has always been a wild child."

"But you never went to the Rainbow Realm? Skye was selling stuff like you do?" asked a curious Holly.

He blew that off with, "Skye and my mother had been friends, then they weren't. It's a long story. Now, you want to get hired." Colin shook his head. "I'm sorry. I've already got two women working the counter. They're sisters who live on the dairy farm down the road. They'd be here today, but they have a wedding to attend."

"I arrange flowers," Holly supplied a bit desperately.

"My mother makes up the floral arrangements, and I help her."

It was going badly, Holly had to do something. She looked to the cabinet across the store. "I-I-I saw the refrigeration unit."

"There are three bigger ones in the back. I've been investing more as our business picks up. With our arrangements, we've got a steady year-round business with local deliveries, walk-in sales, and funeral homes."

Holly brightly reminded him. "I come with my own hearse!"

Colin chuckled but shook his head. "I need a man who can take stock boxes from the delivery truck, muck out the stables sometimes, and maybe pitch in at harvest. And we deliver arrangements to some not so great places."

If she called Paul, Holly was sure she could get a police escort anywhere, but she just said, "I can do that."

That taller black man came back walking from the storeroom two sodas in his hand. "That your hearse outside with that haunt whining?"

She nodded.

"You want to sell them?" He asked, his yellow-rimmed, black eyes gleaming.

"N-n-no." Holly smiled and lowered her head.

Colin turned to his friend. "This is Lapin Le Veau. Lapin, this is Holly Corey, owner of the hearse with a ghost named Bernie in the back."

Ordinarily, she'd offered to give them a ride, but not with the brakes failing so badly. She just said, "I couldn't find The Lady's Cauldron's site on the Internet?"

"Yeah." Colin looked embarrassed too, smiling lopsidedly. "We've got to get a website—someday."

"It's not hard," Holly said. "We've got one for the Corey Mansion Bed and Breakfast. We display our breakfast menus, pictures of the rooms, local tourist sites, and we can take reservations online. It's really helped our business."

"You set that up?" Colin asked with interest.

"M-m-me and Noel–my brother, N.C.–we could help you. You could sell your candles and oil essences by mail. You've got quite a collection." Holly took a deep breath. *He really didn't want to hire her, but she needed to replace the hearse's brakes.* "Do you have anybody else you're considering for the job?"

"Not yet." Colin was obviously trying to be as kind as he could. "The card just went up."

"Okay. Hire me as a temporary until you find somebody else." She stopped to take a calming breath and surprisingly felt a warm wave of confidence spreading over her. *Rather like the feelings she got from Abby sometimes.* Holly started again, "During that time I can work with you on getting your website together."

"But that's not fair to you," he pointed out.

"Well, if I'm working with you, maybe you might find that you don't need anybody else?"

"The job doesn't pay much. And I've got to give my current people first chance at hours."

"That's okay," Holly said brightly.

The dark coon cat sat on the counter, licking his leg. Hearing the sound of air brakes outside, both Colin and Lapin looked up. "Did Esther have something on the schedule today?" Lapin asked.

"Don't matter if it's listed or not," said Colin. "Man your battle stations, the barbarians are at the gate!" He looked to Holly. "You want a job? You're hired. Temporarily--you understand? C'mon, I'll show you how to use the tax calculation chart and the register before the first wave hits."

Holly smiled widely and followed him as he lifted a hinged section of the counter so she could get inside, as a busload of perfectly coifed-haired senior ladies marched in to storm the store!

# Chapter 9

By the end of the week, Holly felt at home at The Lady's Cauldron. Esther and Rachel Goldstein were about her height and two hundred pounds each, with frosted brown hair. Raised on a dairy farm, they worked hard--if they weren't selling, they were dusting the merchandise,  Colin wanted a clean store. Holly's job was to help them by restocking from the back room shelves.

In that large stock room, there were three, five foot by seven-foot worktables, in front of four double-sliding doors, floor-sized refrigeration units filled with flowers. The non-windowed wall dividing the barn had been covered with boards. The cork boards held planting calendars, individual order forms for the floral arrangements, flower resupply schedules, and a calendar for The Lady's Cauldron's Coven events. The day's delivery routes were worked upon a large, school-sized white board with a colored pen for each driver. Holly's was her favorite color--pink.

Colin taught her how to 'green' an arrangement. First, she checked the order for price and description and picked out an appropriate container. Then she cut off and shaped a green foam base that she taped down and wet in the sink. Finally, Holly stuck plant leaves or ferns in to hide the base, in preparation for Colin or his mother to stick in the finishing flowers.

For weak-stemmed flowers, Holly learned how to wire them to a stick; how to use green floral tape to hide stems and to set small water vials on corsage stems. By the end of the week, Colin seemed to be letting her do more and more of the flowers. Just before the shop closed, he always went through the cases, weeded out arrangements or flowers that were beginning to fade or were bruised. "We want our customers getting only the best, so I'd rather take a loss on something that's going, than sell it, and have a customer dissatisfied."

"If you're going to throw them away, maybe I could buy them at a discount?" Holly asked.

"No." He was quite firm about that. "You can have them for free. Since they're destined for the garbage can, it'll save me a disposal problem."

She picked up an exquisite pink lily. "I thought I'd make my own mini arrangements in mason jars for the rooms at the mansion."

"Good idea." He looked over to the shelves. "I have some books on how to do flower arranging. If you want to study them, maybe you could do the displays some days. Maeve really doesn't like coming over to the store that much."

Holly lowered her head and felt herself pinking with pleasure, just having Colin's approval. But she'd worked here for a week and never saw his mother. Then, the sense of male presence just went up. Holly turned. Lapin had come in the back door. He was always so quiet, even in those rubber work boots. Always watching her with those almost black eyes with whites that were yellowish in that burnt chocolate skin. Holly always had the idea that Lapin's aura was enveloping, but that his interest was not sexual. Still, his eyes openly went up every line of her body as he spoke to Colin. "We gonna plant basil before it rains?"

Colin frowned, looking at a delivery box on the counter. "I've got to get those wicks and wax perfumes over to Maeve. She's got to get working on those floral candles—I want them in the store before we get our Beltane crowd."

Lapin looked from him to the sky outside. "Can't Holly take them over?"

"Holly hasn't met Maeve yet," said a tired Colin.

The big black man shrugged. "Holly, gonna work here, she got to meet her."

Holly looked from the box to the trim white farmhouse on the hill. "I can take this up the hill."

"I live in the farmhouse," Colin explained. "Maeve

prefers to live in a cottage in the woods. He pointed to the high pines beyond a big white **PRIVATE PROPERTY** sign. "But that box is heavy."

Holly hefted the package; it was more bulky than really heavy. "I can carry this easily."

"Well, you can take the ATV until you reach the footbridge. Have you ever driven one?"

"Paul took me on a date, and rented two once." She blurted that out before she thought. She didn't want to explain Sgt. Travinski to them.

Still, Colin was watching her closely as he continued with his instructions. "You'll have to leave the ATV on this side of the footbridge." As he pointed across a flowered meadow toward the woods, there seemed to be some sort of pathway into the pines. There was evaluation behind his eyes as Colin explained, "My mother avoids the public." Holly looked at him curiously, so he continued. "She had an accident years ago. The scars are pretty bad on half her face. You'll get used to it in time, but first seeing her is pretty rough."

"If I'm working here, she can't think of me as a stranger," said Holly lightly.

"We agreed your hiring is just a temporary arrangement," he reminded her carefully.

She nodded and picked up the box.

"See that little stream over there with the footbridge my grandfather made? Once you are over it, there's the path worn in the ground. Follow it, and you come out to a clearing above the lake. To your left is a two-story stone and timber cottage. Maeve lives there."

"Are there three bears, too?" Holly asked impishly.

Colin chuckled. "No, Maeve puts out an anti-bear spell."

Holly grabbed a numbered key off the board, picked up her box, and headed out the back door of the barn. She stopped and scanned the land. It was flat land on this back side of the barn. The Ladies Cauldron could put out a deck or a flagstone patio and some tables and maybe serve tea and sandwiches? She'd speak with Colin.

She loaded the box on the ATV and drove down a pathway through a meadow of white, yellow and red flowers, going right down past the **PRIVATE PROPERTY** sign. When she reached the bridge, Holly looked back. Colin was taking his farm-sized green tractor out to the fields, but she didn't like the look of those dark clouds over the hillside. Lightening? Should he be out? Should she?

Parking the little four-wheeled ATV at the stream that was only three foot wide, she crossed on that red varnished, miniature Japanese footbridge. On the other side, Holly found flat, round stones had been sunk into the ground, forming a path she followed into the pine forest. At the beginning of the pine trees, another jarring note, a second warning sign in red lettering: **TRESPASSERS WILL BE PROSECUTED**!

Shifting the box's weight from arm to arm, Holly walked on the spongy path of red pine needles and was pleasantly surprised to keep finding cute little sculptures tucked in alongside the twisting pathway. She spotted a life-like ceramic snail, a stone frog jumping in an arch, a wrought iron pelican looking up at her, and a lurking brown-wood fox that stalked so realistically on the moss. Once she was past a small hill, she could see the glimmer of light through the trees--water ahead. A pond...no, a good-sized lake. *Great, this box was getting really heavy.* Holly kept walking. Finally, the pine forest opened up to a clearing. She stood in the shadows and looked out over a series of brick and flagstoned terraces overlooking sun sparkling water.

The clouds above had opened up for a moment, and sunlight illuminated a cottage that would have been more at home in the Black Forest, with Hansel and Gretel skipping up the path to the witch's oven. Still staying in the shadows, Holly saw that the cottage had an arched, hand-carved door, with a steep roof over a half-timbered second floor. Large windows were made up of small, wood-framed diamond panes.

As Holly stood in the shadows, she saw more clever wood and rock sculptures peeping out of the carpet of short yellow, white, and purple crocuses. She also heard the mellow, ringing tones of stained-glass wind chimes blowing in the wispy breezes from the water. That was joined with a quacking of three or four white ducks, waddling up from the lake, followed by some wild, green and brown-headed mallards.

Holly heard a click, then saw the gothic arched door open. Facing away from her, a slim, full-breasted woman walked out, wearing a blue work shirt, gloves, and faded blue jeans. She was young, with Colin's thick, dark, wavy red hair worn long. A large daffodil colored chiffon scarf covered her shoulders, as she carried a small woven basket to the edge of the main patio.

The growing line of domestic and wild ducks on the terraces quacked excitedly until she started tossing out corn kernels to them. Holly stayed in the cooling shadows and studied the woman's profile more closely. She noted fine wrinkles about the woman's eyes and realized the woman was older than she first had appeared. Holly called out tentatively, "Maeve?"

Like a startled doe getting ready to flee, the woman twisted and stared at her full faced. Holly had a wrenching visceral reaction to the horrifying sight of white puckered scaring that disfigured the left side of her face, even replacing the hair about her forehead and behind the shriveled ear. The woman had a nose, two normal eyes, and lips, but the rest of the face was ruined on the left side. Uncontrollably, Holly found herself giving a shudder.

Probably at seeing the horrified look on Holly's face, the woman twisted away and pulled up the chiffon scarf from her shoulders covering the scarred half of her face. When she turned back to Holly, Maeve had regained her control. Standing tall, as she pronounced in an icy voice, **"You're trespassing! Leave!"**

But as Holly stepped out of the shadows into the warming sunlight, the woman's face seemed to collapse. She took a shaken step towards Holly, crying out, "Hester? Hester, Corey?" Her voice was agonized. "Hester, please forgive me..."

# Chapter 10

The woman abruptly stopped. Facing Holly, she stood silently staring at her, shaking her head as if awakening from a nightmare, Maeve said carefully, "You-you **can't** be Hester!"

"I'm her daughter, Holly Corey."

"One of the triplets?" Maeve turned the scarf covered side of her ravaged face away from Holly and finished in an angry, commanding voice, "Never mind! This is private land. You must leave!"

Holly looked down at the very heavy box in her arms. "Your son sent me. I'm working for him. These are wicks and molds for your floral candles."

"You're working for Colin?" In surprise, Maeve looked back to her full face.

"Yes." The scarf covered the woman's scars, but Holly suddenly felt little waves of nausea. *But from Abby Hoyt, she was learning to determine when that feeling was projected to her by someone else.*

"Why?" Maeve demanded to know.

"I-I-I n–n-need the money."

Maeve stopped for a moment to collect herself and then started again in a measured voice, "I'm so sorry. You must think I'm crazy!" She looked about. "I try to cultivate a nasty hermit reputation, so people will stay away and let me do my work undisturbed. But since you're working here now..." almost defiantly, she stiffened her back and pulled the scarf off her head, letting it fall back on her shoulders. The wide emerald eyes, high curving cheeks, and chestnut-red hair like Colin's were all quite beautiful. She was older than she appeared–but still an attractive woman, except for the puckered white burn scars that marred one side from forehead to her strong chin. And as the scarf shifted, Holly could see that the scarring on her neck also ran down her left arm. "It's not too pretty, but if you're going to work here, you'll have to get used to it," Maeve apologized. "I'm sorry."

"Don't be." Holly could smile genuinely; after the initial shock, Maeve's wrecked face was just another human's envelope, covering the beautiful spirit within. "Can I take this box inside? It's getting heavier."

Maeve moved to open the door again. "Colin shouldn't have you carrying that!"

"I'm strong." They climbed up the wide stone steps to the fairy tale-looking cottage. With stone, stucco, and timbering, it kind of couched in the forest like a cluster of red-topped toadstools. Going in the front door Holly studied the three dimensional, swirling wood carving of a Merlin-like figure in a long robe, with a knotted walking stick and inlaid eyes of milky-green marbles. "Is this your work? It's magnificent!"

"That's Colin's. He carved that in high school, when we remodeled this shepherd's cottage. He has such a talent for capturing physical movement in sculpture."

It was ten degrees cooler inside that slate floored cottage—and darker here. Holly saw working kerosene lamps with metal mirrored sconces on the walls. The furnishings were an eclectic grouping of mostly handmade pieces fashioned of wood. Stump-shaped end tables and chair frames of polished roots that appeared to grow out of the floor were coiled above green multicolored braided rag rugs. Stain glass designs glinted pure colors from some of the smaller windows. Holly had the feeling she was walking in a Hobbit's hole.

Looking at the box she carried, Maeve said, "We'll take that to the studio."

Following Maeve, Holly paused before a five foot by six foot woven hanging. At first, it appeared to be an abstract design in variegated greens, browns, and blacks, but as you looked closer, it coalesced into a twisting swamp scene, with yellow, white and red eyes everywhere. Alligators, turtles, herons and snakes, all woven in a tremendously complex portrayal that seemed to slither and breath damp heat as you watched it. A masterpiece that Holly had seen once before, in a partial state, when it was being created by the warp yarns on Sarah Hoyt's loom–so much for the Sarah and Abby not knowing Maeve Fitzgerald that well!          Each room had built-in bookcases stuffed with oversized volumes. There was a clutter of open research books and project sketches all about the small rooms–rooms that went down a step for one floor, then up two steps for the next room. In what might have been a dining room, Holly saw the table covered with pinned pieces of rainbow colored stained glass being cut to match the pattern sheets underneath them. Next, to that table, a chair was covered with a bright yellow scarf being knitted and several pinecone candle bases being glued.

Each room had two or more crafts projects going. Holly carried out the wick box to a glassed-in porch overlooking the lake. Here the floor was splattered with gray slip and wax from the potter's wheel on one side and some commercial wax shredding and melting equipment on the other.

On one wall dozens of green bayberry and red cinnamon candles hung in pairs from wooden rods on the wall. Those candles were slid from the tin, multi-holed colonial molds hung on hooks beneath them. Below that on the floor were thick pillar candles dipped in multicolored layers of waxes. These were in the process of being hot-knifed carved into curled masterpieces. Again Holly had the feeling of walking through some magical habitat.

Something moved in a shadowed corner. Holly started, but with a whining mew, the big coon cat stepped out. The female, Bast, swept the floor with her thick plume of a tail. Maeve ignored her, checking on the temperature of one of her commercial wax cookers.

Across the windows, three wires had been stretched. The first had twenty or so small, stain-glassed toad stooled sun catchers. "You like mushrooms?" Holly asked.

Maeve shrugged. "People buy 'em."

On the stone-floored porch, Maeve reached down, turning up a propane tank knob then increased the blue flame under a stainless steel wax cooker. With a box cutter, she expertly cut open the box carton Holly had set down, pulling out a bottle of a clear liquid that Maeve poured into the white wax, liquefying in the inner pot of the double boiler giving it the strong smell of vanilla. "Sending this box over is Colin's subtle suggestion that I speed up production."

When Maeve bent over to adjust the gas again, Holly watched as Maeve's long, red hair slid down dangerously near the flames as she worked. Was this fire how Maeve was so badly burned? The scars looked long faded, but after a horrifying burn like that, how could she ever stand to work so closely to open flames?

# Chapter 11

That night, Holly was happy to be driving home. Her muscles ached, but as she was leaving, Colin had looked up and had given her his gentle smile. "Can you work the weekend too?" She had nodded eagerly--more hours, more pay! Her new boss seemed to like her work, so even though she could hear the resident ghost grumbling in the rear, she felt satisfied. "Yes, Bernie. I will wash all the horse manure off the wheels tomorrow. And wax the hearse too, I promise!"

No guests in the mansion until Friday night. Frost had taken his bike to work, and Noel was having dinner with a coworker who would drop him off home afterward, so Holly was looking forward to taking a long, warm rose petal bath to soothe her sore muscles.

Envisioning that indulgence, she forgot to slow down before turning into the driveway and found herself pumping the brakes and yanking hard at the steering wheel, but still driving over onto the grass and clipping one of the high lilac hedges that guarded the Greek Rival columns. Bernie screamed like a banshee.

Gearing down, Holly man-handled the wheel around the kitchen wing and headed for the oversized parking lot behind the mansion. There, her heart leaped up. A shiny blue Ford F 150 truck parked in the lot. Paul Travinski's. He must be waiting for her. There he was, standing tall by the house. Absurdly, she was so, so happy to see him!

Even at rest, Paul's strong planned features always looked a little stern, unless he was kidding around with that silly lopsided smile of his. Today his face looked particularly strict, and his aura was not that of a man seeing his lover. With trepidation, Holly noted the aura lights about him were dark and angry.

Brake pedal to the floor, she rolled to a stop, then tried to appear normal, taking time to get the flowers Colin had given her out of the back of the hearse. Holly found her head lowering with excitement at seeing him. Well, at least he wasn't in uniform, so it was not an official police visit. "Paul?"

"Can we talk?" he asked.

"Sure." She shrugged.

"Inside."

"Okay." Maybe it was going to be an official visit after all. Did he know their rottweiler had run off for most of the day yesterday? She climbed the porch and opened the door, being careful to grab Thor's collar. "Paul, go inside. I'm going to chain Thor out here."

The dog looked to Paul, barked, but really wasn't hostile when Noel wasn't around radiating anger. When Holly returned, she found Paul sitting in her big country kitchen at the wooden table. Her heart sank. This morning Holly had been laying out the necessities to cast the prosperity spell.

On the table were green and white candles, some bay leaves and a green dollar-sized paper resting on a ceramic plate for burning. All she needed to finish casting the spell was more patchouli that she bought home from The Lady's Cauldron. She looked at Paul quickly. Holly didn't think he knew what she was planning on doing. There was something else on the kitchen table. That small, old book of family photographs that Holly had also been looking at before she left.

"What's this?" Paul asked suspiciously, looking at the items on the table.

Holly wanted to get his attention off the spell casting equipment. The book was opened to the picture of the thirteen members of Gault's coven. She pointed to it. "That's my parents and their friends."

Paul scanned the women surrounding Gault and looked at her with eyes that seemed to demand the truth. "Your father's friends?"

Under those stern eyes, Holly finished lamely, "His coven."

Paul picked up the book, looking closely at the picture. "Just women with your father?"

She struggled to remember. "This was another man in the group...but he left. There was some problem..."

The young, wise-eyed blonde farthest to the left was the spitting image of Holly Corey, so Paul gently asked, "Your mother, Hester?"

"Yes." She had to look away from those probing eyes of his. "This must have been taken a month or two before her death. There are baby pictures of the three of us on the next page. The last pictures of my brothers and me together."

He picked up the green candle. "What's this stuff for?"

She tried to turn his attention back to the photograph again. "I think that is Grace Le Fleur on the right."

He looked back to the photograph. There was a question in his eyes, but neither of them wanted to ask it. Was she going up to Grace Le Fleur's Beltane alone?

Holly continued, "I don't know all of them. That woman next to my father on the left was Marium Goldstein, you knew her as 'Skye Rainbow.' And the woman standing close to him on his right is a younger Lilith Hoyt." He looked sharply at that, but Holly just continued. "I don't know who those others are. The two farthest to the left..."

Paul finished for her, "Abigail and Sarah Hoyt." He looked at the picture carefully. "What year was this picture was taken?"

"My brothers and I were five years old."

"Seventeen, eighteen years ago," he finished. "The Hoyts haven't changed much at all," Paul mused.

"Lilith Hoyt had said Maeve Fitzgerald was in this picture. But I don't know which one she is. Maybe that one, with the dark reddish hair at my father's other side. She lives up in North Stonington, on Route 184. I've just met her."

Every morning when he went into headquarters, Sgt. Paul Travinski memorized the license plates of stolen cars and the pictures of new fugitives. He had almost a photographic memory for faces, and there was one he recognized that shouldn't have been in that picture. She was eighteen years younger, but with an unpleasant jolt, he was sure he recognized the woman. She was in Gault Corey Coven before Hester Corey was murdered? "Uh, Holly, I'm... getting a splitting headache. Honey, could you get me two aspirins?"

"Of course," she said, instantly solicitous. "Frosty's bathroom should have some." She hurried into the rooms her brother had at the end of the kitchen wing. When she left, Paul pulled out his cell phone and snapped four shots of the fading photograph, especially getting a close up of that smiling, blonde- haired woman standing near Sarah and Abby Hoyt. He had his cell phone away and was sitting back at the end of the table again before Holly returned.

She came back with two aspirins. "Would you like some herbal tea? Or some peppermint leaves to smell–that some times helps with headaches?"

"Just some water to swallow these down with." She moved to the sink to get a tin cup as he continued very seriously. "Holly, this is not a social call."

"It's about Thor getting out and chasing the neighbor's chickens?" she asked anxiously. "The neighbors complained?"

"The Dohertys are always complaining." He finished, "But  we've got to talk..."

"I thought 'we' were over?" she asked hopefully.

He ignored that. "I've been hearing reports about your driving. That you went through a stop sign and nearly hit another car?"

Not being able to meet his eyes, Holly bowed her head as she got a tin cup from the cabinet. Quickly filling it with cold water from the oversized, triple sink, she brought it over to him. He was sitting down, staring up at her as Holly started,

"I-I-I made a mistake. And since we aren't dating it's not your concern anymore."

"We're not dating, but I still care for you. And as a cop, I'm responsible for keeping the roads around here safe."

"I was going a little too fast because I was running a bit late."

"You're always running late because you start out too late!" He sounded so judgmental.

She looked away, sick of his lecturing. "It was just once!"

Paul raised an eyebrow. "Don't even think of lying to me! It wasn't '*just once*'! You were stopped once, for nearly causing an accident! But other officers have seen you exceeding the speed limit. Rolling through stop lights and signs. You didn't get tickets, because they think you're my girlfriend, and that it's my job to handle it."

Holly hung her head. "I told the officer that we had broken up."

"Tom told me you didn't try to use my name–that's in your favor."

"You're going to give me a ticket? Paul that'll raise my insurance."

"Lady, I'm going straighten out your driving!" He stopped and studied her. "Right now, I'm deciding what would best: giving you a ticket; pulling your license; or putting you across my knee for a real spanking."

"Paul, that stop sign. I did try to stop! My brakes have been a little slow lately..."

"Slow? What are slow brakes?" He looked at her, then stood up abruptly, looming over her. "Give me your keys."

"Paul..."

**"The keys!"**

Reluctantly she held out her keys. He took them and headed outside. She followed, watching as he headed for the 1956 hearse, sitting vulnerable in the center of that great square of cracked pavement. Paul made a point of walking around the car, stopping and looking at both the front and back tire treads. Watching him slide in the red leather lined hearse seat, she softly whispered. "Please, Bernie, just stay quiet for me!"

Paul got into the hearse, put it in gear and started a slow turn around the square lot of parking pavement, picking up a little more speed as he swung the van around and back toward Holly. Then he must have hit the brakes--but just kept going. Holly could see Paul's eyes widening in horror as he frantically tried to twist the stiff steering wheel away from her. The heavy van kept barreling forward, right at her.

At the last minute, Holly managed to dart to the side, as Paul continued to fight the wheel now headed for his new truck. Struggling hard, he managed a slight turn that just barely missed taking off the front bumper on his Ford F 150. **"Shit!"** He yelled through the window. Rolling to a long stop, Paul jumped out, slamming the van's door and strode to her, yelling, **"Slow Brakes?! YOU DON'T HAVE ANY BRAKES!** You press the pedal to the floor, and it just keeps rolling!"

"You have to pump it a little..." she started lamely.

**"Pump it?** Nothing's stopping that van short of a brick building! That monster weights over 5,000 lbs!" He stopped to get control, but was still breathing heavily as he yelled, **"Your brakes are gone! Your tires are bald! There's no power steering! The shocks are shot! No seat belts! No airbags! This death trap shouldn't even be on the road!"**

"I can get it f-f-fixed," Holly tried to explain. "I-I-I've got a job."

He stopped, looked at her, and asked in a surprised tone. "Since when?"

"Ju-ju-just started."

"Where?"

Holly took a big breath. "I'm working at The Lady's

Cauldron."

He thought about it. "That's the tourist barn, selling herbs, corn, candles and stained glass over in North Stonington? What are you doing there?"

"Store clerk. And I'm going to arrange flowers. And I'm going to do a web page for them."

"You're making them a web presence?" He sounded disbelieving.

That insulted her! "Yes...well with N.C.'s help," Holly said proudly.

"What does that pay?"

She deflated. "Not much. It's only three days a week to start with, but they've just said they'll need me extra time this weekend. And business should pick up with the summer crowd. I'll be able to get the car worked on. Soon."

His blue eyes blazed at her. "Soon? When is **soon**? After you crush some family's eco-friendly tinker-toy with this brakeless Sherman tank?"

Holly hung her head.

**"What did I tell you about lowering your head?"** His sergeant's voice barked. "You're being disciplined! You look me straight in the eye, and you say 'yes, sir' or 'no, sir'!"

She looked straight up at him. "We need the hearse! All of us need to get to work. Noel hasn't found another car since you took his!"

"He bought a stolen car. Holly, I'm a cop, I had to take it!"

"I need the hearse to take my brothers to work and to get to my job to get money to fix it," she finished pleading. "I'll just drive a little slower until I get it fixed!"

"Holly." He looked away at the antique van. "Honey, you can't keep up this rotting mansion. Drive that 1950's bomb and working minimum wage jobs for the rest of your life! You know this is like a replay of my mother and my sister Rosalyn–they both just keep making one self-destructive decision after another, while I kept working my butt off to enable them with money!"

He looked about at the yard. Well, she was making some progress. Some of the mansion's rotting woodwork had been replaced and painted, the B&B was getting bookings. The wilder overgrown was getting cut back. Her herbs were growing in neat beds, and some were replanted in pots to be sold. "At least you've got a real job to go to now," Paul said, as he reached into his pocket and fished out his key ring, separated a fob and four keys. These he handed to her. "You'll drive my truck for a while."

"Y-y-your...no!" Holly was appalled. "W-w-what if some-something happens to it?"

"Like the last time?" he said coldly. "This time, you will drive it carefully!"

"N.C. and Frost drive my hearse too!"

"I'm okay with N.C., but Frost...that's a cat of another color."

"Y-y-you kept taking Frosty out until he passed his driving test!"

"Aaup, but if your brother is driving and he's seen a big, overhanging tree, Frost just starts staring at its limbs..." finished a critical Paul.

"There's nothing wrong with that! He's looking for white oaks with natural bends that the seaport could use for keel repairs."

"Nothing's wrong unless you're staring over your shoulder at a tree, while the car you're driving is doing forty!"

"He's driving better now," she finished weakly.

"Tell him if he drives my truck he'd better be looking at the road and only the road!"

Holly lowered her head and shook it. "I don't want your t-t-truck! Wh-what will you drive?"

"As long as I stay in uniform, I can drive the police Tahoe."

"You don't want to do this," she pleaded. "I-I want my hearse..."

"Honey, you're not driving anything in this condition!" He fished out his cell phone. "I'm having your hearse picked up and taken in to get its brakes fixed. And we'll see what else needs to be done to make it street legal." He stared sternly at her. "It may not be fixable! You understand that?"

"I don't have any money to get it fixed," she finished hopelessly.

"My mechanic's a friend. He'll give you time to pay."

"He won't know how to work on a hearse!"

"Quentin Butler has his own garage, specializing in restoring classic, high-end cars. He even makes some of his own parts. Your hearse is a Cadillac. He'll do just fine with it."

"I can't afford custom work by a professional! Paul, can't you just fix the brakes yourself?"

After he got done with his overtime, his master's thesis, the Lewis's plumbing, and Mark's gun lessons? "He'll give you a deal–you'll have time to pay it off."

"**N-no!**" She said flatly.

His stone face had gone very hard. "Holly, you don't have much of a choice here! I'm calling for a tow truck. Either your hearse goes into Quentin's garage or to the police impound lot, and then to the crusher–do you understand me?"

"Paul–no..."

"Honey, it's too dangerous for you to drive!"

He stood there like the rock of Gibraltar. Holly knew she couldn't move him. "Okay–we''ll find out how much it'll cost to fix. But I-I-I've...got to say goodbye to Bernie–the hearse. Before you take it...privately. Please?"

Paul shook his head, his face set in lines of sadness as he walked away to make his cell phone call. Holly walked over to the hearse. "Please, Bernie. Paul is going to have a mechanic look at the Cadillac. He is trying to save it. You can't yell or moan. They won't understand! Please, for me?"

He was getting off his cell phone as she rejoined him. His strong, angled features held nothing but raw pity for her. He was starting carefully, "Uh, Holly...I've been coaching a guy who wants to shoot in competition. Mark. He's a friend. A consultant for the police department. A real bright guy and very understanding. I talked to him a bit about you...he'd like to meet you."

*Paul dumped her, and now he's trying to get her another boyfriend?*

He was continuing, "I'd like you to talk with him. We could arrange..."

Suddenly she got it. "He's a psychiatrist?"

"Psychologist–a very good one."

"I can't pay to fix my car, and you want me to sign up for head shrinking sessions?"

"It'll be free! He owes me some favors, and I'm sure I can work a deal where I'll give him more range lessons for his talking to you. That should give you three months or so. If need be, we can work out something more."

In an icy voice, she responded, "Paul, I don't want to '*talk to someone.*' I'm just fine."

His voice's strained voice deepened. "You're fine? Honey, you're going over to ask your van for its permission to be fixed?"

"No–I–I- d-didn't do anything of the kind! That would be lu-lu-ludicrous!" She yelled back at him hotly; then had to finish lamely, "I just was telling the hearse what to expect."

He was looking down at her with even more pity. Paul started again, "Honey, Mark thinks there is nothing seriously wrong with you. It's just that your outlook on life is a little different than everybody else's."

*He thought she was nuts.* If she took him over to the hearse and got Bernie to make some sort of ghostly scream, he might understand–but Bernie could be like a recalcitrant kid, refusing to utter a sound, even if she kicked his beloved hearse's bumper. "Are we still dating?" she asked.

"No. And you know why. I'm not going to spend the rest of my life, enabling you and your notions. After your van is fixed, we can be friends, but that's all! Aaup?"

Defeated, she asked, "Do you want me to drive you back downtown?"

"Quentin's guy is coming with the flatbed. He'll give me a ride back to headquarters, where I can pick up the Tahoe." Paul fixed her with stern eyes. "And lady, I'm telling my guys to be looking for you and your brothers! So while you're driving my truck, you are to stick to all the rules. Stop at all red lights and stop signs! If you are running late, well you'll just have to be late, because you **will not** speed! I promise you if I keep hearing reports about your driving infractions you are going to be in big trouble with me, do you understand?"

She looked up into those deep blue eyes of his, desperately wishing he would stay, even if it meant him yelling at her."Yes, sir."

"Good." He reached down and gave her a brotherly kiss on the forehead."It'll work out for the best." She looked gloomily at the hearse, thinking of a mountain of mechanic's bills piling up. Then they both made an effort to talk quietly of other things.

Holly always loved talking with Paul whatever he said; she was just so happy to be near him. But in too short a time, the tow truck drove in and angled its flatbed down. Then a wiry, reddish skinned guy ran around. With a rattle of chains, the hearse was tied on and hauled up. Bernie stayed silent.

Then too soon for Holly, the tow truck, Paul, the hearse and Bernie, the whining ghost, were all gone.

Sadly, she went back to the kitchen. Holly had the vial of patchouli she needed to cast that prosperity charm to pay all her bills, but she only wanted to cast one spell–one to make Sgt. Paul Travinski come to her. To want her. To make his hard muscled body long for her as she longed for his. *For that, she needed even more patchouli.*

# Chapter 12

On their day off, Paul had driven Althea in the Tahoe down for a tournament on the police range in Caddemfield. After Paul had taken his turn at the range, Althea got on the line for hers. Paul scanned the crowd of officers, looking for an old friend, who had started as an officer of the Mystic police. Rumored to be an ex-jockey, the short, slightly bow-legged, fortyish Robert McGinnis was now Chief of Caddemfield police. Mac wore a van dyke beard and a perpetual cynical smile that mocked the paradoxical affairs of men. Now he walked to Paul with a young officer at his side.

Mac greeted Paul with, "This is Patrolman Joe Sinclair. My best shot at getting the trophy away from Stan's cabinet this year. Joe, this Stg. Paul Travinski, the guy you've got to beat!"

Joe seemed embarrassed at that intro, but he put out his hand. "Pleasure, sir. Nice a bit of shooting today."

"Noticed you did pretty good yourself," Paul said, returning the handshake.

The patrolman ducked his head. "Well–I do great on the practice range, but seem to lose my edge when I'm in competition," Joe finished ruefully.

Paul nodded. "That might be a breath control problem. You know, in Afghanistan my sergeant suggested all his snipers start practicing Yoga."

"Yoga?" said Sinclair sounding surprised, looking to Mac as if some sort of joke was being played on him.

"Vinyasa Yoga." Paul acknowledged. "Particularly the breathing exercises."

The patrolman still looked to Mac with puzzlement, but Chief McGinnis just nodded and said, "Listen to him."

Paul explained, "Every time you breathe, your chest and your arms move. When you're in a practicing situation, you've obviously got it under control. But probably when you're in a tournament, or more importantly, a hostage situation where sniper skills are required, your body is going to be pumping a flood of adrenaline. That increases your breathing, which can throw off your aim."

"Yeah," said Joe. "I've tried to hold it more..."

"I had a Marine Yoga instructor, training for the Olympics. For the Biathlon he would ski twelve miles, stopping four times to shoot at a round of five targets. That's two standing and two prone positions in snow. The winner had to hit all twenty targets, with the lowest skiing time. You have to have supreme breath control."

Joe looked back at Paul. "Then you're serious about this Vinaa?"

"Vinyasa Yoga. V-i-n-y-a-s-a. Aaup. Try a morning meditation and poses, concentrating on controlling your breath for two minutes to start with. Build up to twenty minutes. Then do some hard running, stop, and try to get yourself into that meditative, controlled state."

"Can that be done?"

"Aaup." Paul watched as Althea was moving to the stand to shoot again. *God, she moved so gracefully.* He paused a second just to enjoy the view, then looked back to Joe. "If your Yoga breathing becomes habitual, you will automatically be able to slip into a control mode under pressure."

"I'll try it," said Joe sounding not quite won over.

Paul nodded. "Start in a quiet room at first, with the poses and breathing, until you get the hang of mediating. Then just try more mental control without the physical poses. Practice after running. Finally, go to the rest stop on I-95 at rush hour and exercise your control with distractions. In a few months, you should be able to monitor and respond to everything around you, but still, have some control over your autonomic physical responses. If you keep at it, eventually when you are in a real stress situation--say under fire--you will be able to stay concentrated on business." Paul passed Joe his card. "Send me your e-mail, and I'll send you some more instructions."

"Thank you, sir." Joe smiled gratefully as he moved off.

The loud smoke exhaust fans were started again as the range officer called out loudly, "**Ready behind, ready on the right...ready on the left...fire at will!**"

Respectfully, they fell silent as the next line began shooting. Paul found himself enjoying watching Althea with her red shooters' ears on, slim in her blue cotton shirt and pants, as she leaned forward to take aim. When the line was reloading, Mac cocked his head to the side. He was also appreciatively studying her, saying quietly, "I know Stan and Evvie are hoping Officer Rogers is the one for you."

"She's beautiful. Smart. Good shot."

"Hear her family has money and influence?" added Mac. "More than Miss Corey's?"

Paul pictured Holly's sweet smile, but said, "Aaup," in a flat voice. "Althea and my life goals are more aligned."

Mac looked from Althea's shooting stand back to Paul and raised a cynical eyebrow. "I've heard guys sound more enthusiastic about going for a root canal."

Paul shook his head. "Aaup."

"How's it coming with the Corey girl?'

"Not coming at all. Holly'll never be a cop's wife. No idea of how to live on a budget. Or plan for the future. Can't dance."

"But when I first saw her skyclad at Grace's she looked really good," pointed out Mac.

"Aaup," said Paul softly, Holly Christmas Corey always looked really good.

"Can she shoot?"

"One of the Coreys with a gun?" Paul looked at him in mock horror, raising a staying hand. "Don't even think about it!" Paul said firmly, "Anyway, Holly and I are finished."

"Are you?" asked Mac with a touch of disbelief, adding, "Cupid usually only laughs at sensible reasoning."

He wanted off this topic, and Paul was down in Caddemfield because he had a bunch of questions to ask. "You've heard about my '*alleged*' involvement in Jim Dietrich murder?"

"I heard the D.A., and the newspaper are pushing to have you up before a grand jury?"

"And pulled from duty. A lot of pressure, but Stan's holding out."

"They still questioning you?" Mac asked with concern.

"Aaup, supposedly because I was jealous that Jim married Margaret. Hell, Mac, right now I can't even tell you what I ever saw in Margaret!"

Mac nodded. "None of us could understand it. She didn't seem to care for anyone but herself."

"At that time, I thought she was the most beautiful woman in the world. Now, I look at her, her features are coarse, her voice grates. She looks at things so stupidly and selfishly..."

"You had a dream–a house on the lake with a loving wife and kids. You ignored what Margaret was, and you remade her in your mind to fit your fantasy. A lot of guys have done that."

"What I felt for her is long gone, but if the detectives don't turn up somebody else soon for Jim's murder, I'm gonna be on suspension without pay."

"If I know Stan, it will be suspended with pay, until they convict ya. And Hiram and his detectives are shrewd." McGinnis laughed, "But with all that free time, you can come up here for Grace Le Fleur's Beltane!"

Paul shook his head. "If I have a sergeant's job left, that would be the easiest way to lose it."

"Is Miss Corey going?"

"I don't know." Paul hoped he didn't sound as worried

as he felt. "Holly said she wouldn't, but those crazy rituals mean so much to her!" He suddenly flashed back to finding a dead woman laying on Grace's lemon silk loveseat. "Mac, are you going to be there?"

"At Grace's for Beltane? Not unless I really want Noreen to divorce me. But Grace has hired a private guard for inside, and I may have an unmarked car stationed up there."

To Paul, that seemed wrong. "None of your guys inside?"

"Grace doesn't want a police presence scaring off worshipers."

The shooters were cranking back their targets. "Mac, we've talked once before about a cold case: Hester Corey's death."

The Caddemfield chief thought about it. "Yeah. She died on May first, didn't she? Part of a Beltane ritual probably."

"You were first on the scene?"

"Second."

"Hester was supposed to be alone at the mill?"

"Never believed that, but nobody else admitted to being there, and we couldn't prove otherwise."

"Her body was burnt in the fire?"

"No. Think the killer meant it to be, but Hester must've dragged herself out of the building. At dawn, we saw a blood trail on the grass. Most of those cuts were shallow, but I still don't know how she crawled out." He shook his head. "Strong, tough people those Coreys."

"If you were the second officer on the scene, who was first?"          McGinnis looked at him strangely. "I thought you read the file?"

"There seems to be a lot missing from that file, including the preliminary contact report."

"First on the scene was the night patrolman in that area, Officer Stanley Lewis." A shocked Paul tried to keep his face neutral with McGinnis studying him so carefully. "Stan didn't mention it?"

No, his chief hadn't. "That abandoned mill is on a private road, deep in the back of the Corey property. Why was Stan patrolling way back there?"

"After midnight, dispatch got a frantic call from Helen Corey. She said her daughter-in-law hadn't returned from a 'walk.' Stan went to the mansion. Mrs. Corey said Hester might've gone to the mill pond. Stan tried to get the cruiser up that old, rutty road. It got bogged down. He got out and smelled smoke.

"Communications weren't too good in those days, but he'd called for a fire truck before he abandoned his patrol car and started on foot. Dispatch had called me to back him up. Stan said when he got to the clearing, the fire was in full blaze. Walking around the mill, he found Hester's body–she was dead, face down and chopped up horribly. When I got there, I could smell vomit on him–we were a lot younger then, and seeing a woman butchered like that..." Mac stopped, then started again stronger, "You never get used it, but it gets easier to cover."

"So at first, they thought it was a suicide?"

"Naw." Mac didn't need to think about it. "From the first, it was a straight forward homicide investigation. The husband...George...Gregor...?"

"Holly's father was Gault Corey."

"Yhep. '*Gault*.' He was the chief suspect. Everybody was trying to build a case documenting his extra-marital affairs."

"He was fooling around?"

"Hell, we couldn't figure out when he had time to father triplets with his wife. He had twelve women in that coven of his! Stan's Uncle, Chief Theodore Lynch, wanted the husband really bad, but Gault had this alibi saying he was in bed in North Stonington, with two of his girlfriends all night."

"Two?"

"Oh, yeah. They had the testimony on that one pinned to the coffee room bulletin board. Very educational. Those Old Craft people are really creative physically."

"Who was he with?"

Mac took a minute to think about it. "Maeve Fitzgerald and Lilith Hoyt. There was only one Mystic Detective then, Hiram, but we were all working at bringing in Gault and his harem for questioning every day, for weeks. Trying to break 'em. Except for that alibi, we had an airtight case. That guy had lovers all over town. The wife was stabbed. He'd even kept the record of the thirteen obsidian bladed knives he'd bought– '*athames*' he called 'em. Ugly looking things–probably the murder weapon or weapons. The shithead saved the receipt for his taxes. "

"The knives were found?"

"Eight of 'em. The rest probably are still in that ruined building under the burned timbers."

"Stan must've been pushing to have Gault charged?"

"At first Stan wanted the guy bad, but Evvie went into the hospital that week. The doctors were saying she might die, so his thoughts weren't on some police investigation that was slogged down."

"But Chief Lynch didn't keep pushing it?"

"Ted? He was like his nephew, bulldog stubborn. Oh, yeah, he was pushing it. Every day, going after those alibis. Going after Gault's mother..."

"Helen Corey?"

"Yeah. Always had the feeling she liked her daughter-in-law a hell of a lot more than she liked her son. And that she knew what had happened. For my money, she was the key. If Chief Lynch and Hiram had kept hammering her, they could've found out what happened that night."

"But they didn't?"

Hiram shook his head disgustedly. "That was Hiram's

first homicide case as a detective, and he couldn't break the witnesses. According to Gault, that coven disbanded just before Beltane. Willow Buckland had just disappeared. We thought she might have been killed too, but we never found a body, and her family wouldn't put in a missing person report, saying '*Willow was just off wandering again.*' As the weeks passed, I thought Miz Rainbow might be getting ready to crack. Chief Lynch had me and the whole rotation parking a squad car in front her family's house, being really obvious. I expected an arrest any day.

Mac paused before continuing, "Then one morning, the chief called Gault Corey into his office. Figured we'd have him in custody, but Chief Lynch just announced that Mr. Corey was allowed to leave town. He did. So did Lilith Hoyt, after her little talk with the chief. We were told the case had gone cold, that we were to concentrate on other things."

Paul couldn't understand it. "It was all over like that?"

"Might've been for the better," said McGinnis quietly.

"How could it be? The Corey triplets lost both their mother and father? They were separated, farmed out to uncaring relatives, and raised to believe their mother had willfully abandoned them by committing suicide?"

"Would they have been any happier to know their father was on death row with a girlfriend or two?"

"It was seventeen years before the triplets were allowed to reunite."

Mac shook his head sadly. "A murder never affects just two people."

So Paul asked, "Why did they end the investigation? The department had a motive, a husband fooling around–possible jealous lady friends. They had witnesses to go after. With that many people involved, somebody would eventually break? Why didn't Chief Lynch just keep hammering away?"

Mac didn't meet his eyes. "The chief wasn't a guy who

felt he needed to explain to anyone."

They stood quiet through another round of shooting, then Paul had to ask, "But you have a theory?"

The Caddemfield chief was silent for a time, then Mac said slowly, "Ted Lynch was a good man. A really good cop, but a pragmatic one. Ted didn't feel the letter of the law was as important as doing the best for all concerned–particularly the innocent victims. Off the record, I'd say he ended things when the investigation turned up something that he felt should stay buried."

# Chapter 13

Paul was locking the gun boxes in the back bed of the Police Tahoe while watching Althea swing herself up into the passenger side. He had to admit that woman could do a lot for a pair of tailored pants. Heading down to I-95, he pulled into a gas station off 154. Althea looked up. "Why don't you fill it up at headquarters when we get back to Mystic? Then it won't cost you anything."

He just smiled, getting out to put the nozzle in. Seeing his sergeant driving the Tahoe instead of his own truck, Chief Lewis had only drily commented that maybe the Mystic taxpayer shouldn't be filling up the tank. Paying for the gas with his personal credit card, Paul then drove Althea back down the wooded land and farms that lined the Haddem River.

She looked at him. "Paul, tell me about the blue shirt club?"

Some idiot illegally passed a cop's car over a double line, and Paul automatically reached for the light bar switch but reminded himself this wasn't his hunting ground. "It's not a real club–just a few of us getting together every two weeks on Friday night."

"But I've heard the guys talking about it? It's at the chief's house, right?" Althea persisted.

"Aaup."

"What's it like?"

"Stan glassed in the long porch that overlooks the river. He's got a snooker table, and a professional pool table, and a wet bar. We all chipped in and bought two big-screened T-V's. Stan gets the sports channel, and Evvie keeps bringing out food. Three hours or so of shooting balls and talkin' bull."

"I'm a patrolman, but I haven't been invited," she said tightly.

Paul was paying attention to the tight traffic. "It's not a departmental event. It's a private social evening at Stan's house."

Althea pressed, "Can you take me along?"

He tried to make a joke of it. "Why do you want to be invited to a bunch of guys belching beer as they yell at the television?"

"I can drink beer."

This was going to be a problem. "Look, Chief Lewis is old school. You know the way the department is run. You respect a lady, you don't tell lewd jokes, you don't smoke a cigar around a woman, and you don't scratch your crotch in front of her. If a woman were attending the blue shirt club, the guys would have to clean up their acts."

"I can tell Stan Lewis a few dirty jokes that he might not have even heard!" pronounced Althea indignantly.

"That I would not advise. You work for Stan, you're one of his family. I screwed up once and got sent out to work on a crew cleaning off a beach full of rotting fish down in Stamford."

"You're kidding?"

"No." That memory stank even today.

"That's sanitation. Not police work!" she pressed.

"Aaup."

Althea tried another tack. "What about Mrs. Lewis? She's a woman? She's slaving over a stove for you guys. She must overhear all of that bad language and belching?"

"Evvie only hears what she wants to."

"But every two weeks she's got to clean up the house and make food?"

Paul hesitated, then explained slowly, "Stan's never talked about it, but I know from other people that they'd both wanted to have a large family. But although Evvie had many pregnancies, her babies never lived. So as Stan made sergeant, then chief, his brother officers became their family. Hosting the blue shirt club for Evvie is sort of like having her sons over for dinner. That's sons–not daughters!"

"The blue shirt club is where the departmental bonding takes place. That's where you got your sergeant's stripes."

*He found himself mildly resenting that assumption.* "I did pass a test or two. Made some outstanding arrests. Showed leadership, and worked a hell of a lot of overtime," Paul commented drily, as he turned up the ramp for I-95 North.

"Paul, I intend to move up! To do that I need to attend the blue shirt meetings! How do I get invited?"

"You have to try harder," he said smoothly as he accelerated to move into the passing traffic.

"Try harder?" she asked, surprised.

"Well, you've got good shooting scores; keep those up. Write more traffic tickets..." she was unconsciously nodded her head as he spoke until he continued with, "and grow a penis."

Althea looked at him resentfully through half-lidded eyes. "That's not fair!"

"Actually it is. Henry and I aren't trying to crash your sister's baby shower."

She spoke with anger, "Attending my sister's baby shower won't guarantee anybody's promotion!"

"In working toward a promotion, you're doing fine, without the blue shirt club. But remember Mystic has a relatively small force. There are only so many openings for advancement."

"What about yourself?"

"I've got a penis." He feigned, looking hurt. "Didn't you realize that the last time you were up in my apartment?"

Her voice did not allow for teasing. "What about your advancement, Paul?"

"My advancement?" He spoke bitterly. "At the moment I'm under suspicion of being a murderer..." He switched lanes, to give an eighteen wheeler more room. "Probably soon to be arrested."

"They'll find the murderer, and it won't be you."

Althea continued with annoyance, "But then you'll be a sergeant for a small police department. Surely you want something better? State Troopers? F.B.I.?"

Paul got a flash of what Holly Corey must feel every time he started hammering on her future plans. He decided they needed a change of subject. "Are you hungry? We could get an Italian dinner at La Luna? They won't have a band tonight, but they'll have canned music. We can dance a bit?"

The lady was anything but indirect. "How about we pick up a pizza on the way to your place?"

Soon they settled on the blue futon of his apartment, with two beer glasses of white wine and an extra-cheese pepperoni pizza.

Althea took a sip, then turned her attention totally to him. "Okay. You said once your chief stuck you and who else on a punishment detail?"

"Two other patrolmen, who shall remain nameless. And a fireman."

"Why have you guys cleaning up rotting fish in Stamford? That's two hours down the coast?"

"Stan couldn't find anything bad enough for us to do around here. A friend of his was Head of Sanitation in Stamford. It seems we were having this humongous heat wave, and a huge school of bluefish was chased into the harbor. Because of a lack of sufficient oxygen, they died. Hundreds and hundreds of rotting fish carcasses washed up on the beaches in the broiling sun. I can still smell it! The four of us got trash bags and pitchforks and got to clean all of it up."

Althea was outraged. "Stan Lewis can't legally force you to do that! Why didn't you put a formal complaint in with the union? Get a lawyer?"

"No." Paul's arm was around her shoulders as he leaned back. "When you work for Stan Lewis you accept his rules or leave."

"But that's ridiculous! What did you do?"

"We screwed up big." He laughed at the thought. "And got caught."

"Doing what? Taking a bribe? Gang raping somebody?"

"No," he laughed. "Nothing illegal."

"Then what?" she persisted.

He thought about it, then admitted, "We were moonlighting."

"Police can work off duty. They do all the time—acting as bar bouncers, or private guards. All you need is your chief's permission."

"We wouldn't have gotten it."

She cuddled against him. "What were you doing? You moonlighted as a ballroom dancing instructor when you were in the Marines? Was that it?"

He found himself flushing but just said with a lopsided smile. "Sort of dancing."

She looked up at him, saw his face, and got it. "Oh, my god, were you stripping?"

Reddening more, Paul laughed. "Four of us got together and formed the Prancing Polish Ponies. It was fun, and we were making really good money out of town with bridal parties and women's birthdays until one day Evvie's eighty-year-old god-mother mentioned to the chief that he had a very well-hung police force. Stanley Lewis was not amused."

"Did he put that on your permanent record?" she asked, sounding upset.

"With him personally, yes. In my personnel file, no."

She looked at his shirt, running her slender fingers down his chest. "You're magnificent just standing still, I can't imagine you...." Althea looked up at him eagerly. "Paul, do a strip for me."

"What?"

"The chief can't object to a private party in your

apartment." She reached up and kissed him deeply.

"You gonna join me?" he whispered, rubbing his stubbled cheek against her hair.

"Depends on how inspiring you are, sergeant," she challenged.

He got up, walked to the CD player, and found a case in the cabinet below. Soon the pounding strains of '*I'm too sexy*' rang out. Paul crossed over to the front door, and from the closet, beside it, he took out a leather jacket and slipped it on.

As Paul turned back, he slowly folded his arms high up behind his head to bring out his chest, spread his massive legs, and then started working it to the music. Althea began sitting there with her ice princess demeanor. He revolved slowly to give her the rear view, then he started playing with the jacket. When he started his deep hip rolls, she began to visibly melt. That was before he even began unbuttoning anything.

By the time jacket was off, she couldn't stand it anymore and had jumped up to join him. Soon they were facing opposite each other, Althea mirroring Paul's every, agonizingly slow, scintillating, sensuous movement as they both stripped it all off. Althea obviously had a talent for all kinds of dancing.

When the long CD finally stopped, his warm arms were around her silky body. He looked across the room and cocked his head. "I've got to redecorate."

"Humm," she said contentedly, pressing against his warm chest hairs.

"Aaup, that corner needs a shiny, brass fireman's pole bolted to the ceiling and floor."

She had a deep, throaty laugh. "Who's gonna polish that pole for you, sergeant?"

He reached down and kissed her, then pulled back and said, "I think some barter arrangement might be worked out." From the WWII marine footlocker he used as a coffee table, he picked up the empty pizza box and headed to his small, open galley kitchen. "You want something more to eat?"

Althea lifted her black lacy bra with its beige lined cups from his futon, then let it fall down, dragging it seductively behind her as she walked toward his bedroom. "Something to eat. Good idea, Travinski, but you're going the wrong way." She stopped at the door, challenging him with her naked body, shimmering from their recent workout.

Slipping in another CD, he hit the button and turned up the volume. The slow build up of Ravel's *Bolero* began. Throwing on just his leather jacket, Paul started to tease her with it again, as he joined her at the bedroom door.

Following his every move with appreciative eyes, Althea said in her husky voce, "Travinski, you are so wasted as a cop!"

# Chapter 14

As usual, Holly was running just a bit late but in Sgt. Travinski's truck she didn't dare speed. It was a treat to drive a vehicle with power steering and brakes that actually worked, but without having Bernie the Ghost moaning in the back, she felt a little lonely.

The Lady's Cauldron hadn't opened yet, but Holly knew the side door that went into the back storeroom would be open. When she went in, Maeve was sticking yellow and white chrysanthemums in a tall, blue vase. Looking up startled, Maeve automatically turned on her heel, showing her back to Holly, as she reached to pull up her concealing scarf.

Holly moved forward. "You don't have to do that for me. Please." Maeve turned and looked a bit relieved as she dropped the yellow scarf back on to her shoulders. "I'm sorry I was running a bit late," Holly explained.

"That's okay," Colin said, looking at the cream-colored lilies he was rapidly sticking in a funeral arrangement. "Bunch of last minute orders. We've got a birthday and dinner arrangement that Lapin is going to deliver up North. And four funerals in Mystic, which will fill the truck with arrangements. Can you deliver all of those in the late afternoon? It may need two trips."

"Sure." Holly looked at the containers that had been set up on the table, alongside the order forms specifying what flowers would be included. Holly started to rapidly green the foam bases. She was starting on the third one when near her was a heavy thump. Bast, the large female coon cat had jumped on the table, sniffed Holly and her arrangements, then with a haughty look walked a bit away, waving her plumed tail in disdain.

Her son, Horus, also jumped up on the counter, coming between Holly and Bast. He sat down and started to lick at his thick, mainly black fur. They both seemed to be watching Holly with intelligent looking green eyes as if evaluating her work. Colin left, then some time later returned with a delivery of long, green cardboard boxes. He looked to the cleared tables. Then to the refrigeration units. Finally, Colin studied the cork board with its orders filled and unfilled neatly pinned up. "We're out of pink roses. Lilies. Yellow chrysanthemums...you guys almost done?"

Maeve nodded approvingly. "Holly works fast."

Holly just smiled but looked to Colin. His auric vibrations were showing more dully than usual, and he seemed a bit down. She asked him, "Having a rough day?"

He gave her a ragged smile, but sounded discouraged, "That temperature drop last night–lost plantings again."

"I'm sorry," she said.

He made an effort to be more upbeat. "I've got loads of stuff in the cold frames and greenhouses. It'll be okay." He cut the taping from the boxes, opening them up to display long-stemmed white, dark red, and lavender roses. Holly picked up each rubber-banded dozen, cut a quarter inch off the stems, set them in tall vases with fresh water, then moved those vases to the bottoms of the refrigeration units. Colin was studying the orders again. "Holly, after four o'clock can you start delivering all these to the three funeral homes in Mystic? Or are the standing pieces too heavy for you?"

"No," Holly said. "That'll work out nicely. Only on the last trip, I'd like to take my truck, so I can just go home afterward."

"Fine." Colin gave her a big smile and then frowned again. "The individual deliveries for North, those Maeve is just finishing. Lapin was scheduled to take them out, but he's not coming in today. Holly, could you take them now?"

"Sure." While she had them both here, Holly decided to talk about her idea. "You know," she started, "the land on the side of this barn is flat with a nice view of the woods. You could set up a patio, and The Lady's Cauldron could serve tea and sandwiches, coffee and cake?" Holly looked from Colin to Maeve.

Maeve immediately pointed out, "Serving food to the public would require all sorts of licenses. Inspections... more insurance. It's not worth it!"

Colin wasn't so negative. "An outdoor tea room might attract another buying segment. It's an interesting idea."

Holly followed up. "Maybe you could just do special items, like ice cream? Or holiday events, like a Fourth of July wine and cheese tasting? There are two wineries, just down the road."

Across the room, Maeve was watching them, and Holly had that distinctly unpleasant sensation again. This time she traced it to an external source, so she could mute it within herself a bit, but she still had a queasy stomach.

Colin was staring at his mother, as he changed the topic, "Holly, are you driving that blue Ford F 150 out there? Is that new? It's impressive."

She found herself reddening. "It's a loaner, while the hearse is being worked on."

"A loaner? A garage gave you that?" he asked.

She started to redden more. "It's a friend's."

"Boyfriend?" he asked just a little too casually.

"J-ju-just a good friend," she explained.

"If you use it for deliveries, The Lady's Cauldron should be paying for gas. Either take cash or pick out something from the store, like those candles or that goat's milk soap you like. But for this morning's deliveries use our van."

Getting the keys from a cabinet in the storeroom, Holly brought up Colin's delivery van. Colin and Maeve were waiting outside with the first arrangements. The three of them soon had the van nearly loaded. While Colin went back to get the biggest, floor standing wedding piece, Maeve stood beside her. "Lilith told me the mill building still stands on your property?"

"The outer shell," Holly confirmed. "The timbers were so thick that the first floor still exists. I-I-I am working to clear it out."

Maeve seemed conflicted about that. "That's where your mother died."

"Do you know why she was there?"

Maeve looked away to the horses in the paddock below. "I didn't know Hester very well."

Holly persisted. "But you were a member of my father's coven?"

The older woman looked sharply back at her. "For a time."

"W-w-what was he like?"

That made Maeve fully turn to her with a sad, half covered face. "You don't know, do you? You were so young." Again, she shifted away, so her undamaged profile was facing Holly. "Your father was an amazing man. Such crackling energy, with that dominating, forceful personality. When he just looked at you, you shivered. You felt those dark eyes of his could see all."

"You were in his last Beltane ritual?" prompted Holly.

"No." Maeve hesitated, then said, "Beltane was coming up. Every one of us wanted to lie on the high altar with him. Receive the renewal of the Earth's energies that continued the cycle of life. But he chose me. I was to be on the altar, as the surrogate for the Lady, and he was to be the Lord."

"He was married to my mother. W-w-why didn't he take her as his Goddess?"

Maeve had the grace to blush. "The special rite that your father had chosen was a new one for the coven. It required a spiritual virgin."

"My mother allowed that?" asked a disbelieving Holly.

Maeve turned her ruined face fully to her. "Your

mother and father obviously had some sort of arrangement. A man as vital as Gault Corey could never be confined to only one woman." She lifted her shoulders in a shrug. "And maybe for Hester, seeing her husband with another lady was a turn on?" Maeve looked to the store entrance as if wondering when Colin was returning. "But just before that Beltane, Gault's Coven broke up. So we never had the ceremony."

"Do you ever go to Grace Le Fleur's?" Holly asked.

Anger darkened Maeve's face. "Her '*Church of Nature's Bounty*'?" she said with contempt. "Eight different altars in her basement? With her party bedrooms on the second floor? Her cocaine sniffing crowd in the foyer? What Grace runs is not a sacred renewal of the union of the Lady and Lord! It's a worship of carnal urges; an orgy of aging sex addicts! Holly, if you want to come to a proper Beltane, join us on the hill!"

Colin had come out carrying a huge display of white gladiolas with yellow and scarlet carnations. Obviously having overheard his mother, he didn't look too happy. "Holly has to study a bit more about Old Craft first."

Maeve had again turned her undamaged profile to Holly. "Study? She was born to it!" She spoke directly to Holly. "This year Colin will reenact the role of the Horned Hunter. You could be his Lady, Holly."

Lowering her head, Holly found herself blushing and totally tongue-tied, but Colin spoke firmly for her, "Mother, we already have a Goddess. Morgane would be very disappointed if she isn't chosen again."

"But perhaps the Goddess has chosen for us...that is why Holly found The Lady's Cauldron?"

Colin stared hard at his mother. "Holly found us because Lilith Hoyt directed her here."

Holly felt her stomach tightening, as if in the middle of a physical fight, but Maeve and Colin were just staring at each other. Finally, Maeve turned away first and walked past him into the store.       Ignoring the tension, Colin just loaded the last arrangement and closed up the panel truck's back doors. Holly felt embarrassed and finally said, "Your mother just wants to help."

"Unfortunately, Maeve can't always have everything she wants. My mother has never really learned that."

Holly wanted to shift the conversation. "You have a Goddess surrogate picked out?"

"Morgane. I've been doing the Horned God for Beltane with her since I was sixteen."

"Do you love her?" Holly asked, feeling the stir of something she didn't want to admit.

He smiled. "She's ten years older–which wouldn't matter. She's very happily married, with kids. Fortunately, her husband approves of her being the Lady surrogate for ritual purposes."

"But how do you feel about her?"

"Morgane is very attractive and lots of fun. One year in the midst of the high ritual, I went down on her. She had slipped a whoopee cushion on her stomach. At the most solemn moment, when I sank down on top of her, there was this horrible echoing fart sound."

"What did you do?"

"I started to laugh," he said still chuckling at the memory.

"That's terrible!" exclaimed a wide-eyed Holly. "The Goddess..."

He cut in, "Must have a tremendous sense of ridiculousness or she could never have created humans! The only people who were seriously offended by it were my mother and some old stick-in-the-muds."

Holly looked at him. "How can you do it with a woman you don't love?"

He shrugged. "I'm great at fantasizing. And at the proper moment, Morgane will arch her back and yell as if she'd just experienced the greatest orgasm any woman in the world has ever gotten. When I was a teenager, I thought I was really doing it for her, then I learned you women fake it! I mean, you can look at a guy and know if he's excited or not, but we just have to trust you, women." He looked to Holly. "If you want to attend our Beltane, it will be only as a guest..."

"Skyclad," she finished."

"Skyclad's no fun. I want you nude!"

Holly giggled. "Skyclad and nude are the same things!"

"Yeah, but nude sounds so, so much more exciting. So while I'm screwing Morgane, I can sneak a look at you, in a purely religious frame of course."

She had a sudden flashback to Yule at the La Fleur mansion, when Gregory St. Clair was pawing her. Again, Holly felt her panic, then her sudden relief, when Paul showed up as her knight in shining skin. That time Sgt. Paul Travinski had saved her, but he wouldn't at this Beltane.

Colin studied her with sudden concern. "Something I said frightened you?"

"I-I-I went to an Old Craft service once, by myself. A man got the wrong idea, and I couldn't stop him."

He looked horrified. "What happened?"

"N-nothing. Others came to help. B-b-but I let myself get into a bad situation."

His face darkened. **"That should never have happened!** It's an unforgivable violation of the sanctuary! If you come to our ritual, you won't be alone. And as long as I'm there, no one will touch you. In fact, I'm going to make that a rule. The first Beltane you come to, you will not be touched by anyone–and that includes myself! "

Holly tried to lighten things by teasing, "You'll fight off a whole, stampeding coven to protect me?"

"Hey, lady." He flexed a muscular arm. "Farming, lifting boxes, and digging makes big muscles. Okay? But any woman or man would be safe at our rituals. Nobody will be doing anything they don't want to. Rules of the Goddess! Well, if someone wants to do anything, a condom has to be worn, but other than that we don't permit anything that violates the spirit of the Goddess."

After Holly finished her deliveries up North, she returned to the store and worked shelving stock. At the end of the afternoon, Holly took the last deliveries in Paul's truck to the Mystic funeral homes. Finally, she was free to head back up Route 27. No guests this weekend, so she really didn't need to get any more eggs, but she passed her mansion as she headed down Chestnut Hill Road to the Hoyt farm. She needed to talk to the sisters.

Tall Abby let her in the door and looked directly at Paul's new truck and smiled.

Holly felt she should explain, "Paul only lent it to me, while the hearse is being fixed."

Abby just continued to smile knowingly, as she led Holly inside. Holly always enjoyed walking into the Hoyt's spacious first floor, with its wide stretch of gleaming yellow oak floor. Now, Sarah sat on the bench before her seven-foot Glimakau loom, weaving a cloth that must be over sixty inches in width. Abby had once told Holly that the loom had sixteen treadles for Sarah's elaborate designs. Today, she was weaving a deceptively simple powder blue sky with white seagulls swooping across. Sarah stood up from her bench, saying, "It's time for a break. Abby, could you bring us some tea, please?"

Sarah moved to the chrome and walnut framed couch, while Holly took one of the matching chairs across from her as Sarah started with, "Our sister Lilith was by and told us you had taken a job at The Lady's Cauldron?"

Nothing disturbed the smooth face of Sarah Hoyt, but still, Holly had the definite feeling that the sisters were unhappy about her being around Colin and Maeve. But at least they weren't pointing out that they told her not to go to the Fitzgeralds. While Abby busied herself in the open, modern kitchen in the back, Holly talked of the hand-crafted candles and loomed scarves that the Fitzgeralds sold. "Sarah, your creations are so beautiful. I'm sure Colin could sell them. Maybe I could take in some wall hangings to show him?"

"I don't think Sarah has anything she wishes to sell," said a tight-mouthed Abby returning with a heavy tray laden with homemade lemon chiffon cake and a teapot of one of her special blends. Every time Holly came, Abby had hot water ready. Did the sisters always have a tea kettle boiling, or did they sense when outsiders were coming?

This tea blend of Abby's smelled of mint leaves and newly mown grass. She set the tray down on the six foot long, highly polished, burled wood coffee table before them. Abby proudly poured the brownish tea in bone china cups with small, silver spoons, set in them to take the heat. The tea and their cake tasted delicious.

Again, Holly wondered about the Hoyt sisters' financial status. They inherited a lot of valuable lands which they still farmed, with at least one helper. In the late summer, when the tomatoes, beans, lettuce, and corn came in, they would put out their vegetables on their farm stand, and probably sold to the local grocery stores. Year round, Abby worked hard milking her goats, collecting eggs, and selling her plucked chickens, but Holly never had the feeling that the Hoyt sisters really needed the money. Finally, she asked, "When you knew I was looking for a job, why didn't you tell me about the Fitzgeralds' farm?"

Abby looked to Sarah, who said coldly, "We've explained to you the Fitzgeralds may not be what you think."

"I know Maeve was in my father's coven–with you both."

The sisters said nothing.

Holly started again. "My mother was killed in a

Beltane ritual, wasn't she?"

"We weren't there," Sarah spoke with total disinterest.

"It was Beltane," started Abigail.

Seemingly annoyed, Sarah added, "The plan was that the coven would celebrate with a high mass Gault had devised. At its zenith, Gault was to take Maeve Fitzgerald's virginity on the altar."

Abby pursed her mouth primly, then pointed out, "But Maeve had already given birth to Colin when she was unmarried and fifteen."          "Whatever," Sarah finished. "She claimed to be '*spiritually virgin.*' Gault knew he hadn't taken her yet, so she was slated for the ritual. But it wasn't the union of the Earth Goddess and Horned God for the land's renewal. The ritual he planned...Gault said was more '*elemental.*'"

Abby spoke with pain. "He built that ugly black altar in the old mill building, with those crude Aztec athames. He wanted to use the rite to increase his powers."

Both sisters stopped talking, so Holly tried again. "My father had sex with all the women in his coven?"

"No!" blurted out Sarah, shocked. "He didn't sleep with me! Or others."

Holly noted that Abby stayed silent and that Sarah did not specify Abby in the '*others*' category. "My mother didn't object to this?"

Abby looked to Sarah, who said quietly, "We never knew exactly what Hester felt. She could shield herself completely. But she mustn't have been happy about it...still, whatever Gault did, Hester made excuses for him. She loved your father so."

And Abby softly added, "And in his way, he loved her."

Holly couldn't understand this. "Someone didn't love her! Was she killed in a ritual? Or did someone trap her at the mill alone?"

Abby looked at Sarah. It was the elder sister who spoke firmly, "We were not there."

"But you know who was?"

"Why do you have to know?" asked an obviously agonized Abby.

"Maeve says there was no ritual that night. Is that true?"

It seemed Abby was about to speak, but Sarah stopped her saying firmly, "We don't know, I've told you this before!" Both Sarah and Abby had closed their faces, auras, and radiations.

But still, Holly pressed, "Where was my grandmother?"

"Helen?" Abby had to think of that. "Well, there were the three of you babies. Somebody had to stay home, and Helen had stopped attending Gault's rituals. She thought the way her son's worship was going violated the mothering spirit of the Earth Goddess."

Sarah nodded. "Your grandfather and his son Benjamin had picked up a crewing job on a fishing boat. They were both away that night."

Holly had to know. "Did my father kill my mother?"

Sarah raised her head in anger. "Again, we don't know! And we wouldn't tell you if we did!"

"But killing Hester on Beltane was a sacrilege!" finished Abby miserably.

Holly didn't know what to say. Her mother's death was more than a violation of religious values.

Trying to change the subject, Abby asked anxiously. "How is Sgt. Travinski doing?"

"They're blaming Paul for murdering that man who ran away with his fiancee."

"And that witch Margaret is back in town," Abby finished bitterly.

Holly looked directly at Sarah. "Is she a witch like

us?"

**"We are not witches!"** said Sarah furiously slamming the delicate teacup down. "Witches are some unnatural hags!"

Knowing she'd made a big mistake, Holly tried to backpedal. "You're wise women, knowledgeable of the Old Craft and skilled in the science of nature's laws."

Abby had wrapped her arms in front of her, and her eyes were staring unfocused across the room. "I've always felt that Sgt. Travinski was under a spell when he fell so deeply for Margaret. I had thought of intervening, but Sarah," she looked at her sister, "was against it."

"It was not our business!" snapped Sarah.

Abby continued, "Margaret was always very elemental. Acting at a low level, but because she's so narcissistic, she can funnel her entire energies toward her goal. That works for a time, but eventually, your victim will grow stronger." Abby looked directly at Holly. "She will try to get Paul again. Holly, you mustn't allow that!"

Leaving them, climbing back into Paul's truck, Holly felt depressed. She should protect Paul from Margaret, but what could she do? Feeling helpless and worthless, she headed back to the mansion. Getting out, she looked up. Storm clouds were beginning to blanket the sky, but it wasn't supposed to rain until sundown.

Noel had the day off, so he would be getting ahead on his baking by making the dough to freeze. Frosty was also home with a fever and a bad cough. He should go to the doctor but didn't want to spend the money. Holly had a healing tea from Abby for him, but there was something she wanted to do first.

Lilith had once wanted to buy the old, burnt mill to reconfigure into a house. They had decided not to sell to her, but maybe if Holly and her brothers ever had to sell the mansion, they could keep that section of the property, restore the mill with all three of them living there? She'd been secretly working on the ruined mill building, trying to clear it out. Holly wanted to go in and change to old clothes, but her brothers would see her and ask questions. She'd parked the truck farthest from the house. Now she pulled out the work gloves she'd hidden in Paul's glove compartment. She'd get two hours of work in before sunset.

Holly walked away from the mansion, heading into the woods on an old, overgrown footpath. In her great-grandmother's time, this land had been vast extended lawns and gardens. Holly passed an ivy overgrown, two-tier cast iron fountain rising out of a cement pond with just a stagnate, green rain puddle in it. The pond's deep blue paint was peeling. Maybe she could someday restore this, but now she wanted to work on the mill.

Way back on the edge of the property the woods gave way to a lush grassy plain watered by the mill pond and dam spillway. The footpath came out where the old dirt road ran along the stone fence property line. The river ran to the left of the stone wall. The three-story stone mill building was set up on the hill, alongside the dam, which was now noisily frothing over with spring flooding.

She never could walk here without sadly thinking of what happened to her mother. Holly played here as a kid, but she didn't remember much of that. When she first came back to Mystic, Holly had come here to sit quietly beside the pond and to try to reach her mother's spirit. But trying to concentrate as much as she could, Holly didn't feel Hester's ghost lingering here.

It was chillier now with the storm coming in as Holly walked up to the building. Part of the roof had burnt out, but the four stone walls, windows, and charred doorway framing still stood intact. Inside there was the blackened first floor, she remembered it was above a deep cellar, where the sacks of grain and barrels of ground mill flour had been stored.

Bracing on the doorway, Holly stepped past a large

hole by the door, getting to the solid wood flooring now filled with burnt timbers from the second floor and roof. She'd been clearing a bit for a while and now had a pile of charred boards outside the door. Amazingly, the first floor of thick, wide oak planks still seemed mostly solid.

With much of the second floor and roof timbers clogging ahead of her, she couldn't properly assess the damage. The wind blew down from the open roof line. She smelled smoke, and what else? Some dead animal in there? No, she didn't sense her mother's spirit, but she did sense death.

Holly pulled at a two by two charred board. This was like a giant game of Pick-up Sticks. You had to pick a timber, then pull that one out without bringing the whole pile down on your head. She needed a construction helmet, overalls, and a saw, but that would mean going home, changing, and trying to lie to her brothers about where she was going.

She just reached for another board and pulled. If she did a little every day, by snowfall, she should have this whole thing cleared. And with the money from The Lady's Cauldron, she could hire a construction engineer to judge the soundness of the walls and have them give her an estimate on what a remodel would cost.

The chill got worse, as the clouds were closing in. It must be near sunset, but she couldn't see the sun, and any wristwatch she and her brothers bought rapidly died on the triplets' arms. Frost thought it was something to do with their internal energy radiating out. Holly wiped the sweat off her forehead, wanting to get a bit more done before she quit for the day. Her gloves were black with charcoal, her watermelon pink pants, and matching shirt were a mess. She needed help. Noel was always too bossy and judgmental, but maybe she could talk Frosty into helping her? If they could attach a tow rope to one of the bigger timbers, and tie it to Paul's truck...maybe the clearing would go faster?

But right now Holly was cold and tired, and she planned to pull out just one more of those ruined boards that looked easy to get, and then head home. Holly walked confidently on the flooring--past the hole by the door--as she started dragging a timber. She was about three foot from the open door when the floor beneath her feet suddenly dropped. With the planking caving in beneath her, a terrified Holly tried to hang on to the charred timber she was holding, but it snapped under her weight.

Screaming, she fell into the darkness below.

# Chapter 15

Going off duty, Paul bit into his takeout crab burger as he drove the sergeant's Tahoe to Classic Car Restoration's garage lot. This garage had been Quentin father's and his grandfather's. His great grandfather had worked on the original Model A's. All the Butlers were master mechanics in their time. Now the old wooden gas station no longer pumped gas; it was a one story, wooden building, with six repair bays on an acre of razor-wire, topped fenced-in parking lot, in a not too great area of town. Outside, under tarps, Paul knew there were donor carcasses, and Rolls Royces, Porsches, and classic Studebakers, all waiting their turn at restoration. Paul could see Holly's hearse parked in the first repair bay, next to the office.

As he got out, Paul smelled the heavy sea air. He looked up to see a swirl of shrill screaming seagulls winging inland, chased by thick, dark clouds coming low and fast. *Have to hurry before the storm hit.* Paul headed over to a thin, short, blue-black skinned man who was listening to a Jaguar's purr. Quentin raised a hand to his assistant. "Cut it." The guy shut down the engine. "Wipe her off one more time, then you and Ed deliver it."

"Yes, sir."

Quentin turned to him. "Sergeant, your hearse is dead."

"Can't it be rebuilt?" Paul asked.

The mechanic started walking to his office. "You can raise the Titanic, and it could be rebuilt. But why do it?"

"Holly loves Bernie."

"Bernie?" Quentin shook his head. "You're in trouble when they start naming 'em." He was walking into his office with Paul following. "Your girlfriend would be a lot better off putting the money into a used Prius or even a hybrid? Maybe if I look around, I could get her a deal?"

"Let's keep on a rebuild. The exterior's still solid,

right?"

"It's okay. But what's underneath is shot! That thing must have over three hundred thousand miles on it, which you would know if the odometer worked."

"Did you look into parts?" asked Paul. The gas station's old office was a Spartan room, with a wall of plate glass window in the front, an old wooden desk center, four chairs, a shiny red coke machine, and new car parts hanging off almost every inch of unoccupied surface. The wall behind the desk held about thirty clipboards. Quentin pulled one off and handed it to Paul.

Paul shifted through a thick sheaf of papers: a needed parts list for the hearse; Internet printouts of parts for sale; Specifications for struts and brakes.

Quentin was watching him. "Paul, I know a guy who runs a car museum up in Springfield. That dinosaur looks pretty classy on the outside. Let me call him. I bet he'd pay a thousand and send the flatbed down to pick it up. That would save your girlfriend from paying to have it hauled away to be junked."

Paul had reached Quentin's estimates for labor. He scanned the numbers, flipped another page, then another. Each one looked worse. Paul looked through the inner door to the repair bay at Holly's long hearse, with its red plush interior and gray-blue scalloped curtains in the rear. "Holly really loves that pile of junk." He looked back down at the bills. "Maybe she doesn't need all of this done now? What if you just fixed the brakes, put on new tires, and installed seat belts?"

"That depends: is she using the hearse as a paperweight or does she expect to drive it?"

Paul exhaled. "This is higher than I expected."

"So she likes driving an old hearse." Quentin typed something into the laptop on his desk. "Yeah, I saw it here. For under ten thousand I can get her a 2004 black hearse,

61,000 miles with air conditioning, radio, airbags. Look. There's a nice 1989 for only four thousand. Hell, I could get you a late model Mercedes for less than your rebuild would cost!" The mechanic shook his head, looking over his shoulder at the figures in Paul's hand.

Paul fingered one of Quentin's print outs. A picture of a Cadillac almost identical to Holly's but smashed up. "What's this?"

"That's a totaled 1957 Cadillac hearse up in Andover, Massachusetts. We could probably get it for seven hundred dollars. The body's gone, but the rest could be used as a donor carcass. That would cut down on your parts' cost. But labor will still kill you. Just the cost of renting a tow truck, gas, and getting some guy qualified to drive it all the way up to Andover is gonna run you four figures."

Paul looked at the specs sheet of the Andover hearse. "1957 and only seventy thousand miles? That's great."

"Yhep. Being sold as part of an estate. Her dad bought the hearse in its first year when a funeral home burned down. He and later his ninety-year-old daughter had driven it to church every Sunday, so it wasn't just sitting leaking oil in some barn. The engine was well taken care of, but the old lady had it parked out in the snow and never washed off the winter road salt. It was rotted through in places, but it was still going strong when some teenage kid hit it from rear and side. Pretty much wiped out the body."

Paul looked back at the photograph. "Looks a mess."

"Yeah. But the mechanic who has it on his lot swears the engine and most of the undercarriage is solid."

"So you could take this engine and put it in Holly's van? Then with new tires and brakes, seatbelts and airbags?"

"Just where would I attach airbags?" objected Quentin.

"Okay. Just three lap belts on the bench seat in the front? Aaup?"

"Paul–it'd be easier to cut your girlfriend's head off

and transplant it to another body. And it would make just about as much sense."

"Work with me here! If we could buy this hearse, I could drive your tow truck up to Massachusetts..."

"You're not qualified to load a van on a flatbed," Quentin objected.

"I've driven trucks in the military. I've stood guard as hundreds of car accidents were loaded. I can do it. I'll show you."

"And if some cop stops you–you don't have a CDL."

"I've got better–I've got a badge."

"Who's gonna pay for the gas to Andover?" said Quentin. "And what if I need the flatbed to pick up a paying customer? I'm gonna have to rent somebody else's truck. You know what that will cost you? Face it, Paul, that hearse needs a hearse!"

"Can't you get this labor estimate down a little?" Paul coaxed.

"It'll still be more than a cop makes in two years."

"I'm not paying for this!" Paul said emphatically.

"So Miss Holly Corey is? With what? Tips from her Bed and Breakfast? Hey, man, it may not look like it to you, but I'm trying to run a profitable business here!"

Paul looked at the damn hearse. "You'll be paid. I'll be responsible for the bill if you'll just let Holly pay on time. Aaup?"

Quentin shook his head in disgust. "That hearse would cost more than painting my mother's monster of a house!"

"Your mother's house?" Paul asked.

"Yeah." Quentin ran a hand through his tightly curled hair. "That yellow, two-story, gingerbread grand folly on Greenmanville Avenue."

Paul looked up from the clipboard. "You're getting estimates?"

Quentin reached down and handed him another

clipboard, with photos of the house's problems; list of needed repairs; painting estimates. Paul studied Mrs. Butler's two-story, rotting wood, mansard-roofed Victorian, buried in its wilderness of overgrown shrubbery.

Sounding defeated Quentin muttered, "So far I've only got one guy who says he'll tackle it. And he wants the yard cleaned up and wood rot repaired before he paints. Hell, just the replacement of that turned wood decoration over the front porch is gonna cost a few thousand, if I can find someone who can do it. You know anybody good who works on old houses?"

"Aaup. Me." Paul looked at him. "We can work a swap here."

"*You paint it?* First, you gotta cut back and cart away a three-decade jungle of rhododendron bushes, poison ivy, and wisteria vines."

"No problem!" said Paul confidently.

"What do you know about painting houses?"

"Started working for a painting crew when I was fifteen. There's a lot of old houses in Boston."

"For this job you got to rip out and replace all the rotting boards, scrape the peeling paint. Man, it's a major shit-pile!"

"Like Holly's hearse. We'll work out a deal! You'll lend me your truck to go up to Andover to pick up the '57 for the parts you need."

"Some of the parts," Quentin corrected.

"I'll buy the wood and paint for your mother's house, and you buy or make any other parts for Holly's hearse. In the end, we'll add up hours and work out two bills. Anything you spend over on the hearse more than the house costs, Holly'll owe you. If the house costs more than the hearse, you're free and clear."

Quentin didn't look impressed. "You're a cop, working all day?" he reminded Paul.

"Got evenings. Can put out lights to paint at night."

Shaking his head, Quentin said, "There's the livery stable out in the back. That's part of the job. One man can't do all that."

"I've got a crew," said Paul confidently. Should he have Holly painting? No. She'd try, but working at night, carrying gallon paint cans up two-story ladders wasn't a woman's job.

Quentin put his hands in his overall pockets and walked to the inner door to the first repair bay, where he gave an evaluating look at the hearse. "You've got a crew?"

"The best around!" Paul pushed. "The Corey brothers. They've been rebuilding Witch House outside of town. Doing a bang up job! And Frost Corey works at the Mystic Seaport Museum Village; he's an expert with 1800's shipbuilding and woodworking techniques. He has access to their tools. Frost can probably turn out identical replacements for that missing gingerbread trim in no time!"

"Holly's hearse for ma's house?" The mechanic took a long look at the hearse. "I think I'll be getting the worse of this devil's bargain."

"Naw—you'll be way ahead!" Paul assured him.

There was a distinct sound from inside the repair bay. Rather like a deep, pained sigh. Paul looked toward the hearse. "What's that?"

"Some sort of gas release from the engine, but it seems to come out the back," said Quentin in a puzzled voice. "That van makes strange noises sometimes. I haven't figured out why." He looked back at Paul. "Okay. With this deal, you're gonna kill yourself! Hope she's really worth it."

*Yeah, he was going to kill himself, for a lady he couldn't have.* As Quentin got on the Internet to buy the Massachusetts hearse, Paul climbed into the police SUV to go break the good news to his painting crew.

# Chapter 16

Paul parked the police Tahoe near his own blue truck in the back of Witch House's lot. He walked around his F 150. So far, no scratches or damage to his truck. Good!  A wet splash hit his cheek. Giving the threatening rain clouds a glance, he ran to the back door and knocked. In a few minutes, Noel opened it, with his hands covered in white flour.

"When's your brother home?" Paul asked.

"He's homesick." Noel looked at Paul's blue uniform. "You still on duty?"

"No, but I've got to stay in uniform while I'm driving the Police Tahoe."

Thor was stretched out on the floor and thumped his tail to see Paul. This time, the big rottweiler didn't bare his teeth or growl–apparently, he wasn't getting angry vibrations from Noel.

Noel awkwardly started to say, "It was good of you to let Holly and us drive your truck–and make her take that beast into repair. We couldn't get her to do it."

Frost came into the kitchen from the dining room, wiping his red nose and looking terrible. "Holly?" he said in croaking voice.

"No," answered Noel, "Paul."

But Paul was already answering Noel, "About the hearse. Getting it street legal is going to cost."

Noel protested. "Holly doesn't–**we**--don't have the money!"

"Well, I've made a sort of barter deal. N.C., it means that you and I and Frost are going to have to repair and paint a house. The rest Holly will have time to pay off."

"Paint a house? When? We all work!" protested an unhappy Noel.

"Evenings. Weekends. Vacation days, whenever–but you two have to help me."

"We don't know how to paint professionally," stated Noel.

"I'll teach ya," said Paul.

Noel didn't look happy, and he started arguing, "I've got a full-time job at the Aquarium, I'm baking for the motels, and working on this rotting dump. I'm not getting any research in on my dissertation for my doctorate, because I don't have the time!"

Paul looked him hard. "You want your sister driving a death trap?"

Wiping his hands in a dish towel, Noel looked helplessly to Frost, who even with a scratchy throat, spoke firmly, "No. We want sis to be safe! We'll chip in whatever money we have, and we'll paint. You want Holly to paint too?"

Paul shook his head. "I don't think it's a good idea. Scraping and painting a two-story house is gonna be a lot of muscle and ladder work.

Frost looked at Noel. "They're giving her more hours at the new job, and we've got more reservations here. Might be better if we said nothing about this to her?"

With a tired sigh, Noel threw down his towel. "I can start tomorrow after 5:30. So can, Frost."

Paul nodded. When the Coreys worked, they worked hard. "At lunch, I'll get estimates on paint. Tomorrow after work, we can scope out the job. Make up a work schedule, and begin cutting down the shrubbery. We'll have to haul it away–we'll need my truck. And we'll have to repair any of the rotted wood and scrape off the peeling paint before we can start. It's a two-story house and the stable in the back."

Frost stared at him closely. "Paul, why are you doing this? My sister said you broke up with her?"

"The police frown on people driving without brakes," Paul said in his cop's voice.

Noel's blue-green eyes stared up into his

incredulously. "You're repairing her hearse–but you're not planning to date her?"

Looking about the familiar kitchen, Paul said sadly, "The two of us wouldn't work out in the long run. But that doesn't mean I still don't care deeply for your sister. And I want her to keep living–especially if she's driving that damned hearse. Where is Holly?" Paul asked, maybe he could just see her shapely body before he left.

Frost coughed. "She was supposed to be back two hours ago, but she hasn't come home from work yet. They've been giving her more hours at The Lady's Cauldron–some big festival coming up."

Paul looked toward the pantry door, puzzled. "You're picking her up, and you don't know when she's coming home?"

"No, she's driving your truck," Noel said.

Paul still looked to the doorway. "No, she's not. My truck is parked in your back lot."

"N.C., did sis come in?" Frost asked his brother, blowing his nose.

"Usually she comes this way...I would've seen her," returned a puzzled Noel.

The three of them walked outside. The strong wind smelled wet and was turning leaves to their light sides.

"Maybe she went out for a run?" said Frost.

"She would've taken Thor. He's still in the kitchen." Noel looked worried.

Frost looked to the woods and low clouds. "All day, I've been sick, feeling bad."

His brother looked at him. "Yeah, you're running a temperature. You shouldn't be out here!"

"No." A concerned looking Frost scanned the yard. "About 4:30, I got nauseous with a splitting headache. I thought it was the cold, but it might've been Holly in pain." Frost closed his eyes, breathing deeply, then said with some desperation. "She's not responding to me!"

**"Will you cut out that psychic shit!"** commanded Noel.

Frost ignored him and ran inside. When he came out, he was pulling Thor with a hand on the dog's collar. "The dog has to find Holly!"

Paul headed to the police Tahoe, with the sun setting behind those clouds it would be dark soon. Should he call dispatch for a search party? But that flaky girlfriend of his might have just gone for a walk. He started pulling out three flashlights from the back of his tool chest.

When he hurried back, Frost was speaking to the dog. "Find mommy! Find Holly!" The rottweiler just sat and looked up at him with its red tongue sticking out the side of his muzzle looking dopey. Frost looked up to his brother. "N.C., come over here. Put your hands on the dog's neck. Picture Holly. Want to find Holly! Need Holly!"

"I can't..." Noel started.

Frost cut him off. **"Yes, you can! Concentrate!"**

Seeming to catch some of Frost's urgency, Noel moved to the great dog.

Paul looked at the huge rottweiler, with his tongue lolling out in that lopsided, stupid grin. No. Thor was no Lassie to send to find Timmy. Still, looking like he was trying, Noel crouched down, closed his eyes in concentration, and put his hands on the dog's neck.

Thor yawned.

Then the dog stopped panting and closed his massive jaws. The rottweiler's eyes were now looking straight ahead, and the dog moved his big muzzle around as if scanning the clearing. Finally, the big head raised as if the dog was smelling the gusts of wet wind coming in or searching for a familiar scent. Suddenly with a deep "woof," Thor stood up, trying to pull out of Noel's hands. Noel grabbed harder to his collar, as Frost ordered. "Release him!"

"**No!**" Paul countered. "Put the long leash on him. Otherwise, he'll run off–we're losing the daylight." Paul passed a flashlight to Noel.

Frost ran to get the lead hanging just inside the pantry door. When he came back, Noel clipped the leash to the dog's collar and ordered Frost. "You're sick. You'll get pneumonia out here in the rain. Stay inside!"

"No–sis is in trouble!"

Paul passed another flashlight to Frost, as he squinted to the lowering clouds, edged red with the sinking sun. "We'll search for an hour, then call in the professionals."

Noel shook his head. "She just might be picking mushrooms in the woods. Holly's always going off and doing some fool thing."

"Aaup." Paul nodded grimly.

Frost didn't go into the house. "She's not responding to me. Holly needs help."

"Does she always respond?" Paul asked. *Which was stupid since he didn't believe in the Corey's supposed psychic abilities, but...*

"Not always...but all this afternoon I've had bad feelings. I just thought it was the cold making me feel lousy, but if it was Holly she might be hurt...or dead." He finished sounding frightened.

"Or you've got a bad head cold, and you feel lousy!" Noel spoke with a touch of annoyance, but let out the leash as Thor barked excitedly and started moving. "Dog's hunting!"

They started past the trucks into the woods as it started raining. *Naturally, Paul thought.* As they pushed through the trees, they all start calling, "**Holly?**" Thor would stop, smell the air, then bound ahead. With the scratching branches and tripping roots, Paul was having trouble keeping up with Noel and the dog. By the sound, the rain was coming down harder, but the thick canopy of leaves above kept most of it off them. Was Holly under sheltering trees? The dog seemed to be following an old foot trail that led to the Northwest corner of the property. It finally opened up to the meadow around a Rockwall damned mill pond and two-story ruined stone building.

**"Holly!"** Frost cried out. All they could hear was the raising water spilling over the dam.

Noel looked around in the sodden rain field. "We told her not to come here!"

"It's news to you that your sister doesn't take orders too well?" yelled Paul bitterly. The rain was letting up a bit, but now they were coming out of the protection of the trees. The ground was soft, and the cold, muddy water soaked into his shoes. With the low, thick clouds, he couldn't see the sun, but it would be setting now, and the darkness would be getting deeper. Paul should have called for backup!

Out of the trees, the cold rain drizzled down on them. Not seeming to hear, Noel dropped Thor's leash, and the dog ran toward the ruined mill building. Frost was just behind him. Thor loped to the gaping door jam first, then the rottweiler stuck his massive head down into the doorway, and he whimpered.

Paul noted there was a stack of heavily charred rafters piled up in front of the ruined building as if someone was clearing the mill. Timbers that could have been lifted by someone Holly's size. "Those weren't piled up there the last time I was here. Were you guys clearing the building?"

"It's too dangerous," said Noel. "If we had the money, we'd tear the whole thing down!"

Frost had run to the stone building, pushing the dog away from the open doorway, flashing his light down. "The floor gave way! It's been holding all these years–but some of it is in the basement now! **Holly?**"

Feeling numb, Paul ran to the doorway, flashing his light down the burnt timbers to water and a flash of sherbet pink. Holly's pants, deep in dirty greenish water. Her head and chest were out of the water, with her lying prone on a tangle of beams. Her eyes were closed. Her skin deadly pale.

As Paul tried to push his way in, Thor growled, baring those formidable yellow teeth.

"**Sit!**" Commanded Noel from behind them. The dog immediately obeyed.

Frost was grabbing at what was left of the rotting door frame, preparing to climb down. Paul pushed him aside. "I'm stronger." He fished for his cell phone. It was back on the charger. Damn! "You guys got a cell phone?"

"Not with me," said Noel helplessly.

Paul looked at him. "N.C., have you got the keys to my truck?"

Noel asked, "Is she dead?"

"**The keys!**" Paul thundered.

"Holly's got them."

*Damn!* Paul fished into his pocket and pulled out another set. "These are the cop car keys. Bring the Tahoe back here!"

Noel looked to him stupidly. "Me driving a police car—is that legal?"

*For God's sake!* Paul went into command mode. "**Do what I tell you!** If your sister's alive, she's gonna need help! You know how to use a police radio?"

"Like a boat's?" Noel asked, sounding not too confident.

Keeping an eye on the big rottweiler with its solid protective stance, Paul was flashing his light around the burned timbers inside the ruined building, trying to figure if any of them could hold his weight. "Use the clicker to open the Tahoe. The mike is wired to the dashboard. Just squeeze the mike to talk, say 'over'—then release it so they can answer you."

"How do I contact them?"

"Dispatch is always listening. We need two cruisers

and an ambulance. Make sure dispatch knows it is **not** an officer in trouble! Chief Lewis will call out the 82$^{nd}$ Airborne if he thinks one of his boys is down! If you can't contact dispatch, run inside your house and get 911 on the phone to get an ambulance up here. Don't wait for the ambulance! Drive my cop truck back here! We need the equipment in it!" Thor still took a wide-legged guard stance at the open doorway; with formidable teeth bared, he started to growl deeply at Paul. "Take this damn dog with you!"

"Thor! Heel!" Noel commanded over his shoulder as he ran into the woods. The formerly savage rottweiler leaped to follow him like a puppy.

Oblivious to rain rivulets running down his face, Frost still cast the sickly yellow flashlight beam down on his sister's stiff body. "Holly's gone," he said in a broken voice. "Sis is dead!"

# Chapter 17

With the over-protective dog neutralized, Paul could get inside the doorway. The heavy timbered floor hadn't totally collapsed. Just a crescent section about ten foot across in front of the door. Paul flashed his light around the remaining supports. Although the fire had burnt out the second floor and the roof above, it had only charred the surface of the dense wood planking of the first floor. Holly must've been walking on the wood flooring when it gave way, but that flooring was awful thick to have gone. It didn't look rotted. Flashing the light farther, he saw fresh cut marks and raw wood. Somebody had recently sawed the supports, weakened the flooring–deliberately.

No time for a forensic study now--he had to get to Holly! Paul put the flashlight in his back pocket, kneeled down, turned backward, and tried to lower himself into the basement floor that must be twelve feet to fifteen feet below him. Paul felt for toe holds in the rough foundation rocks just below the door opening. He didn't want to fall on timbers and damage her further; still, his hands were wet on the slimy, slippery wall. The last three feet were a straight drop into icy water on unseen boards that banged his shin. Carefully, he turned on the flashlight and tried to scope out the best way to reach her.

Holly's head rested on a fallen beam. She probably hit it when she fell, knocking her unconscious, but it kept her from drowning. Her legs were under that black oily, stagnant rainwater that only reflected his flashlight. He moved, and a submerged board shifted under his feet. Trying to balance, he dropped his flashlight, putting him in darkness. Grabbing an overhead beam with his hand, he tried to balance his weight, not daring to press something against her hidden legs. Cold water soaked his pants, as the putrid stink filled his nose. Paul looked up. "Frost! Keep your light on her!"

Paul dug down in the water and muck pulled out his flashlight. It was covered with slippery sludge, but it still put out light! Then he carefully waded his way to Holly. She looked like a child sleeping peacefully. On patrol in Afghanistan, he'd seen bodies like this–young men's faces sweetly asleep in eternal repose. Tightening his muscles, slowing his breaths helped his police training kick in as he bent to touch the soft skin of her neck. Damply cold, but he thought he felt something–a faint pulse. Was she alive?

He moved his hand to her shirt under her breast. Movement of the chest. Breathing–shallow-- but breathing and maybe slight shivering. "**Holly?** Holly, baby?" He tried to pull her up and couldn't. Her legs must be trapped under some of the beams he was standing on.

Lightning flashed above them, and almost a second later thunder rolled. It was too close. "Holly!"

Her eyelids fluttered, then opened. "Paul." She had the red eyeglasses on crookedly as she smiled up at him. "That first step is rough."

"Aaup," he said quietly, straightening her glasses. "Lady, you really stepped into this time. Anything hurt?"

"Everything."

She could speak, that was good. "Anything broken?" he prompted.

Holly struggled to sit but couldn't. Obviously, she was in pain, but she just thinned her lips tightly. "I can't move my legs."

With great difficulty, Paul swallowed, then forced his voice to remain professionally detached. "Your legs aren't responding? Sometimes paralysis is just temporary."

"No." Holly tried to shift again, but couldn't. "It's not paralysis. The timbers are pressing against my legs."

"Do you think your legs are broken?"

"I don't know--they hurt. They're getting numb. I

shouted before. Nobody heard me."

"Cause nobody **knew** you were here!" Frost said uncharacteristically bitterly as he finished climbing down from the other side of the door frame. He splashed into the water alongside them.

"Step slowly!" cautioned Paul. "Loose wood may press down on her!"

She forced a smile. "You're dropping by too, Frosty?"

"I wanted to get out of the rain. Damn, this water's cold! Sis, you do pick the weirdest places to party."

Paul stuck his flashlight in a half sunken beam, then feeling with his hands, Paul gave a testing push against the top beam that might be holding her down. It didn't move. "Holly, what the hell were you doing in here?"

"Nothing."

Frost was getting testy too. "**Holly!**"

"I-I-I was clearing out the mill."

"By yourself?" Her brother finished sarcastically. "Great idea, sis! "

"Well, you and N.C. wouldn't help me. You know it!"

Paul was applying more pressure against the beam he thought was locking her down. It moved only a fraction of inch, and Holly winced. "Am I hurting you?" he asked, feeling sympathetic pain.

She shook her head, but her mouth was drawn even tighter. His professionalism was wearing thin. "**Honey, you've got to tell me the truth**! We're trying to **help** you here!"

Holly gave a half sob. "The wood is pressing against my legs–it hurts when you move it! But you've got to move it! Hurry–the water's so cold..."

Another thunderous clap that seemed to shake the mill's stones. Frost nervously looked up. "Should we wait to get more help?"

Paul rested his fingers on Holly's neck. She was icy,

but her shivering was getting weaker. *Maybe going into shock.* "Frost–get your hands in the water under that top beam that's on her legs. We'll both give it a try." At least Holly's brother followed directions. "Holly, if we can lift it a little, do you think you can pull out your legs free?"

"I-I-I don't k-k-know," she said.

The deathly cold and darkness were wearing Paul down too. **"You will do it!**

Sounding doubtful Frost also argued, "What if we move something that crushes her?"

Paul had had it. **"Frost, get on that other side!** On three, we both pull this toward us, aaup?"

# Chapter 18

Wading carefully, Frost maneuvered for better footing on the other side of Holly.

When he was in place, Paul started. "One...two...**three**." Bracing against a standing post, Paul started to pull. Both men's arms tightened. Muscles rose. Slowly the beam shifted, raising. Straining hard, Paul said, "Holly–try..."

But she had already slipped out her pinned legs. "I think I'm free."

"Get away, if you can, honey. Frost—we'll let it down slow. Aaup?"

Frost nodded as he and Paul used all their strength to lower the beam away from her.

With it down, Paul turned to Holly, relief spreading through him. "Can you stand?"

She started to raise herself weakly, then fell back down into the murky water. Paul grabbed her arm before she went all in, slipping his other hand under her tail and lifting her high up into his arms. Pulling her deathly cold body against his warm chest, he asked, "Frost, can you climb back up?"

Frost flashed his light over the old rock foundation. Then, having apparently picked out his footholds, he put the flashlight in his mouth and climbed up that perpendicular wall like a monkey. For all his thinness and Ichabod Crane looks, Frost was one hell of a strong guy. All the Coreys always surprised Paul.

From the top, another bolt of lightning silhouetted Frost, as he looked back to Paul. "There's a half rotten ladder on the side of the building. I think I can get it down to you, but I don't know if it'll even take Holly's weight?"

Bright red, blue and white lights rotated through the ruined door. Noel must have gotten the Tahoe up the old road and managed to flip on the warning lights switch. "Negative.

We'll use stuff from my truck!"

Soon the third triplet stuck his head through the door. "Holly?"

"Looking good," Paul lied. He could feel Holly's weight heavy in his arms, but it only gave him some very unprofessional thoughts. "Those keys I gave you. In the back of the Tahoe are locked cases. Not the one under the truck bed, that's the guns–but the smaller ones on the side. There's rope ladder in the one closest to the rear door, driver's side. Get it."

Soon they were throwing the rope ladder with its wooden steps down. Paul carried Holly closer to it, then set her feet down in the water again. "Can you climb?"

"I-I-I don't k-k-now."

"Try, honey." From behind, he put both his hands on her waist, preparing to give her a boost up.

Holly reached up and grabbed at a rung, then weakly lifted her foot up to another rung. Tried to pull up, started to rise, but would have fallen backward if Paul wasn't behind to catch her.

"I-I c-can't! My hands are numb. My knees..." Lowering her head, she started to cry. "I'm sorry."

"**Stop crying!**" Paul said sternly, then let his voice gentle a bit. "We'll get you out of here!" With his hands on her arms, he could feel that she had stopped shivering; that meant her body was shutting down. There wasn't much time left for his Holly.

Sounding desperate Noel asked, "Should I get a rope?"

"Let's try lifting one more time with the ladder. N.C., get down on the threshold like Frost and brace your legs on the ground. Both of you put your arms over the door frame. Now, Holly move back. I'm going to get a leg on the ladder, then I'm going to try to lift you up. Your brothers are going to be reaching down."

"I'm s-sorry," she said miserably.

He had to get her stronger, saying angrily, "What did I tell you about apologizing! **Marines and their girlfriends do not apologize!**" In place, he lifted her with one hand under her arms, pulling her close to him. Then he tried to get his first foot on the highest rung he could manage. The ropes creaked with the strain; his and Holly's combined weights were way over the limit for this emergency ladder. Bumping her up on his hip, he got another foot on the ladder. Trying to help him, Holly got a toe on a rung in between, taking some of her weight off of him. *Good.* "One rung at a time, honey."

The cold was sapping Paul's strength. The door jam above seemed so high, and her dead weight pressed so heavily against him. This cellar wall must've been fifteen feet. Paul tightened his left arm on her, shifted his weight and moved his right foot up to the next rung, dragging her upwards. "We're making it."

Still three feet down from the top, he felt Holly raising both her arms. Using his hip, he tried to push her up higher.

"Frosty?" she called out weakly.

He answered, speaking to Noel, "I got an arm, N.C., you?"

"Yeah. Start pulling." Her other brother grunted with the exertion.

"Honey, are we hurting you?" asked Frost.

"It's okay," she said faintly, as they scraped her up and Paul tried to push from below. Finally, her dead weight was totally lifted off him.

In what seemed forever, he heard Frost yell down, "She's out!"

"Don't move her more than you have to! Get a blanket from my truck." Then all that was left for Paul was to take a deep breath and start hauling his own pounds up out of that damned hole. *Depressed lately, he'd been skipping his regular exercising–he'd start his regime again!*

Outside it had stopped raining. Noel had managed to

get the red wool blanket from the Tahoe to wrap around Holly. Paul could hear the siren of an ambulance bumping up the rutted lane.

On the ground, Holly looked up at Paul. "You left your flashlight down there."

He chuckled. "And, honey, it's going to stay down there!"

Frost moved to wave over the ambulance, but Holly stubbornly lowered her head. "I'm not going to the hospital!"

"**Holly!**" Paul started...

"I-I-I'm okay. I can move my legs and arms. I think I'm just b-b-bruised." Well, at least she was shivering again.

"You're going to the hospital!" Paul pronounced.

"You need my permission—I won't give it!" repeated the stubborn Holly.

"She doesn't have insurance," Frost said sadly.

"For God's sake..." Paul started. "I'll pay—aaup?"

Noel came over. "We can take her home. If she seems to be getting worse, we'll call for the ambulance again, I swear!"

"Holly—please," Paul pleaded.

"N-n-no!" she said firmly.

The EMT guys had parked and were slogging over. "Let them at least look at you, aaup?"

Holly nodded.

The EMTs were unhappy but said they couldn't find anything seriously wrong on the surface. Frost lifted Holly into the back seat of the police Tahoe, and Paul drove them to the mansion. With Noel holding the back door, Paul carried her inside. Holly insisted on limping into the kitchen, leaving slimy, inky puddles of stagnant water on the formerly clean yellow linoleum floor.

Frost was following. "There are no guests in the downstairs Library suite. You can take her in there." Paul was following as she hobbled through the dining room and into the front parlor.

"No!" said Holly shivering and dripping dirty water. "I want to go to my bedroom!"

Paul unhappily looked into the foyer, at the staircase curving in a tight spiral upwards. "That's on the third floor. Right?"

"Yes!" Determinedly Holly started to limp forward.

He looked at her, then reached down with one arm behind her shoulders and one under her legs, lifting her up. "First floor linens and furniture. Going up," Paul called out.

Giggling Holly wrapped her arms around his neck as he started carrying her up the curving stairs. At the second floor, he headed for the door to the steep third staircase that led to the attic suite that was Holly's, with her four poster bed and sitting area. He carried her to the back bathroom where there was an old-fashioned claw foot tub and shower head, surrounded by a ringed shower curtain. "Get those wet clothes off," said Paul turning on the hot water, which of course came out cold. He let it run.

She still looked dangerous pale, but her voice was stronger, and he was seeing some of her peach pink color returning to her cheeks. Still, Holly was having trouble undoing the buttons on her blouse, as if she couldn't quite control her fingers. He started on her buttons.

Holly looked at him. "Y-y-you should get out of those muddy pants. I've got blood on your shirt. Take them off, and Frost will put them in the washer and dryer."

"Let's just get you in the tub." The shower was now starting to steam some warmth. He steadied her as she tried to raise her leg over the tall tub. Holly stood with one leg straddling the tub, as bloody mud washed off her foot. She shook her head. "I can't stand. Paul, I'm too weak."

"Aaup." Like a rag doll, he lifted Holly out and set her down on the tub rim. Then he stripped off his shoes, socks, pants, and shirt. Soon he stood there in just his shorts, which were was soaked from the mill.

She giggled. "That looks obscene! Take it all off, Paul!"

He did. Then, grabbing a bar of lavender smelling soap, he climbed into that comforting hot stream of water, reaching out to lift her inside with him. She wrapped both arms around his hairy chest for support, as he reached over and started lathering up her shoulders and then down back to her buttocks. She was warming under his touch, her breasts perking against his chest. Thankfully, in the showers' stream, Holly couldn't see Paul's tears of thanks for her life. He kissed the top of her head; *it had been so close...*

Eagerly she kissed him back, then he was helping her out of the tub, and handing her a fluffy towel as she wistfully asked, "But we've broken up, haven't we?"

He looked down at her. "Not for now." With a pink towel, he wiped himself down fast, then helped her. Finally wrapping her in a fluffy, oversized bathrobe, he carried Holly over to that big four poster bed, with its Texas star quilt and maroon side curtains. She told him where to find a long, soft flannel nightgown for her. He was helping her into it when there was a discrete knock on the door at the bottom of the staircase to the second floor. Paul wrapped the towel around his waist.

"C'mon up," called Holly. It was Frost who climbed up. Over his arm, he carried a green robe of Noel's, not really big enough for Paul, and a tray with two mugs, a thermos that smelled of hot chocolate and two grilled Reuben sandwiches. She smiled at her brother. "Frosty, could you take the clothes from the bathroom and run them through the wash?"

Her brother nodded, so she continued. "You can bring back Paul's uniform tomorrow."

"No," said Paul firmly. "I've got to go to tonight."

Holly reached out a still too cold hand, touching Paul's bare arm. "Must you go? Truce for just tonight? Please?"

"Honey, I'm only going to hurt you more by staying," Paul murmured to her.

Frost looked from one to the other. "You guys work it out. When the uniform's done, I'll knock, and it'll be hanging on the doorknob downstairs. Breakfast will be ready at 6:30. And I'll be sure to get Thor chained up because N.C. is **not** gonna be happy about any of this."

Paul smiled appreciatively, but also asked, "Frost, have you sawed any of that flooring in the mill?"

"No. And I asked N.C. He didn't either."

"But somebody did. I want you all to promise that" Paul looked to Holly significantly, "that **none** of you are going to that mill alone until we figure who did? Aaup?"

"Agreed," said Frost. "N.C. will agree too." He looked at his sister, sternly. "**Holly?**"

At first, it looked like she wanted to disagree, but with the two of them glaring at her, Holly finally said, "Al-all right."

Frost nodded went into the bathroom and came out carrying a mound of muddy, dripping clothes he carried downstairs.

Paul took the food tray, put it on the bed beside Holly and pulled up an empire chair beside her. Trying to control her trembling hands, Holly was already pouring the steaming, dark, hot chocolate into the two mugs. Wood-sashed windows at the front of the house shook behind her with another thunder roll from the storm outside.

She was shivering uncontrollably again, her teeth chattering. Holly lowered her head but still asked. "I'm so cold. How about you climbing in here with me? We can do some old fashioned bundling while we eat?"

Giving in, he climbed into bed beside her, feeling her goose-bumped flesh. God, she was freezing, he put one strong arm around her shoulders as he passed her a sandwich with the other hand.

They both chewed sauerkraut, swiss cheese, and corned beef for a while, then Paul turned closer to her. "Honey, with this last attack, I really don't want you going alone to the spring rites at Grace's."

"I'm not. I'm going to the Fitzgeralds' Beltane."

He still didn't look happy. "You'll be alone, with everybody nude? Drinking? Doing drugs?"

"I won't be attending alone. There will be twenty to thirty people at the Fitzgeralds—maybe more. They make toasts with alcohol, but they discourage other drug use." She didn't say she knew Colin would protect her.

Paul was taking her in his arms. "For me, please don't go?"

She didn't want to, but after tonight the only thing she could say was, "Yes. I won't go."

"Promise?" he persisted.

"I promise," she said.

They finished eating, and he set the tray off the bed, but he still stayed lying back on the mattress beside her. His body heat was good, but she wanted a lot more from him. What had Abby Hoyt told her? Keep silently repeating the invocation: *Blend my body to his, his body to mine. We must be one.*"

Soon they were.

*   *   *

In the morning, Holly opened her eyes, seeing the maroon curtains surrounding her four-poster. The room smelled faintly of Paul's delicious male aroma and honeysuckle. His head was on the pillow next to her. His large eyes were closed, with sandy eyelashes on his high cheeks. His beard stubble was slightly reddish. Holly inhaled his warmth as she gently pulled the pink blanket over his freckled shoulder. Her arm—her whole body—ached from yesterday's bruising, but she had been the aggressor last night. And it had been good!

Holly didn't want to wake him, but she was too wired to stay in bed. She slipped out of the warm covers, used the bathroom across the room quietly, cleaning herself up and rinsing out her mouth, just in case they had time before he left. Paul was still snoring lightly when she came out of the bathroom.

White light spilled down from the roof above. Holly climbed the steep ladder to the square cupola with its four sides of white-wood trimmed windows, and mauve velvet cushioned benches. The storm had scoured all making the world below her sparkle. Last night, trapped in that hole, with no one knowing where she was, Holly thought she was going to die. Now she sat on the soft cushion and folded her stiff legs in a yoga position. She'd never been happier in her life. Paul was in her bed. Noel, Frost, Thor, all of them were safe in the mansion. Holly found herself silently giving thanks for her life–and that of her loves–and the bright morning ahead.

*But what was ahead for them?*

Soft sounds below. Finally, Paul's bare feet were climbing up the wooden rungs to the cupola. He'd put on his uniform trousers, but his muscular chest was still bare. He looked at her lovingly. "Praying to the Goddess?"

"T-t-thanking whoever wants to listen!" she said sincerely.

Ducking his tall head as he finished climbing up to join her in the copula, he sat on the cushion beside her. Putting his long arms around her, he drew Holly gently against him. "Cold up here."

They were silent for a time, then she said, "Thank you for yesterday."

"For last night in bed?" he teased.

"N-n-no." She bobbed her head down. "For saving me, silly."

"You haven't gotten my bill yet," he murmured close

to her ear. He'd used the minty mouth wash too.

She cuddled against him, asking seriously, "Paul, what's ahead for us?"

"Go back to bed for a bit?" he asked hopefully.

"After that?"

"We'll finish getting dressed. Eat breakfast. Go to our jobs."

"That wasn't what I meant, and you know it. What's ahead?"

He hugged her tightly. "I don't know, honey. Let's just see what happens, aaup?"

# Chapter 19

Work that week at The Lady's Cauldron was in overdrive. While Holly carried flower pieces from the storeroom to the sales area, the two Maine coon cats were always underfoot, 'ouuing' constantly. The male swished his tail in frustration that she wasn't scratching his neck as usual, while Bast spits at Holly in annoyance from one of the work tables. *The female must smell Thor.*

When Holly was there, it was part of her job to feed them. In one of the barns, there was an opening sawed in the bottom of a siding board. Colin had shown Holly how to clean out bowls of old kibble and leave more. Following her with his deep purr, Horus would rub against her leg, while Bast would climb up on a hay bale and lick her paw, loftily supervising the whole procedure. After about a week Holly reported to Colin, "For two cats, they don't seem to eat much out of the bowl at all?"

Colin only laughed. "Bast and Horus think that dry kibble is beneath them. They only eat it when nothing else warm-blooded is available. The food bowl acts as bait. They're working cats, keeping down the rodent population. Watch them sometimes, they coordinate a hunt together–it's quite a sight." Holly did one day and saw Bast block a brown mouse's escape, while Horus moved in and pounced, then the male proudly carried his trophy over to drop it at the paws of the matriarchal Bast.

Today Holly just dumped the kibble and hurried back to put out merchandise for the crowds expected for the Beltane preparations. She had recognized a few faces--from Grace Le Fleur's Yule--buying incense, live rose petals, and loose flowers for some altar. They mixed well with the usual tourists stopping in to buy pine pillows and Connecticut coffee mugs, totally oblivious to the Goddess worship aspect of The Lady's Cauldron.

Colin was working behind the counter when Lapin came in, helping a heavy set, an elderly lady who walked with a cane. That cane was cleverly carved with two entwining snakes, and Holly recognized Colin's work. The woman wore a pair of eyeglasses that were twins to Holly's red, only the elderly lady's were blue, and Holly suspected they were the original, not the retros Holly had bought. At his nod, Holly took Colin's place at the register.

Lapin was carrying in an old cardboard box for the woman, setting it down on a small round display table by the windows. The old lady began unloading a bunch of dried, crescent-shaped tree funguses, painted with crude, Grandma Moses type landscapes featuring snowy hills, scarlet cardinals, covered bridges, and raccoons. Over by the storeroom door, a blue veiled Maeve stood watching with tightened eyes; Holly started to feel burning wave after uncomfortable wave of heat, as Colin mother's anger rolled over her.

Colin was bringing a clear plastic multi-level stand over to increase the elderly lady's display area, as the old woman bubbled happily, "I painted a lot more than usual for your service coming up!"

"Good," said Colin. "And I've got some money for you from the last batch. Holly, please get that envelope from the register drawer labeled '*Mrs. Bates,* '."

Holly found the thick envelope and brought it over, knowing that Colin had actually given away most of those '*art pieces*' free to anyone who seemed interested in them.

The old lady's face was surprisingly smooth, with a large mole on her left cheek. Just by feeling the thickness of the envelope, she gave a big smile. "I broke my upper plate. With this, I'll be able to go see the dentist."

Colin frowned, gently chiding, "You should've said something. The Lady's Cauldron can always give you an advance."

"Collie," Mrs. Bates wagged a finger at him, sternly,

"You're running a business!" Then she looked about the store and her tone softened. "Claire and Jim would've been so proud at what you've built from the farm they left you!"

After the elderly lady left, Maeve walked over to Colin. "I don't want that junk out on the counter for Beltane!"

Her son continued to arrange the table display. "Fiona Bates was Grandma's best friend," said Colin firmly. "It stays!"

Even standing away from them, Holly felt wave after wave of hot anger roiling between son and mother. Their fury knotted Holly's stomach, making her feel like Aunt Maureen was punishing her for something again. She could see that Lapin was also getting it, but with over five feet between them, Maeve and Colin Fitzgerald just stood staring silently at each other with narrowed eyes.

Finally--again--Maeve was the first to walk away.

When the door to the storeroom closed behind her, Colin wiped beads of sweat off his forehead, then he looked over to Holly. "You picked that up, didn't you? I'm sorry. I've got to work at teaching you how to shield yourself a little." He smiled ruefully. "Sometimes Maeve and I forget other sensitives are around."

Lapin was still there. Now she saw the big black man use a cigarette lighter to ignite a bundle of dried leaves from the table. These he swirled through the store, leaving a scent of sage smoke. Colin chuckled at some private joke between them. After he left, Holly asked Colin, "Is Lapin going to your Beltane service? He doesn't seem to be too interested in Old Craft?"

Colin now replaced the paper roll in the cash register, he always seemed to be working at something. "Lapin will help with setup and will be driving the hay wagon shuttle up to the hill. He is also bringing his two German shepherds. Our Beltane has a rather risque reputation hereabouts, so he and his dogs will keep patrolling to see we don't have any Peeping

Toms sneaking in the woods. But you're right, worship of the Lady is not Lapin's thing."

"Will the dogs hurt anyone?"

"Lapin has them guarding four-year-olds, but last year some idiot broke into his shop one night, and Diesel and Turbo took chunks of him before he got away."

She looked curiously at Colin. "But I sense a strong spirituality from Lapin?"

"He's from the Caribbean. He practices VouDoo."

"Aren't they calling it Santeria to be P.C.?" she asked.

"The practices are close, but there are differences."

She frowned. "Doesn't VooDoo have a lot to do with Catholic Saints?"

"Lapin prefers 'VouDoo.'" He gave it a French accent. "Come over here." She followed as he walked to a corner bookcase filled with narrow, colored candles poured into twelve-inch high glass cylinders. Each candle had a saint's portrait on the front and prayers on the sides. "You see these? Well--for Catholics--each major saint has a color and a special prayer of intention, like St. Elizabeth here. She was the Virgin Mary's infertile cousin, who--when past the age of childbearing-- was blessed by God and produced John the Baptist. If you are a devout Catholic suffering infertility, you appeal to St. Elizabeth for her intervention of your behalf with God.

"Now, when African slaves were brought to the new world, their cultural and religious practices were banned, but they understood that basic forces were the same whatever name you called them. So to the outward society, they were good Catholics appealing to the saints. But when someone practicing VouDoo lights a red wax candle to Saint Barbara, they are usually appealing to Chango. Saint Patrick is Dumballah, and Saint Jacques is Loa Ogoun."

"Are they prayed to as gods themselves, or as an entity to intercede with God on the petitioner's behalf?"

Unreadable, he studied her. "Why do you want to know? Thinking of changing your religion?"

She lowered her head, blushing. "I-I-I just like learning. I've always been curious about what other people's beliefs were."

Some tourists were coming in and looking about the store as he continued to study her carefully. "Why don't you start your studies with Old Craft? When I was in my questioning teens, my grandmother got me a number of books. One of them was Scott Cunningham's seminal *Wicca A Guide for the Solitary Practitioner*. It explains a lot of the basics. I've got a copy back at the house that I could lend you if you'd like?"

"I'd like that." She nodded blushing more. He seemed about to say something else when a short, heavy woman came up to the counter. Colin turned immediately to her. "Mam?"

The silver-haired lady beamed up at him. "I'm sorry to bother you-all, but I can't reach that red scarf up on the top rack."

"I'll be happy to get it down for you," he said, moving to do it.

A frustrated Holly watched him go. There were so many questions she wanted to ask Colin about Old Craft, but she would read his book and maybe after the rush preparing for Beltane she could learn more.

* * *

Colin had gone back to working outside, hours before Holly finally glanced to the clock on the wall. Twenty minutes to go before they locked up the store, then she'd have to make some flower arrangement deliveries before she could drive home. Her feet hurt and she'd have to cook dinner because both of her brothers were out helping a friend tonight. *Again.*

Only two women were browsing in the store, and they

were coming up to the counter when the bell over the door jangled, and Holly felt herself suddenly wanting to hide. She didn't even need to see the auras to know trouble had walked in. It was that hard-mouthed, red-orange headed woman from the motel, with her tall boyfriend.

The redhead immediately focused on Holly. "Where is Paul Travinski?"

"He's not here," answered Holly in as polite a fashion as she could, while one of the other browsers put a brass Tibetan incense burner on the counter to buy. Holly started to ring it up.

"You're lying!" screeched the redheaded woman. The two shoppers appeared shocked at the anger in her voice. Horsus had jumped up on the sales counter, and the big coon cat was rubbing against Holly's arm, giving his usual guttural, growl-like vocalizations.

As Holly tried to continue calmly ringing up, she found herself reddening with embarrassment at the rude accusation. She could see out the front windows. Colin had been refilling the herb pots on the sale tables outside. Now he seemed to be looking around as if trying to figure out where a bad smell was coming from. Slowly he turned and focused on the barn. Dusting soil off his hands onto his jeans, Colin started walking up the pathway.

Holly was now ringing up several packages of incense cones. "That'll be twenty-four forty-two, mam. Do you want them gift wrapped?"

The woman shook her head, digging into her handbag. "Do you take Master Card?"

"Yes, mam."

"**Where is Paul?**" The redhead yelled at her.

"I told you, not here!" Holly desperately didn't want a scene at the place of her employment, but behind the couple, Colin had walked in. He just stood at the doorway, crossing his arms over his chest, listening and watching.

The abrasive woman announced loudly, "My name is Margaret Dietrich, **Mrs. James Dietrich**." She looked around to see if anyone reacted. "I stopped to buy some incense, and I saw Paul's truck parked in your lot. It is **his** truck because I know his license plate! Is he hiding in the back room?"

The two other shoppers were hurrying out, and Holly was so glad she had the counter between her and that tall, glowering guy of Margaret's. "It is P-P-Paul's truck, but I'm driving it."

"**Does he know that**?" Margaret's sharp words were an accusation.

"He handed me the keys."

The redhead pulled herself up. "Have you been dating him?"

"I don't think that's any of your business." Holly looked around for something to do, to look busy. She started rearranging the jewelry in one of the counter's glass cases.

Margaret glared at her. "I'm Paul's fiancee!"

"You said you were **Mrs.** Dietrich?" Holly returned.

Margaret instantly went from righteous outrage to dignified grief. "I'm Jim's widow and Paul's fiancee."

"And your friend there?" asked Holly.

The woman glanced at him. "Brandon. A friend of mine that my fiancee is aware of."

"Isn't that former fiancee?" Holly pointed out.

"Did you think he is going to marry *you*? He isn't. Not that I'm upset about you--I knew that while I was out of town, he'd have to have some activity to relieve himself." She tried to sound sympathetic, "But did you delude yourself into thinking that sex with Paul meant you were engaged?"

From the front of the store, Colin called out, as he walked forward, "Mam, if you have any purchases, please bring them up, since we will be closing shortly. Holly, start counting the tray for Register 2."

"Yes, sir." She moved to the register and printed out a

cash receipt then opened the tray to start counting the drawer. But felt she should say to Margaret, "N-n-no. Paul is just a f-f-friend."

Margaret glanced back to Colin. "You seem to have a lot of *friends*, don't you, dear?" She had picked up a small violet plant Colin had set on the counter this morning for Holly. While Margaret glared at Holly, she nervously picked at the white flowers.

"Did you want to purchase that plant in your hands?" Colin asked. "You're shredding the leaves."

Margaret looked at the pot and slammed it down on the counter. "Don't you have anything more stylish?" She looked about, then with a smile, Margaret extended her left hand out to Holly, flashing a large, raised diamond. "This is Paul's ring, by the way. We're back engaged."

Holly could just look at the aura's harsh colors radiating about her to know Margaret was lying. "Are you? Paul didn't mention that. In fact, when I last talked to him, he still seemed bitter about you dumping him on your wedding day. That was a bit tacky, wasn't it?"

Margaret set her mouth tightly. "I had reasons."

Holly returned her attention to counting the quarters as she said casually, "Paul doesn't seem like a guy who could forgive something like that."

Brandon had moved closer to back up Margaret as she glared at Holly. "It doesn't matter. Paul finds me irresistible." "Oh, does he?" Holly didn't suppress her smile.          Margaret studied her. "Are **you** engaged to him?"

Colin moved forward to stand near Brandon. "Do either of you want to buy anything because otherwise we are closed."

The boyfriend moved closer to intimidate Colin with his greater height. Colin ignored him as Margaret also turned and glared. Again, Holly got a wave of nausea as Colin just calmly stared back at the redhead. *When Colin and his mother*

*mentally dueled, the angry waves had seemed to emanate
equally from both of them, but in this case, Holly felt the
unpleasant force from Colin's direction easily overwhelming
Margaret's weaker radiations.*

Margaret dropped her eyes first.

Then she spoke angrily, "No, you don't have anything
worthwhile here." She turned back to Holly, smiling meanly.
"I was just testifying today. Talking to a detective, telling him
how bitter Paul was that Jim stole me away. And how
vengeful Paul can be, and the threats Paul made against Jim.
Paul Travinski killed my husband, and I don't know why they
haven't put him in jail yet–but they will! Even Chief Lewis
can't protect him forever!"

It frightened Holly to know that this woman's hatred
could make Paul's situation even worse. Colin looked at
Holly, studying her face with concern, then he escorted
Margaret and Brandon to the door, locking it after them. For
a long time, he stood staring out the window as they got into
their car. Finally, he turned back to her. "Why don't you start
on your deliveries? I'll finish closing up."

Holly lowered her head in shame. "I-I'm s-sorry about
her."

"It's certainly not your fault! Bring up the van, so we
can load the arrangements. You're taking our truck, right?"

"Most of the deliveries are back in Mystic. I thought
I'd take mine–Paul's--so after the last the delivery I could just
drive home."

Colin nodded. "Better idea. But, Holly, there's a favor
I'd like you to do me."

"What?"

"When you drive out if you see that silver rental car
*Mrs. Dietrich* was driving broke down on the road, promise
me you won't stop to help them?"

She was confused. "Okay. I won't stop. Why do you
think they'll break down?"

Colin just gave a little secretive smile.

Holly looked from him to the parking lot. "You weren't near it. Y-y-you couldn't have done anything to her car?"

"Karma always catches up, but sometimes you have to give it a helping hand." Colin's smile deepened.

After she pulled Paul's truck up near the front entrance, Colin helped her load the arrangements, including large two funerals pieces for Mystic. When she drove a quarter of a mile down 184, Holly saw the silver car pulled off the road. The hood was up, and Brandon was standing there looking at the motor with his hands in his pockets. Margaret had her hands on her hips. She turned and imperiously waved one hand for Holly to stop.

Automatically, Holly started to apply the truck's brakes, then remembered she'd promised Colin she wouldn't. She just drove right past. In her rearview mirror, she could see Margaret giving her the finger.

# Chapter 20

Mary told Paul he had an appointment in his chief's office, and since that was a bit formal for him and Stan just to talk, he figured the news wouldn't be good. Promptly at ten, Paul stood before his chief's desk. Stan must have been running his fingers through his thick field of hair, and ruffling it made him look a bit like a white rooster. With a nod of his head, Stan indicated that Paul should sit in one of the two leather chairs before his desk.

Paul decided to start right off. "How's the Dietrich investigation going? Am I still it?"

"All my guys are working on it. Hiram may have trouble booting up a computer, but he's a reliable, thorough detective. He'll get something soon." Stan stopped.

"But in the meantime..." Paul prompted.

"We're getting a lot of pressure. The D.A. is hearing it from Hartford."

"Why is the state capital interested?" asked a confused Paul.

"You've done a hard job well, so you've made some enemies."

"But Hartford wants me up for murder one?"

"Some guys see a chance to knock you down, and they're taking it." Stan obviously didn't want to explain more. "Since you fit the description of the man running away, and since you've had a long-standing grudge against the victim, and you have no substantiation of your movements during the murder, you're a suspect."

"The only one," finished a discouraged Paul.

"No, Hiram's got a few theories he has the boys looking into." Paul raised an eyebrow cynically, but Stan was continuing in a gruff voice, "The Mystic District Attorney would like me to request that you turn in your sidearm until we get this sorted out."

That Paul hadn't expected. "Rubber gun squad, Stan?"

His chief lowered his head. "Just for a time, to keep the jackals at bay."

"You want my badge too?"

"**No!**" Stan looked his old, belligerent self. "You're still on duty drawing full sergeant's pay, but I don't want you responding without a gun."

Earlier this morning--out in the booking area-- everyone had heard Stan's voice raised behind his closed office door. This was probably what that was about. Paul had been expecting suspension with or without pay until this matter was settled, but not being disarmed. "See the Mystic News has been doing editorials about you covering up for me?"

"Not your problem!" Stan snapped.

"Why are they so after me?"

"It's the usual 'anti-Second Amendment,' 'police are brutal' crowd..."

"Stan, I don't want you losing your job over me."

"Son, we've just got to ride out this storm. We will."

Paul shook his head at the insanity of it. "I'll turn in my sidearm, but you know what's in that special built safe in my personal truck bed?"

"Your sniper rifles, body armor, and ammo. I also know about the shotgun and rife locked up in the Police Tahoe, and that arsenal that you've collected up in that apartment of yours, but the *idiots* who wrote this order only specified your sidearm."

"So–I'm off duty?"

"No! You'll do administrative work in the office here. Help out with dispatch, scheduling...Mary will find something for you."

"On a sergeant's pay, you're having me work as a file clerk?"

"That's what our great leaders want. Maybe you can get some studying done toward your Master's degree."

Paul digested that. "You'd need someone to take on the sergeant's duties–Henry?"

Stan obviously hadn't considered him. "He's not senior."

"But he's good! The others respect him, and he could use some administrative experience."

Stan thought about that for a moment. "Okay, I'll try him."

Paul started to fish in his pocket to turn over his keys. "He should be driving the sergeant's Tahoe."

His chief looked pained. "No, Paul, this mess has got to be finished soon. You can keep driving the Tahoe. Now send Henry into me."

*It wasn't pleasant to be replaced that fast.* "Stan, Jim Dietrich was couriering diamonds for a South American group. I've been thinking..."

His chief's face hardened. "Departmental procedure is clear. If an officer is personally involved in a case, he doesn't work on it!

"But if you tried chasing those guys down?"

Stan sighed. "James Dietrich was hired by a rather dicey conglomerate. They've contacted us. Put in a claim for the missing diamonds, as has your ex-fiancee, Margaret or Mrs. James Dietrich, as she's now styling herself."

"The South Americans?"

"No proof they were in the area. Jim was only holding their diamonds for them, so unless they wanted hot diamonds and the insurance money, they had no reason to steal them from Dietrich."

"Who are these guys?"

"Well, that's where it gets interesting. So far, we've only been able to speak to Mr. Juan Manual O'Brien."

"O'Brien?"

"A lot of Irish migrated to Mexico after the Civil War. Passport proves he only entered the U.S. a week after Jim's death."

"U.S. borders are Swiss cheese. Anybody could've come and gone without a passport?"

Stan nodded. " He's dark-haired, 5'6" and 200 lbs. Not the guy seen running away after the shot was fired. The organization he represents is a shell company, owned by another shell company. It gets murkier after that, which is good for you because if it ever comes to trial, that should give your lawyer at least two other viable lines of possible suspects."

Paul looked at him. "You think I'll be indicted?"

"If you weren't a police officer, I certainly wouldn't be putting you into custody on this evidence. There's nothing. No fingerprints. No blood stains, or a gun tying you to the boat. Witnesses didn't see a license plate or even a car. Your motive is weak, a good lawyer should prove it's practically non-existent."

"The South American guys..."

"Hiram brought in a special accountant translator to try and sort through the puzzle box that's their corporate structure."

Paul moved forward, "Sir if I could just look at the files..."

**"Sergeant--I told you—no!"** Stan slammed a fist down on his desk.

Well, Paul had pretty much lost his job anyway, so he decided to go for the whole nine yards. "With the free time, I could look into some cold case files. The Hester Corey murder for one."

"Long closed," said Stan, looking down at some fascinating papers on his desk. "Send Henry into me! I need to run a police department!"

Paul continued to push, "As a patrolman, weren't you

the first officer on the scene?"

Those indigo blue eyes of his chief looked directly into Paul's. "What?"

"You were the first responder to Hester Corey's murder?"

Stan looked annoyed. "That was in the file, was it?"

They both knew it wasn't. "Someone mentioned it," Paul hedged.

"Who? Holly Corey or one of her brothers? Paul, I've told you before, a man interested in career advancement would do well to stay away from the morass that is the Coreys."

"Evvie knew the Coreys didn't she?"

Stan's voice was calm, but his face was draining of color. "Hester Corey's death brought pain to everyone around here. I do not want you bringing those memories back to Evvie! Don't speak to my wife about this! **That is an order!**"

"Why was Gault Corey never indicted for his wife's murder?"

"I was a mere patrolman, Paul. That question should go to my uncle, Chief Theodore Lynch."

"Where is he, sir?" Paul persisted.

"Elm Grove Cemetery. He's dead Paul, like the Hester Corey investigation!"

# Chapter 21

The next day, after that little conversation with his chief, Paul found himself reassigned to permanent desk duty in the Community Police Station. Out on the peninsula where the river poured into the harbor, there was a small, one room, windowless brick building, with three parking slots outside. Inside: a desk, three steel chairs, one bench, a small counter with a sink, and a five cup coffee urn, supply cabinets, and an unmarked bathroom–known among the force as *'Siberia East.'* The substation was envisioned as a way for the community to interact and love their police officers, but the populace seemed too over-awed to drop in. The only people he generally got were lost tourists looking for the Mystic Seaport Museum Village, which they had just driven past. Usually, he did a short two-hour stint being bored here, while catching up on his paperwork.

Now his job was to sit there all day and work on next year's budget requests. And maybe answer any questions from some lost soul who might wander in. Any serious problems, like a robbery or injury, he was to call the nearest patrolling officer with a gun. Acting Sergeant Henry Mackay looked a bit embarrassed when he had to give Paul the assignment.

Paul had to admit that getting out of headquarters was a bit of a relief. Chief Dispatcher Mary was trying to answer a busy board while thinking up make-do work for him; while around headquarters the other officers, his *'friends,'* were giving him stares. He didn't know which he disliked more: the open pity for his plight or the curious *did Paul really do it?* Looks.

On his own, Paul decided to update all the personnel evaluations of the patrolmen under his command. If his guys were coming up for their anniversary up-grades--while he was behind bars--it wouldn't exactly be fair to them. The desk phone rang. It was Mary. They needed a new supply order gotten out today–that was his mission in life now. Maybe he'd fix them all by forgetting to reorder toilet paper.

But while they were talking, Mary dropped an interesting nugget of information. Chief Lewis was headed up to Hartford for some sort of all-day meeting. Mary was going to have to call Evvie to tell her Stan would be late for supper. Paul looked at his watch. He still had another half hour on duty, but afterward, he might have some private time with Evvie. *There were a few questions he wanted to ask.*

He had just finished with that supply catalog Mary had sent over when he heard the door open. Margaret walked in sans boyfriend. Paul couldn't get over how badly she had aged. The makeup was thick as usual, hiding large-pored skin. At one time he'd actually found her darkly drawn, heavy mascaraed eyes as intriguing. Now, he didn't. *Great, this intrusion would top off his day off just fine.*

"Paul." Margaret smiled as she stood with one leg slightly back to make her wide hips look thinner. The tight, gold lame pants didn't flatter her at all. "I saw the Tahoe outside. I know your license plate. "

He'd seen them following him, sometimes together, sometimes only Margaret or just Brandon. For the hell of it, he had even parked down at the marina, gotten out of the police SUV, and sauntered down to have a very long conversation with one of the fishermen there. Still seeing Brandon lurking out of the corner of his eye, Paul walked the pier to Jim's boat. It still had the yellow police caution tape draping it, but Paul was in uniform, so he just climbed on board and tried to get out of Brandon's sight by climbing down the steps to the cabin. This was padlocked, but out-of-sight Paul took his time and loosened his shirt a bit like he might have stuffed something into it.

When he walked back to the car, Brandon was on high alert. Which meant whatever happened to the diamonds, Margaret's partner thought they were still around. *Was that why Margaret was invading his life again?* "Is there some law enforcement reason for you being here?"

"That's a bit formal for us, isn't it?" she returned softly.

"This a police facility and I'm on duty."

"Paul, you used to call me *sweetheart*. I liked that." She stepped closer.

"If not transacting police business, I'm afraid you'll have to leave..."

Margaret pulled back a bit. "I'm filing a report. **I'm in danger!**"

"From who?"

"Brandon. He knows about us!" She moved her head closer to his--from her breath, she must've had fish for lunch.

"*Us* has been over for a very long time," Paul said. She put an appealing hand on his arm. Once her touch had given him a strange tingle, now it just repulsed him. He pulled her hand off. "Please don't."

"I ran away with Jim, but I loved you! When I realized that, Jim still forced me to marry him, but it wasn't working out. That was why I divorced him."

"Gee. He thought he'd divorced you, Margaret? And that he'd placed an Order of Protection against you."

She went on as if Paul had said nothing. "Brandon has realized that I love only you. He's wildly jealous! He's threatened to hurt me. Look! Look at the bruises on my arm."

Paul didn't see any bruises on her heavy arm. "You know." He looked around the small beige-walled room. "I don't have any assault forms here. You'll have to drive to headquarters and fill out a report there. And I'm leaving here soon, so I've got to lock up." He started to stand.

"You're the only man I've ever loved!" Margaret thrust herself toward him as Paul put his arms up in a defensive posture and tried to slide past her.

She kept pushing, "Paul, it can only be us. There will

never be another man for me!"

"If I'm your only soulmate, why is that kid sharing your motel room?"

"Brandon's paying for his own room."

"He doesn't look old enough to have a job."

"His father's got money," she said with contempt.

"Good. Then his father might offer you money to get your talons out of his son."

She went from passion to business instantly. "Jim changed his will! I won't be getting anything!"

Paul smiled. "How dare he?"

"He had millions in diamonds hidden on that boat. I have a buyer for them!"

*It was turning serious here.* "Margaret, Jim was a combat-seasoned soldier and police officer, yet someone got onto that boat and killed him. The owners are looking for those diamonds, and I don't think that they're very nice people. If I were you, I'd shake what I could out of Brandon's parents and move on–unless you want to spend the rest of your life looking over your shoulder for some murderers."

She persisted, "If you don't have the diamonds, who was the first officer on the scene?"

"I don't know, and I don't care." He gently herded her out. "This office is closed!"

Paul locked the door after her. He'd finished all his time here, but he still had work to do. He set up his laptop and downloaded pictures from his cell phone. He hadn't done it for a while. Still had those shots he'd taken of Holly at Cobb's Mill: that sweet face watching the mallards; ducking her head in embarrassment when he told her how lovely she looked; even those silly retro, red eyeglass frames. When Holly said she didn't like them anymore, he'd offered to buy her new ones, but she said no. And he kind of loved seeing her in them.

Yeah, his muscles ached and every night working on

Quentin's mother's house after work was hell with those mosquitoes biting, but it would still be worth it if the car Holly was driving were not a death trap. But he and Holly were over. Paul firmly moved past those photos.

More pictures: one of Althea shooting, some of his Border Collie Sally on her new dog bed. A few of the big bluefish he'd caught with Henry. Then the ones he was looking for–the photographs he'd surreptitiously snapped of that picture in the Corey family album. That old shot of Gault and his twelve-woman Coven. Paul enlarged it more on the laptop screen. Surprising sharp. Must've been real film in a good lensed camera. Again, that vision of Holly to the side was unnerving, but it wasn't Holly, it was her mother, Hester. Her mother died not much older than Holly was today.

He shifted the image right on his laptop screen. More faces. An intense-eyed Gault Corey, scowling at the camera. Showing off. So Gault Corey killed his wife, for who? One of these other women in this photograph? Holly's father had his arms draped around Skye Rainbow and a younger Lilith Hoyt, but they couldn't compare to Hester's beauty.

Paul scanned over faces he didn't know. Then stopped at one. A determined square faced blonde, standing straight-backed, alongside Abigail Hoyt. A face he didn't want to recognize. Couldn't really, one young woman looked so like another.

Paul zoomed in on the screen and looped that face. Isolating it on a new screen. Hair golden yellow, with maybe a touch of red? Eye color? Couldn't tell from this photo. Chin square. Determined. Seemed a bit older than those teenagers Gault charmed so easily.

Fortunately, the lady was facing the camera directly, instead of looking worshipfully at Gault like Lilith and the others. Chief Lewis guarded the Mystic police budget like it was coming out of his own pocket, and Stan couldn't see the necessity for photo recognition software. Paul had put in two requests for a grant from Homeland Security for the software. Nothing yet. So he'd bought his own rip-off program. Into this, he cut and pasted the young blonde's head and shoulders.

Now he needed a shot to compare with. It wouldn't be hard. He went back through his photo archives on the laptop. Over the years he had shot many pictures of the woman who'd taken him into her house when he was beaten up in an arrest that went bad. Who had invited a lonely patrolman for holiday dinners, and stayed up nights at the hospital with him when Paul had double pneumonia. Who rescheduled his root canal when he conveniently *'forgot'* it.

He needed a single, clear, front-facing view of her. He found one, taken at the bar-be-que she'd thrown to celebrate his passing of the sergeant's exam. She was standing between him and her husband, giving a loving smile for the camera.

Paul copied that looped photograph into the identification program. The second woman was older, heavier- -it might not be the same person. If the sex, coloration and racial features were similar, most everybody had two eyes, a nose, and mouth. The real determination in recognition was in the minuscule distance relationships between the features: how long the nose? How close the eyes? That's the basis for a portrait likeness, and how your mind sorts Aunt Helen from the grocery clerk.

This software compared those relationships and came up with a percentage that the likenesses were the same person. He hesitated, knowing what a positive would mean. Then he clicked on the button and sat there frozen as matching point after matching point started to appear on the screen. Finally, the software proclaimed what he had already guessed: Evelyn Fuller Lewis had been a member of Gault Corey's Coven.

Had Evvie been at the mill that Beltane night when Hester Corey died? Had she witnessed Gault killing his wife? Or with thwarted passion, had Evvie stabbed Holly's mother herself--for love of Hester's faithless husband?

# Chapter 22

When he knocked on the kitchen door, Paul had an excuse ready. He needed to look at the shower in the master bedroom that Evvie wanted remodeled. Paul need not have bothered, for his chief's wife opened the door with a warm, welcoming smile, and immediately invited him in for supper.

From the mouth-watering aroma, her homemade spaghetti sauce had been simmering all day in the crockpot. Paul smelled the sweet Italian sausages, with the chopped meat, basil, and oregano. While he petted Sally, Evvie had the water for the spaghetti boiling. She'd already buttered, cheesed and garlic the Italian bread. Now she busied herself, putting it under the broiler. "Honey, can you set the table?"

"Dining room or kitchen?" he asked, reaching for the plates.

"Kitchen. Stan's going to be late. Set a place for him, but we won't wait. Without you taking some of the load, he's got so much more to cover now. We hadn't realized how much you do." Evvie was taking a plastic wrap covered salad bowl out of the refrigerator.

Paul got the bold, black-rimmed sunflower design plates that he had bought her last mother's day down from the cabinet, while she stirred the steaming spaghetti. Paul tried to sound casual as he asked. "Did you know Hester Corey of Witch House?"

"Why do you ask?" she didn't turn around to look at him, but he could see her back stiffen.

"Thought she might have been in school with you?"

"No, Hester Farrington was a few years younger." Not looking at him, she moved to check the garlic bread through the oven window.

"Holly Corey is still very upset about her mother's death."

"That was when she was just a baby," murmured

Evvie.

"As kids, they were told their mother abandoned them by committing suicide."

Evvie was carrying the spaghetti pot over to be drained in the sink. She froze for a minute. "That was a cruel thing to tell them."

He moved to hold the strainer for her. "Hester died in some sort of coven rite–didn't she?"

Without looking at him, Evvie poured the steaming, milky water through the strainer with a pinched look about her mouth. "Did she?"

*This was going to have to be the hard way.* "Holly has a photograph of Gault Corey's Coven. Some of the people she knows. Skye Rainbow. The Hoyt sisters. Some Holly doesn't recognize."

"Well, that's a long time ago. I'm sure they've all changed."

"Would you recognize them, Evvie?" Paul asked evenly.

"Me?" She still didn't meet his eyes. "How could I?" Then those indigo blue eyes of hers locked on his, as she decided to fight back. "Why are you here? For dinner? Because I feel like I'm under some sort of interrogation?"

He had an eight by ten printout rolled up in his jacket. Paul pulled it out and spread it before her, using the little red-glass bird candle holders on her kitchen table to anchor it flat. "That's you there, isn't it? You were a member of Gault Corey's Coven weren't you?"

There were times when Paul looked into Evvie Lewis' square face and saw all his chief's determination and stubbornness. He saw that in her face now. When Stan was on a case, nothing stopped him. Why had Stan's uncle pulled back from Hester Corey's murder? Why had Stan let him?

"Paul..." she started and then just stopped.

**"Were you a member of Gault's Coven?"** he

repeated relentlessly.

She still didn't answer.

So he started again. "Does Stan know?"

Putting the spaghetti pot on the stove again, she sat down as if too weak to stand. "Stan doesn't believe in Old Craft. He didn't know what those weird teas or jellied bull testicles were for." She finally looked at Paul. "He was gone a lot. His Uncle Teddy was chief of the Mystic Police then, and Teddy was training Stan to take charge, getting him ready for sergeant's stripes." Evvie added defensively, "Like Stan and Sgt. Kear trained you."

He wanted her back on track. "So you were attending rituals when he was out of the house and didn't know?" "You make it sound like a dirty assignation! She looked outraged. "Those were religious services!"

"Religious? When the high priest was sleeping with all his acolytes?"

"Not me! I wasn't really a member. Not at first." She looked away. "Gault Corey thought he was the Goddess' gift to womankind." Finally, she looked back at Paul again. "But Hester Corey–she was the real power in that coven. The true magic came from her! The strength, spirituality, the focus."

"If it wasn't for sex, why did you join his coven?"

For a long time, he stayed quiet, thinking she wasn't going to answer, but finally, Evvie started slowly, "Even before we married, Stan and I talked about us having kids. He came from a family of ten brothers and sisters. I was an only child. I always wanted a brother or sister. We planned to have seven kids. I got pregnant the second month of our marriage, and Stan was so proud.

"For the first months, I had terrible morning sickness, then it seemed to get better, but I went into labor early at seven months. Babies can live at seven months." She was silent for a moment; the raw pain on her face cut at him deeply. He wanted to reach out, try to take that pain away; instead, he was going to interrogate his surrogate mother about the evidence she may have concealed in a murder investigation. A cover-up that might cost her husband his career.

In a lifeless voice, Evvie was continuing, "The baby was born. A perfect little boy. We named him after Stan. During labor, they'd told me his heartbeat had stopped, but I didn't believe them. They took the baby away, and I never saw him again. I was in the hospital when they buried him in Elm Grove Cemetery." Paul allowed another long silence before she spoke again. "But the others...I was at their burials. I got pregnant within two months of little Stan's death. Lost Chris at four months.

"We didn't pay for an expensive funeral that time. My aunt had a beautiful cherry wood keepsake box. My cousin, Reverend Kermit, presided, and Stan just dug a hole in the old Hoyt family plot by one of the Fuller Graves. Sarah and Abby let us bury all of the others there.

"The doctors said to wait a year before trying again. The doctors said to take thyroid, estrogen suppositories, give up caffeine, walk, stay in bed, take injections, take a vacation, relax...I did it all. And I had baby after baby die."

"Evvie..." Now Paul wanted her to stop reliving that endless pain, but she couldn't. She just kept pouring it out. "At first Stan had more hope then I did, but as each baby died, he took it harder and harder. Then he wanted to stop trying."

"But you didn't, so you joined Gault's Coven?"

"Sarah and Abigail Hoyt were old friends of my mother's. They introduced me to Hester Corey. She was a few years younger than me, a gentlewoman that seemed to bring the sunlight with her. Abby said Hester was more in tune with Old Craft than they were. More powerful. When I begged for them to help, they all kept making up special teas and prayers for me, to help me carry to term. Their efforts seemed to work. Each miscarriage was coming later and later.

"Then Stan found out. He acted at first like it was a

joke; a scam; then he got frightened. He said they were poisoning me! Killing my babies. He went behind my back and threatened the Hoyts first. Forbidding Gault and Hester from even talking to me.

"Hester defied Stanley. She was this slender girl that looked like a breath of wind would blow her over, yet she wasn't afraid of anything! Stan found out that Hester was still coming to our house. He and his Uncle Teddy set the department on the Coreys.

"Ticketing them for speeding. Ticketing them for parking. When Gault held a ritual, if anyone parked on the street, they were questioned and ticketed. A zoning man showed up at the mansion. The fire chief discovered violations. The whole town was after them, and the Hoyts, and the Le Fleurs and anyone else who admitted to being Old Craft.

"Of course the Coreys were a stubborn lot! They didn't back down. My mother said that was why we had those constant rains and flooding throughout that year. That the Grandmother Helen was praying a curse over the whole seaport!

"I promised Stan that if he would just leave the Old Craft people alone, I wouldn't go near them. There was some sort of truce for nearly two years. But try as we could, with all those expensive fertility specialists I couldn't even get pregnant again." "Why didn't you adopt?"

"At first, we thought it was just a matter of time until our own babies came. My mother had lost five sons before she had me later in life. But we wanted our own, so I went back to Witch House. The grandmother was afraid of Stan, but I begged them. Hester finally agreed. I was initiated into Gault's Coven at Yule. At Ostra, I discovered I was pregnant again."

"What happened?"

She kept looking away from him. "Why do you have

to know?"

"Evvie, please!"

"Hester died. My baby died. Stan's patrolmen became his boys. You guys have been my babies. Not all of you, I've always picked out special ones, like you, Paul, and Sgt. Kear. He was married here in this house. Having you and the sergeant and Rose for Thanksgiving dinners was like having our family with us. Then Rose was killed, and the sergeant got cancer. Now they're taking you away too." She started to tear up. Evvie was usually so strong, so sure right would prevail, now she seemed to be collapsing like a dam that could no longer bear the flood against it.

"Evvie..."

"You give me mother's day cards. You've been looking after Stan more and more, like a true son. **Paul, don't end it all!**"

"Were you at the Corey's mill on the night Holly's mother was murdered?"

"Honey, please don't dig up this horror again..."

"You were a witness! That's why Stan's uncle killed the investigation? To keep the fact hidden that you were attending a witchcraft ritual? That you knew who killed Hester?"

"Yes, I do know who killed her." She looked directly into Paul's eyes. "I killed Hester Corey."

Evvie said that so flatly. So plainly. So finally, yet Paul couldn't believe it. He felt his strength, his very life draining from him. He'd dug this truth from her. *Why had he ever started this?* Evvie said it as if her guilt was an undeniable fact, yet Paul knew it couldn't be true! This woman who had become a second mother to him couldn't kill anyone! "You hated Hester Corey enough to stab her over twenty times? Why?"

"**THAT'S ENOUGH!**" The voice behind them could have cut cold steel. Chief Stanley Lewis stood there, his blue eyes blazing, his legs spread in a fighting stance. Paul noted his chief was still in uniform, still wearing the utility belt that held his gun. Stan was yelling at him. **"WE'VE TREATED YOU LIKE OUR SON–AND NOW YOU ACCUSE MY WIFE OF MURDER?"**

"Sir, I just..."

His white-faced chief glared at him. "That Corey girl bounces her boobs before you–and you turn on us? Holly Corey's father stabbed his wife to death! **THAT'S A FACT!** You investigate the mother's murder, you're only going to rub the daughter's nose in it!"

Stan was moving protectively between Paul and Evvie. Had Stan ever killed a man? Because Paul felt his chief was ready to now. And Paul knew he could never harm Stan.

Like a trapped animal, Evvie Lewis had kept stepping backward until the wall behind stopped her. A hand covering her mouth she looked in horror from Paul to Stan, unable to stop the two men she loved most from attacking each other. "Stan, it must come out...We've always known it."

**"SHUT UP!"** her husband yelled.

"Evvie..." Paul started.

But he was cut off. Gaining back his icy professionalism, Stan's voice became even more deadly cold, "Don't ever talk to my wife again!"

Paul tried, "I mean no harm!"

**"GET OUT!"** yelled his chief. "You're suspended! You try to come back to duty, I will make your life **HELL!**" He paused as if to be absolutely sure of what he was going to say next. "Paul–I'll kill you before I let you destroy Evvie!"

# Chapter 23

With the sun just coming up, Holly drove her brothers to work. From the back of the cab, Noel was arguing again. "Okay, Paul's been decent about his truck, but if he really cared about you, Holly, you'd be engaged. The sergeant wants a play partner--that's all!"

Sitting beside her in the passenger seat, Frost argued back, "They haven't known each other long enough for marriage."

Holly was just concentrating on driving past that half hidden cop's car at exactly thirty-five miles per hour, while Frosty continued, "Paul doesn't want her doing Beltane down at Caddemfield."

"He's right on that!" barked Noel. "You went to that ritual last time, without telling us!"

*That took the first prize!* She angrily pointed out, "N.C., **you** went up to Grace's without telling me!"

"Yeah," said Frost. "And you both wound up involved in another murder."

They fell silent, with Noel closing his eyes, trying to get a little sleep. Frost had to be at work earliest, so Holly drove past the Aquarium and onto the back lot of the Mystic Seaport Museum. She stopped just at the entrance gate. With the motor running, she waited for him to get out, but Frost had turned to her and was searching her face. "Holly, if you are going to do some ritual at The Lady's Cauldron, tell me, and I'll come with you."

"I'm not going up the hill. Colin will be paying me to keep the store open late that night. Then at two a.m., I'll serve coffee in the parking lot to the participants as they leave. That's all. I promise."

She waited while Frost lifted his bicycle from the back of Paul's truck. Tonight Noel had the promise of a ride home with one of the guides at the Aquarium. Noel hadn't mentioned names, but both Holly and Frost sensed a woman. Holly turned the long cab truck around with difficulty to get back on the main road with morning commuter traffic.

Next stop was the Aquarium parking lot, almost empty, hours before opening. With the hearse, Noel always had her drive him to the Olde Shopping Village lot so he could walk the rest of the way, but with Paul's hot new truck, N.C. wanted to be dropped off right at the entrance. Now she looked back in the seat. Noel was sleeping restlessly, dreaming again. He had dark circles under his eyes, and Holly hated to wake him, but, "N.C."

He sat upright, looking afraid. "Damn."

"Another bad dream?" Holly asked softly.

"Yeah, every time you drive me to work in this truck. Today I was stranded on a freezing ice slab, floating in a dark sea of white icebergs."

Holly said, "That sounds better than yesterday's shattering glass palace."

Noel smiled weakly starting to get out, but then her brother stopped, looking back at her. "Holly, when Beltane comes, call me if they start pressing you to go up on that hill!"

"You couldn't come--I'll have the truck."

Noel's lips tightened. "I can borrow something! Get an Uber. I'll get there! Just don't let them talk you into dancing naked with them!"

"Colin would protect me..." she started.

"Yeah. I'm sure he'll see you nude and just keep thinking of his *religion*! Get real, sis, he'll be trying to get you on his altar for some very secular sex!"

Careful not to answer, Holly watched him go. Her getting on the altar might be the only way she could save Paul. At the moment of the God and Goddess' union, Colin had said he would be picturing her, appealing to the Lady on her and Paul's behalf. As Holly drove Paul's truck at the speed limit, she stopped to deliver the Mystic Motel muffins, then Holly still had three hours before she was to start at The Lady's Cauldron. And she had some questions that could only be answered down in Caddemfield, so Holly turned onto I-95 South.                    In Caddemfield there was a quarter of a mile of curved driveway before Grace Le Fleur's yellow Italianate mansion, set on its acres of park-like property edged with old growth woods. Holly drove up front and stopped, then had second thoughts. This was Paul's personal truck, and out front, it might be seen by Chief McGinnis, who was also friends with Chief Lewis. Innocently saying something, Mac might get Paul into more trouble.

She started the engine again, backed up in the driveway and took the spur off on to the right, that went past a small barn, and behind the house to the bigger livery stable. The grassy yard was filled with tulips blooming in yellow, white and lavender. Holly was surprised that with this much woods around they weren't all eaten by deer. *Maybe Grace cast some special spell to protect them?*

There already were two blue vans parked by the kitchen door with '*Swenson Cleaning*' on them. Men wearing yellow overalls carried an industrial floor waxer between them toward the back door. Holly found herself just following them in, walking on stepping stones through Grace's budding herb garden. Inside that old-style country kitchen, Holly recognized Nora, a member of Grace's coven. The smiling, rotund witch was preparing several commercial-sized trays of hors d'oeuvres, probably to be frozen and reheated for Grace's Church of Nature's Bounty's Beltane on Saturday.

Wiping chili powder from her fingers on to her apron, Nora asked eagerly, "Holly! Is Paul with you?"

Holly shook head. "N-n-no. Is Grace about?"

"Downstairs working on the high altar."

Opening a white painted door, Holly headed down the old wooden stairs to the dirt-floored basement that smelled of myrrh and damp earth.

The red framed, glass, electric-lanterns cast weak light on the eight altars that lined the huge, unobstructed room that ran the length of the mansion. Slender, looking much younger than her years, Grace Le Fleur had short, meticulously styled black hair, with just the barest touches of silver.

The high altar to the North end held three foot high, carved sculptures, representations of a full stomached Earth Goddess and the Horned Hunter. In form-fitting designer jeans, Grace was cleaning wax drippings and replacing the two-foot high green and red pillar candles with fresh white ones. She looked up and smiled. "Holly, it's been so long! Is Paul with you?"

"N-n-no."

"Are you coming to Beltane?" Grace's face shadowed. "I'm so sorry about what happened to you last time. Mac insisted I hire a private security guard for every Sabbath going forward to see that it never happens again!"

"Will Chief McGinnis be here?"

Grace looked sadly at her altar. "No, Mac's wife doesn't like me or my church." She stopped,  then softly continued, "I had a chance with Mac once, before Noreen. But I wouldn't give up my rituals, and he wouldn't give up being the Chief of Police. He didn't need a job–I have more than enough money, but male pride is such a ridiculous appendage."

Holly intuited Grace's great unhappiness and felt moved to say, "Mac still loves you. I've sensed that. He's very protective of you."

"We still are friends, whatever Noreen wishes." Grace looked up to brush away old memories. "You being here, does this mean you'll both come back and join us again?"

"Not this time...perhaps someday."

Ignoring Holly's slight evasion, Grace continued, "Beltane is difficult for newcomers. Lammas will come up, less pressure for you and Paul. Now on my Church of Nature's

Bounty web site, I have referrals–would you like me to put up a link to your Witch House Bed and Breakfast?"

"O-o-only if you call it the C–C-Corey Mansion Bed and Breakfast."

Grace nodded. "That sounds better."

Holly studied the long, packed dirt-floored room. There were eight altars down here. Each one was to a different God or Pantheon. Grace's high altar stood before a low oriental framed couch with a ticked mattress. The red velvet cover must be being cleaned in preparation for the surrogate mating of the God and Goddess. "They're gone," said Holly.

"What's gone?"

"The two machete knives you used as athames."

Grace wrinkled her nose in distaste. "Gregory talked me into those, but since he's not coming back, they're gone!"

"What will replace them?"

"The wand will be of lightning struck oak from this property. For the athame, I've commissioned a goldsmith. He's creating a truly beautiful dagger, with a haft formed of a staghorn entwined with English Ivy leaves. The leaves and decorating berries will be of red gold with enamel tracings, the blade will be of white gold."

"It sounds magnificent," said Holly, thinking of all the great Catholic church commissions that kept fine artists alive and creating masterpieces throughout the centuries.

"I just hope it will be done in time!" sighed Grace. "Beltane is almost upon us. Oh, I do hope Paul will change his mind and come up here again," she said wistfully. "Holly, what a pair you would make on the High altar! What strength you both would bring to our worship!"

Holly felt she had to admit, "P-P-Paul and I have broken up. He says our goals are incompatible."

"I'm surprised." She looked at Holly curiously. "You seemed such a fated pair, I'm sorry... but maybe he'll change his mind."

"No," said Holly, sadly, "I think Paul is right."

"If you aren't seeing Paul...but I feel such a strong male presence about you." Grace looked at her, reached her hand out, and she stopped, asking, "May I?" Holly nodded, and Grace extended her perfectly manicured fingers lightly touching Holly's cheek. "Yes. That glow I see about you is for a new male. A formidable man. Strong in body and spirit like Paul, but dangerously powerful in the Craft." Grace looked truly puzzled. "Holly, who are you going with?"

"I'm not g-g-going with anyone." Holly pulled her cheek back, breaking the revealing contact.

Grace studied her. "There are not many males that strong around here?"

"C-C-Colin."

"Maeve's son?" Grace's voice lowered to a whisper, and she sounded upset, even frightened for Holly. "Colin Fitzgerald?"

"He-he's very kind. Gentle."

Grace ignored that. Her voice had a touch of foreboding. "How did you meet him?"

"The Hoyts."

"No." Grace shook her head. "Sarah and Abigail would never have introduced you to the Fitzgeralds!"

"It was Lilith," Holly admitted. "She was visiting her sisters. I was looking for herbs that Abby didn't have, and Lilith mentioned that I could find them at The Lady's Cauldron."

Grace spoke slowly, as if to a child who was not too bright. "When Lilith was staying at your bed and breakfast, she influenced the emotions of you and your brothers. You and N.C. and Frost started fighting. Lilith does that with people. She enjoys watching anger and pain, she psychically feeds on it! Maybe Lilith is the reason you've broken up with Paul?"

Holly wanted to change the conversation. "You used

to know Maeve. You both were in my father's coven. Why don't you still worship together?"

Grace's mouth tightened. "I feel that worship should be a joy, a true union of like spirits, a renewal of energies. Maeve doesn't approve of my gatherings, she says they're too frivolous. She doesn't mind sex or drugs, but she believes one must only worship her way and only her way." Grace's face darkened, and she looked a bit older. "And I find some ways Maeve uses her powers to be irresponsible, and quite unethical." Grace seemed to want to say more, but wouldn't, then it rushed out, "Beware of them, Holly, the Fitzgeralds will seem kind, but they are powerful and are capable of creating an illusion about themselves. They can appear as anything they wish!"

# Chapter 24

Holly ignored that--she needed answers. "Was Maeve in love with my father?"

"She had a young girl's crush on Gault. We all did." Grace looked away to the dark corners, seeming to remember. "It was almost unnatural the way we all felt." She looked back at Holly with an ironic smile. "Maybe Master Gault Corey was a lot better practitioner than I thought."

"Others were in love with my father? The Hoyts?"

"Not Sarah, Abby—maybe a little." Grace gave a tiny smile again. "Abigail does have a strong sensual inclination."

"Lilith Hoyt?"

Grace paused to think. "She was very possessive of your father. She wanted to be on the couch for Beltane. I think by elevating Maeve to 'Goddess' instead, Gault was disciplining Lilith. Showing her who was in charge."

*Probably something her father shouldn't have done, Holly thought.* "But you think Lilith loved him?"

Grace shrugged. "I think she only wanted Gault because all of us also wanted him. Lilith only loves Lilith."

"Could Lilith Hoyt have created your passions for her own reasons?"

Tilting her head to the side, Grace took time to think about that. "Lilith can only magnify what is there. She can increase jealousy, she can't create it." Grace thought about that and elaborated, "I think Lilith saw herself as High Priestess to his High Priest, but Maeve had equal powers, and she too was very possessive of Gault." Again Grace warned, "Maeve Fitzgerald will be the same way about her son. She can't help herself. If you stay around Colin, be careful!"

"My mother died on Beltane. The police said she went to the mill alone."

"Gault was doing his own thing at that point," said Grace firmly, again looking to rearranging the candles on the main altar.

"But it was the night of Beltane, Hester wasn't alone when she got there, was she?"

"I wasn't there," said Grace with finality, not meeting Holly's eyes.

"But you know who was supposed to be there?" Holly persisted.

Reluctantly Grace turned away from the altar and looked at Holly. "The coven was breaking up. Your father had gotten off the worship of the benevolent Earth Goddess, and he seemed to be building a sex cult with him as its head. Not that I think sex can't be part of worship, but he seemed to use it to put people against each other. For Gault, that generated a dark energy, a dark power."

"Why did my mother put up with that?"

"Hester loved her husband and chose to ignore his many failings." Grace kept finding things to move around her altar. "According to Gault, he and your mother had an arrangement. An *open marriage*–of course when Royce Doherty joined the coven and started paying attention to Hester, and your mother looked back, Gault cut that '*open*' bit off fast."

"Royce Doherty?" Holly frowned. "That name sounds familiar?"

"Royce is the widower, who--with his son Randall--lives on the property that runs along your mansion's Western border."

Holly leaned back and had a sudden fearful vision. "For a time he was a member of my father's coven, but then one day, Royce came over...he, and my father were arguing...fist fighting....it was terrible!"

"That is long over." Grace turned back to her altar.

Thinking about it, Holly slowly said, "I remember playing with Randy as a kid. Do they still live beside us?"

Grace looked back at her tightly. "It would be better to

stay away from the Dohertys. To forget all of this!" Although her face was unlined and calm, Holly saw Grace's hands were shaking. "Holly, your mother, went to the mill and was killed. Our Old Craft community splintered permanently, and I don't want to talk about it anymore!"

Frustrated, Holly had to walk away.

* * *

She made some time on I-95, but when Holly got to the seaport's local roads, she didn't dare speed, so she was late when she got to The Lady's Cauldron. Holly started up the pathway to the store, but someone was calling from down below in the paddock.

"Holly?" It was Colin. He had the dark seal-brown stallion saddled, and was taking a pancake looking saddle off the red-gold mare's back, but the horses didn't look like they had been ridden yet.

"I-I-I'm so sorry...I-I'm late." *Why did being around him always make her so silly?*

"Don't sweat it." He was holding the saddle. "Do you ride?"

"No." She shook her head, lowering it. "I've always wanted to take lessons."

"Maeve was going to ride, but she's working with Lilith Hoyt today."

"Lilith?"

"Well, for Beltane, Lilith has commissioned two large flower arrangements from us, for the disrobing pavilions. She wants to help make them up with Maeve, so my mother won't be riding Gem, but the mare needs some exercise."

Holly looked up. "But the store?" Those green eyes of his were so warm, always crinkling a bit, like he was getting ready to laugh with you. *He couldn't be the deceiving monster Grace warned of.*

"Esther is working the store. Did you want to get a riding lesson with me, while I check on how the hillside is coming?"

Lowering her head, she nodded excitedly. She would love to be alone with him, away from Maeve's critical eyes.

"Okay. First, you have to learn how to put on a saddle." He looked at the red saddle pad already on the horse. "This is an English saddle. A western one would be easier for you to start with. I'll get one." While he took the saddle back to the tack shed, shyly Holly walked to the mare and stroked her velvet nose. Gem had a white star on her light-red forehead and four white stockings on her legs.

When he came back, Colin quickly showed Holly how to throw on the western saddle with its high pommel. He had her tighten the girth herself. It took several tries. She was taller than Maeve, so Colin lengthened the stirrups. The closed rein bridle was already on.

While he worked, she moved to the other side, closer to the dark looking stallion. "Watch him," Colin warned. "Jacobite is high strung and will bite or kick occasionally. He's an Irish hunter." Finishing, he said, "Now come over here. You always mount on the left side. Move closer to Gem's flank, it'll be easier to pull your body up. Put your left toe in the stirrup and use the pommel to pull yourself up. You really should have heeled boots to prevent your shoe from sliding forward and getting caught in the stirrup. To get started riding, you can hold on to pommel for balance, but you should be staying on by pressing your legs against the horse's barrel."

Holly followed directions and soon found herself sitting on top of the tall, slim legged, red-gold mare. When Colin left her to walk to the nervous looking stallion, the mare shifted between Holly's legs and stepped forward in the paddock, scattering a bunch of black chickens before them. Off balance and falling, Holly frantically grabbed for the leather covered pommel and Gem stopped moving.

Mounting the stallion, Colin turned him around, looking over at her. "Gem stopped because the horse feels your weight shifting, which is part of your communication with her. Gem's got a tender mouth, so only pull lightly on the reins to stop. To turn left or right, rest the rein on her neck on the opposite side. Shift your weight forward or make a clucking sign to move forward. "

Bending from his horse's back, Colin unhooked the paddock gate, letting her ride out first. Then they walked past more sheds and the plastic covered, commercial-sized greenhouses. Colin rode forward on Jacobite, looking back often to see how she was doing. Holly just hung on as Gem followed.

It was a little scary at first, bouncing in the saddle, but Holly loved it. Colin was riding out along the edge of his newly planted fields and heading uphill to the woods. A first he trotted ahead, then he pulled the spirited stallion back to ride alongside her. "Gem's a natural pacer. It's a comfortable gait."

Holly nodded. The sun warmed her, and she smelled coppery tomato plants and basil as the horses headed upwards.

"Since you're not used to riding, you'll probably going to be sore tonight. You have a bathtub you can soak in warm water for an hour?" asked Colin. She nodded. "When we get back to the store, I'll give you an herb bath packet that should help."

Straddling a horse was a stretch she wasn't used to, but Holly felt excited to have Gem moving between her legs. "Can we go faster?" He shifted forward, and his stallion broke into a faster gait; the mare followed with a smooth pace. With wind pulling back her hair, Holly felt like she was flying. But she noticed that she bounced against the saddle, while Colin seemed to rise and fall in perfect union with Jacobite.

They were on a farm road climbing up through the trees. Actually, it was just two dirt tracks chewed out by the tractor wheels. Here the woods were thick with old growth oak and elm. They stayed in the shade climbing until Holly saw bright sunlight on white meadow flowers ahead. Colin was trotting out to a pasture of high grass.

There was a boarded fence section at the base, then the grass field above was wide and open to an arch of the hillside with powder blue sky behind it. She could see someone had taken the tractor and mowed a wide circle around the hilltop. They tied the horses to scrub growth, then Colin led Holly up into the meadow.

She looked over the field. "This is where you'll do Beltane?"

"Yhep. Got some measuring to do." On the ground was a tarp, which he opened to take out a three-foot-long stake wrapped in a red cord and bags of five colors of marking chalk. "We're laying out circles that will enclose the five pentagrams."

"Five?"

"We're planning on twenty-five people, maybe thirty-six actually worshipping, maybe more. Figure about nine worshipers to each circle."

"Why not one big circle?" she asked.

He didn't look too happy. "Could do that. But some people feel nine is the maximum for a circle of protection.

Holly inclined her head. "I would think the energy would be stronger in one big circle? All of us holding hands, concentrating?"        "Actually," he looked around the field, unwrapping the cord from the stake, "I agree with you, but our High Priestess Maeve wants several individual groupings."

"She's your mother, why do you always call her '*Maeve*'?"

Handing the other end of a five-foot cord with a bag of blue chalk dust to Holly, Colin stuck the three-foot tall stake into a clump of grass and with effort, pushed it down. "She is eternally 'Maeve'–a   charming, endlessly high spirited gamin." Holly unrolled the cord he'd given her, pulling it tight, and started walking a circle marking a line on the grass with the blue chalk dust around theperimeter.

"Who must always be the center of attention?" asked Holly.

He smiled appreciatively. "Teddy Roosevelt's daughter remarked that her father wanted to be the bride at every wedding, the baby had every christening, and the deceased at every funeral. That's my mother all right."

"What was it like when you were a child?"

He didn't seem to like the subject, but he still talked, "I had a warm, lovingly mothering childhood. All home-baked cookies and chicken soup–from my Grandmother, Claire Fitzgerald." He looked at her. "Well, did your mother wait at home every day with oatmeal cookies?" His face filled with pain. "That was an incredibly stupid thing to say." He stopped again, seemingly angry with himself. "After Hester's..." Colin stopped and tried again. "You were raised by?"

"My aunt," said Holly. "I called her just *'Maureen'* too."

Whatever she said, he always seemed to be reading her auras. "Then she didn't love you?"

Holly lowered her head, looking at the ground as she chalks dust marked. "She tried."

"I'm sorry," he said with a great deal of understanding. "But she didn't teach you of your Old Craft heritage?"

"No, if I tried to heal a puppy or make my own herbal teas, I was punished. Maureen always said, *Do that, and you'll wind up like your mother!*"

He shook his head, angrily. "Your aunt was a fool!"

Holly wanted to change the conversation, and she looked to the top of the hill at a huge rough-cut blue stone, approximately four foot long by three across and three foot high. "That big flat stone will be your high altar? You'll put the couch in front of it?"

"Just an air mattress covered in washable green corduroy. That'll be set out just before the service, Morgane hates spiders."

She looked directly into his eyes. "There you'll play the role of the Horned God renewing the earth by having intercourse with the Goddess surrogate?"

"Yhep, out naked in an open field, in front of thirty to eighty people. No pressure. Last year it started a cold drizzle, just before I was supposed to get it up, and I got a bee sting on my foot as I processed up to the couch." He finished ruefully, sitting down on the grass to look around.

"What are you going to do, if you c-c-can't..." She started blushing again.

"Get up it?" He smiled up at her impishly. "Every hear of faking?"

She was horrified. "That's not right! The whole ritual won't work."

Those clear emerald eyes of his studied her. "Holly, whether I get it up or not, whether I stick it in or not, Spring will come. And the Summer's laden fields, and Fall's lush harvest. The Lady is very understanding of mortal failings." He reached up a hand. "Join me in my boudoir, my lady."

The hand that guided her down was gentle but so strong. Holly fell into the soft grass as his other hand went around her back. She wasn't going to fall into this trap. "Maeve set us up here, for you to talk me onto that couch?"

"Yes, mam," he admitted. "But I'm not. And we don't have to wait until Beltane to celebrate life." He drew his arms tighter, pulling her towards him. She smelled his shampooed hair and body heat.

Suddenly frightened by his strength, Holly started to pull back, realizing that she should have never come up here alone with him. But at the same moment, Colin let go of her and laid back on the grass, saying, "Hell, babe, I am **not** into rape!"

Breathing hard, Holly sat up but didn't run as he just lounged back in the grass, saying calmly, "Yes, the High Priestess herself would like '*us*' to happen–that doesn't mean it will. Or that it should."

"I-I..." She started.

He cut her off. "You are not ready to be the main act on Stage One. And that's fine with me because I'm already paired with Morgane as this year's Goddess. At midnight, under the stars and torchlight, Morgane will be under me. At the appropriate time, I will thrust magnificently, and she will arch her back and scream as if it was the greatest she'd ever gotten–whether I get it up or not!"

"That's wrong," protested a horrified Holly. "The union of the God and Goddess is important." Holly reached down and touched the earth. "To treat it otherwise is a sacrilege."

He sat up and took her hands his. "I will **never** disrespect the Lady! This, I swear to you. I have always done my best at Beltane without a condom. At first, because Maeve wished it, but later because I felt the energy flowing through me into the earth. That is sacred to me. But again, the Lady has made us. She understands that mortals must worship, and mortals must play. Despite what Maeve and Lilith proclaim, I'm sure the Goddess respects worship done in Grace Le Fleur's bedrooms as much as she respects what we do on this hill. The Lady knows us better than we know ourselves and is forgiving."

Through his hand, Holly could feel his life force, know he believed as much as she did. Holly could read his aura, and there was raw sexual hunger for her, but also a desire to protect her. "Maybe your mother is right, that I should be with you on the couch. Maybe that's why I found The Lady's Cauldron. The Goddess has directed it."          "No!" He pulled his hand back. "Lilith's plotting directed you to The Lady's Cauldron, with maybe a bit of pushing from my mother, I'm positive of that!"

Holly sat there beside him. Should she tell him? "I know it's unconscious, but when Maeve sees me close to you, she lets out a vibration–th-that is un-unpleasant."

Briefly, he laughed bitterly. "It is unconscious because she really does want us to get together."

"For magical grandchildren," Holly finished unhappily.

"Hey, she likes you. You should see what Maeve did to my prom date in high school, and every other woman I was foolish enough to bring home. Poor Amber wound up vomiting on my Grandmother's living room carpet, and kept it up for three days."

"But if your mother wants you happy?"

"Maeve wants my happiness to be waiting on her with undivided devotion. Even as she wishes us to mate, she unconsciously realizes that it would divert my attention from her."

"Then you can't ever have a girlfriend?"

"I can date, and I do. Not around here. I go up to Grace Le Fleur's sometimes, but not too often, because building this farm has taken a lot out of my life–but The Lady's Cauldron is getting to where I want it, so I can loosen up now, and have a little fun." He put his arm around her. "Still Holly, when I decide it's time for me to start a family, I can promise you I will not be doing it to increase Maeve's coven."

"But if I were your Goddess?"

The line of his jaw stiffened. "I don't put my foot down with Maeve often, but this time I have! Holly, you can attend our Beltane, but **not** as the Goddess surrogate."

That didn't please her either. "A friend of mine--Paul Travinski– is wrongly accused of murder and needs help. My brothers and I are trying to hold on to the mansion. We all need the Goddess to look favorably upon us."

Colin sighed. "All the circles will be blessed at

Beltane. The Lady should look with favor upon you and your friends. Morgane and  I will beg her favor for you."

Was that enough to save Paul? "Can you and I do Beltane now?"

"Now?" He sounded surprised, almost shocked.

"Yes." She searched his eyes with hers.

"Are you on the pill?" he questioned slowly.

"No, but I feel it's right to do it now, and I should be safe." She knew he wanted her, Holly put a hand on his leg.

"I-I..." He looked about at the meadow, then back to her. "No man could look at you, Holly and not think about it a little, but I don't have any protection."

"It'll be all right." She reached up and started to unbutton his shirt. "It's not sex, it's worship."

"Isn't that supposed to be my line?" he said making a thin joke; but while he was not joining in, he wasn't fighting her, and he was beginning to breathe heavier. "I want you–but not as some sort of altar sacrifice. Not on the spur of the moment. We don't know each other enough to know each other in the Biblical sense!"

She took both of his large hands in hers. "Know me, Colin, in every sense. Because I know you."

Leaning forward, Holly kissed him firmly on the mouth; he returned it passionately, soon they rolled in the grass, still dressed. Then she pulled at his pants, and they were both undressing the other. For a time he lifted her above him, taking the scratchy straw grass on his backside, letting her ride, but finally, he pulled her off of him and laid her on the grass.

Rolling over on top of her, supporting most of his weight on his arms on either side of her, Colin kissed her. Then he murmured an invocation in an ancient language she didn't recognize. Silently Holly added a prayer for Paul's exoneration. Slipping between her legs, Colin bore down and thrust.

She came, with him, as the Horned God's energy shot through her into the Earth.

Resting back, he finished the invocation in English. "May the land renew, the plants grow, the animals be nourished at the Goddess's breast. May she protect her own, especially the innocent Paul Travinski." Then rolling alongside her, Colin took her in his arms. Exhausted, they blissfully lay together. *Oh, Lord, one minute she longed for Paul, then next she wanted Colin—what was the matter with her?* She decided to just lay back and savor the moment.

Soon she felt impish and teased. "You do this with all your ladies?"

He flushed a bright red. "**No!** And as tight as you are, Lady, I don't think you're doing all the other guys either." Colin seemed to think about that, then looked back at her concerned. "This wasn't your first time, was it?"

"N-n-no!" She settled back against his shoulder, not willing to tell him how few times it was. *What if Paul found out?* But he was the one who said they were finished. She had to get on with her life. And this had been an appeal on his behalf. "Do you think the Goddess heard us?" she asked a little afraid.

"She always hears. And I think we had some fun too."

Holly lowered her head. "That's wrong..."

"No." He wrapped his arms around her. "Worshiping can be fun. It can be a joy. In fact, it should be!"

Colin lay, resting his head against her breast. Holly looked up at the sky. Felt one with the Earth. She looked to the two horses, grazing with their bridles still on. Those bits would be a sticky mess to clean up. Now the wind was changing, coming from the bottom of the hill.

The mare raised her fine head, pricking up her ears, and looking intently down the valley. Gem must have picked up a familiar scent.

Sliding Colin away a bit, Holly raised herself on her

elbows and looked down the meadow to the tree line. A dark figure. Watching them. Holly recognized the hooded blue cape. Maeve. How long had she been standing there?

# Chapter 25

Paul took the Police Tahoe down to the elementary school where the Mystic Horticulture Society met on Wednesday. No Evvie. He also lurked outside the next meeting of her Bridge Club. Still no Evvie. *Did Stan put his wife under house arrest?* Knowing Evelyn Fuller Lewis, Paul knew that wouldn't last long. But still discouraged, he went back to his apartment to stare at the walls.

On suspension, he was still getting paid, but without a job, the days seemed endless. In his high ceiling bedroom, he looked from the California king water bed to the three, five-foot tall gun safes and his exercise equipment. He'd already worked out twice and really didn't feel like doing much more. He'd shut off the police radio that normally played 24/7 by his bed. It made things easier, not hearing normal police calls that he might have responded to.

N.C. Corey had called with a VIN number for another car the brothers were thinking of buying. On suspension, could he just waltz into headquarters and go onto the computer? Call in the VIN from the Tahoe? Well, he still had the keys to the Community Police Station–use that computer? Knowing Stan Lewis' temper, all of those seemed like really bad ideas. *Maybe he should have it out with his chief, demand that the three of them talk about Hester Corey's murder?* That didn't seem like a good idea either. Finally, he called Henry's personal cell phone and asked him to check out if N.C.'s possible car was stolen.        Not long after that, the phone rang, and it was the head dispatcher, Mary. She sounded stressed, "Paul...I don't know what's going on between you and the chief. He won't talk to me!" She stopped. It was obviously something she didn't want to say.

Paul expected it and finished for her. "Stan wants my resignation?"

"Yes," She hesitated, then forced herself to start again.

"I'll be sending two guys out to pick up the Tahoe..."

"Aaup. Just have them come up, and I'll give them the keys and my badge and my resignation." *What would he do without a car?* "No, don't send them to the apartment. Have them meet me at Quentin Butler's Garage, Classic Car Restorations. I've got to get a loaner."

Mary had been with the department when Stan Lewis was only a patrolman. She sounded like she wanted to cry. "Paul, what is going on?"

"It's between the chief and me," he said firmly.

"Don't quit! If it's about this Dietrich murder–Paul, we all know you couldn't have done it! Sure, Stan's getting a lot of pressure about firing you, but the chief has hung tough before!"

"It's not the Dietrich thing, Mary." *No, he was trying to pin a murder on the chief's wife.*

"Well, what is it?" Mary persisted. He didn't want to answer, so she sighed and continued, "If it's something personal, just wait a bit! Stan will cool off. He can't fire ya, without putting something on your personnel record, which-- since I do the filing around here--I know he hasn't! You know the chief. The squall blows up fast and furious, then it's just blue skies again."

No, this wasn't blowing away. Paul going after Evvie was something that Stan Lewis could never forgive. Yes, Paul could refuse to resign, he could fight it, but he and Stan could never work together again as a team, so he wouldn't. After Paul got off the phone, he wrote a brief two-line resignation to take effect on June 15th. That'd give Paul a month of pay to find another job, and Stan time to choose his replacement–*unless he was arrested before then?*

Paul tried to force himself to think beyond his own problems. Evvie Lewis had confessed to killing Hester Corey. He didn't for a moment believe she could've done it, but by Paul's cop instincts, he also knew that Evvie wasn't lying. *So what did happen?*

Evvie admitted she was a member of Gault's Coven. That Paul believed. Had she seen Gault stab his wife, then because of fear, she didn't tell anyone? That did not square with the assertive Evvie he knew. Or, because she'd been a second mother to Paul, could he only see Chief Lewis' wife as some sort of untouchable saint?

*Had she lied?* As a coven member, had Evvie been having an affair with Gault Corey? Had it become so passionate that Gault was willing to kill his wife to marry Evvie? Had Evvie confessed guilt over Hester's death because she felt their affair was responsible for Gault's murdering his wife?

That made more sense then Evvie grabbing a knife herself...but there were divorce courts in those days. No need to murder the wife. And Gault didn't sound like he wanted to be tied to any woman, much less one married to a gun carrying cop. *Because after Hester was killed, what in hell would they have done with Stan Lewis?*

Paul had spoken to Mary the other day, asking her if the chief had ever been forced to kill while on duty. She remembered that as a young officer, Stan Lewis had been forced to kill on two separate occasions. A proud, short-fused man like Stan, if he found out that his wife was having an affair, Paul could see him hurting, maybe accidentally beating Gault Corey to death in a fit of fury. But a brutal, premeditated stabbing of his rival's wife in revenge for Gault's transgressions? No, Paul couldn't envision his chief ever doing that.

None of this was adding up—the Corey murder or Jim's death. Paul was the number one suspect in Dietrich's murder, and he didn't do it. Apparently, Margaret and Brandon had alibis, but if they had murdered Jim to steal his diamond shipment, why in hell were they still hanging around town? Paul needed to clear his mind and then get more facts.

He moved to his bedroom closet. Cool for April. He'd need a warm jacket and old pants that could get dirty. As he was pulling out his painting jeans, he stopped and looked across the closet pole: his blue uniforms hung neatly together; winter long sleeves; summer short sleeves; all with his sergeant's stripes sewn on. At the end of the pole, he still kept his Marine dress blues with their pressed white pants. All uniforms he no longer would be wearing.

Paul had had job offers in the past, but anything in law enforcement was probably closed to a guy under suspicion of murder. Especially since it looked like no one other than himself was being investigated. Could he be a private detective? Open his own office? Try to hook up with some detectives he knew? Louis Rodale's agency did department store thefts, skip tracing, and marital investigations. *Is that what the rest of Paul's life would be?* He looked sadly at the line of empty police shirts. This was the first time since he turned eighteen that he wouldn't have a uniform to put on.

But now he had a resignation to turn in, and transportation to worry about. Holly still needed his truck. Paul could rent something, but with his salary ending, no prospects of a job, and having to hire a lawyer, he had better start worrying about how long his money was going to stretch. When he got to Quentin's garage, Holly's hearse looked permanently ensconced in that first bay.

Paul walked over to Quentin, bent over a silver Rolls Royce's engine. "How's the hearse coming?"

"Slowly, but getting there," replied Quentin. "They built those dinosaurs to last. But with this murder business, are you going to have time to paint ma's house?"

"It's getting done." Paul looked about the lot. "Look, I'm going to need transportation for awhile..."

Quentin only shook his head, saying, "All I've got left in loaners is that gray and yellow wreck over there."

Paul eyed the bondo cemented Honda. "Does it

actually run?"

"Sometimes."

Well, beggars can't be choosers. He followed Quentin into the office for the keys. Soon, looking shame-faced and unable to meet his eyes, Henry and Tom came to collect the Tahoe, his badge, and Paul's resignation.

After turning the key three times, The Honda's engine finally caught and Paul drove to the deli. There he picked up two bottles of iced tea and a thick roast beef sandwich. Then to keep from being made, he parked the Honda in the tourist lot at the Seaport Museum and hiked down the road to the 1880's brownstone arching gate of Elm Grove Cemetery. On what now was prime real estate, tombstones and monuments seemed to flow down to the river on mowed grass.

Paul headed toward the older family sections. Back here were the Farringtons, Scofields, and Hoyts. While acid rain had scrubbed marble transcriptions, gray granite, and in some of the oldest plots, blued slate, Paul still recognized Revolutionary war and Civil war graves with their starred flag holders. Finally, he came to a large plot with metal pipes set in granite shafts surrounded it. No great granite obelisk or angel statues, just rows of generations of stones from pre-Revolutionary War in the back to two modern matching, angled stones before him. Rose Marron Kear, '*Wife of George*' and beside her, Sgt. George W. Kear. '*82ⁿᵈ airborne and Mystic police*'.

A lump caught in Paul's throat. He hadn't been here since they buried the Sergeant. When Rose, his wife, was murdered three years earlier, George didn't really have a family after that. Well, he had the Mystic Police. Like the Sergeant, to Paul, the Police Department had become his chosen family, with Stan and Evvie as surrogate parents. Only now that family was gone forever, for the Sergeant was dead, and Paul-the-cop had hunted his chief's wife.

Paul studied that polished stone. He had had other

sergeants--he had been one himself in the Marines and had taken George's place in Mystic, but to Paul, George W. Kear would always be '*The Sergeant.*' Biggest thing in the sergeant's year was opening day of the trout season. That last Spring, with his lung cancer, George could barely walk, much less wade into a river swollen with snow runoff.

But Paul told him they were going fishing. He waded in behind his sergeant, holding George by his waist against that rushing, icy water, so the weakened sergeant could cast his line in. Hell, toward the end, Paul thought they were both going to be frozen and washed away, but, as he reeled his last trout in, the look of happiness on the sergeant's face had been worth it.

Paul bent his head in a short prayer. Aaup. He hadn't been here since the funeral, but today was George Kear's birthday. Still, Paul had work to do. What had his first sniper trainer said? *Find a shooting site, where your quarry wouldn't expect you to be hiding.* He scanned the cemetery for hiding spots, seeing old oaks, granite obelisks, tall pines, and marble markers.

He remembered coming here as a rookie. Some clown in a ski mask and running suit had been ripping off the pocketbooks of elderly widows putting Christmas wreaths on their husbands' graves. *The Mystic Police Department wanted that Ghoul so bad it hurt!* After each attack, Stan ordered a week of stakeouts.

They tried decoys, but the clown was smart enough to avoid a pattern. Over the next six months, the ghoul kept harvesting his handbags without falling into a trap. Elm Grove cemetery was on Paul's first beat. He got to fill out the reports from tearful elderly ladies, who'd lost their month's social security, their eyeglasses, and Medicaid cards. The bastard never threw the emptied handbags where Paul could find and recover them.

Off duty, he took to haunting that cemetery. Folding

his height behind moss-covered crypts and rhododendron bushes. As the days grew longer and warmer, he got a thermos for his hot tea and found an ancient pine tree with low enough branches for him to climb up and sit in. He'd hunt until the gates closed at sunset. Only then, stretching his stiff, pained muscles, he'd find a tree to relieve that bladder pressure, then he heads home to open a can of stew for his dinner.

Paul was in his impromptu sniper's perch one day when both Sergeant Kear's SUV and the chief's cruiser pulled into the cemetery and parked. His superiors got out and started walking on the gravel paths, scanning the tombstones. It had been a while since the last theft, so they were expecting another. Stan Lewis was looking at the ground and mausoleums, but a former sniper himself, Sgt. Kear took in the whole landscape. At one point, Paul had the feeling that the sergeant was staring right at his tree, but George gave no indication of seeing him. Feeling a bit like a fool, Paul decided to just sit tight until after they left.

But their walking reconnaissance gradually drew closer to his hiding place. When they were standing under his tree, they stopped and Sgt. Kear pulled out two cigars. They lit up. Tantalizing white smoke rose to Paul's nose, while the officers below talked about the frustration of being beat by a purse snatcher. Finally, Sgt. Kear looked up into the branches, straight at him and said, "What do you think, Travinski–are we going to get him?"

Chief Lewis looked up in shock, and Paul remembered grinning back a bit sheepishly. The story got around, and in the precinct, they started calling him '*Tarzan of the Tombstones*'. When he walked past, there were a few monkey calls behind his back, but almost a month later, he was in his tree when the Ghoul grabbed old Mrs. Mooney's handbag. On legs that were stiff as hell, he dropped to the ground and after a half-mile ran the guy down, triumphantly dragged him by the collar of his yuppie running suit into headquarters!

Today, Paul didn't feel like climbing, and there wasn't much leaf coverage, but he found a massive growth of rhododendrons to crouch in. And again he waited for his chosen quarry, as patiently as he had held his sniper rifle in Afghanistan.

# Chapter 26

Nearly three hours later, Paul looked up, as a silver van pulled to a stop on the white graveled lane. He'd almost given up, but now his target got out and opened up the back of the van. As silently as ever, Paul slowly stood up, his body painfully stiff from his hours of crouching. His quarry was now facing away from him, carrying a pot of red geraniums and a trowel to Sergeant George Kear's grave.

Under a cloudy sky, she approached the stones and kneeled down in the mown grass. As Paul quietly stepped closer, he heard the sound of metal scrapping stone and dirt as Evvie used the trowel to weed the encroaching grass around the two stones. Paul just found himself watching as she took out a cloth and polished the pink granite. Cars were passing on the road in front of the cemetery. He could be caught out here at any moment, but Paul couldn't disturb Evvie's private time with the Sarge.

After she cleaned a bit, then dug, Evvie set her pot of red geraniums in that hole. In that moment the clouds shifted, and the sun illuminated the polished granite of the two graves. Only then did she bend her head in prayer. Paul bent his head too, as a gentle breeze cooled his back. Finally, when she was finished, Evvie leaned back on her heels. Looking out over the mowed lawn rolling to the glimmering river water, she raised her left arm and without turning to look at him said, "Paul, could you help me up?"

He moved forward to take her arm. "How'd you know I was here?"

"Smelled your citrus aftershave, dear. The ladies must love it." She leaned heavily on his hand to rise. "And I've been expecting you since our conversation was so rudely cut off the other night."

"Evvie, we have to talk."

"Honey, if Stan finds out you are talking to me, you're

going to be in even more trouble. He's already got you on suspension, but if you just let him cool off a bit..."

"Actually, he asked, and I've handed in my resignation, valid June 15th."

"Why?" she looked shocked. "That is so dopey! All you have to do is let the storm blow over!"

"The chief and I can't work together anymore. Not after he thinks I tried to hurt you."

"Honey, you'd never hurt me!" Evvie reached up to put a hand on his arm. "And if Stan would only cool off a bit, he'd realize that. But you two stubborn males are bent on head butting–to see who's got the biggest! That's so silly." Her voice turned to firm command. "Now you are going to have to apologize to him!"

"Me? Why do I have to apologize to him?"

She smiled up at him. "Because you're the bigger man! Physically and mentally."

"Lady, you're really shoveling it."

"Paul, he's the chief. He has to be in charge. For you to go back on duty, you've just got to make the first step."

"I can't go back on duty. Evvie, I'm being investigated for murder one."

She waved that away. "Which you didn't do! Stan's got the detectives on overtime." Her voice took a worried tone. "But I've talked to Hiram, they just aren't finding anything!"

"I didn't kill Jim."

"We know that. Maybe the day Margaret left you at the altar, Stan and I were worried you would hurt him. Stan had a cruiser give them a 'lights and siren' escort out of Mystic to start their honeymoon."

"What?"

"Well, after that bitch so nicely sent the flower girl down the aisle with the note to tell you she was eloping with the best man, we wanted them out of town! Then you made your announcement that the wedding had been postponed, but the guests were still invited to the reception dinner."

He shrugged. "I'd already paid for it."

"While I was talking to you to keep you busy, Stan made sure they were safely gone." Evvie put her hand in the crook of his arm, and she started them walking toward the river to get out of sight of the road. "I never liked that woman anyways. What you ever saw in Margaret..."

"That's past!" Paul broke in. "I've got limited time because I bet Stan is keeping an eye on you. We have to talk about the Hester Corey's murder!"

"I told you. I killed her." She started to turn away from him.

"**No, you did not**!" He said, following her. "Hell! When Stan was at the Police Convention in San Francisco, you called me at two a.m., to come kill a groundhog that some car half flattened on the road."

"It was suffering!"

"I told you to just take a rock and drop it on the groundhog's head!"

She lowered her head. "I couldn't. I'm sorry...I shouldn't have called."

"Of course you should've! You need me--you call! Evvie, you've been more of a mother to me than my own mother. You and Stan..." He stopped, then continued. "A woman who couldn't club a groundhog to death could not have mercilessly stabbed Hester Corey! Even if you had the hots for her husband."

"Hots for that **pig**?" She looked up at him incredulously.

Paul looked at her. "You weren't in love with Gault?"

Evvie looked as if she couldn't believe him. "He was a creep--staring at you with those intense eyes; so puffed up with himself, believing himself to be the Goddess' gift to womenkind. Always trying to touch you with those nasty, womanish fingers. That bastard repelled me!"

"Then you didn't have an affair with him?"

"Of course not!"

"I heard he was attractive to women?"

"He was skinny, with narrow shoulders, dirty blond hair, shifty eyes, and a continual five o'clock shadow. Gault thought he was some sort of male icon, that no woman could resist. And to some women, I guess that is appealing; there were women who liked Charley Manson. But I had Stan Lewis. Stanley wasn't tall, but he had solid abs, and was so cocksure, and walked like he owned the world. After I saw Stan, there could never be another man."

"But you were a member of Gault's Coven?"

"I said prayers and lit candles. I laid flowers on an altar. That's not having sex with anyone! Especially Gault! How could I, after what he did to Hester and those other foolish girls!" Evvie shook her head sadly.

"You think he stabbed Hester?"

She seemed to be thinking that out. "I've never thought so.  In his strange way, he loved his wife. And he was so proud of fathering those triplets."

"Great way to show it. Screwing everybody he could get," Paul finished bitterly.

She paused before trying to explain, "Things were looser then. We were all younger. Wilder. For Gault, it was more than the sex. I think he really believed that intercourse with the coven women was going to give him power." She looked out over the smooth river.

"Who killed Hester? I know it wasn't you."

"But it was." Evvie sighed and looked up at him. "I killed her. At least I'm responsible for her death."

"How?"

"We all knew the hero worship–sex cult had gotten out of hand. Maeve, Marium...

"Marium...?"

"Marium Goldstein. Well, then she had started calling herself 'Skye Rainbow.' All of those foolish girls were after him. Gault liked his side dishes young and gullible. Skye had been the 'in' lady until Maeve Fitzgerald swung her ample hips up to the altar."

"She was to be the sacrificial sex at Beltane?" Paul asked.

Again Evvie hesitated before speaking. "The religion that Gault was pushing wasn't Old Craft or Wiccan. It was more power based, control oriented. More to the dark side."

"Satanic?"

"I'd say so. The stuff they were doing at the mill--the goat sacrifices, the invocations--they grew less and less a tribute to a loving Earth Goddess and more and more obedience to Gault's '*Master*'...I'd learned Old Craft from my grandmother, and what Gault was doing frightened me. It wasn't the old teachings."

"But you kept going?'

She stopped and sighed at the memory. "I was pregnant again. I wanted to carry the baby to term. There were those in the coven that I trusted: Hester, her mother-in-law, Helen, Grace Le Fleur, Sarah, and Abby. Especially Abby."

"The Hoyt sisters?"

"Yes. Sarah is dominate, but Abby has always been the stronger practitioner. Of course, Hester was the strongest of us all."

"Why did you say you killed Hester?"

She stopped, her face taking on a deeply pained expression. "That night there was to be a Beltane ritual, to quote Gault '*a rite to end all rites.*' He was going to culminate everything by taking a virgin on the high altar he'd built within the mill. I hated that altar! A forbidding, ugly disgusting concoction with thirteen obsidian athames, black and red candles surmounted by a curling-horned ram's skull. At Samhain, Gault had decided to take Maeve at Beltane, but

Willow and Skye were still jockeying for the honor. And of course, Gault was immensely enjoying playing one against the other."

"His wife said nothing about this?"

"This time, Hester had enough! She wasn't upset that Gault was having sex with any other women, or that he was finally doing it publically. She just felt that the wrong gods were being honored. The wrong powers were being summoned. That Maeve was too young, too innocent..." Evvie stopped walking and looked out at the water. "Hester was wrong, of course. Maeve Fitzgerald wasn't an innocent. Maeve knew exactly what she was doing!"

"How did Holly's mother plan to stop her husband?"

Still not being able to meet his eyes, Evvie kept looking at the shining river. It seemed to calm her. Paul allowed silence until she was ready. "Hester was planning to go to the mill the night of Beltane. She would confront them and force them to stop. That day, she turned to all of us–Grace Le Fleur, Sarah, Abby, Nora, and myself and begged us to join her."

"What happened?"

"It sounds silly now. We were all terrified of Gault and his supposed powers. I was so afraid, I actually loaded one of Stan service revolvers, and I took it with me!" She looked back at him. "With the clouds, it was a dark night. Hester's mother had broken her ankle. She was staying behind at the mansion to take care of the triplets. I don't know where the grandfather was or her brother-in-law, but they weren't in Witch House that night."

Police sirens were heard in the distance. Both of them stiffened and looked to the road, but Evvie continued. "Grace Le Fleur said she was sick. Sarah and Abby just refused to come. Then it was only Hester and myself. I had Stan's gun in my handbag. A storm was coming in, with the sky dark and the wind turning the leaves. Hester and I started to walk from the mansion, not by the road, but by a shorter path in the woods that Hester knew. Stan had forbidden me to go, and I was afraid of Gault's powers, but Hester needed me...then my stomach cramped. I stopped. I told Hester we shouldn't go farther, that Maeve wasn't really any virgin, and that this was all nonsense! But Hester was so sure of herself, confident of her powers.

"From fear, I was getting more cramps. Hester knew I was pregnant, that I shouldn't be out this night. She insisted that I should go back. I could see the mansion's lights behind us, through the skeleton trees. The wind was picking up..." Evvie's voice broke. "I was a coward! I told her we both had to go back! That the forces against us were too strong. She looked at me so sadly, but just said firmly, '*You go back. I can take of this myself.*'

"I left her. I almost ran back to my car. I stopped when I got in the car–she shouldn't be going alone." Evvie held his arm, seemed to be pleading for forgiveness. "Paul, I almost went back, but then I thought of the baby I was carrying. We'd named this one 'Teddy.' I got in the car, and I drove home. I never even once thought about giving Hester Stan's gun. If only I had given her the revolver–she could've fought them all off."

"Them? It wasn't just Gault?"

"It must've been more than one. I visited Stan in the department, and I saw some of the crime photos on his uncle's desk–one person couldn't have done all that to her."

"Evvie, who else was there that night?"

"How should I know? I turned back and ran, leaving Hester to die!"

"Who did you expect to be there?"

She thought about that. "Well, Gault, of course. Maeve Fitzgerald."

"Skye Rainbow?"

"Oh, yes. And maybe Willow..."

"Willow?"

"Willow, really Susan Buckland. Another of Gault's enamored young things."

"Anyone else?"

"Lilith Hoyt."

"Also, his lover?"

Evvie stopped at that. "I just can't see Lilith being in love with anyone but herself. I know she pictured herself as the next Mrs. Gault Corey when Hester was out of the way. She just wasn't powerful enough to get rid of the wife. Lilith could only needle Hester. Try to humiliate her. Try to make her leave Gault."

"You think Lilith Hoyt stabbed Hester?"

Evvie shook her head. "That isn't the way Lilith works. She puts people up to things; she doesn't bloody her own hands."

"Who do you think killed Hester?"

"I don't know. One of them? All of them? I don't even know if she stopped the ritual. I don't know if she angered Gault, or made the others jealous?"

"When the police questioned you..."

"They didn't."

"They didn't?" Paul couldn't believe that.

"Stan came in very late that night. I was in bed, but I knew something was wrong. When he asked me if I had been out, I lied and said, '*no*.' I know he didn't believe me. Then I asked him why he was late? He said '*no special reason*,' so he lied too.

"In the morning, while Stan was showering, the phone rang. It was Grace Le Fleur. The police had questioned her and told her Hester Corey was dead. Stabbed to death. When I got off the phone, those terrible, deep cramps had started. I reached down, and there was blood between my legs. When Stan came back into the bedroom, he saw blood on my hands and knew I was losing baby Teddy–losing our son–I lost him as punishment for killing Hester Corey!"

"You didn't kill Hester!"

"If I had gone with her..."

"Two women against five? You probably both would've been stabbed to death!"

"I had a gun!"

"And you never would have used it against friends! You would've threatened them with it, and Gault would have taken it out of your hands, and used it against you!"

"Paul, I could've saved her!"

"Evvie, if a meteorite hit the mill, Hester also could've been saved! You didn't kill her–Stan must've told you that!"

She pursed her lips, then said, "Stan and I never discussed that night."

Paul reconstructed it in his mind. "But Stan and Chief Lynch found out you had been in the Gault's Coven–they probably knew it before. Stan had asked if you were out of the house, which meant he suspected something. He'd probably felt the heat on your car hood or saw the car was parked in a different position, or someone said they saw you. Maybe the grandmother? Did Helen Corey know you were with Hester?"

"Yes, but I don't think Helen would have ever said anything to the police."

"Stan knew if you were lying to him about being home, that you may have been involved. I'm sure he never once believed you could have stabbed Hester, but he probably thought you might've witnessed it. To save you, Stan and his uncle shut down the police investigation and hustled Gault Corey out of town."

They were walking back to Sgt. Kear's grave. When they reached it, Evvie stopped, put her trembling hands in her jacket pockets, and looked down at the sergeant's headstone. "George always liked bright geraniums. *'Such proud, upright flowers'* he used to say."

"It was good that you let his wife and him be buried in

your family plot."

"Rose and George were adopted family to Stan and me." She turned and looked up at Paul. "Just as you are."

He looked down at the grave. "I should've come here more often. He was a great guy."

"No, you shouldn't. I don't know why I come here–I just feel a little closer, I guess. But George's spirit isn't here. I've felt it sometimes–that horrible blizzard when Stan had his emergency appendectomy. I knew that George was there with us when you were fighting to stay on that snowy, icy road to get Stan to the hospital in time. The sergeant was looking over us–guiding you.

"Then there was that terrible hurricane two years ago, with the flooding and lightning. I knew you were on patrol at the shoreline. Then you were overdue, and Dispatch couldn't reach you. When Stan told me, I knew he was so scared. That night, I felt Sgt. Kear was beside me. Just briefly, touching my hair, then I knew George left to be with you." Tears that had been filling her eyes were starting to pour over and run down her cheeks. "Paul, this mess has to be straightened out between you and Stan! I couldn't bear it if you left us too."

Feeling a little choked up himself, he reached down and held her to him in a tight squeeze. While mentally he was totting-up the list of suspects: Gault Corey, Skye Rainbow, Maeve Fitzgerald, Willow Buckland, and Lilith Hoyt. All in a Beltane ritual fueled with jealousy and power, igniting with hate. One or more of those suspects probably were responsible for taking the life of Hester Corey.

Now another Beltane rite would be coming up–a rite twisted with religion and Lilith's hatred. Would this Beltane take the life of Hester's daughter, his Holly?

Stiffening, Evvie was looking past him. Paul turned to see Chief Lewis' cruiser pulling in behind Evvie's van. In uniform, Stanley Lewis got out of the car, slamming the door. "Travinski! I knew if I followed my wife, you'd show up." His face was white and grim. Ignoring Paul, he turned on Evvie. "I told you not to talk to him!"

"You don't give me orders!" his wife shot back.

Paul started to step between them. "Stan–you know I'd never try to hurt her!"

His chief stopped and glared at him. "Not willingly, but you keep digging into things that are better long buried!"

"No!" Evvie sobbed. "It's time it was out! I wanted to tell Paul the truth about what happened to Hester."

Stan cut her off. **"Evvie! We've got other problems!** Your boy's in a hell of a mess. Paul's about to be arrested for Murder One."

# Chapter 27

"What?" Paul got that kicked in the gut feeling. "The Mystic D.A. is going to have me taken in?"

"No. Norwalk has your apartment staked out, and they've got cruisers on the roads."

"Norwalk? That's a good two hours down the coast from here?" said Paul, not understanding at all.

"The D.A. here will not proceed without more evidence, but there's some sort of technicality. James Dietrich was murdered on his boat, which is registered out of Norwalk Harbor–so Norwalk claims that the murder scene and the entire investigation is under their jurisdiction."

Paul couldn't believe what he was hearing. "That's **bull!**"

"They got a Norwalk judge to go for it." Stan stopped, looking back to the road as if he was worried they'd be interrupted. "Son, you've made a lot of enemies over the years. The guy who I think is pushing this, is that prosecutor from Hartford..."

"Alejandor Harnell?" Paul finished.

"Why is he after Paul?" Evvie asked.

"In the line of duty, I shot a cousin of his. The family tried to sue over the death–it was ruled justifiable. Then Harnell got up a dossier on all my cases, tried to get me on reckless homicide, brutality, racism. When he couldn't get those charges to stick, he pushed for a Federal charge against me on Denial of Civil Rights to his cousin."

Stan looked beat. "That cousin of Harnell had already shot his wife to death and was holding a gun threatening his mother-in-law and his kids, and he would've killed them all if Paul hadn't gotten a clear shot from the water tower."

Evvie stared hard at her husband. "You're scared, Stan. What aren't you telling us?"

Her husband pressed his lips tightly. Finally, he gave

in with sinking shoulders. "The prosecutor has told the Norwalk judge that segregation is not needed in Paul's case."

She grabbed her mouth in horror. "They're putting a cop in with the prison population? The other inmates will kill him!"

Her husband looked grim. "I think that's the general idea! Let a policeman know what it is to be incarcerated. Maybe get roughed up a bit."

Paul stood numb as the realization of just what he would be facing hit him.

"Stan, you can't let them do it!" Evvie looked at Paul. "You've got to run. Head for Vermont! My uncle's cabin is on the Derby Line. Canada is just across the river." Evvie looked to Stan. "He'll need money. I'll withdraw what we have from our savings. Is there time to pull anything out of the money market?"

Stan shook his head. "He'll be on the run for the rest of his life!"

Evvie was continuing to Paul. "You'll need clean clothes and food."

"Gorp," Paul responded. "If I'm gonna drive to Canada, I'll need lots of Gorp. But not the new stuff, it's got too many raisins, not enough peanuts and no red M&Ms."

**"What the hell are you babbling about?"** yelled Stanley Lewis in his strident chief's voice, as he glared at Paul. "You think this is funny, Sergeant? **Everything is always a joke to you!"**

"Sir! First, I'm not a sergeant anymore, because I've handed in my resignation. Secondly, you don't think it's ludicrous to hear the Chief of Police and his wife discussing drawing out family funds to help a presumed murderer run to Canada? Immigration won't let me in."

"They let those draft dodgers in!" said Evvie.

"Draft dodgers weren't an ex-cop running from a murder charge," Paul countered.

She cut him off harshly. "You will go into the woods and wade cross that river! You can do it! We have friends in Canada."

Paul started again, "Evvie, all your friends are cops! They..."

Only to be cut off by Stan. "You aren't an ex-cop! I haven't accepted your resignation! You're still my sergeant. You're on suspension, but still on my payroll! And you're not going to those jackals in Norwalk!"

"How can they arrest Paul?" a desperate Evvie cut in. "They don't have a case against him!"

Her husband ignored her. "Son, you run from arrest you're gonna look guilty as hell!"

Paul finished quietly, "What kind of pressure are they putting on you, Stan?"

"**Don't worry about me!**" his chief yelled. "Are you going to run or stay?"

"Run!" said Evvie.

"Stay," said Paul firmly.

Stan nodded approvingly. "Then we can't let you be taken in by Norwalk for custody or let Hartford run this! I've spoken to Rudy Lee. You name the time and place, and you can surrender to the State Troopers. We'll do it at a Service Center on I-95."

"Why can't you arrest him here? Stan, keep him here!" she pleaded.

His chief looked torn.

"**No!**" Paul said. "That's putting too much on the chief! He already accused of favoritism. I don't want him losing his job and maybe his pension too. Evvie, what would you guys do without that money? I'll go with the State Troopers."

Stan nodded. "I'll call Rudy and make it for Madison at ten this morning."

"Later," said Paul, thinking. "One p.m. I have

something that I must do first."

Stan looked at him as if he was crazy. "Those sons-of-bitches are patrolling my roads, looking for you. If they catch you first..."

"They're not going to arrest me here. It's out of their jurisdiction!"

"I don't think the niceties of police relations are going to apply here! Tom's already ticketed a Norwalk patrol car trying to get through on a yellow light that went red."

Paul couldn't believe what he was hearing. **"We ticketed an out-of-town police cruiser?"**

Stan smiled smugly. "Tom got the same guy for a taillight out, and no proof of registration in the car!"

A horrified Paul commanded, "We're not starting an interdepartmental war here, Stan! This nonsense has got to stop!"

Evvie took Paul's arm, pulling it. "To be safe, you have to turn yourself into the troopers now!"

"No." They looked to Paul questioningly, and he explained. "There's someone I have to speak to first."

His chief's eyes darkened. "Your girlfriend?"

A confused Evvie turned to Paul. "Surely Althea wouldn't want you to take a chance at being thrown in among other prisoners that could kill you?"

"It's not Officer Rogers that he's going to see," finished Stan, anger weighing his voice.

Paul ignored the question on Evvie's face and stated firmly, "Tell Captain Lee at one p.m. I'll be at the I-95 service station, South above Madison to turn myself in, aaup?"

Knowing Paul was as stubborn as he was, his chief just nodded. "And you'll need a lawyer. I've already spoken with John Hagen. As soon as the troopers take you in, he'll work on getting your release through the Norwalk courts."

Evvie finished, "Then you'll stay with us so that you'll have an alibi in case they come up with any other idiot charges!" Paul looked with doubt between them, so she looked to her husband and said firmly, "Stan?"

# Chapter 28

Stan nodded. "He can come home if he can hold off trying to pin Hester's murder on you!"

Paul had to speak. "Look, Stan, Evvie did not stab Hester Corey."

Stan looked wounded. "I knew that! She couldn't."

"Did you know that she wasn't a witness to the murder?" countered Paul, as a startled Stan looked to Evvie. "She was not a witness because she left Hester walking to the mill. Evvie didn't go to that ritual."

Stan looked at his wife. "Why didn't you tell me that?"

"Why didn't you ask?" she returned.

Paul wanted to keep this focused on the case. "Chief Lynch didn't have Evvie questioned?"

Stan shook his head. "My uncle knew Evvie was friends with those people. He even may have known about Evvie being Old Craft–he never mentioned that. Uncle Ted knew after the miscarriage that the doctors were concerned about Evvie's fragile mental state, and my uncle thought she was home in bed that night. I...I never told him differently."

Evvie looked at her husband. "But you knew I wasn't?"

"You weren't looking too well that day. Pale. Before I made my patrol swing up North, I stopped off at the house to check on you. Your car was gone. Figured it was Beltane and you were out dancing with those nutcases!"

"You knew I'd be at the mill?"

"No. I would have dragged you back home if I'd known where you were! The doctor had you on bed rest."

"Why did you go to the mill?" she asked.

"Dispatch got a call after midnight. Helen Corey was frantic. Her daughter-in-law hadn't returned. When I got to the mansion, she told me to take the dirt road to the old mill building. I didn't know it was still in use. Couldn't get the old cruiser up those dirt ruts. Had to get out and walk. Smelled smoke, called it in. Started running. The mill was a blazing inferno when I got to the clearing. Flames up to the second floor going onto the roof."

"Hester was in it?" said Evvie in a trembling voice.

"Found her just outside the door. Even fatally wounded, she had dragged herself out. Tough lady. But she was gone then. Hell–Evvie, when I saw that pale-haired woman laying face down, I thought it was you!" Stan said brokenly. "When I got home you were in bed, pretending you hadn't left. In the morning, before I could talk to you, you started miscarrying. At the hospital, you went into seizures. The doctors didn't know if you were going to make it. Then you were so depressed over the miscarriage. Kept saying it was all your fault! I couldn't ask you questions about Hester Corey."

Remembering, Evvie looked to the distance. "I knew that morning. Grace Le Fleur called."

"Shit," said Stan as he seemed to be reviewing the case in his mind. "It wouldn't have made a difference. If you weren't on the scene, we still wouldn't have had a witness tying Gault Corey to his wife's murder."

"He may not have done it," suggested Paul. "Evvie thinks there might have been at least four other people in the mill with Hester that night."

"Four?" asked Stan.

"Lilith Hoyt, Skye Rainbow, Maeve Fitzgerald, and a Willow Buckland."

Stan was remembering. "We questioned anyone connected with that witchcraft mob. They all denied being anywhere near the mill that night. Maeve claimed Gault was at her cottage the whole night, having sex with her and Lilith Hoyt–a happy threesome."

"Probably lying," Paul said.

"Yeah. Gault was wearing overalls a size too

big–probably left his clothes in the mill. Uncle Ted always thought it was just an alibi set up, but we questioned them separately, constantly for weeks. They all kept tightly to the script. Could come up with the sex acts they supposedly performed on each other all night–some quite enlightening sessions."

Paul asked, "What about the grandmother, Helen Corey? She must've known what went on?"

"I think she did. But you can't expect her to turn her son in, as the murderer of the mother of her grandchildren. As it was, I think Helen told her son to get out of her house. Gault started living at the Fitzgerald farm with Maeve. When Uncle Ted figured we'd never be able to get the evidence to convict Corey, my uncle started pushing him out of Mystic."

But Paul looked off into the distance. "There is no statute of limitation on murder."

His chief shook his head. "The grandmother is long dead. Evvie wasn't on site. Willow Buckland has been out of town for years. Skye Rainbow is gone..."

Paul finished for him. "But we still have Maeve Fitzgerald and Lilith Hoyt. Maybe we could get Gault Corey. We should go back and revisit Hester's murder."

Stan thinned his lips. "Let's forget about a case that's been cold for eighteen years and start worrying about what will happen to a cop turned out into a general prison population of guys he's arrested!"

"Oh, honey," whispered Evvie looking at Paul. "Don't go to your girlfriend. Turn yourself into the State Troopers now, before Norwalk gets you!"

# Chapter 29

Even though she was early, Colin wanted the close parking for his customers, so Holly parked Paul's truck way in the back of the Fitzgerald farm lot. A lot more customers today. She looked at license plates of the cars as she headed up the path to the barn shop: Rhode Island, Washington, Alaska, Florida, California–all just tourists passing through? But Lapin had said The Lady's Caldron Coven's worship drew members from other states, and even from overseas. Their visitors would be increasing, as Beltane drew nearer, and Holly now had four coven couples with rooms at their bed and breakfast-- Colin must have recommended them.

She hurried inside. There were about twenty people browsing through the goods, with a line at the counter. There Colin rang up a woman's purchases, and Holly lowered her head, moving quickly to wrap the women's glass candle holders in newspaper. "You should've called me to come in earlier."

"Yeah." He gave her a crooked smile but immediately headed for the storeroom, leaving her alone to check out a long line of customers. When he finally came back from the storeroom, Colin was carrying a large, blown glass goblet. It was clear, with blue streaks and had some kind of dark brownish liquid in it, that had the oily sheen of swamp water, and it smelled of kerosene.

Finally having checked everyone out, Holly crinkled her nose and looked up at him. "What's that?"

"We were a little careless the other day. The early Colonists documented that American Indian women compounded herbal potions to keep from getting pregnant. My grandmother corresponded for years with a Mohawk medicine woman. This is her formula."

That stuff reeked and there must be over twenty ounces

of it. "It's unnecessary, " Holly said, shaking her head.

"Just in case. I'll drink the first half and you drink the rest," he offered.

"If it's to keep a woman from being pregnant, why are you drinking it?"

"To show you how good it is?" They both eyed the evil looking potion, as he continued lamely. "Okay, it's because if I screwed up on the formula, I'd be the first to die."

"Colin, don't you think I would know if I had another soul floating within my body?"
He almost seemed to plead. "Humor me?"

"Alright." She reached for the glass, he pulled it back, then with one swallow, he drank the first half with a gagging sound.

It took a moment before he could speak in a strangled voice. "You know, I added half a cup of sugar to make this taste better. It doesn't." Holly took the goblet from him. "Try to drink it down in one shot," he counseled.

She did, and it was terrible! After Holly finished feeling like she was going to vomit it all up, she looked at him. "This stuff protects from pregnancy because the Indians never wanted to have sex again. Colin, are we going to have to drink this every time?"

He shook his head. "**No way!** Next time I will be prepared. I promise you!"

God, that stuff had a horrible aftertaste, but more buyers were coming up to the counter. Holly put the goblet on the work table behind her and starting checking them out.

Later, face half covered with her green silk niqāb, Maeve came out to help Holly with the busy counter. They both worked as a team until Maeve turned and saw the goblet. She walked over to it and ran her finger over the gritty, black dregs and tasted it.

With shocked eyes, she turned on Holly. "You think you're pregnant?"

"N-n-no."

"With who? **Colin?**" Maeve demanded.

"N-n-no," protested Holly weakly.

Maeve looked on her son. "Colin, she's pregnant?"

"That's none of your business, mother." The eyes he turned on Maeve were narrowed and cold.

The eyes Maeve turned on Holly were wide open and colder.

Suddenly Holly's abdomen painfully cramped, and ignoring everything, she lifted the countertop and made a desperate run for the bathroom as Colin glared at his mother.

*   *   *

Burning oil with a trail of blue smoke, Paul drove Quentin's crappy loaner car up Route 184. Quentin's Honda didn't seem up to doing more than forty without a bad engine knock. The Fitzgerald Farm's parking lot was three-quarters full, and Paul had to park back near his Ford F 150. He walked around his truck. No dents, no scratches--so far, so good. Quentin said the hearse was getting fixed–how could Paul keep his end of the deal up if he was in jail? He turned back toward the barn store and was unpleasantly surprised to see Lilith Hoyt heading down the parking lot pathway. She was dressed in daffodil yellow slacks and a matching sweater, Lilith stopped when she saw him. She always stared at him with such hatred in those weird gray eyes of hers. Was it because she hated all cops or just him? He just kept walking past.

Paul remembered that when the Fitzgerald grandparents had been alive, their store had been basically a glorified vegetable stand only open in the Fall for corn, pumpkins, and jellies. Now when he walked inside the barn, Paul saw that three sides of small-paned windows now lined the walls transformed the old red barn into a spacious selling space. Looking about, he saw brightly colored, fresh flowers in refrigeration units, art glass, candles, incense, and tourist trinkets. Paul also noted high-end costume jewelry, with Mystic tour books, handwoven capes. He found himself nodding in approval. This looked like a good place for Holly Corey to work.

\*   \*   \*

Holly was ringing up a silk flower, pink tea-rose diadem for a middle-aged woman when she looked up and saw Paul Travinski walking into The Lady's Cauldron. Just seeing him always brought waves of happiness welling up within her. That stern planed face of his looked a little stiff today, but his eyes still brightened to see her.

Holly moved to let Maeve take the next customer, as Paul walked to her.

"Nice place," he said softly.

She nodded. "You're not on duty?"

He looked away. "Not today. Can you take a break for a few minutes?"

She nodded her head without even asking. "Maeve, can you take over?"

Paul wasn't reacting to Maeve's head cover, so Holly figured he must have heard about her disfigurement. Maeve was studying Paul closely. As Holly moved to the section of the sales countertop that lifted up, Maeve moved back to the working table in the center and picked up Colin's goblet. Holly felt herself going cold; she could guess what was coming.

Walked over to him, Maeve asked, "You're Holly's boyfriend?"

"A friend." Paul finished. He was looking at the glass goblet in Maeve's hand. "What is that?"

Maeve's voice sounded happy with herself. "Just some medicine for Holly."

"She's sick?" Frowning, Paul looked from Maeve to Holly.

"N-n-no..." Holly started.

Maeve smugly cut in. "Holly and my son were rehearsing for Beltane, and Colin had forgotten to bring protection, so he made this potion just in case Holly might have gotten pregnant."

Paul's eyes widened as he looked from Holly to Maeve. "Pregnant?"

"I-I-I was never p-pregnant! I-I just drank his potion to make him feel better," Holly finished weakly.

"And we *do*." Maeve emphasized the '*do*' as she smiled prettily and walked over to help a customer.

Paul looked around. "Holly–can I talk with you?" He pulled her to the side of the store, but before he could say anything, she put a finger to her lips and led him out to the grass above the parking lot.

"There was no p-p-pregnancy..." she started, hating Maeve with a passion.

"Well, Colin and his mother think there's some chance of it? Which means you two are doing more than just staring into a crystal ball together!"

"C-C-Colin's a nice guy. B-B-Better than Gregory.

"Aaup, I like him better than Gregory St. Clair. That's not saying much!" He didn't want to sound as unreasonably angry as he felt. "You went from virgin to sleeping with a guy you've just started working for? What did he tell you? That it was some kind of new employee perk?" Face going white, Paul looked about at the farm. "Did that son of a bitch give you something funny to drink? Was **that** how he did it? I'll have a talk with Mr. Colin Fitzgerald!" He finished savagely.

Holly put both hands on his chest."No! Paul--I like Colin! And I did what I wanted to!"

Paul made an effort to dampen his emotions. Finally saying slowly, "Then is he your new boyfriend?"

"N-n-no. Maybe. I don't know." *She sounded so lame!*

He stared down at her. "You're not quite sure of how you feel about him, but you're having sex with him?"

She stood up and stared straight back at him. "Paul, you're not my father or my brother. You're not even my boyfriend anymore!"

Twisting his lips with irony, he smiled gently down at her. "You're getting pretty good about keeping your head proud and standing up for yourself."

Holly nodded thankfully. "Because of you. But you dumped me, and I didn't hear you joined a mon-mon-mon..."

"Monastery." He got a quick vision of Officer Roger's black lace garter belt and silk stockings that she had worn under her uniform pants at his apartment. He finished, having the grace to be ashamed. "Aaup, I didn't."

Holly still kept going. "I hear you're out dancing with that police dog–I could warn you off of her!"

He chuckled at the reference to Althea, then smiled tightly. "Holly, I came to tell you I'm going to be out of town for a while."

Seeing his paling aura and sensing something was wrong, she touched his arm. "W-w-where?"

He ignored that. "It's not important. Beltane is coming up, and I can't be there for you. Do you really trust this guy, who has sex with you, but can't even come up with a condom?"

She pressed her fingers harder against his arms. Holly was feeling fear. For herself. But more for himself. "Paul, what's the matter? Where are you going?"

"Nowhere." He mumbled, tried to evade.

"Someplace bad? It must be--because I feel you want to run?" She pressed both her hands harder on to his chest.

He gently pulled them away. "I'm going into temporary custody with the State Troopers. No big deal."

But she saw it differently in his eyes. "You're going to

jail?"

"Just holding, until my lawyer can get a bail set up."

She searched his face. "You're going to be held with people who you've prosecuted?"

"I just arrest them, honey."

"I'm sure that makes them very happy," she returned tartly. "Paul, we can hide you in the mansion!"

"No." Trying to be strong for her, he was regaining his resolve. "I'll be surrendering to the State Troopers. My chief's arranged it. They will keep me segregated from the prison population until John Hagen can bail me out." He pressed his lips against her hair. "But Holly, honey, don't go to Beltane!"

She wanted to please him, but tried to explain, "At Beltane, I might be able to free you, if I can appeal to the Goddess' mercy directly!"

"For me, can't you just skip this one?" He hugged her hard, kissing her on the lips, then released her. "I've to go—I'm late."

"No." Holly lowered her head. "T-t-there's something I've got to t-t-tell you first."

"Aaup?" He waited. Knowing the signs, he slipped his fingers under her chin, to lift her head up to look him in the eye. "What did you do?"

"I-I happened to be at the Mystic Motel..."

"Working as a maid for Alice?"

"Only two rooms."

"Alice gave you the pass card?" he sounded unhappy.

"N-no-not really," she looked at that stern face. "I kinda found it."

"Great! You stole the card and illegally searched..."

"Margaret's and Brandon Uberstat's rooms." She admitted. "Margaret saw me coming out of the room, but Alice covered."

"What did you find?"

"Paul, she had three poppets."

"Poppets?"

"Little cloth dolls. They're used in magical rites to cast a spell, cause misfortune, or gain control over an individual..."

"Honey, witchcraft is not against the judicial code. It's been over two hundred years since we've hung a witch in Connecticut."

"She also had books."

In surprise, he laughed out loud. "Margaret is reading?"

"All books on diamonds: how much they sell for, where to sell them, and how to know if they're real."

"That figures. Jim Dietrich was a security courier, and he was carrying a load of diamonds before he was murdered."

"Did they find the diamonds?"

"Nope. They claim I stole them and have been searching everywhere I've been. Surprised they haven't searched your mansion yet."

She looked shocked. "They searched your apartment?"

"Aaup, Norwalk had warrants. They want to even search that bomb of a loaner car I'm driving."

"They haven't searched your truck. I've got it."

"Doesn't matter if they do search it, they're not going to find anything."

"Paul, do you want me to bring it in?" she asked.

"If the **Mystic Police** want it, you'll bring it in! Those other guys will just have to learn to word their search warrants correctly." He still frowned, Paul always looked so stern when he frowned. "In this illegal search, did you find anything else?"

"No."

He studied her carefully. Something about her lowered head made him wonder. "Holly, are you sure? Nothing that seemed out of place? Or something that just hit you as wrong?"

She hesitated and finally said. "There was something

odd. I looked in Brandon's closet."

"Margaret's new piece of meat?"

"His taste in clothing seemed tropical or cruise oriented. Loud palm tree patterns on the shirts, cargo pants, khaki shorts, and smart-mouthed t-shirts."

"Aaup, from what little I've seen of him 'teenager' seemed to be his style. Margaret has truly acquired a younger accessory," he finished.

"But hanging in his closet was a pair of plain, dark blue trousers, and at the other end of the rack, a plain blue, long sleeved shirt." Paul absorbed that as she continued. "The shirt had some loose black threads on the sleeve, like something had been hand sewn on, but ripped off?"

"Sergeant's stripes?"

She thought about that. "I didn't find any, and the boyfriend has dark hair."

"There are wigs or spray paint to temporarily change color hair," Paul reflected.

"He's about your height, Paul. But because I searched his room without permission, none of this could be evidence, right?"

"It's inadmissible unless somebody could get a warrant to do an official search. And only if the pair didn't have the smarts to dump the stuff after seeing you in Margaret's room."

"Should I go to the police?" Holly asked.

"No. I'll talk to someone, but now I'm turning myself in." Paul looked down at his watch. "And I'm running late."

He started to leave, then had to turn toward her loveliness one more time. Taking her up in his arms, he kissed Holly hard. "Don't do Beltane! For me, please?"

Giving in, she nodded. "I won't."

Then he left.

She was alone. Holly had promised Paul she wouldn't celebrate Beltane at the farm. But he didn't understand how important the ritual was. They must get into the good graces of the Goddess. She and Colin had worshiped on the hill, but they were still arresting Paul! But if Holly allowed herself to have sex on the altar with Colin, with the support and energy of his coven, she might be able to save Paul. Still, if he ever found out, he'd never forgive her!

# Chapter 30

Paul turned the old clunker of a loaner car onto Route 184 and headed for 27. He had to be back in Mystic to pick up I-95 and go surrender himself to the State Troopers before Norwalk caught him and made him into a sacrificial goat in a yard full of guys he'd arrested.

Flashing lights and a blaring siren burst behind him, and Paul's spine turned to ice, as he pulled the loaner off the road. *Norwalk had him!* He'd stayed too long talking with Holly. Could he challenge the arrest on the grounds of jurisdiction? A brief panic, then Paul gritted his teeth. If he had to fight in some prison yard–he fight! He'd teach them what it was to attack a cop–even a disgraced one! He glanced in the rearview mirror.

He was being pulled over by a silver, unmarked police car. It was too close to see the plate. Automatically he reached for his wallet and license. What about his revolver hidden under the seat? He'd been required to turn in his service pistol. Did this limping mess of a car have a registration in the glove box? He reached to open it. It stuck. He couldn't get the damned glove box open as he heard the other car's door close. The cop must be walking over to him.

Paul applied force. Finally, he yanked it open, almost ripping the glove compartment door off. It was stuffed with a rat's nest of papers. He grabbed them all and turned to face the officer walking to his car. Silver sunglasses on a tall, athletic blonde, with that big, familiar rack. Officer Althea Rogers. Paul smiled his relief. "Was I going too slow in this clunker?" he asked.

"We're supposed to have an eye out for you, the chief's worried."

Because he was late? *Or did Stan think I might have second thoughts and run?* "How'd you find me?"

"Thought you'd be here, saying goodbye to your

girlfriend."

"Holly Corey is no longer a girlfriend, but she's still a good friend." Althea smiled ironically at that, but Paul continued. "I've got to be above Madison before one..."

She eyed his bondo filled car and cut him off. "You think you're going to make the Service Area with this heap? That's quite a distance."

"Aaup," said Paul.

"How about I drive you?"

He automatically slipped into his sergeant's voice. "You're on duty, officer."

She wasn't phased. "I'll call Dispatch. Tell Mary I have an urgent personal matter in Madison and need time off. She knows you're going to turn yourself in."

"Everybody knows I'm going into custody?" said Paul hating it.

"Officially, no. But word gets around, and nobody's too happy about it. Besides, somebody must own this wreck? After they take you into custody, it will be sitting in a parking lot way down at the Service Center?"

She had a point about leaving Quentin's car up here instead of Madison. "I don't have time to make Quentin's lot–I'll drive this to the Mystic Motel, so it can be picked up. Then we'll switch to your cruiser."

A fast nod and she was gone. Althea could move, and as Paul watched those graceful, trim hips recede from him, he wished he had just a little more time as a free man.

At the motel, Althea waited while he was parked the loaner. As he was getting out of it, his police Tahoe pulled up alongside. Well, it was the 'Sergeant's car.' Not his any longer. Henry was driving it, and Henry MacKay would make a good temporary sergeant. Well, hell, Stan probably planned for him to take Paul's place. *Everything was going so great, Paul thought bitterly.* Henry was the sergeant, while Paul was going to jail. Holly probably was lying, and she would be dancing with the witchcraft worshipers, who killed her mother. Damn, there was even a fresh scratch on the passenger door of his sergeant's Tahoe.

Deeply depressed, he locked up the loaner and started to the passenger side of Althea's cruiser as Henry walked over. "Let's take the Tahoe. I'll drive."

Althea looked unhappy but bowed to the inevitable. "Yes, sir." She turned to Paul. "I'll do whatever I can..."

Henry shook his head. "Hold it, officer. Lock up your car, Althea. We'll call it a lunch break, and we'll take you along, as a witness. You two love birds can have the back seat, but no loud funny stuff!"

"Uh, there's one thing." Paul signaled for Henry to join him at the loaner. There he unlocked it, reached in and slipped his friend the revolver for holding. Then Paul locked the car and handed Henry the keys. "Can you drop these off to Quentin Butler at Classic Car Restoration?"

"Sure."

Then it was only climbing into the back seat of his former Tahoe with Althea. Henry jerked the wheel and took off to accelerate onto I-95 South.

"You guys are certainly eager to give me a send-off," complained Paul sourly.

"You're running late," said Henry slipping into the speed lane and hitting seventy. No need for lights and sirens doing only seventy on I-95.

Althea hesitantly started, "Paul, my family has some political influence. Mostly in New York, but they have friends here that could help you..."

"All help gratefully received," said Paul.

She looked at him, surprised. "I didn't think it would be that easy. Male pride and all that."

"Mam, I'm in trouble."

"My cousin, the one you met at the political fundraiser..."

"David Rogers? At the Stardust Ball?" Yes. *That had been something.* Officer Rogers was the best dancing partner Paul had ever had. If only Holly Corey could dance. If only Holly would even try taking lessons...

Althea was continuing. "He's been talking to people up at the State Capitol. Alejandro Harnell seems to be the problem. "

"The prosecutor who's vowed to get me?" Paul asked.

Henry spoke from the front, as they drove along treed hillsides, then brick factories. "Stan was called up to the State Capitol a few days ago."

Althea spoke softly. "They wanted the chief to cut you loose. Make your suspension without pay. Find reasons for you to be fired."

"They're still going after Stan Lewis because of me?" Fear was giving way to a feeling of anger for Paul. This endless nightmare was getting to him.

Althea continued. "Stan told them he wouldn't give you up. Said they can't fire a police chief for no real reason. And that he is pretty politically well connected himself. Finally, they *suggested* that he take early retirement before he was criminally charged in covering up your guilt."

"What?" Paul couldn't believe that.

"They said if he didn't give you up, then they'd get both Stan's job and his pension."

"Hell!" said Henry from the front.

Jaw tight, Paul looked down to Althea. "What did Stan say?"

"Well, he listened patiently to all they had to say, then he made one short comment. Didn't get the exact words, but my cousin said what Chief Lewis told them to do was physically impossible."

Paul chuckled. "That's Stan." He was silent for a bit then he sighed, "But he shouldn't be ending his own career because of me."

Althea rested a hand on his leg. "Paul, worry about yourself! You're going to need lawyers. Maybe cash up front. I can lend you..."

"Hey." This was going a bit too far for Paul. "My sergeant's pay is more than your patrol woman's."

"I have a trust fund or two," she said. "You can pay me back later."

"In trade?" He teased, looking deep into her eyes.

Knowing Henry was listening, she blushed.

"There is one thing," Paul said without really thinking. "When I'm gone, there's an Old Craft ritual coming up, Beltane. Holly Corey's got herself mixed up with this witchcraft crowd. She promised me she wouldn't go–but Holly doesn't take orders too well. I don't want her to be up there alone."

That made Althea furious. "No! There is a lot I'll do for you, but babysitting a rival is not one of them! Of course, if Ms. Corey gets herself into trouble, I'll be happy to arrest her. Or her rapist?" Althea finished helpfully.

Paul patiently explained, "Holly's mother went to one of those rituals and came out with over twenty stab wounds."

"She lived?" asked a shocked Althea.

"No. Hester Corey was very dead."

Henry spoke up from the front. "Paul, a couple of merchants back in Mystic have started a Sgt. Travinski Defense fund. It's been catching on. Alice at the motel set you up with a support site on the Internet, and there are collection jars in a lot of the stores."

"Thanks." It was kind, but it made Paul feel ashamed. And there was another problem. "Henry, I've made a barter deal with Quentin Butler."

"Classic Car Garage?"

"Aaup. After work, I'm painting his mother's house on Greenmanville with N.C. and Frost Corey."

Henry thought about it, then said, "Okay. I'll take your

place, and I'll ask around to see if I can scare up any other happy volunteers."

"Holly Corey again?" Althea asked in a disgusted tone.

"Police business. Keeping an unsafe van off the road," Paul defended.

"Althea," Henry cut in, "If it isn't the Coreys, you can bet it will be some other lost soul that Paul is always trying to rescue."

They sat in silence for the rest of the way with Paul reflecting on how weird it was to sit in the back of his own police car. He found himself getting a little slap happy: going to MacDonald's to get a cheeseburger, fries, and get imprisoned; everybody gets your guns to go to the family burger palace... But he didn't have a gun–he was on the rubber gun squad. Now he was on suspension leave with pay. When he was taken into custody, would he still be getting his salary? Probably not. Getting to the end of the month and bills had to be paid. How much did he have in savings? *Shouldn't have bought the new truck.*

Soon the three of them were climbing the steps to the sprawling, one-story Service Center with its cluster of fast food counters, restrooms, souvenir shop, and soda machines. He saw someone familiar walking over to the table section, well, at least his uniformed back. Chief Stanley Lewis was just carrying his food tray to one of the eating areas' sticky tables.

# Chapter 31

As Althea and Henry got on one of the long lines to the registers, Paul asked him, "Get me a bar-be-que beef, big fries, and a coke, while I talk to the chief, aaup?" Henry nodded, and Paul walked over and slipped into the booth seat opposite Stan, who was starting on his Big Mac. His chief looked up with mild reproof. "Finally got around to showing up, sergeant?"

"Figured I wasn't coming?" kidded Paul.

Stan shook his head, saying with quiet confidence. "No, I knew you wouldn't run."

Paul's face fell into stern lines. "Stan, I hear they're going after you. That they want you to cut me loose or retire early?"

"You also hear what I told the hyenas?" his chief mildly returned.

Paul smiled appreciatively. "Aaup." He looked around. "I thought Evvie might be here?"

"**Hell, no!** Bring the wife?" Stan shook his head. "When the troopers came for you, Evvie might've grabbed one of our guns and tried to break you out of the Service Center!"

Paul smiled at the absurd picture, then turned serious again. "Listen–I don't want to bring both of you down with me. I mean it, Stan."

Those quiet, dark blue eyes turned up at him. "Son, you're innocent, and we all know that. The process will work. We'll make it work! We've just got to keep you safe until my detectives can come up with the real killer."

This was going to be hard, but Paul had to do it before Henry and Althea got back to the table. Before he was hauled off in cuffs. "Stan, there is someone who will remain unknown, who may have done a little unauthorized searching...." Paul stopped. This was ridiculous. He couldn't go through with this. "Never mind."

Stan looked sharply at him. "You were late. Officer Althea Rogers stopped you down the road from The Lady's Cauldron, where Miss Holly Corey is presently employed. I assume you went to say goodbye, if not to the nutcase, at least to your truck that she's driving until her hearse is rebuilt. What is that rebuild costing you, Paul? You, Evvie and I are gonna have a little talk about that some time. Now I assumed Miss Corey did the illegal search. Of what? Dietrich's boat?"

"It might have been a motel room..."

"Motel?" Stan thought about it. "Margaret's room?"

"And the boyfriend's," Paul confirmed.

"We didn't search their rooms." Stan frowned. "Hiram didn't think it was necessary and didn't want to spook them. I did speak a bit with Alice and the maid there. They didn't see anything that I should get a search warrant for. I know Margaret had some books on diamonds in her room. And that she and Uberstat are obviously lovers, with both connecting doors unlocked, but that only strengthens their alibis as to being together when Dietrich was killed."

"The boyfriend likes to wear loud print shirts and cargo pants."

"Who cares?" said Stan, looking mystified.

"In his closet, he may have a plain, dark blue shirt and matching trousers."

"Shit! Like a cop's uniform?" Stan stared at him, as the consequences of that sunk in and fermented. "And he's about your size. Of course, you're a blond. Uberstat's dark-haired."

Paul pointed out. "Maybe Uberstat's got a wig? Spray can dye job–that washes out?"

"Your nutcase girlfriend find any of that?" his chief demanded.

"No, but she says the blue shirt sleeve has short, black threads hanging from it. That shirt may have had something sewed on it, like sergeant's stripes?"

"If anybody finds out your girlfriend was nosing around random motel rooms that would invalidate anything we could find as evidence."

"Margaret and Brandon Uberstat caught Holly leaving the room. Alice just put on a show like Holly was the maid. And Holly does fill in there sometimes."

Stan ignored that. "But if Uberstat used that outfit to commit a murder, wouldn't he and Margaret have been idiots to keep it?"

"Trust me, I didn't want to marry Margaret for her I-Q. And I hear that boyfriend makes her look like Einstein! Maybe they planned to use the fake uniform again?"

Stan didn't seemed moved. "A dark blue shirt and blue trousers isn't really proof of anything." The chief stared off to the tables by the windows, obviously weighing options. "Hiram's lead detective. He doesn't think he has enough for a warrant."

When the troopers came, Paul would be totally out of the game. He had to push, "You'll need probable cause to get a search warrant and I can't testify as to where the tip came from, but the murder victim had a restraining order against Margaret. Her alibi is her new boyfriend, which is pretty weak. There's stuff missing–the diamonds-that might indicate a robbery. With all that you should be able to get warrants to officially search two motel rooms?"

Stan didn't look happy. He pulled out his cellphone and looked around at the screaming kids, whose parents just sat nearby calmly eating their chicken wraps. "I'm going outside to call Hiram about this, but, Paul, I've put him in charge! And going forward, I don't want you, your nutcase, or anybody else *'helping'* us with the Dietrich investigation– **do I make myself clear**?"

As Stan left, Henry arrived with a tray loaded with yellow wrapped burgers, fries, and three oversized drinks. "What do I owe you?" Paul asked, reaching for his wallet.

"Althea's treat," said Henry.

"Thank you," said Paul, as Officer Rogers slipped into the booth, sliding down the seat so that her shapely leg pressed hard against Paul's thigh. He smiled appreciatively down at her. Henry unwrapped his bacon cheeseburger; Paul unwrapped his bar-be-que beef and just looked down at it. Althea didn't even bother to open hers up.

Then they talked brightly about everything that had nothing to do with why they were there until Chief Lewis returned to the table looking grim. "Saw a State Trooper's cruiser pulling in outside-- probably our guys. Paul, give me your wallet and any other identification."

# Chapter 32

Paul reached in and pulled out his wallet, handed it to his chief, who shoved it into his other pocket.

To cover his panic reaction, Paul reached for the icy coke. *Again that cold, falling feeling of being trapped–of wanting to run. Of being captured. Tortured. He had to get over this!* Calm down. With an effort, he cleared his mind and began to consciously focus controlling his breathing--in and out--to steady down, as if he was on the shooting range going for the championship.

Stanley Lewis had settled down opposite Paul again. His chief's indigo blue eyes were watching him carefully. Did he sense Paul's cowardice? Stan was speaking quietly to him. "Son, over the years you've made a few enemies, but you've also made a hell of a lot of friends. Trust us to get this straightened out for you."

Paul decided to utilize what little time he had left as a free man. "Does Hiram have any lead on the diamonds?"

Stan hit the table impatiently. "I told you to stay out of this investigation!"

"They're coming to arrest me, Stan. Ignorance doesn't seem to be working out too well for me."

"No diamonds have been found," Stan told him. "Dietrich's clients have filed a theft report and an insurance claim. The insurance company apparently has sufficient proof that the twenty-nine million dollars in diamonds actually existed. Either the killer got them, or Dietrich hid them before he was shot."

"Margaret seemed to think I or some policeman might have them," Paul stated. "If she and the boyfriend had gotten them I don't think she would be smart enough to keep hanging around here."

"So maybe she didn't do it?" asked a skeptical-sounding Chief Lewis.

"Stay on the diamonds," Paul advised. "Maybe check the public lockers at the beach near his boat slip?"

Stan looked tired. "Hiram got the pass keys, and we went through all the locked ones. Picked up a gun that's being tested for the murder weapon, a kilo and a half of marijuana, and some really nasty child porno. All locker accounts were paid for with cash. Paul, other than yourself, did Dietrich have any more *'friends'* he screwed?"              "I don't know anyone else that he hung with." Paul tried to remember. "There's the Dockmaster, Larry Scofield. They talked."

"Hiram spoke to him," Stan stated. "Larry said Jim Dietrich dropped by to say hello. Larry let the detectives search his office, the docks, the yacht club, and his boat and his house, just in case Dietrich stashed anything." His chief sat back. "Did Jim scuba dive? With a wet suit maybe he stashed 'em below the waterline?"

"No." Paul shook his head. "Jim had inner ear problems. Wouldn't have done any diving."

"Family graveyard? Church? Gun club? Any place he had access to that was unlikely to be disturbed?" Stan kept digging.

"I can't think of anything." *All Paul could think of was being placed in a box with a barred door.* John Gotti had coped by doing push-ups. In that air-conditioned restaurant, Paul found himself sweating, as he saw two tall men in gray state troopers' uniforms and silly fedora--looking hats. They scanned the room, spotting their table, and headed over.

Paul forced himself to concentrate on the problem at hand. "I don't think there is anyone Jim could trust in Mystic. The murderer probably got the diamonds...unless Jim had time to hide them. If he did, he needed a place where his stash wouldn't be disturbed; a place that wouldn't be connected to him; and a place handy, so he could eventually retrieve them." Paul was just repeating what Stan had said--panic was freezing his brain.

Stan looked a little ashamed. "Paul, Norwalk got a warrant and searched your apartment, but Hiram also had to get it on the record as having done it. He's got a warrant and is searching it right now."

They wouldn't find anything, but Paul still hated the thought of investigators going through his refrigerator, sweaty laundry, and *Playboy* magazines. "Should've been done sooner, Stan. You and Hiram have to turn the whole murder investigation over to the State Troopers. Otherwise, you're vulnerable to cover up charges!"

"Sergeant, **I'll** run my own department!" said Stan crisply. "Go over that meeting you had with Dietrich again."

Paul desperately tried to remember it all. "Henry and I were going fishing, I didn't even think about Jim being in town. He came over wanting to talk. Jim admired my truck and apologized for running off with my fiancee. Jim told me he was fully punished for that one." Paul tried to keep focus on the problem at hand, but he kept watching the two grim-faced, gray-uniformed men, making their way over to the table. *Paul couldn't keep from getting that irrational feeling of being a trapped animal going down,* as he forced himself to continue, "Jim offered me a job. That seemed to be why he came over. He mentioned Margaret's interest in the diamonds he was carrying," Paul finished hopefully.

The two senior troopers loomed above their table. The first respectfully nodded to his chief. "Stan, good to see you again." Then he looked to his partner. "Chris, we've got Sgt. Travinski here. Let's see, how many points did the sergeant beat your score in the pistol finals?"

Chris' tight-lipped reply was, "Only five. Travinski beat your score in rifles with that seven-point spread, Rudy."

They both looked at Paul, with impassive cop faces.

Paul forced a smile back. "Sorry to make you guys drive all the way down here."

"Naw, taking you into custody, sergeant, it's gonna be our pleasure," said Rudy, again totally deadpan.

The second trooper asked, "Just what are we pulling him in on?"

Rudy looked, Stan. "What were you guys gonna use?"

Stan thought about it. "We're on the harbor. We could've brought Paul in for questioning about his possibly poaching lobster pots."

Rudy shook his head. "He couldn't be stealing sea life on I-95."

"Paul drives pretty fast," suggested Henry helpfully. The trooper captain shook his head. "Naw, we don't take them into overnight questioning for speeding."

"Well, he could resist," his partner suggested helpfully.

"Then we'd have to shoot him. Too much paperwork" replied Rudy laconically. "Got to get something else."

"Paul's been looking longingly over the fence at Bronsen's ewes," supplied Henry sounding concerned.

"Beastiality?" Trooper Chris looked to his superior. "Rudy, what is the age of consent for having sex with a sheep in Connecticut?"

His captain pretended to think about it. "Sheep? You know with Travinski's height, I always thought of him more as a cow luster."

Even as he knew the teasing was friendly, with Althea there, Paul found himself flushing.

"Naw, cattle abuse usually isn't in the State Troopers' jurisdiction anyway," finished Rudy.

Althea smiled prettily. "Paul was over my apartment for dinner two nights ago and left a check..."

"That was for your niece's girl scout cookies!" Paul protested.

Ignoring him, she continued playfully. "If the check's good, maybe we can go after him for solicitation..."

Henry cut in helpfully, "And if the check bounces,

you've got him on rape!"

"Thanks, guys." Paul looked to the troopers. "Isn't it great to have friends?"

Rudy turned to his partner, saying seriously. "Wasn't there a truck hijack and armed robbery at the Fairfield Service Center, late March? That's still open, I think. We could presume the perpetrators could have escaped off the Mystic ramp?"

"But those were three Hispanic looking guys, all under 5'5"." Trooper Chris cocked his head to the side and eyed Paul. "He may have bleached his hair. Grown a foot or so. Yeah, he might be one of them."

"I think so," agreed Rudy. "Witnesses are always off a little."

Chris took over. "Sir, what is your full name?"

"Paul Kenneth Travinski."

"All right, Paul, where were you on March 23$^{rd}$ in the evening?" said Rudy amiably.

"You know–I don't remember," Paul said. "And I do not wish to talk to you."

"Do you wish a lawyer before speaking to us?" asked Trooper Chris.

"No, sir, I just don't wish to talk to you."

His captain asked, "Do you have any identification to prove who you are?"

Paul patted his jacket. "I seemed to have misplaced my wallet," he said, finding this ritual oddly comforting.

Chris looked to his senior. "Maybe he has ID in his car?"

"Actually," Paul said, "I also seemed to have misplaced my car."

"Sir, since you do not have an alibi for March 23$^{rd}$, you can't provide verifiable identification, and since you are refusing to talk to us, we are forced to take you into custody."

Althea looked to the untouched burger in front of Paul.

"He hasn't had time to eat anything yet," she spoke with a pained voice.

"I'm not hungry," said Paul.

Stan stood up and moved to stand between the two tall troopers. They towered above him, yet his body language said he was their equal, maybe their superior. Rudy quietly said to Stan, "What's with the chief down in Norwalk? I thought you, and he were buddies?"

"Chief Fergerson is on medical leave. The Acting Chief--Alan Zellman--is in his thirties, refused to take my calls. I drove down to see him. He explained to me that he's *'against the old boy network way of doing things.'*"

The senior trooper raised a disbelieving eyebrow. "He's gonna try to go it alone? We'll certainly see how that works out for him."

Stan spoke tiredly. "There's a lot of pressure on Norwalk to go after Paul, some of it coming out of the prosecutor's office up in Hartford. And then there's the usual anti-police reporters and the 'professional victims crowd' that claim Paul is anti-whoever they are trying to get donations out of this week."

A muffled cell phone rang. Close. All of them automatically looked to their utility belts. Henry fished his cell out. Listened, then he said, "Shit!"

Chief Lewis looked at him. "What's the matter?"

Henry looked from him to the State Troopers. "Uhmm."

Stan Lewis glared hard. "**Report!**"

After looking from the troopers to Chief Lewis, Henry said, "Norwalk's dug up a judge who signed an order against you personally, sir, as *'obstructing Travinski's arrest.'* The Mystic Police are ordered to hand Paul over immediately. There are two Norwalk officers back at Headquarters waiting to arrest the sergeant or to take you into custody, sir."

"Arrest you in your own precinct?" Rudy laughed

heartily.

Stan shook his head in disbelief.

Althea looked to Stan. "It's an illegal order! We can fight that in court!"

Stan looked at Paul. "While he rots or worse in open custody?"

It really was getting to Paul. "I'm not dragging you down with me, Stan!" He looked at Henry. "Call headquarters, call all our guys in. I want a seaport presence when the chief returns."

Stan turned on him with full authority. "Sergeant! You've just been taken into State police custody! **Get the hell out of here!**"

Appearing sick Althea looked to Stan. "It'll be on the computers. Norwalk's prosecutors will find out where Paul is. Their homicide warrant will supersede the State Troopers' questioning detention in a cold robbery investigation." Her voice was rising with her fear.

Solid faced Chief Lewis looked up to Rudy, and the senior trooper just smiled tightly. "Well, our guys can be really bad with paperwork, mam. Could take days, weeks, longer. And, first, those guys from Norwalk have got to find the trooper who processes our interdepartmental paperwork."

He looked to his partner Chris, who finished. "Yeah, we keep losing that guy, don't we?" Chris smiled at Paul. "Sergeant, we know Chief Lewis. He can take care of himself. But let's get you out of here before some judge starts writing arrest warrants for my captain here."

Paul started to rise slowly. "I'm going to raise my hands, interlace my fingers behind my head and turn around for the frisk." The senior trooper scanned the room of burger eating families, as a screaming five-year-old ran past him. "Don't do that, Paul. These people could get nervous, seeing an arrest. We'll just walk out quietly."

Paul shook his head. "Guys, I don't want anybody else

getting in trouble because of me."

Chris walked to his side to lead him out, saying firmly, "We'll go by the book, sergeant. I'll pat you down by the cruiser."

Giving up, Paul just followed Chris. Rudy nodded to Stan, then saw the anguish on Althea's face. "He'll be fine, mam. We'll feed him, then my sergeant will tuck him in a nice warm, private, holding area. Nobody's taking the sergeant from us," said the senior State Trooper reassuringly.

Sad-eyed Althea watched Paul being marched away.

# Chapter 33

Before dawn, Holly was setting up Noel's four oversized muffin trays with paper liners, while he vigorously hand stirred the batter in a huge steel bowl. *They needed a commercial mixer.* He started pouring batter into four regular sized bowls, one each for blueberry, cranberry, streusel, and one for chocolate. Watching him, she said, "I'll need three guest baskets for the mansion tomorrow. Four couples staying for Beltane at The Lady's Cauldron."

"Good," said Noel, who mixed blueberries into the first bowl, then handed it to Holly to pour into the baking trays.

Doing that she asked, "You guys got in late last night? Who drove you?"

Noel did not want them on this topic. "A friend. Holly, did you take my cinnamon again?"

She blushed. "I'll get the cinnamon. I was trying to cast a spell for Esther." Holly hurried out of the kitchen.

"Spell? I wish you wouldn't fool around doing that stupid stuff!" Noel called after her.

Although it was still dark outside, Frost was returning from walking Thor. Now he moved to the sink to fill up the Rottweiler's water bowl. "Since Holly has only good thoughts, casting spells are harmless."

Noel was not amused. "If it's harmless, she shouldn't be wasting her time!"

Holly came back with the cinnamon, salt, and vanilla extract. "Esther's cat is sick. I'm trying to make her feel better."

"Esther or the cat?" asked Frost.

"Both," she said, as Holly looked at him curiously. "Where have you guys been the last four nights?"

"Out," said Noel.

"Yeah," agreed Frost. "Out."

Holly reached up to touch Frost's pale-blond thatch. "There's white paint in your hair?"

As Noel glared at him, knowing his sister's psychometry abilities, Frost quickly moved to the table to evade her probing fingers. "I was painting a bit."

"At the museum?" she asked.

"Yeah," Frost said, at the same time Noel was saying. "No."

She looked from one to the other, knowing something was going on, and that they were shielding from her.

Frost explained quickly, "Yes, I have been painting at the museum, but I'm also helping a friend I work with...paint his house. And Noel is helping us too."

That sounded good to Holly. "We're getting paid for this?"

Noel looked to his brother. "Are we getting paid for this?"

"No," said Frost, shooting a warning look to his brother. "It's for my friend's mother...she doesn't have much money."

While Noel started slipping the muffins trays in the ovens, Holly walked into the parlor and opened up the roll top desk to reveal his computer. She checked for bookings on the Internet and updated the mansion site with May's breakfast menus. With guests staying, she didn't want to use the vacuum before they woke up, but Holly got a wash started with tablecloths and began the endless dusting of all the oiled wood and Victorian bric-a-brac.

At 6:30 a.m. Noel was packing the boxes of baked goods for the motel. Frost had finished chopping more of the wood they'd need for the mansion's many fireplaces this winter. He came out of his room in his bright blue Mystic Seaport Museum guide's polo shirt, with it's white embroidered whale tail on the pocket. Now Noel, in his Aquarium's red shirt with its black embroidered seal on the pocket, hurried from the back suite carrying his boss's laptop.

"You finish those statistics for Dr. Morjessky before you fell asleep?" Holly asked.

Noel nodded. "Yes, but this weekend I've got to get some work in on my thesis."

Frost looked at him. "We gotta paint, remember?" Giving him a very significant look. "And we might be short-handed."

"You guys need my help?" offered Holly.

"No," said Noel quickly lying, "We're almost done. But we'll need Paul's truck after dinner."

"Okay." Holly tried to reassure them. "This weekend, I'll cook all the meals and do the motel baking–basic stuff only."

"That'll help," said a tired sounding Noel gathering his jacket for his day job.

Into pale early daylight, they headed out to Paul's king cab truck. As she walked around to the driver's side, Holly ran her fingers over the un-dinged, un-faded side door. She felt so rich to be driving a truck that wasn't six months old yet. *Yes, it was fun to be driving Paul's fancy truck, and feeling his manly vibrations, but she wanted the ghostly Bernie and her hearse back*!

Frost sat beside Holly as she drove. In the back, as usual, Noel just closed his eyes and managed a few winks on the short drive. She pulled up to the Aquarium entrance plaza first. Holly looked in the rearview mirror. Eyes closed, Noel was tossing his head restlessly. "N.C.'s having another of those nightmares again. Wake him gently, Frosty."

Frost turned around in his seat, saying softly, "Hey, Buddy. We're here. N.C.?" Noel shook his head groggily. "You okay?" prodded Frost.

"Another stupid dream," said Noel wearily.

"What was it this time?" Holly asked.

"I'm in this truck, and we're headed into a green

tunnel. It's full of rocks falling inside–Holly, I try to tell you to stop, but you won't listen,  and the windshield shatters. Bright light glinting off the shards, blinds you, Holly, and you crash the truck."

Frost shook his head. "That's better than yesterdays, with the garage-sized, green hen laying balls of blue fire. If you go back to sleep in the morning, you get rotten dreams." Frost rubbed his own arm, grousing, "At least it's not a strained shoulder from that damned painting...that pain doesn't go away when I wake up."

After Holly dropped Frost off, she headed back to the Mystic Motel. When she carried two boxes into the lobby, Alice was on the phone. She just waved to Holly. In the breakfast area, Holly rapidly started loading the clear plastic dispensers with Noel's muffins and bagels. Alice joined her, pouring new coffee grounds in the percolator as she reluctantly said, "Honey, I hate to tell you, but the State Troopers arrested Paul Travinski."

"He-he's with the other prisoners?" Holly asked fearfully.

"No. I know a State Trooper. He said they're treating Paul fine. They have him in the barracks dayroom watching t-v, giving the guys tips on their shooting. A trooper goes out and gets him take-out food, and he's by himself at night."

"But they're still going to put him on trial," said Holly miserably.

Alice sighed. "Chief Lewis has Hiram and his detectives working on it. They'll get it sorted out."

Later at The Lady's Cauldron,  Holly worked in the storeroom, as Colin and Lapin were carrying in boxes of flower deliveries. They'd both been planting herbs since dawn and looked pretty beat. Holly smelled male perspiration and manure, as she smiled shyly at them. "I could've carried those in."

Lapin put his warm wide fingered hand on her back.

"Lady, we don't want you working too hard." Holly wasn't used to being touched by him, and Lapin's hand left her feeling a little uncomfortable, and even drained. It felt even more awkward when she looked over at the angry face on Colin. His green eyes had narrowed and darkened, and the line of his mouth was tight as he stared at her and Lapin. *Holly wondered if he was angry with her for letting Lapin touch her?* But she and Colin didn't really have any sort of relationship that justified him feeling jealous if another man just put his hand on her back.

Seeing the stormy look on Colin's face, Lapin moved away from her. To avoid Colin at the side exit, Lapin went out the door into the store, which with his mucky boots, he usually didn't do. Darkly, Colin's eyes followed him.

Holly looked at Colin. "I brought my brother's laptop to show you how the web page is coming. Y-Y-You don't have Internet in the store here?"

Colin slipped back to his normal, gentle smile. "I have it up the hill at the house."

"N.C. was saying that you could maybe move it to the store instead? Depending on how much you use the Internet in the house?"

"Or I could pay for another setup," suggested Colin.

"N.C. said it would easier for you to take credit cards with the Internet, instead of by the phone. And if you have Internet, he can get you a cheap program that gives you unlimited phone use countrywide for only sixty-nine dollars the first year, then thirty after that."

"Good. N. C. Seems to knows a lot about computers." He studied her. "It is Noel Christmas, Holly Christmas, and Frost Christmas Corey isn't it?"

She gave an embarrassed smile. "We were born on Christmas Day. My father wanted us to be born on Yule, but it didn't happen, which was good because I don't think I would've like being named  Solstice Yule Corey." She was pulling up draft pages on the laptop screen. "These are some of the web page ideas we have for The Lady's Cauldron."

Taking time, Colin studied the five layouts.

"They're just rough d-d-drafts..." she apologized.

He smiled. "I like them all."

"Frost did most of the designing. He says it would probably be better to get one look, like that photo of the old cauldron we had in the woods, and put that on every page for unity. Maybe keep the site colors the same, but you can change the pictures every month or seasonally. Show what's growing, feature two or three store items. We'll have other pages with sales and product lists." She looked directly into his emerald eyes. "You're very knowledgeable about herb growing and usage, especially with American Indian medicine, so maybe we could put up a page with your photo as the 'Warlock's hints'..."

He interjected, "Make that 'the Farmer's' hints."

She nodded. "Those might get picked up by the search engines. And your site will be able to take credit cards and Paypal, and we'll mail the stuff from here."

"Have to give you a pay upgrade as my Web Master," Colin said. "Looks like your brothers have done a lot on this. I should thank them in person."

Holly smiled. "Y-Y-You could come to the mansion and have dinner with us, and we could ta-talk about the website."

He smiled back at her. "Or, since you are all working as consultants for me, I could treat you three to dinner at a real restaurant?"

She lowered her head and smiled shyly. "That would be fun." *It would be a foursome with her brothers, but it was sort of a first date...*

\* \* \*

Late that afternoon from the paddock Colin watched Holly driving away in Paul's truck.

Lapin looked up with shrewdly evaluating eyes. "She goes from that cool hearse to a whippin' truck?"

"It belongs to a guy who Holly knows, but she says he isn't her boyfriend."

"Sure," Lapin scoffed. "He don't care about her, he just lends her fancy wheels to drive around in." Lapin's eye's glittered between lowered lids. "Every time I walk past that thing, I inhale pure gold. It intoxicates my mind."

"Holly didn't say much about him, but I get that same feeling from that truck." Colin didn't sound happy.

"You gonna spell her away from him?"

"**No!**" That angered Colin.

"Maybe she already does that to you? That lady is powerful Old Craft. Yes, sir, farmer boy, she seems to have put the hex over you. More than just those wide curves, I inhale witchin' from her."

Colin studied Holly's blue truck turning out onto 184. "Holly is totally unaware of what she is capable of. Her paternal line is Corey, and the maternal family was Farringtons. She's one of triplets. Her two brothers may also have some powers that Maeve and Lilith are interested in harnessing."

"And seeing what they can breed out of you and the blonde?"

"It's been mentioned," said Colin distastefully.

Lapin raised an eyebrow. "But you don't want her? Maybe I take blue-green eyes. Does she know what I am?" Lapin asked.

Colin stared at the larger man, levelly. "She probably senses that hyped male sex aura you're always pushing out, but I don't think she realizes you are a Bokor or even knows what that means. Her family apparently told her nothing about what we do."

"They Old Craft, but don't tell her?"

"Yeah." Colon ran a hand through his thick hair. "They didn't want Holly practicing. In fact, her aunt punished her when she did what came naturally."

"Pure shame. She being that powerful and not trained how to channel it."

Colin took a wide-legged stance before his friend. "I saw you touch her back! I know what you did to her."

Lapin shrugged. "I was tired, I needed a pickup, so I draw off a little juice. It don't hurt her, she don't even know what I did. That one has too much magical energy, it sloshes off her."

Colin leveled his eyes at Lapin. "Don't **ever** do that again! She's not sophisticated enough to ward you off--so until she is, Holly Corey is under my protection!"

Lapin flashed wide, white teeth. "You gonna tell Maeve and Lilith that?"

"Yhep." A grim mouthed Colin finished with a hard glare at his friend.

# Chapter 34

Sunset would be the start of Beltane. Holly arrived early that day at the farm to find rows of cars, campers and RV's parking in the lot and overflowing into the meadows, even before the store was to open. The hay wagon was gone from beside the barn, so it must be on the hill ferrying people up. Holly saw Colin saddling Jacobite and Gem. She walked over to him. "You're taking the horses out?"

"They need exercise whatever day it is. Maeve decided she doesn't want to ride today. I need help on the hill. Want to come with me?"

Happily giving a soft stroke to the mare's smooth neck, Holly moved to mount Gem. The smell of warm horse and oiled leather always excited her. Colin led off, going faster now that Holly was riding better. They trotted along growing shoots of lettuce and dill. Farther on, other plants were poking up in neat, even rows. To contain the fast spreaders like mint and lemon verbena, Colin had planted them in pots, also set in lines. In the center of the fields, Holly could see two robed figures. Maeve and Lilith were stretching their arms high. Holly shifted her weight forward, to bring Gem up alongside Jacobite. "What are they doing?" she called out to Colin.

He looked over. "They're trying to ensure the forecast rain doesn't come until after our festival."

She looked to the low, dark clouds moving in. "Can they?"

With a smile on his face, Colin shrugged. Reaching the woods, they moved to a canter. When they came out, the wild hill had been transformed. The colored circles Holly had worked on now had chalked pentagons within. The rock altar was bracketed by two large floral arrangements, and a small table stood above it. Down below, just above the pasture fencing, were the rentals: two large, enclosed, white-wedding pavilions, and over on the other side was an open-sided "cook" tent with tables before it. Several women of the coven were putting out empty, chafing trays on folding tables, and Holly could see large white ice coolers, some aluminum beer kegs, boxes of wine bottles, and stacks of commercial insulated-transport bags, some from La Luna pizza.

Another woman tended a four-foot long pit dug in the ground. Holly smelled the smoke and savory meat aroma and realized they were roasting a whole calf. Colin dismounted near the tractor with its hay wagon and tied both horses up to a tree branch, asking her, "Could you help us decorate the two disrobing pavilions?" He was lifting two boxes off the hay wagon and handing them to her indicating: "One for the ladies, one for the men."

She smiled and took the boxes from him and walked to the first eighteen foot by an eighteen-foot white canvas tent. The tent had closed sides and inside a twelve-foot high ridge pole leaving a clear area below. Holly found a red oriental carpet had been laid on the grass with a number of items on it. Two portable clothing racks had been set up with hangers. There was a folded card table that she set up and spread with an ivory damask cloth. From the first box Holly took out a small, fresh flower arrangement of white roses with pink centers; a cut glass candy dish she filled with red jelly hearts; a box of individually wrapped combs; packets of hand wipes printed with lilies of the valley designs, and some spray deodorant and bottles of patchouli perfume from the store. There was already a nail on a side pole to hang up the full-length mirror leaning against it.

Holly finished by setting up six folding chairs for the guests in the tent. Then she hauled the second box over to the men's pavilion. Colin and Lapin were just finishing rolling out the blue flowered carpet in the second tent. Colin left to direct the guys delivering three porta johns, while Lapin set up the clothing racks and helped Holly with the folding chairs. She decorated the men's table, which including a box of condoms, as Lapin hung another mirror. To finish, he hammered two staked signs before the tents, elegantly printed with '*Warlocks*' and '*Witches*' in gold lettering on polished maple wood. As a last touch, Holly hung unbroken glow sticks around the signs for tonight.

Soon Lapin took the tractor and hay wagon back down below. Colin and Holly carried up boxes to decorate the rock on the hilltop as the high altar. She spread a moss velvet cloth, embroidered with scared symbols in gold thread across the rough cut blue stone. She watched as Colin set out a five-inch silver pentacle disk in the center, with a bowl of salt above it for Earth; then a bowl of water to the right side; a red candle for Fire beneath it; and on the right side an eagle feather for Air. On the feather, he laid a flat, black, polished stone.

"What is the significance of the stone?" Holly asked.

He smiled. "Keeps the feather from blowing away."

She inclined her head. "The altars at Grace La Fleur's had mostly the same items, but each of them were laid out differently?"

"Old Craft rituals aren't codified by a Pope or some central conference," Colin explained. "Remember what Abigail Hoyt told you? You put it out, hold your hand over it, and go with what you sense is right." He was setting out two silver chalices to the left, with a small iron cauldron on the right. Then at the top on opposite ends, Colin set up two art nouveau styled, twelve-inch statues of the Mother Goddess and the Horned God. Holly added white and green candles in the holders beside them, as Colin placed a shallow bowl with a floral arrangement of white and lavender flowering bulbs in the center top.

Finally, from the box, he took out a slender, polished oak wand and an athame, laying them on the bottom right. The knife was wood, but it had been masterfully shaped and sharpened to a pointed blade. Holly found herself shivering. He must have sensed her reaction because Colin looked at her. "What's the matter?" He followed her eyes to the wooden knife.

"It's athame, Holly. You know—or maybe you don't--it's used in the ceremonies to point and focus the power."

"It's wood, and it's sharp..." she said in a mechanical voice.

"The early athames were wood, so I fashioned this one. It couldn't really function too well as a cutting instrument." He stopped, looked at her, and got it. "You're thinking about what happened to your mother on Beltane? Of course, that would upset you." he looked around. "You know, we're finished here, it's time we go back. Lapin can set up the couch."

"I'll see the athame at worship tonight," Holly said resolutely.

He looked over the hillside. "No. No, you won't, because you're not joining us."

"You said I could come just to watch?" she protested.

"Yeah, well, I've changed my mind," he smiled lopsidedly at her. "Your boyfriend, Paul..."

She cut in, "My **friend**, Paul."

"You said he doesn't want you attending Beltane, and he may be right. In our coven, you would be perfectly safe, but you know, I'd personally rather not have the added pressure of you watching me perform on the High Altar." He gently ran the back of his hand along her cheek. "It's uncomfortable enough to be having sex with a woman who knew me as a kid."

She couldn't understand. "Even if I won't be here, you'll have twenty to thirty other people watching?"

"I'm not trying to date them." He looked unhappy. "Holly, I won't stop you if you insist on coming, but I'd rather you didn't. And we've already made an appeal to the

Goddess."

"Paul is under arrest. He didn't do it, but innocent people do get convicted of murder," she said miserably. "I wanted to go to appeal to the Goddess on his behalf again."

"Holly, you don't need a fancy ritual, with a cheering crowd on top of a hill. Tonight is a ceremony dedicated to the worship of the Lady, but it's also a social blowout for our people to reconnect and strengthen bonds, even have some fun!"

Staring at her intently Colin continued, "After we go up on the hill, close to midnight, take one of the incense burners out of the store and a few cones of pine or whatever scent you feel close to, and go outside. Take off your shoes to properly connect with the earth, light your incense, and whisper your own direct appeal to the Lady."

"Do you think she can save Paul?" asked Holly.

"Could she, yes. Will she, I don't think so. What I think the Goddess will do is give **you** the strength to go ahead and save him yourself."

"I'm not r-r-really good at being religious," she started miserably. "Paul is in so much trouble..." Holly looked at him with those ocean blue-green eyes. "C-c-ould you..."

Shaking his head in disbelief, Colin looked to Holly. "You want me to appeal for him? Knowing that we're rivals for you?" Daring not to say anything, Holly's eyes searched his. Finally, Colin surrendered. "Oh, Holly, you make it so hard for a man. Figurative and literally! Tonight when I am before the altar, and I am performing the Spring fertility rites, I will silently pray to the Lady for Sgt. Paul Travinski's vindication."

She stretched up and kissed him briefly on the mouth. "Thank you."

He returned her kiss stronger, then reached down, and took her hand as they walked back to where the horses were tied. Sunlight illuminated Gem's smooth coat to a glowing golden red as the mare stretched her neck to chew new leaves.

"C'mon. I'm hungry. The calf's not ready for cutting yet, but we can get some pizza and beer before things get too crazy." He started into the cook tent with its stacks of insulated pizza carriers.

She'd need money. "I don't have my handbag."

"We never charge for anything on the hill. You like pepperoni? Sausage or meatball?"

"Bacon and pineapple?" She asked.

He smiled. "Not today, but if you like it, I'll put it on the order next time."

Sitting across from him on the grass, holding a foamy beer in a plastic cup, she bit into a gooey cheese masterpiece. "Renting these tents, and all the food you're providing for free, you aren't charging for this?"

"There are donation boxes in the store. Some of our members are very well off and are quite generous. Others just contribute by their presence." He shrugged. "Sometimes we break even with the extra traffic to the store, sometimes not. So far this Beltane, we seem to be making a profit, but that's not what this ritual is about. The store services the Cauldron, not the other way around."

Finishing up, they untied the reins and mounted. Holly easily turned Gem toward the path down, but Jacobite was fighting the bit, sidestepping, and bucking. His flank was dripping with foam as Colin explained, "He feels the energy building as more coven members arrive. Animals are sensitive to it. Easy, boy." Jacobite fought for the bit. Colin seemed to be controlling him, but said, "Holly, do you mind going down by yourself?"

"No." She reined Gem turning to keep facing him.

"I want to run off some of his nervousness by jumping him a bit."

"C-C-Can I jump too?"

"Have you ever jumped a horse?" he asked.

She shook her head.

"First we've got to get your legs stronger for holding on. Then I could teach you, starting with low jumps. But not on Gem. Maybe we can borrow Morgane's mare."

"Why not Gem?" Holly asked.

"Gem won't jump, she always refuses. I tried for the longest time to get her to–she won't even jump over a board lying on the ground."

"Okay." Holly patted Gem's warm neck. "I'll watch you."

He pulled the left rein lightly, and Jacobite spun around. Then, by just tightening his legs and leaning forward, Colin started Jacobite galloping off. Colin was riding him parallel to the wood board fence before it made a right-angled turn. There Jacobite gathered his legs and took the fence in a high, smooth, powerful jump. Holly had the feeling she was watching a centaur–man, and horse together as one. Colin matched his horse's movements completely. As Holly watched, they took two more broad jumps across a log and a stream before they disappeared into the woods headed down toward the cottage at the lake.

When she could no longer see him, Holly gently reined Gem's neck, turned the mare, and paced down the hill to the paddock. The parking lot was completely filled up. People were walking up the hill to the store. After taking care of Gem, Holly joined the line of people. An enthusiastic threesome in their twenties told her, "We came all the way from Reno for this!" Another fiftyish couple, excitedly pronounced, "Allentown, PA. It's been four years since we could make it up here again."

Both Rachel and Esther were ringing up lines of people on the two registers in the store. Holly started by bringing out more fresh flower diadems from the back room to restock the front cooler. Then she moved behind the counter to bag for Esther. Wrapping two ruby, blown glass goblets, she looked up to see Maeve and Lilith entering.

Their auras were flashing out an excited orange, and Holly had the uncomfortable feeling of being targeted. Wearing a gold niquab veil over her lower face, with a shoulder-length headscarf of black chiffon, Maeve moved behind the counter to help. Lilith settled in front of her at the counter. Although they were talking to each other, Holly had the feeling they were speaking for her benefit.

"Oh, Maeve, it's going to be marvelous," Lilith gushed. "So many people. They're already parking out on the road."

Maeve nodded. "Yes, the energy raised this Beltane will be phenomenal!"

They both looked to Holly, as Lilith said sympathetically, "You need that abundance for your mansion, I hear your bed and breakfast isn't doing too well?"

"That's a shame,    Holly," team tagged Maeve. "Perhaps if you did a direct appeal to the Lady...?"

As if it was a sudden thought, Lilith looked Maeve. "Could Holly take the part of the Goddess' surrogate?"

Maeve seemed to be doubtful,   "We already have Morgane, but if Holly really needs the renewal–maybe it is the Goddess' will..."

Lilith was nodding in concert. Holly knew they were both trying to push her onto the couch again, but Paul was in such trouble, and she had been worried about the unpaid bills lately. "I-I-I..." she started.

The voice from behind them all was angry and definite. It was Colin's. "As I explained that to you last night, mother, that is **not** the Goddess' will!" He and Lapin were carrying a seven-foot floral piece gate from the storeroom. He raised his voice, speaking to all those in the room."When the hay wagon comes down again, we'll start bringing up the worshipers who need rides. Anyone else, I suggest you start getting into your processional robes. You can change in the marked barns below or the tents above." He said less loudly, but more deliberately, "Mother, you should be changing."

Under his stern eyes, Maeve and Lilith retreated to the storeroom to change, but when Colin walked away, Holly still felt conflicted. Excited customers emptied the store as they headed up on the hill.  Esther and Rachel were not in the coven and finally left for home at sunset. Watching them go, Holly stepped outside the store looking to the sky with its drifting purple clouds turning bright orange. She could smell kerosene from the Tiki torches that ran every thirty feet or so along the trail to the woods. For safety, in the woods, there were battery lanterns.

The very young, the elderly, and anyone else who didn't want to walk up started loading onto a hay wagon pulled up by the tractor. For three wheelchair-bound people, Colin had also rented a four-person golf cart, which one of the coven was driving up and down. The walkers gathered together on the road beyond the barns, milling as the energy seemed to increase, giving Holly a tiny electrical charge running along her arms.

It seemed a laughing and happy gathering. Then a commanding clap of hands,  as the high priestess walked to the head of the procession. Still wearing her gold niquab veil and shoulder length black headscarf, Maeve was now dressed in a long, flowing tan robe gathered by a belt wrought in the shape of ivy leaves. In her hand, she held a tall staff with a clear, round crystal on top. This she raised, and the worshipers felt silent as they formed two lines behind her.

Holly felt that tingling along her arms and legs growing more intense–strong energy rising. Maeve started walking, and the others followed with the chiming sound of bells, cymbals, and sistrums. Those who would be worshiping skyclad in the inscribed pentagons would disrobe up at the hill meadow.

Seeing Lilith looking at her, Holly noticed the woman

had now dressed in a lavender kimono. Lilith chose to walk at the very end of the line. Would she be skyclad up on the hill? Just before Lilith entered the woods, she stopped again and turned to look back directly at Holly. Under those staring eyes, Holly felt a growing need to join the group, which she fought down with great difficulty.

Finally, Lilith rejoined the others and walked into the growing shadows of the pines.

When they had gone, Holly felt so isolated–so alone, so insignificant. *Had her mother felt that way her last Beltane? Was that why she walked to the mill alone? Had Hester felt the same irresistible pull?*

# Chapter 35

At eleven thirty Holly walked down to set up two folding tables in the parking lot. She stopped for a moment and faced the hillside, looking up to the starred sky. Now it was a cloudless black velvet. The sliver of the crescent moon had set with the sun. The guttering torches still flared every thirty feet up the pathway, and now the sky's blackness was pierced with sharp stars.

Driving the tractor, Lapin carted a group of latecomers up the hill, as his German shepherds, Diesel, and Turbo, ran alongside, barking excitedly. Wistfully watching them, Holly returned to the store to carry down a basket of coffee cans, cream, sugar and tea bags to the tables set up at the edge of the parking lot. Later Lapin carried out the filled water urns that were plugged into long extension cords, before taking his dogs on peeping tom patrol. With the rising dampness, she'd wait until after midnight to bring out the cookies. Alone again, Holly found herself restlessly walking to the end of the parking lot with its hay bale markers. It was so frustrating–others celebrated Beltane while she just stood there. *Paul was in jail for murder, and Colin had said she could save him–but she couldn't.*

As midnight approached Holly restlessly paced the outside to the edge of the parking lot and looked up to the trees before the hilltop. When she listened very carefully, and the wind was blowing downhill, she could hear distant chanting. Not understandable words, just waves of sound rising in worship. Holly returned to the tables, took off her shoes, and dug her toes into the cold, loose earth. She had taken the brass dragon-shaped burner they used in the storeroom and some cones of jasmine incense. Holly lighted one with a flaring match; when the cone ignited in yellow flame, she blew it gently to glowing coal. It was too dark to see the smoke, but she smelled the rich jasmine of her sacrifice to the Goddess and Horned Hunter.

Alone, she added her prayers to the tide on the hillside. *Watch over Paul Travinski. Help him prove his innocence. Please help me make a success of the Corey mansion so Frosty and N.C. and I can rediscover what it is to be family. Let N.C. finish his dissertation and earn his doctorate, and Frost find his happiness.* Was that asking too much of the Goddess? Holly quickly amended, *"But above all please, please protect Paul–you made him such a good man!*

She listened carefully. Silence...then the rhythmic chorus of peeper frogs. Finally, she heard loud cheering from the distant hillside, and someone actually set off firework shells that arced in gold, silver, red and green sparkled trails across the black sky.

By twelve-thirty, the first of the hayrides were bringing tired worshipers down the hill. Holly had paper and styrofoam cups stacked, coffee perking, and hot water urns ready, with plates of shamrock-shaped Beltane cookies set out. By two a.m. There were still stragglers coming down. The cookies were long gone, but Holly started to make some more coffee. Lapin parked the hay wagon near her, as subdued, robed or street clothes dressed worshipers climbed down. One guy was staggering to the parking lot. Holly hurried over with a steaming Styrofoam cup. "Sir, wouldn't you like to have some coffee?"

"Naw." He stumbled hard against a parked car.

Holly followed persisting, "Sir, I don't think you should be driving. Do you have a friend who could take you home?"

"I'm flying, girly," he leaned over to kiss her. Holly quickly ducked, but the guy just staggered on past her. Darkness moved behind him, and she saw a flash of yellow eye whites. Holly realized it was Lapin.

"He shouldn't be driving," she said to Lapin quietly.

Not answering her or saying anything, Lapin took the

man by his shirt collar, and turning him around, forcing the man to look at him. Those yellow ringed eyes staring down at him. The guy looked, stiffened, and then slumped. Lapin dragged him behind the straw bales marking off the parking lot, as he thinly smiled to Holly. "He sleep awhile."

Colin was coming over, wearing jeans and a shirt now, glanced at the clouds coming back. "Lapin, can you take the tractor wagon back for any stragglers?"

"Sure, boss."

"Holly," Colin turned to her. "You should've left already. I'll walk you to your truck." He put his arm around her shoulder.

"I've got to put the coffee urns away..."

"Naw, I unplugged them. I'll take in the sugar, cream, and anything that would attract animals, and we can bring the rest in tomorrow in the daylight."

As he walked alongside her in the velvet darkness, she looked at him, saying softly, "How do you think it went? The people coming down seemed very happy. Their auras could just about light up the night."

He pulled her closer. "Holly, with the energy that channeled through me tonight, we should have the most abundant year ever."

They'd reached Paul's truck. "Good," said a satisfied Holly.

She realized Colin was looking at her lovingly. He was going to kiss her, and not thinking, Holly found herself leaning up to him. But Colin had also put a hand on the front fender of Paul's truck. He pulled back, looked at that truck again. "Damn, it's hard to go up against a guy who's so wealthy."

"W-w-what?"

"This is your boyfriend's truck, right? I've got to admit he's got bucks."

"Paul Travinski?" She asked in a surprised voice.

"Paul's a police sergeant, still paying off college loans. He saved his overtime for years to buy this truck."

Colin backed away, studying it. "Yeah, I know what a Ford F 150 costs. My new tractor cost me more than this." Colin appeared puzzled. "But when I'm next to this truck, I have a feeling like being alongside a Silver Ghost Rolls Royce. I mean..." he put his hand out on the passenger's door again, touching it with his palm flat out. "Don't you feel it, Holly?"

She focused on the truck, letting the sounds of cars leaving and people talking and everything else drain away. At the front end, she felt tremendous wealth–exorbitant, unconscionable riches. With her hand resting on the car's dew-wet surface, she walked the length of the truck. There was still that feeling of richness, but it weakened in the rear.

Holly walked around the back of the truck, running her hand along its metal. Still feeling the wealth, but sensing she was away from it. She cornered and walked along to the driver's side of the truck. Again the richness increased as she got to the cab, then to the front fender. But it was slightly weaker on the driver's side. Holly walked across the front of the truck. The wealth feeling started to increase again.

Colin was already there with his hand on the front hood, passenger side. "It's here. Whatever it is, it's here." He ran his hands down to the front fender. He looked up. "Holly, is there a flashlight in this truck?" Colin asked, getting down with his back on the mashed grass.

She got Paul's light from the glove compartment and handed it to him. He was flashing it at the undercarriage, behind the bumper. Then he whistled lowly.

"What is?"

"A mass of duck tape. Holding something."

Holly climbed down on the wet grass beside him, sticking her head under the bumper and looked up to where he was holding the beam. She could see the gray tape and something darker behind the tape.

"Don't touch it," he said.

"What is it? A bomb?" she asked.

He put a tentative hand held open near the duck tape, but not touching it. "I don't think so. I don't think it is mechanical."

"But it shouldn't be there?"

"No." He shook his head. "It's definitely not part of the truck." He rested his hand about three inches from the 'thing.' "It's not good. What is in there is inert–but people lust after it. Want it enough to hurt other people."

"This is not Paul's–I don't feel anything from him around it!"

"I bet he doesn't even know it's here," finished Colin.

"Take it down," she said, reaching up, starting to claw at the heavy tape with her nails.

"Shouldn't you talk to Paul first?" Colin cautioned.

"I can't. They've arrested him for the murder of Jim Dietrich, but Paul didn't have anything to do with it. This will be proof!"

Colin didn't look so sure. "Holly, there's immense value here. Someone hid it here. They might be coming after it. Someone who may have already killed a man, and they might hurt you to get it. Leave it alone! Look–drive this truck back to the sergeant's place. Park it there, let him deal with it when he gets out–you and your brothers can drive the store's delivery van, okay?"

"No!" She pulled down a leather pouch trailing duck tape. "I prayed to the Goddess. This is her answer. I bet this was why Jim Dietrich was killed! It won't have Paul's fingerprints on it. It'll prove Paul is innocent!"

"I don't know." He had slipped out from under and now offered a hand to help her up.

"No!" Stubbornly Holly was positive on what she should do. With confidence, she said, "Paul is innocent, this will free him!"

"Or give him a motive for killing the guy," warned Colin.

# Chapter 36

It started to rain as Holly headed for Mystic. Now she drove along black roads shakily lit with fog-wet, yellow lamp reflections. She parked Paul's truck in the parking lot of the Mystic Police. There were lights on inside, but the doors were locked. Holly just hammered on the front door. Finally, a sergeant she didn't recognize opened it up. She stood there with that leather, heavily zippered pouch in her hands. "I need to get this fingerprinted."

"Mam?" The officer asked, sounding surprised.

"My name is Holly Corey. I'm a friend of Sgt. Paul Travinski's."

"Oh, yeah, Paul. Come in."

She followed him into a building mostly dark, with only minimal lighting in the booking area. A man dispatcher sat taking calls at the board. Two patrolmen were coming out of the back with coffees. One of them was a tall, blonde. "Althea!" called out Holly, carrying her pouch over. "Althea, make the officer listen! We need to get this fingerprinted!"

Althea seemed shocked to see Holly. "If it's to be printed, you shouldn't be touching it without gloves. Where did this come from?"

"I found it under Paul's truck." Holly put the green leather pouch on a table. "Taped to the inside of the fender, but Paul didn't know about it! Somebody else put it there!"

"What is it?" The mystified sergeant asked.

The other patrolman, a slightly built black man Holly recognized as Tom studied the lock holding the zipper to the end of the pouch, and its dragging rigging of gray taping. "Looks like a courier's pouch."

Althea went paler than normal. "They've been looking for one."

Tom looked at it. "Yeah. The diamonds from Jim Dietrich's boat." He looked to Holly. "You found that taped to Paul Travinski's truck?"

"Yes, but he didn't know it was there. He didn't put it there!" she repeated desperately. Holly put her hands out in front of her, palms flat down, inches above the bag on the table. "Can't you feel it? Paul's vibrations are **not** on the bag or its contents!" They just looked at her. With a sinking heart, Holly realized she was trying to describe colors to people that had been born blind. She tried to put in their terms. "When you fingerprint it, you won't find any of Paul's! I'm positive!"

Althea's voice sounded dead. "Holly, that pouch is oiled leather, with faceted diamonds inside. They aren't going to get too much in the way of prints off any of it. That duck tape looks like it has been driven under a car in the rain."

Holly turned back to her psychometry. Her fingers detected a man's essence. She had a brief mental glimpse of a man, big like Paul, but dark-haired, no one she recognized. There were others–to faint to determine.  Hopelessly, Holly looked back to the cops. She saw mostly pity for the mad woman, who inadvertently convicted Sgt. Travinski of theft and murder. By turning in these diamonds, she'd screwed up irretrievably.

The night sergeant was speaking. "Mam, please get away from that pouch. Officer Rogers, get her fingerprints for comparison. I'd better call Chief Lewis."

\*   \*   \*

Depressed the next morning, Holly didn't even feel like going in to work at The Lady's Cauldron. She just slowly cleaned up the mansion after her last guests left. Carrying a bundle of dirty sheets downstairs, she heard Thor barking from the foyer, as the sound of the doorbell chimed from the front entrance. Only guests used that. Dumping the laundry into the Library bedroom, she hurried to the front door, opening it to see a slim, blue uniform. That blonde cop was on her porch.

"I wanted to let you know what's happening," Althea said in a husky voice. "According to the insurance company, it was Dietrich's diamonds you found."

"I sank Paul," said Holly not wanting to cry in front of this perfect woman.

"Maybe, maybe not. They got fingerprints, not many. Some from the bag side that was against the car, and some on the paper envelopes that were holding each individual diamond. There's no report yet, but I heard Hiram telling the chief none of them were Paul's. Some were yours on the outside. And at least two other people's... Did anyone touch the duck tape with you?"

Holly realized they were probably Colin Fitzgerald's, but she wasn't going to tell the police. She'd made enough of a mess for one guy she loved.

Althea was continuing, "Some were from Jim Dietrich, which would line up with Dietrich taping the bag to Paul's truck, probably while Paul was out fishing. But the prosecutor could argue Dietrich was in on the theft with Paul.

"Does Paul know the diamonds were found?" Holly asked hesitantly.

"In his truck, by you, yes. The chief called and talked to him last night. Paul's not too happy."

"I never should have turned them in. I just wanted to help," Holly finished miserably.

"We both know Paul is innocent, but we have to leave it to the detectives," said Althea as she started to turn away. "And if I were you, I would try to stay out of the way of Chief Lewis for a while."

Althea started down the steps. Standing there in pain, Holly smelled the early blooming honeysuckle that entwined the lilac hedge that hid the mansion from the road. A big yellow butterfly flitted by. Early for monarchs? Or a message from the Goddess? "Althea. **Wait!** Please." The patrolwoman stopped, and Holly ran down to her. "Paul and I are finished.

He dumped me. I only want to help him now, do you believe that?"

Althea gave her a measured stare, then said, "Yes, I do."

"Have they announced the diamonds were found?" Holly asked.

"No—when Paul is put on trial they'll have to bring it out, but the police like to keep certain facts about a crime quiet to trip up the perpetrator. Chief Lewis thinks Margaret and her boyfriend are hanging around Mystic, trying to find those diamonds."

"I've been in her room. I know she's guilty of something, I can sense it—but I can't prove it," murmured Holly. "Althea, can you get those diamonds?"

Looking at her strangely Althea said, "No way in hell! They woke up a bank manager last night to open the vault to store them because the department's lockup is a tin box."

Holly looked at her rival and said slowly, "What if a crooked cop, who was first on the scene of Dietrich's murder found the diamonds, but didn't know how to make money with them?"

"A cop not knowing how to fence something?" a skeptical Althea asked.

"One who needed to go to Margaret for her help to cash them in?"

Althea seemed to be weighing her options. "She's gonna want to see the diamonds."

"Maeve has some up-scale craft stones that she uses for her jewelry. They look real. How many do I need?"

"Eight very large ones. But I don't think glass would fool Margaret," said Althea.

"If she's buying books on diamonds she can't know too much about them."

"Who is going to be your crooked cop?" asked Althea, already knowing the answer.

"Margaret knows I'm not a cop. She may have even seen you in uniform. You could save Paul." Confidently Holly stood back. *This was going to work! This was the Goddess supporting them*! "Paul got a wire for me to wear once to secretly record a criminal, but if you go through the department, you'll have to explain why you need one..."

"I've got a cousin who owns a security firm in New York. I can get one," confirmed Althea.

Holly eagerly asked, "Do you want me to call Margaret at the motel, and try to set up a meet?"

For a moment Althea said nothing, then, "I'll do it. There's still a pay phone in town that won't show up on a phone log. But damn you!" blurted out Althea. "We're only working together until this is over and Paul is free!"

"Then you can have him," said Holly sadly. *For her help, the Goddess would demand a worthy sacrifice.*

"Oh, you worked this out great! If you win Paul, you were better than me, if I win him, it's because you gave up him up! No, Ms. Corey, when this is over do your damnedest. I am going to win Paul because I am **better** than you!"

# Chapter 37

Stopping fast in the precinct's ladies' room, Althea taped on the wire under her bra, then touched up her makeup, using a Kleenex to pat away sweat beads from her forehead. Back in the booking area, she clocked out. *Now all she had to do was go to the Mystic Motel and get two murderers to confess.*

"Officer Rogers." Althea looked up to see Mary was standing at the counter. "Chief Lewis would like to see you."

"I can't now. I'm late."

"**Officer Rogers**!" Mary turned very official, and the other cops started to look their way. "The chief's office–**now!**"

Glancing at her watch, Althea did a fast turn on her heel. *No time to chat with Stanley Lewis today, she had to get this over with before she totally lost her nerve!* The chief was sitting at his utilitarian desk before a wall of green filing cabinets. Two brown leather cushioned chairs were in front of that desk, but Althea had no intention of sitting. "Sir, I'm off duty, and I have to leave for a pressing engagement."

"An important engagement, patrolman?" With his head of white hair, Stan was giving her a benign grand-fatherly smile, but those dark blue eyes held the look of a hungry spider watching a fat fly entangle itself deeper into its sticky web.

"It's a personal one."

"But I like to know what my officers are doing?"

Althea realized she had not been asked to sit down, and she was automatically taking an *'at attention* stance'. "Respectfully, sir, my personal life is not the department's business."

"Stg. Travinski mentioned you were interested in coming by my house?"

That surprised her. *Was that what this was about?* "Yes, sir. For a meeting of the blue shirt club. That's on

Friday,s, I believe."

"Let's start with you coming home with me now for dinner and meeting my wife, Evvie."

"Tonight? Unfortunately, I can't." Especially since she felt like throwing up.

"Your personal appointment, patrolman?"

"Yes, sir."

"The one you have at the Mystic Motel?" His voice had lost the fatherliness tone and had slid to burnished steel.

She instantly got it. "You got the motel manager's permission to tap their telephones?"

"No, officer. We are going to have to see you get a refresher course in obtaining admissible evidence for court. We got a judge to sign warrants to tap the phones and bug the motel rooms of Margaret Aster and Brandon Uberstat, so we were surprised to hear one of my patrolmen wanting to sell Dietrich's diamonds back to them. Let's talk about that, shall we, Officer Rogers?"

Althea only fastened on one thing. "You've been listening to them?"

"Yes, mam."

"Anything incriminating?" Althea asked eagerly.

"Great incriminating plans for the diamonds–if they can get their dirty hands on them. Margaret believed that Paul or another policeman had stolen them. But neither of them ever talked about Paul killing Jim, assumably because they knew better. They didn't tumble onto Miss Corey's possession of the diamonds."

"Then that doesn't help Paul," Althea said regretfully. "Holly was afraid of that."

"Holly? **Oh, God!**" Stan's voice dripped with poisonous sarcasm. "Is Miss Corey helping us too? After she turned in the material evidence that is going to convict my sergeant of both murder and grand theft, what else has she got in mind to help Paul?"

Althea was focused on only one thing. "The surveillance, sir?"

"We have tapes with references to Brandon being afraid they shouldn't still be holding onto '*it*.' My detectives think that '*it*' may be the gun used to kill Jim Dietrich."

"Would they be stupid enough to keep it?" Althea sounded disbelieving.

"Knowing Margaret, I think so. But we've searched their car, rooms, and anywhere else we know they'd been, and we can't find it."

"If we could get that gun, we'd have our proof! They're meeting a crooked cop, they're probably going to feel a need for a gun. Maybe '*the*' gun?"

A delighted sounding Stan Lewis finished for her, "And if they shot you with the same gun, at your autopsy we could cut out the bullet and prove Paul's innocence! A patrolman for a sergeant, I'm trading up." Chief Lewis rubbed his forehead with stubby fingers like he was getting a bad headache. "Paul Travinski is in custody in the State Police Barracks, but my department is still being run like a Polish joke!"

"I'm not planning to get shot, sir."

"You're not? That's reassuring," said Stan, continuing sarcastically, "and you're making plans with the likes of Holly Corey, so whatever could go wrong? What is Miss Corey's brilliant strategy this time?"

"She gave me some large fake diamonds, thinking that if Margaret has books on diamond,s, she can't know much about them."

"Holly knows that?" Those blue eyes of Stan's were darkening with anger. "Yes, Miss Corey did an unauthorized search of Margaret and Brandon's rooms. However, where money is concerned, Margaret Astor's always had the blood-homing instincts of a great white! She's going to know those stones are fakes!" He looked off into the distances as if trying to work out the logistics. "And the real diamonds are locked up in a bank already closed for the day..."

"I'm going to show her just one." Althea reached into her shirt pocket and pulled out a small, manilla packet. She opened it and poured out a large, unset, round cut diamond onto Stan's desk. It glinted brilliant mini rainbows on the beige desk pad.

Stan was not impressed. "With the size of that, even Margaret can just look at it and figure out it's a fake," he said disparagingly.

"Actually it's real, sir."

Stan looked from her to the diamond in shock, then turned even sterner. "Miss Corey held back one of Dietrich's diamonds?"

"No, sir. My cousin brought this from my grandmother. It's a rare, flawless diamond, an absolute 'D,' which means it's a true colorless stone; insured replacement value is two million, seven hundred and fifty thousand."

Stan was having trouble with this. "Your grandmother sits around with a few million in unmounted diamonds in her bathroom medicine cabinet?"

"My grandmother's fourth husband left her the major interest in the Yales jewelry chain. This was the showiest stone she could get on short notice."

"You told you grandmother that you needed a diamond because you personally were prying a confession out of two murdering, would be jewel thieves?"

"No, sir." Althea bit her lip, then confessed, "Sgt. Travinski had escorted me to a family wedding. Grandmother Harding was very impressed with him, and she is under the impression that our relationship has progressed to the stage where if Paul thought a suitable diamond was available--from the family as a wedding gift--he might be persuaded to propose."

"You've been working on these con games for a while

haven't you, patrolman?" said Stan, not sounding too pleased. "What happens if you lose this *engagement* diamond?"

"That's not going to happen, sir," said Althea. "I'm wired, and my cousin will be out in the motel parking lot taping everything."

Stan looked like that major headache was getting worse. "Althea, I am sure that you are dealing with two idiots–but even those two fuc..." he paused for control, seeming to suddenly remember the patrolman he was reaming out was a patrol-lady. "Those two clowns can still panic and pull a trigger. "

She stood stiffly at attention before him. "I'm willing to take that chance."

"But it's what chances I'm willing to take? Because if I allow you to go in there and get yourself shot, I know Paul Travinski would ever forgive me! Hell, I'd never forgive myself!"

# Chapter 38

Dry-mouthed, Althea parked in the Mystic Motel lot. She was still in her blue uniform, but if she was going to deal with these guys, she couldn't go in wearing her utility belt. Margaret had specified she shouldn't bring a gun. Reluctantly, Althea unbuckled the belt and safely locked it in the trunk of her car. Then, never feeling so alone, Althea climbed up the outside staircase to the second floor.

The window curtains were pulled closed on the oversized plate glass windows on both 213 and the adjoining room beyond it. She knocked on 213. No one answered, but she could hear shuffling movements inside. *Were they as afraid as she was?* To calm herself, Althea looked away from the motel over to the quiet park next door. She relaxed slightly at the sight of carefully trimmed shrubs, tall green trees, and mowed lawns. Suddenly Althea realized she was looking at the marble tombstones of Elm Grove cemetery–just where she might end up today.

The motel door was opened by an orangey-red haired woman, who walked like she was beautiful but wasn't. "Officer?" she asked brightly.

"Althea. I called?"

Margaret eyed her, then looked up and down the balcony corridor, and out into the parking lot. Finally seeming to accept the fact that she had come alone--and was unarmed--Margaret smiled prettily and pulled back, allowing Althea to step into the beige motel room. Althea looked around fast: two queen beds, one messed up with the comforter down; a desk against the wall; a cluttered bureau; and in the front under the window, two wing chairs on either side of a small round table with a glass top protecting its tropical palm design table cloth. The two doors to the adjoining room were open, and the tall, solid-chested figure of Brandon Uberstat was leaning against the wall–*another complication.*

Margaret waited, then started, "You said you were the first responder to my late husband's death? It was such a shock for me–poor Jim dying so suddenly."

"I'm sure." Althea smiled back, then said nothing more.

"You also said you might have found some of my property?" Margaret coaxed.

"Actually, it was Jim Dietrich's, but let's think of it as **our** property now," Althea finished smoothly

"What are we talking about?" Margaret asked her voice, hardening with business.

"Twenty-nine million in diamonds."

"Which you generously want to share with me?" Now her voice was tinged with disbelief.

Althea was ready for that. "I'm a cop. I can't fence twenty-nine million dollars worth of hot diamonds, but I think you can. We'll share fifty-fifty."

Margaret gave a relieved look to Brandon. Greed, she understood thoroughly. "You give me the diamonds, I'll sell them and send you your share."

"Hell, no," yelled Brandon. "No, fifty-fifty! One third for you, Margaret, one third for me, and one third for the cop!"

The deep lines around her mouth tightened, obviously, Margaret had no intention of giving Althea any share. But for Althea's benefit, Margaret corrected him sweetly, "Baby, we're sharing. You and I."

"Well, sharing two-thirds is better than sharing a half right?" he said, sounding not so sure of it himself.

Since Margaret seemed to be having trouble working that out too, Althea groaned inwardly and helped them out with, "Half would be fifty percent. You're right, two-thirds are sixty-six percent–that would be fairer. You did have to kill Dietrich to get them." She dropped that bomb casually.

And Margaret picked up the ball, turning to Brandon. "That was a mistake! He shouldn't have been killed. I told you!"

"Like you were there? He was coming for me!" Brandon's voice was bitter. "The diamonds weren't even there." He pointed to Althea. "She had them!"

Margaret looked to Althea. "How did you get Jim's diamonds?"

"Jim wanted to take Paul on as a partner, so Paul told me about the diamonds. By pure luck, I was first on the scene, but I might have been suspect, so when I found the courier's pouch, so I hid it in Paul's Travinski's truck."

That stopped Margaret, who studied her carefully. "You're Paul's girlfriend?"

"I was until I caught him screwing Holly Corey. Then the fool let her drive his truck! But I knew where she parked. Now, I'm perfectly happy to let you dump the guilt for Dietrich's murder on Paul."

Margaret smiled meanly. "I've already signed a deposition saying that Jim was afraid of Paul. That Paul told me he was going to kill my husband. The sergeant is on his way to prison!"

Althea nodded. "Which is what the two-timing bastard deserves! From now o,n, I'm looking out for myself, and I am not letting the diamonds out of my sight until I get the cash in hand."

"But we'll only get a percentage and have to share with the jeweler in Miami..." whined Brandon.

"You're not going to sell Dietrich's diamonds back to their owners for the insurance?" Althea asked, her mouth going dry. *This was getting too complicated.*

"No—those syndicate guys are killers!" confirmed Margaret. "I have a connection in Miami, who put me onto this job. Told me what Jim was transporting."

"You want to take the diamonds to Miami?" Althea paused. "Okay. I'll go with you."

Brandon actually had a clear thought. "You're a cop.

You just can't take off? Won't they'll notice?"

"I'll get the time off," said Althea positively.

"How can you be so sure?" asked Margaret suspiciously, then a wide smirk spread over her face. "You're sleeping with Chief Lewis aren't you?"

"Not yet, but Stan wanted to take me out to dinner tonight. I'm sure I'll have no trouble getting any time off I'll want."

"How do we know you really have anything?" Returned Margaret shrewdly.

"Anything?" asked Althea innocently.

"Jim's diamonds!" Margaret glared at her. "We haven't seen them yet!"

What Althea wanted to see was the gun that killed Jim Dietrich, but she didn't, so she slowly reached up to her breast pocket, took out the manila paper envelope, and made a show of carefully pouring the large diamond out onto the small glass-topped table near the door. It rolled to its side.

*Diamonds are a girl's best friend.*

Margaret stared at the jewel with a palpable hunger that Althea could smell and almost taste. The curtains were still closed, but even in those weak motel lamps that diamond flamed with an internal fire. Margaret was breathing heavily, wetting her lips with her tongue, obviously getting an orgasm just staring at that hunk of priceless ice.

"It's fake!" pronounced Brandon. "Look at it! It ought to be decorating a fishbowl, next to the pirate's chest!"

Margaret looked at him, torn. "The dealer in Miami said the courier pouch held eight diamonds worth twenty-nine million in total. Each one of them must be pretty big?"

Althea stayed quiet, not wanting to overplay her hand. She still hadn't really gotten a prosecutable murder confession out of either of them. With no substantiating evidence, they always could claim they were lying to her. Margaret picked up the huge, round cut stone, bringing it up to the light, studying it, then she stared back to Althea. "This is paste!"

"Only real diamonds can cut glass," Althea softly offered.

Glaring at her, Margaret looked at the stone between her fingers. Twisting it so that the pointed bottom was down, her hand hovered over the small round table with its glass protector. Focusing hard, Margaret swung the stone with a scraping sound. As it cut glass, she got excited, pulled it around, drawing a big plushy heart with it. She looked up at Brandon in triumphant as she transferred the stone to her left hand. Then with her milky-violet contact lens covered eyes narrowing, she turned on Althea. "Where's the rest of them?"

"I'll bring them with us to Miami."

"First, I must see all of them." Margaret kept her fingers tightly grasping the diamond, as she stepped back away from Althea.

Althea decided to try to get something more incriminating on tape. "You're dealer is going to know they came from a murdered man. Do you think he'll still do business with you?"

Margaret had reached one of the queen beds, bending fast, she slid her right hand under the pillow coming back up with a thirty-eight revolver. At her moment of triumph, Althea felt herself going deathly cold.

"Don't shoot her before we get the diamonds!" Brandon helpfully supplied.

"I'm not going to shoot her. We're partners, right, Althea? You're just moving a little slow, and I want you to know who the senior partner is."

Althea glared back at her. "I'll take you to the diamonds, but you'll still need me!" Feeling absolutely terrified Althea surprised herself by being able to sound and function so coolly. Especially, as from their standpoint, once they had the diamonds, they wouldn't need her.

Margaret pointed to the door with the gun. "Fine.

We'll follow."

"You can't show the gun outside." Brandon looked about fast, then ran into the bathroom coming back with a towel. "Give me the gun, baby."

"I gave it to you last time, and you killed Jim before you got the diamonds!"

Brandon covered her gun hand with the towel, while Margaret was careful to stay out of Althea's striking distance, saying, "You are going to walk out slowly. This diamond must be worth millions." She pushed it in the front of her blouse, stuffing it into her bra cup. "If I have to, we'll shoot you and leave with just this one. Brandon, get the run bag, then hold the door from the outside while she walks between us."

He picked up a small suitcase, and Althea turned toward the door, wondering exactly what she was going to do next. Brandon went out first, holding the door before Margaret allowed Althea to walk through.

Outside was four-foot of open concrete corridor and then a wrought iron railing with a one-story drop. Althea turned to walk to the down staircase, but the pathway two rooms down was blocked by a maid's steel cart. And with a sinking feeling, Althea realized that the maid in jeans carrying a vacuum was Holly Corey, just as Brandon called out. "Didn't the maid already do the rooms this morning?"

* * *

Down in the Mystic Motel office, the nervous manager, was checking in a family. Alice glanced over to the little glass computer booth off the main room. Two men in t-v repair overalls were working there, supposedly fixing her computer, but she recognized Chief Detective Hiram Warren of the Mystic Police. The other, taller, solidly built man was called 'Rudy.' Hiram had told her to say nothing. They'd gotten the maid's pass cards from her, but were staying in the lobby. This was great. How was Alice expected to run a motel for tourists, with the police endlessly staking out her guests?

Hearing a gun report, she looked abruptly upwards, as both men came tearing out of the glass-doored booth with drawn guns.

# Chapter 39

Getting her pocketbook after seeing the last of her bed and breakfast guests out, Holly was about to leave the mansion when the phone in the parlor rang. Answering, she recognized that controlled but sexy sounding female voice on the line. "Holly, he's almost free!"

Joy surged within Holly. *At midnight she would light a dozen candles to the Goddess in thanks.* "I'm so glad!"

"Dealing with Margaret was your idea. And it worked," acknowledged Althea.

Holly could give credit too. "You were the one that grabbed Margaret's gun."

"When you swung that vacuum at Brandon, you broke his jaw." Althea continued, "John Hagen is still processing Paul's legal work, but the D.A. has the surveillance tapes, and Forensic has already matched Margaret's gun with the Dietrich murder weapon. The idiots still had the fake uniform shirt and pants in Brandon's closet, and some of the yellow, temporary hair spray dye. The State Troopers are returning Paul today. The department is planning a welcome home pizza party for him at La Luna at seven. He'll probably want you to be there," Althea finished generously.

"Then it all worked out all right?" *The Goddess wasn't usually that neat.*

"Not totally," Althea sighed. "I'm to tell you that you and I have a joint appointment in Chief Lewis' office tomorrow at 10 a.m. to review this whole investigation. I don't think he's going to be congratulating us."

Holly didn't care. *Paul was back!* Even if Althea got him, he was safe! Holly would just be so happy to see him free and patrolling the Mystic roads again. But she would not be going to his welcoming home party. "Tonight is yours. I'm working this evening at The Lady's Cauldron."

There was silence on the other end of the phone for a

minute and then Althea said firmly, "To save Paul we've had a truce. Now, Miss Corey, it is over. May the best lady win!" And from her superior tone, Holly knew Althea planned it to be herself.

\*    \*    \*

To honor the Sabbath ritual and to give everybody a rest, Colin had declared The Lady's Cauldron closed until sunset. That evening, when Holly drove into the parking lot, there were still some coven members in campers and RVs. Knowing Paul would soon be celebrating at his La Luna party without her depressed Holly, so working hard physically at the store would help tonight. Alongside the parking lot was a long row of filled trash bags and stacks of used pizza boxes. It was always a little melancholy cleaning up the sad remains of a big party.

On the tables by the parking lot, the coffee and tea water urns were gone, but Holly stripped off the green plastic tablecloths and the pieces of scotch tape. Then she turned the tables on their sides, to fold up their legs. These she started hauling back to the storeroom, as Colin and Lapin were bringing the hay wagon down with the pavilions and equipment that had to be picked up by the rental place.

Coming back from the storeroom Holly was going over to help them when Maeve called to her from the paddock. Holly walked over, seeing that Maeve had an English saddle on Jacobite, and the bronze haired woman was throwing a western saddle over Gem.

Holly pointed out, "Aren't Colin and Lapin planning to take them out for a run?"

For a moment Maeve stopped, to adjust her brown toned headscarf, then she continued tightening Jacobite's girth."You know–I need some exercise more than they do. Would you come with me?"

Holly squinted to the sky. "The sun is nearly setting."

"We'll still have enough twilight and Colin doesn't like me riding alone. He and Lapin can finish packing things away. Holly, please. Just a quick ride?"

Well, Esther was in the store, and she could handle the coven people still parked with campers in the lot. "Of course." Holly moved to tighten the girth on the mare. Jacobite seemed more skittish than usual. "Do you want me to ride the stallion, I may be stronger?"

"No," said Maeve smiling. "I can handle Jacobite." She laughed. "He's a male!" With Maeve and Jacobite leading, they took the pathway up into the trees, toward the ritual meadow. Maeve reined the stallion to drop back alongside Holly's mount. She spoke softly, so Holly could barely hear her over the pine-needle thudded hoofbeats. "It was a good Beltane. You should've been there."

Holly agreed with that but only said. "I am sure the Goddess was pleased."

"I think it was the best Beltane we ever had."

"You've been to a lot of them?"

"Since I was sixteen. Then my family couldn't stop me." She started to laugh at the memory. "Two years ago, it rained–poured--for a week. We called 'mudtane.' After the 'Lady' and 'Lord' renewed the earth, we all started to mud wrestle on the hillside. I remember another one, in the eighties that ran for four days."

"Four days? What were you doing?" A startled Holly asked.

"Everything and everybody! We had home brew, mead, and beer kegs, and all sorts of mushrooms, buttons, and Maryjane brownies. Everybody looked handsome and alluring." She laughed easily.

The sun had gone down behind the hill, but there still was a pinky glow across the sky. Yet in the dark shadows of the trees, fireflies flickered. *Holly decided now was the time.*

"You were at the Beltane ritual the night my mother died?"

Maeve stiffened, and the stallion shifted to a nervous side prance, pulling at the bit as she tightened her gloved hands on the reins. "Yes, I was."

Could Maeve tell Holly want happened? "Who else was there?"

"Gault. Skye. Lilith and Willow... It was supposed to be the full coven of thirteen, but Grace, Abby, the others said they wouldn't come. Your grandmother had hurt her leg and wanted us to call off Beltane. In defiance, the rest of us decided we would worship without them."

"My mother was there?"

"Not at first...it was just the five of us by lantern and candlelight, inside the old mill building. Gault took off his red robe and was naked. He sat in what Lilith called his 'throne chair' beside the altar. After Willow drew a huge pentacle of blue chalk on the rough floor, we all undressed before Gault, all nubile young women competing for his attention.

"Lilith turned on the walkman, with music from *Night on Bald Mountain*, while before the altar, we oiled our bodies with musky essence. Gault had bought dancing scarfs of almost transparent silk–rose pink, emerald green, and sunshine yellow. They were over ten foot long, nearly three foot wide. We draped them over our budding breasts; trailed behind us like royal trains; then ran with them with arms raised forming wings behind us. Gault watched smiling, while Lilith moved to the master's side to pour her home-brewed, blood-red wine into his carved-skull goblet.

"Skye, Lilith, and Willow had wanted to be the Goddess surrogate to Gault's Horned Hunter. But he hadn't taken me yet. He chose my virginity to be sacrificed on the altar. That Beltane it was to be him uniting with the Goddess through me.

"We began to dance before the altar covered in black velvet and bone." Maeve raised a gloved hand and waved it before Holly. "Willow picked up one of those ugly obsidian athames. You father had thirteen of those ceremonial daggers arranged in a semi-circle on the altar. Each of us picked one up, holding it high, as we circled and danced before him, teasingly brushing the transparent silk veils over our youthful bodies. I was the largest breasted in the coven." Lilith glanced to Holly's chest. "With the exception of your mother, of course.

"Lilith had taken a position next to Gault by the altar. She kept pouring more wine into his goblet as she watched us with half-lidded eyes. I was afraid she'd try to usurp me from Goddess coupling, but as we danced past she just handed us glasses filled with her intoxicating, scarlet brew. We drank it as we swirled seductively before the Master.

"But as we danced, Gault seemed to be slumping in his chair. We were swirling, dipping, and jumping in ecstasy, and our lord and master was falling asleep." Maeve laughed softly at the irony. The pink and gold light blued in the sky. It just barely lit the trail as the horses trod from pine-needles onto the high grass meadow. Holly felt they should start back, but Maeve seemed to want to ride on.

"Could the brews Lilith fed him and you been drugged?" Holly asked.

Eyes widening, Maeve twisted in her saddle. "They may have been! I never thought of it before." Her laughter was bitter. "That would be just like Lilith! The Hoyts were renowned for their herbal knowledge. Lilith wasn't as accomplished as Abby or Sarah, but she was always compounding something strange. I remember once when Lilith gave me some dill biscuits, and I started hallucinating. She said it must have been a flashback to some peyote I had chewed ritually, but she and Willow kept giggling over some secret joke." Maeve remembered, as her lips twisted and she pulled the scarf off her head, so Holly could see her scars. "Yes, Lilith might have drugged Gault, so he couldn't take me on the high altar."

"Do you think you were drugged?"

She was silent for a time, then said slowly "My thoughts were so wild, so free. But we were young. Excited. So sexually unrestrained then..." her voice trailed off. She wasn't allowing the horses to move, but Holly didn't want to say anything to break the moment. Finally, Maeve did speak, "I've never been that alive since that Beltane. I died that night."

Holly had to know. "When did my mother get there?"

Maeve was looking away to the hillside. "We were dancing. It could have been minutes. It could have been hours. Then the door opened, and Hester walked in with the storm winds blowing her cape. Suddenly the party was over. Your mother marched like a prim, schoolmarm. She called for an end to this '*Bastard Beltane.*' She called it an *abomination in the Goddess' eyes. A sacrilege!*

"We stopped, just staring at her. I looked back at the altar. Gault was propped up on one elbow, looking at Hester with eyes he couldn't seem to focus. He tried to rise and stand–but then just fell forward face down on the planking.

"I was nude, Gault was nude, the others were skyclad too, but it was your mother in her long skirt and flowing cape that looked out of place. She looked at Gault laying there on the floor and again began shouting orders. "*This will end now! I'm taking my husband back home!*"

The older woman loosened the stallion's reins to start him walking again, and Gem followed, but Holly stayed silent in her saddle, having the feeling that Maeve wasn't even aware she was there. Instead, Colin's mother was reliving that night at the mill. "Mockingly we chanted and danced around Hester..."

Afraid of breaking the spell Holly still had to ask. "Lilith too?"

"No." Maeve peered into the gathering darkness as if

she was seeing it all again. "No. Lilith always stood watching. Skye, Willow, and I swayed and dipped and spun around Hester, tangling her in our long veils, as she tried to make her way across the floor to Gault."

"Did she ever reach him?" Holly asked quietly.

Maeve shook her head. "I don't know who stabbed her first–I think it was Skye--but suddenly we were all stabbing Hester. With her bare hands, she tried to fight back, but there were three of us wielding those horrible, cursed obsidian athames...

"Hester was down on the floor of the mill. An ecstatic Skye jumped over her and danced above her. But Willow and I looked at our hands covered in dark, dripping blood. Willow backed away, terrified at what we had done. I just stood frozen, looking down at Hester. She was moaning. Moving. She was still alive. I reached out to her–but my hands were sticky with her blood. I couldn't touch her! Your mother looked up at me.

"Then, she stiffened. I was certain Hester was dead! I looked around. Willow was trying to drag Gault up from the floor. With his arm over her shoulder, she was trying to pull him outside. When they reached Hester–Gault stretched his hands out. Touching her body. Covering his hand with his wife's blood--but I don't think he knew it was her! He was acting like a sleepwalker trapped in some horrible nightmare.

"Willow screamed for me to help with Gault. I looked at Lilith. She had climbed atop that monstrous altar and was pouring the sacred oil down on the black velvet cloth, down to the floor. Lilith kicked the guttering candles down into the oil. The flames followed the spilled oil like a bright yellow river. And with one of the empty candlesticks, Lilith swung and overturned the brazier with its burning coals.

"When the coals flamed into the oil, the whole thing went up! Skye had grabbed Gault's other arm as she and Willow were dragging him out into the storm." Maeve seemed to see Holly again. "I thought your mother was dead! But then the police said that she dragged herself out of the burning mill building." Maeve stopped with a little sob, then started again. "Lilith grabbed my arm and pulled me out of the mill.

"Outside, Gault was groggily walking like a man hip-deep in a rushing stream. We were halfway down the back path when Gault finally started to come out of it. Smelling the acrid smoke, he stopped. We all could see the clouds in the sky above, reflecting the inferno that was now the mill. Gault kept looking around, calling out '*Hester! Honey, where are you?*'

Maeve stopped. Then spoke slowly, "He truly loved Hester. We knew he'd be furious that we killed her! So when he started to ask for her, Lilith told him that he had stabbed Hester! That in the middle of the Beltane ritual, his wife had come in, and that a demon had taken control of him! That he stabbed Hester again and again and we couldn't stop him!

"Skye told Gault that he had commanded us to follow his lead and to stab Hester too. That it wasn't Hester we were killing, but a devil that had taken her form!

"Gault pulled away from us and ran back to the mill. We followed, but it was all in flames! Nothing could be alive in there! Lilith pulled at his arm. She said the police would never believe he was possessed by a demon. That we'd all go to jail. Get the death penalty!

"We four managed to drag him back down the trail again. Lilith kept talking, saying that Hester's body would burn in the fire, destroying the evidence. That the police would believe while she was doing some ritual there by herself, a candle had overturned, and she was caught in the fire.

"Gault looked so helpless, I wanted to protect him. I wanted to tell him the truth–but I was afraid he'd hurt me for killing Hester! When we got to the mansion parking lot, he babbled about going inside to wash his hands of Hester's blood!

"I said we should go to my grandparents' farm. Say that the four of us were with him all night. That we started drinking and having sex and that we never went to the mill for the Beltane ritual! We would alibi each other. They could never break us if we all stuck together!"

Maeve stopped as she stared into the darkness. "A light came on, flooding us. The porch light at the mansion. Then I realized we were all naked, except for that stupid veil around my neck. I saw Helen at the back door..."

"My grandmother?"

"Yes. With her cane, she limped out onto the porch. Over the trees, she could see the flames reflected in the dark sky clouds above the mill. Your grandmother looked down and saw the black blood on her naked son's hands–on all our bodies. Gault babbled that he *'didn't mean to kill Hester.'* Your grandmother just raised her head, her lips grimly closed in condemnation as she glared at us, then with contempt she said, *'Get out! Don't ever come back!'*

"I ran around to my car, where my handbag was with the keys. Lilith helped Willow push Gault into the passenger side of my car, and then she went to her car. Willow was screaming and crying by her parent's van. We were all going to my studio, but Willow must have gone crazy. She left Mystic that night, and we never heard from her again.

"I drove Gault, while Lilith followed in her car. Skye came in hers too. We had to park at the barn. My family was asleep in the main house, and it was so cold without our clothing, as we ran through the woods in the rain. Your father was sobbing. Skye, Lilith and I had a horrible time trying to drag him over the footbridge to the cottage I used as a stained-glass studio.

Reining Jacobite in, Maeve stopped them. "Skye came in to borrow some of my clothing–but then said she was going home. She said her parents would be angry if she didn't sneak back in, but if questioned, Skye'd say that she was here with us at my cottage until after midnight.

"Digging around, I found overalls for Gault and robes and painting smocks for me, Skye and Lilith. Gault just fell back to sleep on my couch." With a jangle of the bit, the stallion raised and lowered his head, impatient to be moving again. Maeve went silent.

Finally, Holly spoke, "That doesn't sound like drunkenness or natural tiredness. The shock of the fire, seeing my mother stabbed—adrenalin should have kicked in and woken my father up."

Maeve allowed the stallion to walk again, his hooves stamping on the dirt trail. Holly's mare followed. "What does it matter?" Maeve said hopelessly.

"Your burns? Your face and hands?"

"Not that night." In the darkening woods, Maeve looked down at the gloved scarred hand that held the reins, like she didn't recognize it. "That night–it was like I was outside my body, watching somebody else stab Hester. Someone I couldn't control." Maeve was repeating her story, telling it all again, like she must have done to herself a hundred times. *A hundred thousand times...*

"I think it was Lilith Hoyt," said Holly quietly. "I've been under her control myself, but I didn't realize it at the time. I was depressed, thinking terrible things, thinking it was my own thoughts, but when you're free of her control, you can look back and realize what she's been doing. I think Lilith wanted to marry my father, and she realized that getting rid of my mother was the only way. Maybe she wasn't even conscious of the hatred, the murderous thoughts she was sending out."

"It doesn't matter. I cut Hester's flesh," whispered Maeve. "But I killed most of myself that night. I had to keep living for Colin. Keep being punished for what I had done." She seemed to remember Holly was there again. "The scars inside are so much more terrible than the ones you can see."

"But you said you weren't burned that night?"

"About six months later, I couldn't stand the nightmares every time I fell asleep. I tried to commit suicide. I locked myself in a small shed on the hill. Then set fire to straw stuffed in a woodpile, with gasoline poured over it. Instantly the flames whipped to the ceiling, the heat was horrible–suddenly I didn't want to die! I started to stamp it out with my hands. My long hair caught in flames, burning the left side of my face." Maeve stopped then started again. "My parents got the door open and dragged me out. Beat out the flames. My mother yelled that Colin was still a baby! No matter what I'd done, what punishments I had to bear, I had to keep living for him!"

Holly felt Maeve's unbearable pain. "You were so young. Maybe drugged. Probably being controlled by a stronger will than yours. I can forgive you. My mother would've forgiven you," said Holly softly.

Maeve twisted in the saddle and peered at Holly intently. "Seeing you looking so much like Hester has brought all the horror back. I thought that if you and Colin got together, maybe married, that somehow it would make things right. But nothing can ever erase the stain of what I've done. Lilith is back, and now your father is coming back."

"My father?" *Could it be true?* "You've heard from Gault?"

"He sent me a letter."

"From where? Please tell me!" Holly begged.

"It doesn't matter! He's coming back here to Mystic. I don't want to see Gault. I can't relive it all! Can't start the nightmares again! Colin is grown now–I no longer have to live with my punishment!"

Wanting to comfort her, Holly reached out, but Maeve swung forward, whipping the stallion's flanks with the rein. Jacobite took off at a dead run.

Twisting forward herself, Holly desperately kicked at Gem's barrel. At first, Holly thought they had a chance to catch up to Maeve, but at the end of the woods, they reached that turn at the lower pasture fence. Maeve gathered Jacobite up to a jump that cleared the four-foot high fence.

Desperately Holly kicked Gem's ribs, but the mare pulled up short. Holly found herself flying forward. Only by grabbing around Gem's neck was she able to keep from tumbling over the mare's head.

In the pale moonlight, Maeve was continuing her mad ride—racing down the field in the direction of the trees and her cottage. Any second the horse could stumble, and Maeve's neck would be broken. Holly yanked at the right rein and kicked the poor mare. She must get help. *There would be someone back at the barn that could save Maeve!*

Down the hill, her horse's neck was splotched with nervous foam, yet Holly kept kicking poor Gem's sides as they raced into the stable yard. In the light from the security lamps, she could see a dark figure had heard Gem's hoofbeats and was opening the wooden gate to the paddock. It was Lapin. Behind him, Colin was carrying a sack of feed to the stable. Holly choked out. "Y-y-you're mother!" She took a painful breath and then stumbled with, "K-k-killed my m-m-mother! It wasn't her fault!" Colin had grabbed the foaming mare's bridle, as Holly slid to the ground. "Maeve said she can't live with it! S-S-She was headed to the cottage!"

Colin dropped the reins, then started running out the stable yard. Holly took after him, as he ran down the pathway toward Maeve's studio.

But as they reached the wooden footbridge they smelled kerosene and smoke.

# Chapter 40

Even with the weak moonlight, Holly lost sight of Colin in the pines ahead. Branches ripped at her, but she kept running, hearing him calling out, "Maeve! **Mom! Don't do it** !" When she reached the clearing the cottage's windows were filled with flames. Colin stood silhouetted by the ravenous yellow light. Holly ran in front of Colin, grabbing him. "You can't help her! You'll be killed!"

In agony, he stared past her calling out, **"Maeve!"**

Holly blocked him with her body, wrapping her arms around his chest. She had to yell over the roar of the fire. "The wax! The alcohol! There's propane! The cottage will explode!" The light and intense heat was growing. She felt her back burning. *If he kept going forward, he would be killed!*

He was looking over her shoulder. His eyes widened. **"Mom! I see her! Holly, look–she's in the window! MAEVE!"**

Still blocking Colin tightly, Holly looked over her shoulder. Flames filled all the windows. Colin was pushing against her, struggling to throw her out of his way. She turned, pressing her forehead against his chest, digging her heels in. *He'd die in that fire!*

Now Lapin was pulling Colin from behind. What if both of them couldn't hold Colin?

The explosion hit with a blanking of all sound, slamming her forward, knocking all of them up the path.

\* \* \*

Coming to--feeling queasy--Holly found herself leaned against a tree, watching the burning house frame collapsing--in a strange silence.

Then sound of collapsing timbers. That was new, she could hear again. Men in fireman's suits were trying to spray the trees with a single hose. The cottage was only a flaming foundation and burning timbers. A limp body was being loaded onto a stretcher. A dark figure–Lapin–followed the stretcher. Holly struggled to get up.

Large, firm hands pushed her down. "Easy, honey." It was Paul Travinski in police uniform, looking at her, very concerned.

She pointed to the silhouetted stretcher. "Is that Maeve?"

"No. Colin. He was hysterical about his mother. They gave him a shot. But he'll be okay."

"Did he go into the flames?" Holly asked in terror. "It was only me and Lupin to stop him."

The firelight reflecting on his rugged face above her as Paul quietly answered her in a professional tone. "No...you were able to stop him. From what Lapin says, by yourself." Paul looked down at her anxiously. "Can't leave you alone, lady. What happened?"

"Maeve is in there!"

Paul looked to the remains of the burning cottage and then looked back to her. "They're draining water from the lake, with a portable pumper back on the other side of the footbridge. The stream's weak, but it's the only water source. They'll be bringing the stretcher back for you. We can't get any cars back here." She struggled to sit up, so he murmured, "Just stay still, honey."

In the distance, Holly could see Jacobite chewing grass at the pond's edge. "One of the firemen should catch him." Holly murmured as she pulled up her legs and moved her arms. She had a vague memory of Colin beating burning sparks off her clothing with his bare hands. She tried to rise, but Paul still held her down. "I'm all right," Holly said. "Poor Colin saw his mother suicide."

Several hoses had been clamped together to make one long hose and were spraying water at their loose joints.

Volunteer firemen were all over the place, but they only had that one working hose. Its weak spray flattened, arched down, then spurted up and out again. Most of the other guys were using canvas rectangles to stamp on embers that flew down from the funnels of superheated air. They were trying to keep the woods from burning. The firemen were ignoring the cottage, which was just white charred timbers now.

"Maeve was in there?" Paul asked quietly. "You saw her in the fire?"

"We both did. She must've set the fire to suicide, then changed her mind and tried to get out, but couldn't." Holly turned back to look at the fire. "Colin said Maeve was in the living room. The big window that was there." She pointed to where it had been.

"Colin said it? Was Lapin here?"

She thought about it. "Not then."

Paul seemed to be pushing her. "But you did see Maeve? Think carefully, Holly. If you saw her, describe to me exactly what she looked like?"

She tried to picture that intact cottage, then the cottage with the flames behind each of its windows. Huge flames that looked like dancing demons. But where did she see Maeve? As she struggled to remember, Holly tried to stand up again but started to fall.

Paul grabbed her. "Stay still, honey! You had the wind knocked out of you from the explosion."

"I caused Maeve to suicide," said an anguished Holly. "We went riding. I made her confess to stabbing my mother! With Skye and Willow. They were performing a ritual before the altar in the mill, dancing in some sort of ecstasy, and my mother tried to stop them."

"Your father was there?" he asked.

"He was sitting by the altar, but Lilith was feeding him alcohol or worse, and he passed out. The three girls stabbed my mother, then dragged Gault from the mill, as Lilith set fire to the altar."

"All of them left your mother bleeding?" Paul asked incredulously.

That did seem unforgivable, but Maeve had been so tortured by it. "They were young! Crazed! Maybe drugged too! They were afraid my father would punish them for killing my mother. When he groggily woke up, Lilith told him he had killed Hester."

"Aaup." Paul said slowly. "This is what Maeve told you? That she helped murder your mother?"

"I don't think it was Maeve's fault! She was drinking Lilith's brews. Maybe being mentally controlled by Lilith Hoyt!"

"Controlled?" He said flatly and very cop like. "People aren't *'mentally controlled*,' Holly."

How could she explain to him what Lilith was capable of? "Your infatuation with Margaret. Don't you think there might have been something unnatural about that?"

Paul stared at her with just a hint of doubt. "Like I can't get you out of my mind?"

"**No!**" she was horrified. "I never p-p-put a love sp-sp-spell on you!" *She'd thought about it, but never seriously did.* He pulled her close and kissed her hair, seeming to be just so glad she was alive, but Holly had to keep talking, "My father has contacted Maeve. Said he was coming back to Mystic." Holly spoke with excitement. "That might be another reason for Maeve to kill herself?"

"Or it might be a motive to have everybody think she's dead–allowing her to just disappear and avoid all the problems," he murmured into her hair.

"No! I pushed her over the edge by making her confess!"

"Holly, look at me." Firm fingers forced her face from the fire to look into his eyes. "Lapin showed us a letter that he found. A letter Maeve left in the barn that Lapin read while he was calling the firemen. It's Maeve's suicide note."

"What did it say?"

"Something like, '*when Hester died, I died too. Now I must cleanse my sins in fire. Colin, I will always love you, but I can no longer live with my guilt.*"

"Then I did kill her!" whispered an anguished Holly.

Paul was frowning. "You're not paying attention to the time line! Maeve must have written that letter before she went out on that horseback ride, where you supposedly forced a confession out of her. And when Maeve ran off, Lapin didn't call the police–he called the fire department, probably before he could smell smoke or see flames reflected in the clouds."

With the pain of the explosion and small debris cuts, Holly was having trouble thinking straight but, "You think..."

"That Colin made an on-the-spot witness of his mother's alleged suicide and you were a convenient back up."

Feeling weak, Holly shook her head as she leaned against his strong chest. Now they both stared at the burning cottage. "Maeve's guilt over stabbing my mother was just overwhelming."

"Eighteen years after she did the deed? Talk about your delayed reactions?" he commented cynically.

"Colin saw his mother in the window..."

"But didn't rush in to save her?" he asked.

"He tried to. I held him back," explained Holly.

Paul stared down at her hard. "Holly, you've always surprised me by being way stronger than you look, but, honey, you were pushing against a grown man, who makes his living doing hard physical labor. If Colin was shooting adrenalin, I don't know if I could've held that guy back. You certainly couldn't have." They heard the sound of the roof remains collapsing into the white ember bed, as yellow sparks showered in clouds of black smoke. "The fire chief is going to have a forensics check made, but he thinks with that fire's intense heat they won't be able to find anything, even if there was a woman in there."

"If Maeve didn't die, she's shouldn't be running, it isn't her fault..."

"If Maeve Fitzgerald didn't die in that fire, we'll find her and talk about that."

Holly thought of Lilith and her mind control. Nothing possible to explain in a court of law, but having been under Lilith's influence, Holly fully understood that Maeve could have wielded that knife, but not be responsible for Hester's murder. "What would you have to find to know Maeve was dead?"

"Teeth...or shrunken bone with DNA matching her son's. But after that inferno, I don't think they can find anything, even if it had been there."

She wanted him off of this topic and was so happy just to see him back. "You're in your blue shirt and pants. You're back on duty?" she asked hopefully.

"Well, it seems two ladies got together and managed to get incriminating statements out of Margaret and the boyfriend. And the expensive lawyer Brandon's father hired-- seeing the kid was up for murder--had Brandon go state's witness. The kid's really rolling over on Margaret–so I'm released by the D.A. Stan, and the department held a homecoming party for me tonight. I was kinda hoping you'd show up?'

"Althea asked me, but it was her night." Holly frowned. "Paul, she said I've got an appointment with Chief Lewis tomorrow at ten to discuss..."

"Performance review? Aaup. I've had a few of those. The chief's pretty unhappy that you two planned to go to that motel with no more back up than Althea's cousin with a tape recorder."

"Maybe I could beg off because my injuries tonight?" she asked hopefully.

"Get it over with. From what I hear about the Battle of

the Mystic Motel, you both deserve a good blistering. But you and Althea made a truce?" he asked suspiciously.

"Temporarily," Holly confirmed. "But long term we have seriously conflicting objectives."

"Which are?"

"We both want to land the same clueless man."

"Aaup."

A sadness came over Holly. "Only since I guess officer Althea Rogers can dance and I can't, she's got the edge."

He arched an eyebrow. "Fortunately, you know a guy who used to teach dancing."

She smiled up at him.

His eyes turned serious. "Did you go to the Fitzgerald's Beltane ritual by yourself?"

"They had a lot of people there–nobody was by themselves," Holly evaded neatly.

"That wasn't the question I asked, lady." He put a bent crooked finger under her chin to lift it up so he could look directly in her eyes.

"No. I did not go to the Fitzgerald's Beltane. Or to Grace's Le Fleur's." Holly stopped as she thought. "But I should've. You're okay, but me, and the mansion, and my brothers–we all need some changing luck." On shaking legs, she started to stand again.

He helped her up, letting her lean on his strong arm. "This Beltane–must it always be performed before a crowd?"

"No, there are solitary practitioners."

"The Fitzgerald's did Beltane on Thursday, May first, but I heard Grace Le Fleur's was done on the weekend?"

"Grace felt it would be more convenient for worshipers to gather." She perked up at that. "I think the Goddess would allow some leeway if say jail prevented a handsome man from participating. I'm sure Grace Le Fleur could arrange another Beltane ritual. She's got the couch and the altar waiting. She already sees you as a Greek god!"

"No, mam, I'm not performing at Grace's Le Fleur's Couch of Good Times! But I've got something else in mind. We can talk about this after you go to the hospital."

"No, hospital!" she said definitely.

"Holly!" He got stern.

"No insurance, remember? I've got some cuts and bruises, but I feel okay. I don't need an emergency room bill to confirm that."

*He silently cursed her stubbornness!* "I want the ambulance guys to look at you, and they will make that decision. Aaup?"

"Paul..." she shook her head.

"If you let the paramedics look at you, then we can talk. Maybe you can take a dance lesson or two, and then maybe we can have a private Beltane?"

Now, smiling a little, she ran her hand along his broad chest. "Aaup."

# Epilogue

After their morning run, Thor bounded to the porch door ahead of him. Frost shifted the mail to his other hand to let the rottweiler inside. In the pantry, he could smell the mouth-watering bacon frying and the eggs benedict that a harried Noel was preparing for a mansion full of departing guests.

"Need help?"

"Gonna need that cantaloupe cut up." He turned to the refrigerator. "But first, in the dining room, finish setting up the coffee urn and get that started."

Noel had already filled the dog's dish. Now Thor was noisily chowing down on his kibble, as Frost felt a long, white envelope on the bottom of the stack in his hands–an envelope giving off vibrations that were troubling. Putting down the rest of the mail he looked at the printed return address: the firm of Keen, Widdle & Barstal. Nobody he knew. His name and address had been printed out by hand, not an advertising circular. Frost took a paring knife from the counter to slit it open.

"Don't use cooking implements to open filthy letters!" His brother admonished as Noel mixed hollandaise sauce and flipped the bacon on the grill with his other hand. "Holly shouldn't have gone away with a full house here!"

"Sis deserves a break once in a while. It's only for this weekend."

Noel nodded his head. "Holly deserves a break–but it should be with a guy who cares for her! Not one who's just up for partying."

"Paul has put in an awful lot of time and sweat trying to get that hearse back in working condition."

"He left us stuck painting that house!"

Frost was unfolding the stiff, typed document in his hand. "N.C., he was in custody! And all his cop friends came over and helped us finish up." Frost looked off to the distance.

"Despite what he says, I think Paul really loves sis. But it's up to them." Frost looked down at the paper in his hand. "Shit!"

"What's the matter?" Noel asked, still staring at his eggs.

"You know how Holly always wants to locate our loving father?"

"Who disappeared after he thought he'd killed our mother?"

"Yeah," said Frost disgustedly. "Daddy's located us. Or at least his lawyers have."

"What?" Now Noel stared at him.

Frost scanned the document. "They're writing to us to take over this mansion. This paperwork claims it's our father's property."

Noel's bacon was smoking, but he still stared at Frost. "Grandmother Helen deeded Uncle Ben a life interest, then left the mansion in trust to us after we were over twenty-one."

"According to this, our grandmother had no right to do that! Gault's claiming Witch House..."

Noel glared at his brother. "It's not Witch House! It's the Corey Mansion Bed and Breakfast."

Frost ignored that. "This is from the lawyers representing the Thorenson Corporation. They state they have already given our father a deposit on the property."

"He's sold it? He doesn't own it?" Noel couldn't believe the nerve. "Gault's own mother threw him out of here for killing mom!"

"Well, Holly says our father didn't stab our mother. Not that he knew that. This document is my eviction notice from this property. There are two more envelopes. One for you, and one for Holly."

The kitchen ghost started its high pitched laughter in the background. Noel threw down the red-checkered dish towel. "Maybe daddy dearest can just have this ghost infested rat trap!"

"You don't mean that, N.C. Just the acreage in this area alone would be worth a small fortune." Frost looked up. "Shall we call Holly? You got Paul's cell phone number?"

Noel searched the stack for his own envelope and ripped it open. Silently he started reading his own eviction letter, then he looked around the worn kitchen. In the last few months, he'd really gotten used to the place, kitchen ghost and all. "No, We've got a whole thirty days to live here. Let's wait with the bad news until after sis has her weekend."

* * *

Holly looked from Newport Harbor to Paul driving his truck. The sergeant's strong features that could look so stern now glanced to her with a loving smile and fast wink. "Almost there, honey."

She bobbed her head down, shyly smiling back, as she found herself blushing.

Earlier, to make losing her virginity a very special time, Paul had found this motel with its fancy bridal suite. Holly remembered the small kitchen nook and shades of golden and ivory living room with its bubbling hot tub. She loved the luxurious cream-marble bathroom with its ceiling of raindrops over the double sized shower stall. But grandest of all was the huge, gilt trimmed bedroom with its oversized, round bed covered by gold satin sheets.

For her first time, Paul had arranged for champagne and chocolates to be delivered before they arrived. Now when they walked in on the thick carpet, she found that this time he'd had a basket of fruit, with a cheese platter, and a bouquet of yellow roses delivered to honor the Goddess. Still, being a thrifty Boston boy, Paul brought a couple of bottles of wine from home.

Holly kicked off her shoes to run her toes in the deep carpet pile, then turned, reaching up to him on tiptoes for a kiss. He leaned down, and her cheeks brushed against his short stubble of beard. Intertwining his fingers under her bottom, Paul lifted Holly up closer to him. When they were finished kissing, he asked, "Where do you want to set up your altar?"

She looked around. Set it up on the marble flooring around the hot tub in the living room? Or in the bedroom, before the velvet, goldenrod comforter? As Colin had said, *the Lady doesn't go by clocks or calendars. The Mother of All goes by the intentions in your heart.* Beltane–the renewal of the earth, the reigniting of their passions, the revitalization of the life force and year's energy going forward--this they would accomplish here tonight, by the surrogate union of Earth Goddess and the Horned Hunter. "We're setting up in the bedroom."

He carried in their suitcases, while she carried one of Frost's hand-crafted wooden tool boxes that she had filled with her sacred implements. Holly stopped on the threshhold. She hadn't remembered how beautiful this room was. "Oh, Paul, it's so lovely–but I always thought the bridal suites would have mirrors on the ceiling."

"We could've had that. The suite across from this has a hot tub too, black leather furnishings, nail-polish red walls, with gold dust mirrored ceilings tiles over the entire suite. You want me to see if we can still switch to it?"

"No." She shook her head, smiling happily. "This is 'our room.' Can you move that low table over in front of the bed for the altar?"

Paul moved it, putting it a safe distance away from the bed because of the open candles flames. From Frost's toolbox, Holly took out a powder blue satin cloth, the color of the sky in the morning. This she covered the coffee table with. She took off the duck tape holding the top during transit and set out a heart-shaped, cut glass candy dish holding pure, white salt.

Bubble-wrapped, carved ivory figures of the Horned

God and Goddess that Holly borrowed from the Hoyt sisters followed. Then her own brass candlesticks, with the pure white candles, and the scarlet one that Colin had given her from The Lady's Cauldron.

In front of that, she laid her grandmother's art nouveau styled silver letter opener for an athame; knowing what had really happened to her mother took away much of her fear of the ceremonial knife. Holly added a matching handled wand from Abby, fashioned from lightning-struck oak from Grace's land. Holly unpacked a pewter bell,   two tall vases for the roses, and almond soap for purification. She also set out a ceramic plate for Paul's chocolate offerings and poured a shallow bowl of spring water, that she had carried from near the mill, in her grandfather's old glass lined lunch thermos.

"What happens next?" Paul asked.

"I've questioned Abby Hoyt and Grace Le Fleur. The theology is a little loose, but with a short invocation Grace gave me, we will be summoning the Lady and Lord, asking them to look with favor upon us. Asking them to enter our bodies, so that we may honor them by consummating their spiritual union this day of our Beltane."

He reached down and kissed the side of her neck. "At the price of this suite, I hope this is going to be more than just a spiritual union?"

"Oh, yes, sir." She kissed him back, finally withdrawing and shyly saying. "We can start soaping in the rain fixture stall, then warm up in the hot tub, before we will come back in here and light the candles, chant out our requests to the earth and sky and then..." She looked to the bed.

He followed her eyes and smiled. "I'm getting this religion." Paul looked down at her. "So, first we've got to get undressed."

She started unbuttoning the pale green cotton shirt over his long, muscular chest. "I'll help you–if you'll help me?"

Paul smiled and started on the pink buttons of her

lavender flowered blouse. Throwing it aside, he was running his big hands over her full, lacy bra cups. She always loved the way he excited her body.

As she unzipped his pants, Holly reveled in the knowledge that this would be her first Beltane celebration with Paul, one that she would always remember the rest of their lives.

The End

*The Seaport Psychics Murder*

The first in the Mystic Triplets mysteries. When their Old Craft worshipping mother dies of stab wounds on Beltane, her young triplets are separated for seventeen years. Raised without knowledge of their witchcraft heritage, Holly Corey returns to the Connecticut Seaport of her birth. Reunited with her two brothers, her only goal is on turning 'Witch House' into a viable Bed and Breakfast to keep the three of them together; that is until she meets Sgt. Travinski, the handsome policeman, who is determinedly pursuing both Holly (for love) and her brother Frost (for murder).

*Murder at the Altar*

In the second of the Mystic triplets mysteries, brother Noel is accused of poisoning a fellow Beluga trainer at the Aquarium. When Holly Corey starts investigating, she visits her Old Craft mentors, Sarah, and Abby Hoyt. Unfortunately, against their advice, Holly accepts two new long term guests at the Corey Bed and Breakfast: Lilith (once a member of her father's coven) and Lilith's younger warlock architect (and sometimes lover) Gregory St. Clair.

Lilith is pressing to buy the old mill that the triplets' mother ritually suicided in, while Gregory is trying to seduce Holly up onto the high altar at Grace La Fleur's Church of Nature's Bounty. Afraid of the Wiccan ritual, but needing to know more, Holly drags Sgt. Paul Travinsky up to the beginnings of the naked Yule celebrations that wind up being raided by his fellow cops. While the sergeant is being told to stay away from Ms. Corey or give up his job, Holly finds herself in danger of losing her life--or her soul--to the combined efforts of the Rasputin like Gregory, and the powerful, mind controlling Lilith.

## OR MURDER SCIENCE BASED:

### ORR: The Nobel Prize Murder

Turned down for this year's Nobel, fortyish genetics pioneer Grace Farrington finds out the new head of Oyster River Research is the man who had stolen her prize! When Dr. Marshall is murdered on ORR's house boat, Grace finds herself chief suspect and is further implicated when following an1800's witch's Curse of Three, two more people die in Oyster River Harbor. While finding herself romantically involved with a billionaire patron and a red-necked colleague, Grace must use her scientific reasoning and her eclectic group of friends (scientists, cops, psychics and some other slightly eccentric New Englanders) to solve the murders before she's arrested or killed herself.

### ORR: Fatal DNA

Grace Farrington is considered a genius in her field, so it is not a surprise that when doing some special DNA sleuthing she discovers a convoluted motive for murder as she attempts to desecrate a body in a funeral home. Her life suffers further complications when her new age friend Freya involves her in a seance that triggers a desperate search for a lost Revolutionary War ransom. Of course, no one has found the treasure in over two hundred years, but they didn't have Grace's skill at reading the secrets of Colonial DNA.

Distracting entanglements are the three men on her romantic horizon: rough-edged fellow scientist Kurt MacKay; old moneyed David Gardiner; and a new billionaire, the handsome Jack Stuart who arrives in the New England town of Oyster River Harbor with an intense interest in both her research and her body. Grace is determined to keep her mind on mitochondria, even as Kurt is attacked by a local fisherman. But when her sometime lover is accused of murder, Grace has to act, only to find out too late that the next targeted victim is herself!

### ORR: Murder Genetically Engineered

In the third book in the Grace Farrington DNA mystery series, Grace is returning from winning the prestigious Guru award, when she finds Oyster River Harbor Research is being picketed by Anti-Genetic Engineering protestors. Her rival, Dr. Huang Wong, has signed a research grant with a conglomerate run by the handsome, wealthy bachelor Axel Jensen. C.E.O. of Humanity's Harvest, Axel has a reputation for marrying brainy women and is under the impression that his generous contract also includes Grace.

Tension is building up with the demonstrators, as Grace and the other researchers start getting anonymous death threats. These threats are ignored until a body is found floating in the Connecticut harbor. Humanity's Harvest tries to cool things off with a December outdoor-in-the-snow bar-be-que, while Grace is hunting for traces of the elusive *"food for the Incan Lord God"* in the University Museum. In New Haven, she stumbles on to an intriguing DNA puzzle left over from the Conquistadors conquering of Peru. Can even Grace solve it all before the next murder?

## ORR: *The Tell Tale Y*

Just trying for a relaxing vacation, Dr. Grace Farrington discovers what might be missing evolutionary DNA from a fisherman's net on the island country of São Tomé and Principe. Later, in a rustic beach cabin with Kurt, their overdue romantic interlude is interrupted with the news that her best friend, Freya, has been arrested for murdering a man in Senator Kincaid's boathouse.

Cutting her vacation short, Grace returns to New England and Oyster River Research, where Freya isn't talking. Unfortunately the Kincaid's mysterious *"caretaker"* was murdered with the same tenth-century trimming ax that Freya uses to build her Viking ship reconstructions. Furthermore, although Freya is trying to hide it, this dangerous, blackmailing deadman may have been her son Mac's real father! But even while Grace investigates to prove her friend innocent, she's drawn into another complicated genetic code mystery, this one involving the last Czar of Russia and his missing daughter, Grand Duchess Anastasia.

## PARANORMAL SURPRISES:

### *Adam's Unorthodox, Unnatural Legal Practice*

Inheriting his Great Uncle Quentin's unconventional law firm in Missouri Adam Martin finds himself defending the rights of a succubus, zombies, a semi-senile seer, mermaids, a dryad, and gorgons. Soon he is writing contracts for werewolves, consulting with ghosts, and protecting unfairly accused fire starters. While this is going on, he is trying to stand up to his six foot tall *'Cherokee'* law secretary, and deal with his staid, disapproving family of conservative lawyers led by the formidable 'hang them high' Judge Jeremiah Martin. Yet while struggling to save his clients and his law practice, Adam still has time to romance some very intriguing and unusual females.

**FANTASY ADVENTURE:**

*Centauresses of the Silver Dragon*

Jace a centaur of Clydesdale proportions, leads of 'The Regiment,' a band of sword and shield mercenaries. Having won all their battles on the field, they are betrayed by a treacherous prince and outlawed. In unchartered lands, Jace desperately searches for a patron to keep his band together. He finds that mainstay with the lovely Silver sisters, tall shes with long legs, pale gray hide with black stockings and cream dabbled hindquarters. To Jace alone, the ravishing Silver Star promises endless wealth if his Regiment clears her clan's mines from a ravaging dragon.

But there are problems: Jace is sure his alluring patroness is lying, as he does not believe in dragons; Some of his warriors are rebelling against his leadership and he is desperately trying to conceal a leg wound that is worsening. His brutal choice: abandon the Regiment and the Lady Star or face a challenge to his leadership that will only end in death!

**For more books by Lynn or to contact the author, please go to lynnmarron.com**